MW00641621

A
GENTLEMAN
NEVER
TELLS

A GENTLEMAN NEVER TELLS

JODI ELLEN MALPAS

FOREVER

New York Boston

Forever
Hachette Book Group
1290 Avenue of the Americas, New York, NY 10104
read-forever.com

First published in Great Britain in 2023 by Orion Books, an imprint of The Orion Publishing Group Ltd., a Hachette UK company. First Forever ebook edition: July 2023

First Forever trade paperback edition: February 2024

Forever is an imprint of Grand Central Publishing. The Forever name and logo are trademarks of Hachette Book Group, Inc.

The publisher is not responsible for websites (or their content) that are not owned by the publisher.

The Hachette Speakers Bureau provides a wide range of authors for speaking events. To find out more, go to hachettespeakersbureau.com or email HachetteSpeakers@hbgusa.com.

Forever books may be purchased in bulk for business, educational, or promotional use. For information, please contact your local bookseller or the Hachette Book Group Special Markets Department at special.markets@hbgusa.com.

Library of Congress Control Number: 2023948828

ISBNs: 978-1-5387-2620-4 (trade paperback), 978-1-5387-2622-8 (ebook)

Printed in the United States of America

LSC-C

Printing 1, 2023

Also by Jodi Ellen Malpas

Belmore Square Series
One Night with the Duke

This Man Series
This Man
Beneath This Man
This Man Confessed
All I Am: Drew's Story (a novella)
With This Man

One Night Trilogy
One Night: Promised
One Night: Denied
One Night: Unveiled

Standalones
The Protector
The Forbidden
Gentleman Sinner
Leave Me Breathless

To the younger version of me. Who knew?

Chapter 1

I am nose-to-nose with the white stallion. My body as still as can be. But my heart? It thunders in my chest. My pulse? It booms. My God, I am more alive than ever. Whether it be with fear or excitement, I cannot tell. I allow my eyes to slowly travel up the horse's nose to its rider. The horseman is staring down at me, their eyes hardly visible past their low hat and high scarf and the shadows they cast. Curious eyes, I'm sure, that are slightly narrowed, inspecting me. Then a small sparkle. Smiling?

I inhale and step back, needing to get the horseman in my sights, arms, body, legs, and all, for I am certain I am not looking at a horseman at all.

But the impressive stallion moves before I do, rising up on its back legs on a neigh, loud and intimidating as I expect is intended. I stagger back and fall to my backside on the stones, but I somehow succeed in keeping my eyes up. The rider laughs but stops abruptly.

"My God," I whisper, watching as she slides down from her horse and approaches me slowly, despite the warning of her two fellow, male—they're definitely male—riders, who remain just a few yards away, their horses treading the ground impatiently. She holds out her gloved hand, and I take the dainty thing, getting to my feet. I must be at least a foot taller. She comes closer. Closer. Closer. Reaches up on her tippy toes. I close my eyes and breathe in, holding my breath. The skin of my cheeks heats, feeling her breath on my face from where she's pulled her scarf down. And then her lips push into my rough cheek.

Magic.

Her face. Does she want me to see it? For she has removed her scarf.

I quickly open my eyes and blink, so very confused, my heartbeat ferocious in its pace, and find nothing before me. At least, no human, but the horse remains, and the rider is still upon its back.

What in the name of God just happened?

I reach for my cheek and feel it, as my sister hurries to my side and helps me to my feet, looking at the impressive white stallion as she does. I spend the few seconds I have before the rider kicks the horse into action committing every detail before me to memory, until all three of them gallop off into the distance, kicking up dirt, making the ground vibrate. I turn on the spot, mesmerized, in a trance, speechless, my head just about ready to explode with the pressure of words swimming around my brain.

I bolt up in bed on a gasp and glance around, a little disoriented, and exhale when I find I am, indeed, in my bed and not at the mercy of the highwayman. Or woman. It *has* to be a woman. Each time I dream the dream, a little something else is added. This time, a kiss. My God, I am obsessed.

I jump out of bed and go to my writing desk in the window, collecting my quill and dunking it in the pot of ink, not taking a seat—I don't have time—my mind needing to get the words out. The smell of the horse. The tickle of its coarse hair when we stood nose-to-nose. The gallop of my heart that I'm sure pounded harder than the hooves of the horse at a full canter. I write until my hand aches and I drop my quill, exhaling, running a hand through my hair as I look up out of the window.

I lean forward and pull the half-drawn draperies aside, focused on the floating form of a girl across the cobbles. Lady Taya Winters. Also known as my brother-in-law's little sister. The woman does not walk but floats. She's quite a vision, I admit. Her bright green eyes shine, her dark blonde hair is adorably wild, her cheeks blushed, her lips plump, and her lashes long and fluttering.

My God, she is beautiful.

And completely forbidden.

From the day I met her, when she returned to Belmore Square with her mother, Wisteria Winters, and her brother, Lord Sampson Winters, I have been wary of her. I am not without female attention. I am, however, without the thrill one would expect from female attention. That has died a slow, painful death over the course of my time in London—a sign of my overindulgence, I suppose. I cannot tell you whether it be her aloofness or simply her unusual, wild, unconventional beauty, but when Lady Taya Winters glanced at me that fateful day, I felt as though I'd been struck by lightning. Twice. I walked away telling myself I need to keep my distance from Taya Winters, for she is sure to get me into trouble, and I need no trouble, no complications, especially now when I must convince my father to let me publish my story. I have never desired to write for our family newspaper. I have hardly expressed any interest in the operations of our family newspaper, *The London Times*, doing the bare minimum I could without doing nothing at all. Porter helped run the business with Papa, until, of course, his untimely death, and my sister wrote the most popular stories. I had very little enthusiasm for work or writing, so I made myself useful elsewhere. Usually in a woman's bed.

How odd it is to feel this new sense of purpose. To be inspired. Motivated. *Excited*. This enthusiasm to write is rather refreshing.

I watch Taya Winters pass through the gilded gate, ready to disappear into the greenery of Belmore Square Gardens. But she stops, stands still for a moment, and then slowly turns, looking up at my window.

I think I move before she catches sight of me or my bare chest.

I think.
I know I didn't.

Belmore Square. What a weirdly wonderful place it is, the home to an eclectic mix of people, all stinking rich, it must be said, with a wildly vibrant color palette, from the shrubs and flowers of the gardens, to the frocks of the residents that grace the cobbles. It even sparkles—the gilded railings enclosing the square gardens that the thirteen homes circle polished and ever shiny, as perfect as the homes, the clean cobbles, and every petal and leaf on every flower and bush.

Money, power, and respect, they are all contributory factors to the idea of perfection. It is a lovely notion, if unrealistic. Perfect is an illusion, and my family breaks that illusion most days with the stories that we print in our newspaper. Our success is not only attributed to the invention of the steam printing press, but to the talented hand of my sister, who has always penned the most riveting of tales for readers to indulge in. Not that the readers knew it was, in fact, a woman entertaining them. No. Every story was credited to me, Frank Melrose, for the idea of a female journalist was, much to Eliza's dismay, laughable. Unheard of! But the arrangement suited us both, for my passion to write did not match my sister's.

Oh, how one quite inconsequential encounter with a horseman has changed that. Suddenly, I wholly appreciate my sister's drive. I understand her desires to write and entertain the ton with wild, elaborate stories. Wild and elaborate but true. Her recent tales have been received rather well. Of course, anything concerning to the Duke of Chester is guaranteed to pique the interest of the ton, their raging curiosity about him and the murder of his father begging to be settled. My sister is doing a terribly fine job of settling said curiosity and answering the questions that have lingered for some time. Of course, it helps that she is to marry the duke in question, and she now has a walking, talking reference guide on all things connected to the Winters family. But the story that has dominated the front page of *The London Times* for some weeks now is almost told, for the happy couple will wed today. I smile. Eliza will be whisked away on a bridal tour, and the people will still wish to be riveted each week by a good story. In her absence, someone needs to maintain the momentum Eliza has set. Sales need to keep growing. Our reach expanding.

I stand on the steps of our home on Belmore Square and cast my eye around as I fasten the buttons of my new jacket, bracing myself for the upcoming celebrations. I honestly never thought I would see the day. My sister is as independent as a female could be. Almost to a fault, if truth be told. She has gotten herself into many scrapes because of her headstrong ways and ambitions. Me? I've spent most of my adult years finding pleasure through intimacy. I cannot deny it, I have been quite lavish with my affections, and my focus has most certainly been misplaced. If I didn't appreciate my sister so much, I might see her as an obstacle in my way. If I didn't love her so much, I might not have approved of her marriage to the Duke. Unfortunately, to my own detriment, I appreciate her more than she'll ever know, and I love her dearly, so I must be patient. It's hard, I must say. I have always found writing to feel like I'm pulling teeth. These days, my hand simply cannot keep up with my brain. But I am not foolish enough to go up against my sister in a war to win the front page. Not only because I could never be at odds with her, but because I have spent too long taking the credit for Eliza's words. She must have her time, for she has more than earned it.

We sold ten thousand copies the day after Father finally gave Eliza his blessing to write her story and sign her name as the author. Ten thousand! It's a record, and not at all surprising given the interest in the notorious, deadly Duke. He might be a stoic beast of a man with a questionable past, but there is no denying the love he holds for my sister. Not to mention, he's a duke, and it is easy to forget one's past when one has a title to paper over the cracks, not that any of us are likely to forget his or his family's past, for it is still the talk of the square. And on that thought, I wonder how the Duke's sister, the floating, *forbidden* Lady Taya Winters, has taken to being back on Belmore Square.

I hum, just as a newspaper lands at my feet. I kneel and pick it up, smiling at the first few words of the headline. My sister's words.

Imagine if...

"Yes, imagine if," I murmur, folding it up and slipping it under my arm.

I rest my hat upon my head, collect my cane from where it is resting against the door, and take the steps down to the cobbles, starting a wander around the square, breathing in the new day, swinging my cane casually. I circle the square anticlockwise, relishing the sounds of the morning bustle, horse's hooves on the cobbles, wheels or carriages bumping across them too, people calling out their polite greetings to everyone they pass. I have never appreciated the benefits of early mornings, for my nights are too late, being spent in a gentleman's club, indulging in too much liquor and even more female flesh. The mornings are quite delightful, it must be said.

"Good morn to you, Melrose," Mr. Simpson, Belmore's resident shipbuilder, says, tipping his hat, prompting me to tip mine too. "I look forward to the celebrations later."

"As do I, Simpson," I reply, carrying on my way. "Good morn to you, Casper." I lift my stick in hello to our family lawyer—a kind man with kind eyes and a kinder smile.

"Good news about the sales," he says. "Long may it continue."

"We'll be expanding to ten pages in no time at all," I assure him. "Let me know if you require any more advertising space, Casper."

He waves his cane, looking up at the clear blue sky. "What a wonderful day for a wedding."

"Indeed," I say quietly, passing by the Hamsleys, whose daughter, Esther, one of the only women on this square who hasn't caught my eye, is on her fifth season. Fifth! I am not surprised; she is rather frosty. I have never once seen the girl smile.

"My lady." I nod politely to Annabella Tillsbury, Baroness of Shrewsbury. Her eyes fix to mine. Her smile is demure. She is an understated, beautiful, soft lady, whom Mama has become rather friendly with, and it is for that reason alone, and a crying shame, I must admit, that I have avoided her advances, as I have Lady Blythe, Marchioness of Kent, our local famous author who has a silver tongue and a wicked sense of humor.

I smile fondly at the thought of Mama, who is currently breezing around the house in her morning coat singing orders to our staff, while Emma, her maid, scampers along behind her trying to fix her hair, and Clara, my gorgeous baby sister, whinges and whines about having to wear frills. It's a stark turnaround from when we arrived in London. Back then, Clara was most impressed, dazzled by the fancy frocks and sumptuous surroundings. Until she realized that those fancy frocks are quite restrictive, and I don't mean literally. She can no longer dirty herself in mud, pick apples in the orchard, take some home for Mama to bake and throw the bad ones at the boys in our village while yelling blue language. It was rough enough accepting Eliza has come of age and will now marry. Clara? She is just sixteen. Sixteen and overflowing with attitude. Of course, I love it. Of course, it is not suitable for our life these days. So imagine my displeasure when I discover from Eliza that our little, wayward sister is in love with a stable boy. A stable boy! It is not so much that he is a stable boy, although, naturally, that is a problem. She is my baby sister, and I should like to keep

7

her as such for as long as possible. In addition, such a scandal will very likely ruin the family name, and we've all worked too hard to allow that. Therefore, the stable boy has had a polite warning to stay away from Clara. Poor thing looked terrified as I casually stroked a hoof knife and nippers. Good. Although, admittedly, I did feel a trifle guilty. I have hardly led by good example when it comes to suitable company to be keeping. Perhaps that changes now.

Perhaps.

I spot Lady Rose, the Countess of Somerset, who resides at number nine Belmore Square, a pointed, haggard old woman, crossing the cobbles up ahead, the feathers on her bonnet looking like they came from a decaying pheasant. The hat must be as old as she is. "Melrose," she sneers, her nose high. Christ, she looks quite frightening.

"My lady," I say, tipping my hat and bowing as she breezes past. "Will we be seeing you for champagne later?" I ask, forcing her to stop. I smile on the inside, for I know Mama has not invited her.

"I only attend the weddings of aristocracy."

And we are not that, as she so often likes to remind us. Lady Rose does not like very many people around here, and the feeling is mutual. Mama always looks like she is sucking on a lemon whenever she encounters the old Countess.

"Well, my sister will be a duchess, my lady. And she is marrying a duke."

"Scandalous! He should be locked up for his crimes."

"And what crimes might those be?" I ask, rolling my eyes. "I believe it was your friend Lymington who was proven to be the criminal. Haven't you been reading *The London Times*, my lady? It's very informative."

She snarls and marches away, and I laugh to myself as I amble on, casual and without rush, mulling over the first part of my story once again. It's informative. Explosive. Intriguing.

I've never felt so impatient about anything in my life. It has been mere weeks since my encounter with the highwayman, whom I believe to be a woman, but it feels like I've been waiting centuries for Eliza and Johnny's wedding so that I may claim the front page when she leaves London for her travels.

I look down at my pocket watch. The hour draws closer. I cross the road as a carriage rumbles up to number eight Belmore, where that crook Lymington used to live. His son, Frederick, the man my sister was once promised to, before the Duke returned to Belmore Square, shockingly very alive, has absconded to Cornwall to be with his one true love, which means the house has stood empty for weeks.

"So what snooty lord or lady will be gracing the cobbles of Belmore Square next?" I ask myself, taking the steps back to our house and entering, hearing the chaos of the women in our family getting ready upstairs.

I decide Papa's study is the safest place and enter, pouring myself a Scotch and taking a precious moment of quiet. I sit down and sip, seeing an ornate silver-plated mirror on Papa's desk—definitely not his. I pick it up and spin it before looking at my reflection. My blond hair is pleasingly tidy, my blue eyes bright after a good night's sleep on a belly of water instead of gin. My new rich blue velvet coat complements my gaze perfectly, my fair hair too. I lean closer into the mirror and tweak my hair as the door flies open and Mama bursts in, scanning me up and down for a brief moment, smiling her approval at her boy, before she clocks the mirror in my hand and runs at me, snatching it and running back out.

"I've found it," she yells, slamming the door behind her, making me jump at the loud bang. Mama. Dear, *dear* Mama. She will be in her element today. Loud and proud. There is no question, Eliza's marriage to the Duke of Chester will put the Melrose family firmly on the ton's map.

The door opens again, and Papa enters, fixing his cravat. It prompts me to check mine. "Are you ready, son?" he asks, tweaking his blond hair too.

He has been a different man these past few weeks, since being freed from the financial chains and blackmail of his investor. That crook Lymington had Papa fooled, had us all fooled, until his crimes were exposed. Now, the newspaper is ours again, and Papa is lighter, happier. "I am," I say, getting up and pouring him a Scotch. "We need to replace Porter, Father," I say, handing him the tumbler and going back to the chair behind the desk.

"Indeed we do. We shall advertise for a new journalist very soon. I wouldn't want Eliza to feel like we're replacing her."

I bite at my bottom lip. "I'll write for the newspaper again," I say, bracing myself for his reaction.

"You?" he blurts. "You've always hated writing, Frank. What's changed?"

A mysterious highwayman that I think could be a woman! "Just considering our options."

Looking somewhat taken aback, Father pulls on his jacket. "I must say, I'm surprised, son. I know you've struggled to adapt to business in London since we arrived." He cocks his head, and I smile mildly over the rim of my glass. It is true. I have struggled, my heart definitely not in it, but I have not, however, struggled to fit into the social scene. Or the women's affections.

"Let us discuss it another time. It is your sister's wedding day, a joyous day!" He collects me and leads us out of his study.

"Indeed," I say, as Mama flies past us, Emma still in pursuit, looking worn out. We stop and collectively turn our heads to follow her path. "Where's Clara?" I call, receiving a waft of her hand through the air, dismissive. Everyone is quite distracted today, understandably, and my little sister needs a watchful eye on her. The stable boy may be terrified of me, but my wily baby sister is not.

"I am here, brother," Clara says, appearing at the top of the stairs. I restrain my smile, for I'm certain I will receive a whack if I show my amusement. She looks sickly in lavender and peach frills.

"Clara," Papa says gently. "You look beautiful, my darling."

I cough over my laugh to disguise it. "Striking," I add. Her nostrils flare, she picks up her dress, and she stomps down the stairs, muttering something. I cannot be sure what, something unladylike I expect.

Papa smiles, bright and happy. "She's a live one, isn't she?" He has no idea. Mother flies back across the hallway, and we both step back to avoid being taken off our feet. "Your mother is very keen to become a patron of Almack's, you know." Papa collects his cane and hat from the stand near the door.

"Oh, I know," I reply, laughing.

"So as to have the pick of the crop lined up for Clara to choose from when her time comes to be launched into society."

"Oh, yes, because I am certain it is all about Clara's prospects and not Mother's desire to be one of the most popular ladies of the ton."

"She is already that, my boy. God bless her soul, Florence Melrose has certainly fallen seamlessly into high society."

And, it must be said, she is the source of the best gossip, ladies hoping to be treated to a sneak peek of the next day's news. Mama always obliges, throws them scraps, entices their interest, all to ensure *they* ensure their husbands invest in the next day's edition of *The London Times*, which is a ploy we cannot be opposing of, especially in the wake of the recently levied tax on newspapers that has come to light. It's absurd. At one time, not too many weeks ago, when Lymington was an ally, not an enemy, we were hopeful that he, since he was rather friendly with the Prince Regent, might have a quiet word and deter him from passing the new tax, for it would certainly affect sales, and the family has worked so hard to boost them. Unfortunately, with Lymington gone, although where is yet to be determined, as we have seen neither hide nor hair of him and heard nothing regarding his whereabouts, so has our only opportunity to stop the tax being enforced. Four pence in every seven!

"But she still bakes," Papa goes on, resting his hat atop his head and polishing the gold topper of his cane with his hanky. "Did you know that, son?"

"Yes, I knew that," I say, smiling as he opens the door for me. "She's been at it all night, banging her way around the kitchens."

Papa chuckles. "Let us do your mother proud and show Belmore Square how we Melroses throw a party."

I step out and breathe in, feeling the eyes of many women fall upon me.

"You get your good looks from me, you know that, don't you, Frank?"

I turn a smile onto my father, and it drops the moment I find raised eyebrows. I am certain I am not going to appreciate what comes out of his mouth next. "Maybe it is time to devote those looks to one woman and one woman alone. Be a bit more responsible."

One woman? Good God. Who? There is not one lady in London—not one!—who has succeeded in keeping my interest for longer than one encounter. Perhaps two at a push. A lifetime? I laugh to myself.

Never.

Chapter 2

Eliza and the Duke are entwined in quite the passionate kiss, much to the shock of the clergyman, who is standing looking increasingly gormless with The Book of Common Prayer resting across his palms. I do not claim to know the Duke of Chester particularly well, although, arguably, better than I did a few weeks ago when he came to me with quite the shocking news of betrayal and scandal that cleared his name, but I do know, as do most of Belmore Square and beyond, that when it comes to my sister, he has no boundaries. He will kiss her, touch her, and do as he so pleases with her, whenever he so pleases, and wherever he may be. Frankly, it makes me feel quite uncomfortable, but I'm not about to argue with a rather passionate man.

I look across to Father and see him rolling his eyes, as Mama starts to clap for the happy couple and the rest of the congregation, just family, joins her. "Disgusting," Clara groans from beside me. "God, Frank, why does he feel the need to practically eat our sister alive?"

"It's their wedding day."

"You say it as if it does not happen at every opportunity he has, brother." Clara claps slowly, bored to tears. "Is it finished? I want to go home."

"You will stay put," I say firmly, earning myself a snort of disgust. I look down at her with a cautionary eye. I am not stupid. As I have said, the stable boy may be terrified of me, but Clara is not. She is quite the devious little thing. She is also beautiful and intelligent, not to mention stubborn. She is not in love with the stable boy. She is in love with the excitement of breaking rules, and there are certainly many to break since we arrived in London. Mama and Papa would burst a blood vessel if they were to discover her antics. It was quite a shock that the Duke of Chester had somehow won their eldest daughter's affections. And he's a duke! Disgraced, granted, but still a duke. The stable boy? Lord above, our parents have worked so hard to earn respect for the Melrose name, and now we are related to the Winterses? We cannot risk Clara ruining that with an immature calf love. And we cannot have *me* ruining it with my old sexual escapades. So perhaps Papa is right. I need to be responsible. Responsible sounds utterly boring. "You are sixteen," I remind her, rolling my shoulders, an odd shudder plunging down my spine.

"Am I?" Clara gasps and swings shocked blue eyes my way. I can't say I care for her sarcasm, so we are both dissatisfied in this moment. I return my attention forward, scowling, but not at Clara, more at the tingles on my skin. It is rather cold in here.

"You really do say stupid things, Frank," she goes on. "And who are you to judge who I fall in love with?"

I nibble my bottom lip, my eyes narrowing at the space before me, as Clara continues to drone in my ear, words I am not paying attention to in the least. I discreetly peek over my shoulder, and all is answered when I find Lady Taya Winters on the row behind me. She looks up from her hymn sheet, her bright green eyes shimmering, and I quickly turn back, catching a breath. How is it so a woman can do that? Quite literally steal the air from my lungs? Is she a witch?

"Who are you looking at?" Clara asks, looking over her shoulder.

"No one." I grab her arm and swing her back to face the front. "Now shut up."

"What did you do to Benjamin?" she hisses, quite out of the blue.

"Nothing too brutal." I say, pulling myself back into the room for the joyful occasion, facing the happy couple once again, pretending the enticing sight of Taya Winters isn't lingering behind me.

"Frank!"

"Don't make me take further action, Clara."

She huffs, and it is disrespectful, although completely expected from my littlest sister. And to think when she arrived in London for this season she was full of enthusiasm and couldn't wait to party with the poshest. That all changed rather quickly when she grasped the constraints she faced. "And what will you do?" she asks with a strong voice that she would do well to manage.

"Send you back to the countryside."

"You wouldn't," she whisper-hisses, outraged.

"Try me." I smile and nod to Papa and Mama as they follow Eliza and Johnny out of the church. "A stable boy is a stretch too far, Clara."

"Oh, but a murdering duke is just fine."

I roll my eyes and edge out, walking out of the church with the rest of the family, making a conscious effort not to allow my eyes to fall anywhere near Taya Winters. She makes me feel… uncomfortable. "You know as well as I do that the Duke is not responsible for any murders."

"Unfortunately, yes, I do." She trails me as we leave the church. "It is all right for you, Frank, for you may do as you please and have dalliances galore."

Apparently not. Not anymore. "I know not what you speak of," I say stoically, making Clara roll her eyes.

"Where has that snake Lymington disappeared to, anyway? There has been nothing written in the newspapers about what has happened to that old heathen. Why?"

Clara is right. Absolutely nothing, and I am suspicious. It's no secret the Prince Regent favors *The London Times*, but he is also Lymington's friend, so I expect the fact that Eliza revealed Lymington to be the murderer of Johnny's father and the reason the Winters family left London, for their safety, may change that. Time will tell. "I know not, sweet sister, but rest assured justice will be served."

"Sweet?" she questions, nudging my shoulder as we come to a stop outside the church doors. "Oh, please. And if you want justice served, just put Lymington in a room with our lovely new brother-in-law. I'm sure the Duke will teach him a lesson or two. After all, murder is punishable by death."

I smile at Clara's candid attitude; she'll make a great reporter one day, I'm certain of it, but my smile drops when I catch Taya Winters approaching me. Oh God. I begin to shift, uncomfortable. What the hell is wrong with me? I usually laugh in the face of a pretty girl. Knock them back with my killer smile. Look at them with a million promises in my eyes. This woman, though, has me in a bit of a fluster. I haven't even ever spoken to her. How is this possible?

I bow, as one would expect in the presence of a lady. "My lady," I say politely, keeping my eyes low.

"Mr. Melrose," she replies simply.

And those two words set my insides alight. Good grief, her voice is soft, almost a whisper, sweet without being sickly, seductive without effort.

And dangerous.

My heart thrums. My breathing diminishes, my skin prickles. It is all so very odd, but completely unstoppable, which is most unfortunate because stop it I must.

"Brother?"

I blink myself out of my daze and find Clara looking up at me in question. Then I glance past her and find Lady Taya watching me closely, in interest, as if she has mind-read my mental analysis of her attractive assets and my body's reactions to her. I suddenly feel so very exposed and vulnerable. I blink and look away, claim Clara, and walk us on. I remind myself that I have never been short of a pretty girl to bed, none of whom, I further remind myself, are related to me. "I am all right," I assure Clara as we approach the happy couple, and they are so very, very happy. Sickeningly so. We join Mama and Papa in wishing them well, and I take the needed moment to gather myself. Or, failing that, distract myself.

"You look beautiful, sister," I say, taking in her simple muslin gown that is, naturally, made of the most luxurious material. I cannot even comprehend the level of excitement Eliza must be feeling, for now she will fulfill some of her biggest dreams, the first one being to travel far and wide. I expect she will return with glorious stories to write.

She smiles, a true smile, one that has been so very rare since we moved to London. For that alone, I will forgive the Duke for being a tactless beast, for he is quite tender with Eliza.

"As do you, brother." She reaches for my jacket and tweaks a gold button. "*Another* new coat?"

I wrinkle my nose at her and swat her hand away. "Of course."

"Well, I suppose for a special occasion, it is acceptable."

I roll my eyes and kiss her cheek. "Congratulations."

"Thank you," she says. "You know, I read your story last night while I was trying to get to sleep."

"I hope it did not *send* you to sleep."

She laughs. "It did not."

"What a relief."

"It's very good, Frank, I must say."

I try to be nonchalant, as though of course I know it's good, but Eliza knows me too well. It would be a waste of energy. "You really think so?"

"Yes, I do." She removes a piece of paper from the satin pouch dangling from her wrist and slips it into my inside pocket. "You've always been a good writer, brother; that we all know. What you were lacking was desire, and desire is what makes authenticity. I'm very happy to feel the passion in your words."

"Thank you." She knows that means an incredible amount to me, to know she thinks my words worthy of the front page that she has dominated for so long. I look at Johnny, who is approaching, and shake his hand, clearing my throat as I do. "Make sure you look after her." I frown to myself. "Your Grace," I add. Must I still have to honor him with his title, since I am now family?

"Frank!" Eliza gasps.

"Really?" the Duke asks, his hold of my hand tightening somewhat.

"Yes, really," I confirm, not backing down. "Don't make me hurt you, Winters."

"Papa, please," Eliza begs. "Make him stop."

"Or don't." The Duke squeezes harder, making my teeth clench and my jaw start to ache.

I move in closer, my eyes narrowed, my hand, too, tightening.

"Boys," Mama breathes. "Come now."

Johnny yanks on my hand, forcing me forward, and then his serious, rather deadly expression cracks. And he smiles as he releases my hand and hauls me in for an uncharacteristically friendly hug. "You ass," he says over a laugh, as I discreetly shake my hand back to life. "Perhaps next it will be you walking out of the church with a bride."

I snort, pushing myself out of his embrace. "Let us not get excited," I mutter, making him laugh, and Mama, Papa and Eliza look at me, all with tilted heads. "I'm too busy."

"Doing what?" Clara asks. I give her another warning look. She has too much to say today, and I can't say I appreciate much of it.

"Oh, you are a treasure, my boy," Papa says over a light laugh, waving for Wisteria Winters, the Duke's mother, to join us. "Come, come," he calls, and she does, bringing Johnny's brother, Sampson, and his sister, God help me, Taya, with her. I remain focused on Eliza, not only to avoid Taya, but also because I have never seen my sister looking so radiant and it is quite the vision. I always knew she would need a strong, somewhat determined man to take her on. Frederick Lymington was, bluntly, never going to survive such a task, so it is just as well my sister fell into the affections of another man. Johnny Winters has got what it takes, I'm sure of that.

"Ah, here is your transportation," I say, watching my horse, Figaro, which I have gifted to the newlyweds for a time, for he is fit and steadfast and sure to last the journey to the sea, pulling a remarkably ornate carriage up the lane. "I do hope you enjoy your bridal tour." I wander over when it comes to a stop and helpfully open the door for my sister. "Be sure to make plenty of notes and bring home many tales of your travels."

Eliza smiles, picks up the bottom of her dress, and proceeds to kiss the cheeks of Mama and Wisteria Winters before finishing with Papa, who smiles down at her fondly. Then she goes to her husband, and he helps her up into the carriage before turning and nodding to us.

"We will see you very soon," he says, tipping his hat.

I smile, not looking forward to missing my sister, but very much looking forward to not having her stories to compete with. She's an exceptional writer, could make even the most boring of tales riveting. We wave them off on their travels as a further two carriages are pulled up the lane to take us back to our house to celebrate.

A footman opens the door for me, and I move forward to climb in but stop when I see someone out the corner of my eye. God damn it. "My lady," I smile tightly, my eyes low, sweeping my hand out in gesture for Taya.

She picks up the bottom of her dress and walks past me, stopping just shy of the steps up into the carriage. She keeps her attention forward, and my senses are bombarded by the most intoxicating scent. Lord above, what is that? I discreetly inhale through my nose, fighting off the dizziness. Honeysuckle. It's honeysuckle, delightfully sweet. I find myself leaning forward, drawn to it, and she looks at me, tilting her head. I withdraw and swallow, as she removes her bonnet and shakes out her hair. Long, unruly hair. Hair that is unmanageable, I expect. She climbs in, I close the door, and make my way to another carriage. A safer carriage.

And I vehemently ignore the pulse that's erupted inside my breeches.

"I'm afraid there is no room, Frank," Mama says, shifting up close to Lady Wisteria.

"I'm sure there is space in the other coach," Papa says.

I look back at the other coach, the coach I abandoned only a moment ago, seeing Sampson Winters climbing into it, joining his sister Taya. *Jesus.* The carriage carrying Mama, Papa, Lady Wisteria, and Clara rolls away, and I am left standing on the dirt contemplating my options.

Then Sampson's dark blond, curly mop pops out of the window. "Come on, Melrose, we haven't got all day."

"Pray for me," I whisper to myself, wandering over and climbing up into the carriage. I lower to my seat, which is, unfortunately, opposite His Lordship and Her Ladyship, so avoiding eye contact could be somewhat tricky.

The carriage starts rumbling along, and Taya pulls out a fan, wafting it leisurely in front of her face, blowing her unmanageable hair around her face. My God, what is she doing? I don't know, but I'm beginning to think that the hair matches the owner. Unmanageable. Let it be known, that fan is not there to cool Lady Taya Winters down, for London is hardly boasting soaring temperatures today. No, that fan is a tool, and by God it works.

She gazes out of the window, smiling over the top of it, and I swallow, as Sampson declares his departure, virtually diving out of the window.

"What the bloody hell are you doing?" I blurt, practically lunging for his leg to save him from falling to the cutting stones. Of course, I miss it, for the man moves fast, and I look out of the window, turning my head to see up onto the roof. He's sitting up there, relaxed, taking in the view. "Such a waste to be cooped up like chickens in there," he says happily, turning his eyes to me. "Behave, won't you, Melrose, while I am up here, and you are down there with my sister?"

I huff and pull myself back into the carriage, and I get as comfortable as one can in such a situation. Which is what, I ask myself. What is the situation? Just an attractive lady? I am used to those. But this one? Perhaps it is because she is forbidden, for everyone wants what they cannot have.

I reach into my pocket to retrieve my story and distract myself by reading for a time, so I may ignore the rather pleasant feeling of her eyes on me. I frown, feeling around in my pocket. My heart begins to race. "Oh no," I murmur, scanning the floor at my feet. The bench either side of me. My lap. "Bugger it all, no."

"Looking for this?"

I peek up and find Lady Taya waving a foolscap folio before her face, the piece replacing her fan. I gasp and reach forward, snatching it from her grasp, and she recoils, surprised. My God, did she read it?

"I'll take that as a yes."

I scowl to myself and tuck it away, looking out the window. "I apologize. I did not mean to act so sharply."

"What is it?" she asks.

"Private."

"Oh? You won't tell me? Not even if I promise to keep it a secret?"

I peek at her, and she starts wafting that fan again, her smile hardly seen. *Unmanageable!* "Oh please," I say, unable to stop myself. "Your tactics are insulting." Does she think I'm that shallow? And then it occurs to me that perhaps she does. My God, does *everyone* think I am so shallow? One dimensional? That a seductive smile and a silent promise may influence me. I feel sick. Wait. *What is she promising?*

Frank!

She laughs, and it is like sweet whispers in my ear. "I do not have tactics, Mr. Melrose. I'm simply curious."

"Well, my lady." I smile, and it is forced. "A gentleman never tells."

. "Tells what?" she asks quickly and strongly, coy, letting her smile loose. She needs to stop smiling at me immediately. And laughing. In fact, she shouldn't talk to me or look at me either.

I raise my eyebrows and return to admiring the view, ignoring her question, but am disturbed from the challenge of pretending she isn't here when she starts shifting in her seat. I peek out the corner of my eye, watching her, as she rootles in the top of her dress. *What is she doing?* I gulp, my eyes rooted on the creamy flesh of her chest, until she eventually pulls something out and unfolds it. She settles again, pulling a pencil from her pouch, and starts tilting her head back and forth, concentrating as she studies the paper, taking the pencil in every so often and flicking it here and there. I frown, craning my head to see what it is she is doing.

Her hand stills. She glances up. And I quickly redivert my attention to the view. I can feel her smiling eyes on me, and I sigh, looking at her, making her aware that I am aware of her tactics, though why she is doing this is beyond me.

I scowl and she smirks. My God, she's infuriating. I try to settle, I try so hard, but I continue to fidget terribly, the tension thick. Sexual tension?

"So," she says, and I blink, snapped from my brief silent wondering. "What do you think of this marriage between my brother and your sister?" she asks.

"Is it not a trifle too late to be asking for opinions on this joining?" I don't look at her.

"Perhaps," she muses. "But do you think it is a good coupling? I love my brother dearly."

"As I love my sister, too, my lady."

"Well, my brother is a duke. Our family is renowned."

It is as if she thinks it her responsibility to look out for her brother. For Christ's sake, her brother is an athletic, six-foot four-inch bison of a man, and she is a petite, slender, willowy female with, I realize now, an air of self-importance about her. "Your family, my lady, were renowned for being dead." She flinches, as do I. *Did I just say that?*

"I beg your pardon?"

God damn me. "I mean…" Hell, what do I mean? "My sister is a beautiful woman inside and out." I level Lady Taya Winters with a serious look, forcing myself to withstand the beauty which is now glaring back at me. "Our family owns the most successful newspaper in London, and soon beyond." How dare she question our position. Our worthiness. We've worked hard for it. I inwardly wince. Papa has worked hard for it. Eliza has worked hard for it. Me? "Stop the carriage!" I yell, making Taya shoot forward abruptly when the horses skid to a stop.

"Oh my!" she shrieks.

"Hell!" Sampson shouts from the roof.

I catch Taya and ease her back onto her seat. "I think I shall walk from here," I say gently, getting out of the carriage, feeling suffocated by both the enclosed space and who is in it, and by my apparent shortcomings.

"Mr. Melrose, I didn't—"

"Good day to you, my lady."

"Where are you going, Melrose?" Sampson yells, righting his splayed body on the roof.

I slip on my hat and start the long walk home, pulling my story out of my inside pocket and reading it for the thousandth time, getting tingles from top to toe once again. Imagine, I think, as I wander alone, how new eyes will feel reading it for the first time if I myself am awed?

This is better. Air to breathe freely. My focus reset.

The nerve of that woman.

Dislike her. I must dislike her, and she has given me good cause.

It will be a hell of a lot easier than lusting after her.

Chapter 3

As the bridal party took a little detour around the royal park en route to the house, they are only just arriving when I round the corner into Belmore Square, which is alive, loud and bustling, talk of the newly wedded couple now venturing off to lands far and wide fueling the excitement. I go to the first carriage and offer my hand to Mama, who breezes down as if she is floating, her chin high, daring anyone on the square to question her status, for, let it be known, Florence Melrose has arrived, and she is not going anywhere. The fact Lady Tillsbury and Lady Blythe, both respected ladies of the ton, have become rather fond of my bright, chatty, unconventional mother has helped her cause, no doubt as well as her eldest daughter's marriage to a duke. Ladies of the ton want to be friends with ladies in the know, and Florence Melrose, wife of the owner of the most successful newspaper in London, is certainly in the know. Who needs a gossip paper when we have Florence Melrose?

"Thank you, Francis," Mama says, linking arms with Father, who is waiting for her on the cobbles, and letting him lead her up the steps to our home. They are both floating now, and they both look so very happy. It is a new era for the Melroses, one without stress and financial pressures. One where I shall step up.

I pull my jacket in and take one step but pause when I notice something is missing. I look left and right, then back to the carriages. "Bugger," I hiss to myself. Where the hell has she disappeared to? I look toward Mr. Fitzgerald's house, the architect who designed Belmore Square and also the stable boy's employer. I must go there and have a word with him. Ask him kindly to threaten the boy with his job if he continues to see Clara, because my word of warning, I fear, has had no effect whatsoever. Yes, I must. And there is no time like the present.

"And where are you going?" Taya Winters asks as I pass her, my eyes purposely avoiding her willowy form.

"I don't believe that is a concern of yours," I say, being as polite as I can be, smiling tightly, my eyes low as I walk away from her. Since my body's reactions are quite unstoppable around this woman, I must not look at her. Or smell her. In fact, avoiding her is imperative; if she would only stay out of my way.

"I'm not sure my brother, or, equally, your sister, will be too pleased about your absence when they arrive home for the celebrations."

I stop and frown at the intricate, gilded railings that circle the gardens of Belmore Square. Whatever is she talking about? "My sister and her husband"—who, highly distressingly, is Taya's brother, therefore there is no getting away from her—"have left for Paris, where they will spend a few days being all romantic, I suppose, and then sail to Italy and a few other European destinations, before they head for Ind..." I fade off, not just because Taya is showing amusement, but because another carriage has just turned onto the square, and pulling it is a horse I recognize. *My* horse. Figaro.

"Ah, here they are!" Wisteria sings, prompting Mama and Papa to turn at the top of the steps, where all the residents of Belmore Square can see them perfectly well.

"What is going on?" I ask no one in particular.

Taya Winters is quick to enlighten me. "They decided to postpone their bridal tour."

"Pardon me?" I turn a stunned look onto her, one which I can tell she is relishing. Postpone? But they cannot. I have a story to publish. News to tell.

"Their bridal tour, they are not go—"

"Yes, yes, I heard you the first time." This is rather unfortunate, I must say.

Taya blinks her surprise. "You are very rude, Mr. Melrose."

I laugh under my breath. This woman is quite unbelievable. "I am rude?"

"Yes, you are rude," she says, folding her arms over her chest, and, as a consequence, further pushing her breasts up. Naturally, and unstoppably, my eyes drop to the swelling, peachy globes that are only partially covered by her dark blonde waves.

"I apologize," I say over a swallow, ripping my eyes away, feeling rather hot.

"Maybe I won't accept your apology."

"That is your prerogative, my lady." I smile and relish the slight tilt of her jaw. I'm certain she wants to take my apology and push it down my throat, and because I am truly concerned she may do just that—for she apparently has sass for days—I climb the steps to my rather pleased-looking parents. "Eliza is not leaving to travel?"

"Not yet, dear," Mama says.

Papa shrugs. "She claims to have work to do, and I have long stopped arguing with your sister on matters of work."

Well, this is perfect. My plan has just gone up in smoke. I would like to tell Eliza's new husband to insist. Unfortunately, I cannot do that without risking upsetting a great many people. Bugger it all, what now?

I turn to face the square as rapturous applause breaks out, seeing the carriage come to a stop. So now they love the Duke, do they? Idolize him? The hypocrites. These people gave the Winterses hell. Snubbed them. Practically chased them out of town, and here they all are celebrating the Duke's happy ever after.

I watch the ton welcome back the previously disgraced Duke with open arms as I lean on my cane, feeling that familiar burning sensation again. Eyes on me. *Don't look, Frank. Do not look.*

But my eyes betray me, and I peek up. She is standing at the back of the carriage, and when I catch her eye, she quickly looks away. I watch in fascination as her chest slowly rises and falls. Watch her flustered hand brush her hair out of her face, and then she peeks at me again, and I catch it, as well as the flush of her cheeks.

And it occurs to me in this moment...she's attracted to me, too. "Oh dear," I murmur, my eyes absorbed by her. "This is rather unfortunate."

She watches me murmur the words, but then, as if snapping out of a trance, she shakes herself back to life and her eyes narrow on me, as if she has just this moment remembered that I have upset her. Good. The hostility, it is a good thing.

I shake my head to myself and take the steps down to the cobbles, circling round the back of her, and I get my mouth as close to her ear as I can without rousing suspicion or attention. *What are you doing, Frank?* "You're not my type." I simply cannot help myself, feeling as though the power is now in my hands.

Taya laughs, and it causes chaos behind my breeches. "I have heard *every* woman is your type, Mr. Melrose." She turns toward me, and her face is suddenly so very close to mine, so close, in fact, I can feel the heat of her breath on my cheeks. I swallow, and it is extremely lumpy from trying to be discreet. She has heard? Damn it, what exactly has she heard?

"Fortunately, you are not *my* type." Her green eyes blink slowly as she, equally slowly, scans my face.

"No?"

"No," she whispers, her voice but a purr, "I am not partial to rakes."

"Thank goodness," I murmur, my eyes falling to those lovely, full, kissable rosy lips. It's almost a travesty that God would bless a woman I cannot touch with such beauty.

"I suppose you desire a woman with not an ounce of steel in her." Taya blinks and her lashes flutter. She bites her lip. And completely and helplessly mesmerized, I find the space between our mouths closing, the heat of her breath getting hotter on my skin, our surroundings disappearing. *Kiss her. Taste her.*

"I beg to differ," I say, smelling the pleasure to be had.

"And what do you think you are doing?" she asks in a whisper, so quietly, but so very loud too. I stop just shy of her mouth.

Lord above!

That is a very good question. *What the hell am I doing?*

I gulp, move back, quickly look around us, relieved to see everyone is distracted by the happy couple, thank God. I shake myself back to life, resisting adjusting myself.

"I think it's best if we stay out of each other's way," Taya says, and I laugh.

"Fine by me." I value my life *and* my relationship with my sister. "Enjoy the rest of your day, my lady." I bow and force a smile, backing away.

"Oh brother." Clara's singsong voice is high and distant, one might say satisfied too, and I follow the sound up the front of our house to her bedroom window, where I find her casually leaning on her forearms, looking down at me. "Are you all right?" she asks, somewhat cheerily.

Bugger everything to hell.

"Quite all right, sister," I assure her, cringing, not bothering to question how much Clara might have seen from her view up there, as I am sure it was quite a lot while I was briefly lost in a trance. At least I know now she is not with the stable boy. It is a small mercy.

I leave Taya behind, and by the time I have made it back up the steps to the door, everyone is in the drawing room drinking champagne, including, and I'm still not over it, my sister and her new husband. I swipe up a glass and join them. "So you have delayed your bridal tour," I say as casually as I can, taking a little sip of my drink, looking around the drawing room, appearing as nonchalant as I sound.

I sense Eliza's small smile and find her. "We have," she says simply, with no elaboration, which, I have no doubt, is intentional, for she knows, as we have spoken about my encounter with the highwayman who we think may be a woman at great length, that I am very keen to publish my story, but there is little point when Eliza is dominating the pages of *The London Times* with her extended, quite riveting story of the Winters family. Over the past few weeks, there has not been one long report, but many reports, the whole, unbelievable story being broken down into segments, a business tactic that I myself recommended. I didn't, admittedly, realize that this would become a long-term feature, and by long-term, I mean longer than the few weeks in between Johnny asking for Eliza's hand, them actually getting married, and then going off around the world. "If, dear brother," she goes on, "you had bothered to take the time to read my work this morning, you would have realized the story is far from finished."

God damn *me*. "I was busy."

"Purchasing another new jacket?"

"I do not support this, for the record," Johnny says, looking stoic and unimpressed, making me swing shocked eyes his way. Oh? Well, this is interesting. How might my determined sister react to a statement such as that from her new husband? Is he stupid?

"You do not support my career?" Eliza asks, indignant. "Am I to remind you that—"

"Never a need to remind me of anything, my sweet duchess." The Duke pulls her into his side and pushes his mouth into her hair. "I simply hoped that after weeks of you writing as if you may never write again, I might get you all to myself for a while."

"Well," Eliza says, practically sighing. "I'm sure you can wait a little while longer."

A little while longer? And how long is that? "How far can you possibly stretch this story?" I ask. "Christ, Eliza, write a bloody novel if you want to drag this out."

She laughs a little. "Need I remind *you* that it was, in fact, your idea to break my story down into segments? For the benefit of sales, I might add." She raises her glass. "A very prudent business move, I must say, brother."

I scowl but quickly correct it, for clashing with my sister will not help, and, actually, I love her too much to argue with her. So I shall appeal to her softer side, as I know she has one, even if she conceals it, and since it appears I may have the support of the Duke, I am open to try. "Come now, Eliza," I implore with a soft voice. "You must start married life and enjoy it."

"I'm sure your encouragement is purely selfless."

"He is right, Eliza," Johnny says, raising my hopes. If anyone can get through to my sister, it is her new husband. He has his methods. I refuse to acknowledge what, indeed, those methods are, as one does not wish to think of their sister in such a way. "I fear you are becoming a little obsessed with the story." He pouts a little, thinking as he takes a sip of his wine. Obsessed. I certainly know how that feels, so I can sympathize. But I do not have a marriage to concentrate on. "Not unlike how obsessed you became with me, I suppose," he adds, thoughtful.

She swats his arm, prompting a chuckle from both him and me. "Be warned, Winters," Eliza says in a steely tone that even I am wary of. We both pipe down.

"Consider me warned." The Duke shrugs, giving me sorry eyes, and I inwardly deflate. I should know by now, after nearly twenty years with my sister, she is a determined little thing. I'm not going to win this, therefore I shall have to revise my battle plan. "Now, I need to feed my wife," Johnny says, "so if you will excuse us." He places a hand on Eliza's back and pushes her onward, and I grimace when I see her look up at him all dreamily.

Love.

"God, I'm surrounded," I mumble, switching my empty glass for a suitably full one.

"Surrounded by what?" Taya asks, joining me. I look out the corner of my eye to her wild blonde hair splayed unconventionally all over her shoulders as she, too, enjoys some champagne. "I thought we agreed to avoid each other?" My eyes fall to her lips as they press to the glass. A slither of her pink tongue appears. Her neck lengthens as she sips, extending the smooth, flawless skin.

"You don't like me, do you, Frank?"

That is a very loaded question. "No." I laugh lightly, and it is without humor. "I do not."

"You're such a gentleman." She looks up at me. "Tell me, what is this breaking story you're preparing?"

"Excuse me?"

"I overheard you speaking with Her Grace just last week."

"Her Grace?" I ask, in a complete muddle.

"Your sister, Mr. Melrose. She is a duchess now."

Of course. How could I forget? "You were eavesdropping?"

Her indignance is quite charming. "No, I was passing the library and overheard." Her eyes drop to my breast pocket, her teeth sinking into her lip. "I don't suppose it has anything to do with the piece of paper you dropped in the carriage, does it?"

Good Lord, did she have a peek? I back away. "It's been a pleasure as always, my lady."

Her smile falters, and I quickly turn away before she can correct it, taking a few deep breaths as I go. I finish another champagne, replace it with yet another, and start to mingle with the partygoers. I will—as everyone else seems to be doing, even the bride and groom who are supposed to be on their way to Paris, damn it—enjoy the party.

Chapter 4

Quite some hours later, I am far more intoxicated than I should be, along with the rest of the family, including—and it's a surprise, for I have never seen her drunk—Eliza, but not including—and it's no surprise because he is somewhat of a control freak and quite committed to taking care of my sister, something I cannot fault—my new brother-in-law.

I have consciously and successfully avoided Taya Winters, though it has not been without difficulty. After all, we are in the same house. Unfortunately, as a result, I have forgotten to check up on Clara, a fact I am reminded of now as I sway in the hallway admiring a family portrait of the Melroses. Clara's whereabouts are something that should be quite a priority given her recent jaunts and vanishing acts, but, and it is of great comfort, Clara would most certainly struggle to escape the house, for the party has spilled into every room on the ground level, including the hallway, where Dawson has spent most of his evening opening and closing the front door, announcing and sending off well-wishers, one of which included Lizzy Fallow and her new husband, the decrepit, and quite repulsive, in my humble opinion, Viscount Millingdale. Avoiding her was quite easy, for she could not leave her husband's side, and as luck would have it, her husband can hardly walk, so they were stationed in the drawing room and did not move for their entire visit, which, as luck would have it again, was not very long at all. I imagine the old Viscount needed his bed. I shudder, wondering how the fresh *young* wife of Millingdale may be coping with the quite unthinkable chore of being the new viscountess. Lizzy Fallow's faults, and I know her to have many, and not all as admirable as ambition, may be the end of her. She looked thoroughly miserable this eve. Well, she asked for it. She always told me she would be a true lady. That was when she was talking to me, of course. She no longer does, and I am yet to fathom if her disdain for me is because I didn't beg her not to marry old Millingdale, or if I dived out of bed before she had a chance to finish telling me that she suspected the old Viscount was unable to sire an heir. I knew she was an ambitious young lady, who would not settle for a title-less man, but I never anticipated she would suggest I should be her secret lover and help ensure she fulfills her obligations as the new Viscountess. I have never gotten dressed so quickly, and as soon as I was decent, I went straight to Kentstone's and lost myself in the rooms there. That was until Eliza and Johnny found me and carried me home, for I was as drunk as a sailor on blue ruin and quite determined to indulge in the body of any old Barque of Frailty who didn't have a hidden agenda. It was quite eye-opening, I must say. Alas, Lizzy Fallows is quite determined, as proven at the Prince's birthday celebrations when I was pulled into the corner where she kissed me. She kissed me like a desperate woman until I firmly but gently removed myself from her clutches. The incident did not escape Eliza's notice. Nothing gets past that girl, I swear it. And for some strange reason, Eliza holds me in high regard. For that reason, it was easy to let her believe I was affected by Lizzy Fallows's marriage to Millingdale and that was indeed the reason why I got ruined on the ruin. She thinks I have a heart. I suppose I do, for my love for my family knows no bounds. But it is quite dead beyond that. I seek only pleasure. Nothing more, and I will only venture where it is safe to do so.

I shudder as I make my way to the stairs and climb them slowly, tugging at my cravat, which appears to have become tighter as the evening has progressed. I approach Eliza's room and stop, thoughtful for a moment, before I clasp the knob and push the door open. Her bed is pristine, and it shall remain that way forevermore now she is wedded and residing with her new husband at number one Belmore Square. I smile, wondering how she will take to life as a duchess. Like everything Eliza does, I expect she will be quite wonderful at it, and I will surely miss my sister, despite her living a stone's throw away, just across the square. But still, and it saddens me, our conversations over breakfast were one of my most favorite times of day, even when, and she often did, Eliza exasperated me. Be that as it may, I am also delighted for her, that she has found a man who may complement her rather than suppress her, a rarity in today's world, we all know. She really does deserve a honeymoon and a break, and I know her to be eager to travel, something Johnny is equally eager to fulfill. I would not usually wish my sister away—I will miss her dreadfully, but as long as she remains in London, I know she will not be able to resist writing, and as long as she writes, the front page will be hers. I would hate her to see me as another oaf ready to discredit her efforts and ambitions, so I shall bide my time. It pains me, but I must.

I close the door to her room, carrying on to Clara's. Without knocking, I enter and am greeted by darkness and silence. "Bugger," I curse, squinting, trying to see but failing, so I step back and take a candle from the table at the top of the stairs and hold it before me, illuminating my youngest sister's room. I smile when I see her bundled up under the covers, as still as could be. "Sweet dreams, sister," I say quietly, hoping her dreams are ones perhaps a little more realistic than the stable boy, although I fear my hopes are wasted, as I pull the door closed. But before I can release the knob, I still and think. I think very carefully. I think about Clara and her craftiness. I think about how distracted everyone has been all day, including me. I think about how well I know my little sister.

I open the door again and march across her room, tugging the sheets back, discovering a quite convincingly shaped pile of pillows and blankets before the waft of the sheets extinguishes the candle and I am in darkness again. "The little scoundrel!" I rush to the door.

And walk straight into the frame, my forehead bouncing off the hard wood. "Bugger it all to blasted hell!" I yell, rubbing at my head with one hand and feeling my way to the top of the stairs where I am eventually blessed with the candlelight streaming up from the table by the front door. "I'm going to strangle her," I declare to no one, taking the steps fast, but slowing down to a less urgent pace when I encounter Mama at the bottom with Wisteria Winters. Damn it, I was hoping to slip out quietly, locate my youngest, wayward sister, and return her to our home without being detected by either Mama or Papa, after, of course, I have given her a thorough bloody scolding.

"Frank!" Mama is slurring terribly, a sign, I am sure, of too much indulgence on this eve, though I can hardly begrudge her the luxury of all the champagne, and she has certainly made the most of it. She's as drunk as only a man should be. "I was telling Lady Wisteria that I may be voted a patron of Almack's!"

I nod to Johnny's mother. It is no rumor that she is unfathomably beautiful. *Her daughter has inherited that.* "My lady," I say, and she smiles softly before Mama drags her to the drawing room.

"Come, I must tell you about Lady Tillsbury, too, for I am certain you will love her. Oh, did you see my cake? I made it, don't you know."

My mother's relentless and tiresome need to be the most popular lady on the square has not waned in the wake of the scandal. In fact, I believe now she is more determined than ever to show all members of the ton what she is made of, which is endurance. Add in her congeniality and, some might say, vivacity, Florence Melrose is making quite the impression on the other ladies of the square.

I pull the front door open and come to an abrupt halt once again, this time finding Eliza and the Duke in my way. I frown when I see him holding up my sister, and frown harder when she grins at me. "I'm a bit top heavy, Frank," she slurs, hiccuping.

"I can see that."

She falls into Johnny's chest. "Oh dear," he says, smiling down at the back of her head. I roll my eyes. He's even smitten when she's drunk. "Come, my duchess, let me take you home."

"Yes!" Her arms lift with much too much effort and hook over Johnny's neck, where she practically hangs, looking up at him through squinted eyes. "Take me home and do wicked things to me, Your Grace."

"My God," I murmur, pulling the door closed behind me. "You've corrupted her."

"Oh please, Frank," the Duke says, hoisting Eliza up and virtually tossing her onto his shoulder. "Your sister needs no corrupting I can assure y—" He jolts, his eyes widening a fraction.

"What is it?" I ask, frowning, craning my neck to see around his big body to my sister hanging down his back. He turns to assist, and Eliza comes into my view. So do her petite hands, which are currently, and quite outrageously, squeezing the Duke's derriere. "Oh for the love of God," I grumble, disgusted, looking at the Duke, hoping to find disapproval as potent as mine. I am hoping in vain, for he looks delighted, his grin as wide as Belmore Square.

"How I do love my wife."

"Please remember, *Your Grace*, that your wife is my sister, and I can't say I appreciate such brazenness in my presence." I feel somewhat corrupted myself, and the Duke jolts again as the sound of Eliza's hands slap his backside, making me flinch, along with Johnny. "I cannot bear it," I say, passing them quickly. "Is it not punishment enough that I must deal with one barmy sister?" I say, walking with conviction and in long strides toward Mr. Fitzgerald's house. "But two?"

"Where are you going at this hour?" the Duke calls. "Pray do tell I will not be forced to venture into town and drag you from the arms of any naked light skirt."

I scowl at the darkness and rub at my sore head before looking back, finding an irritatingly cocky smile. He is a fine one to speak, as I know he too has frequented the rooms of Kentstone's before he courted Eliza, so if I am being made to feel disgraceful, I shall extend the same kindness to His Grace. "I hope you have cancelled your membership now that you are a taken man, Your Grace."

His face drops. "What the hell happened to your forehead? It's as red as a baboon's arse."

"Don't ask."

"And where the hell are you going?"

"To rescue another sister from the arms of *another* highly unsuitable male."

The Duke smiles, starting the walk across the square to number one. "I do so hope you have better luck this time, Melrose."

"I will," I reply quietly, walking on, my head beginning to pound, and, let it be known, it is not through alcohol. Clara has a lot to answer for.

When I reach Fitzgerald's house, I stomp up the steps and bang on the door with little finesse or care for disturbing anyone sleeping in their homes nearby. It swings open rather swiftly, and Fitzgerald's butler looks me up and down. "Mr. Melrose?"

"I must see Fitzgerald," I say, pushing past him, hearing movement at the top of the stairs where I find Fitzgerald pulling on a robe.

"Melrose, what of this ungodly hour?"

"Have you seen Clara?"

His sleepy face scrunches up as he takes the stairs to join me in the hallway. "Young Miss Melrose? Should she not be in bed at the hour?"

"Indeed she should, except she is not."

"And why, may I ask, would you believe I would know of her whereabouts?"

I falter in my approach. Hell, to openly ask about the stable boy, I risk ruining Clara, especially if my suspicions are correct and she is, indeed, with him. Why didn't I consider that before? Perhaps because I am full of champagne. *Or because your mind is elsewhere!* "Ummm…" I clear my throat, coughing into my balled fist. "I believe she had a question she was quite insistent on asking your fine self." What question? I must think on my feet once more, for I am certain I will only get away with this ridiculous performance if I act it well. "We were discussing it earlier, you see, and, impatient as she is, she wanted an answer to her inquiry quite promptly, so I thought perhaps when I noticed she was missing from her bed, she had come here to clear up the mystery." What on earth am I rambling on about? Fitzgerald must think me mad. Or ape-drunk. And on that thought, I start rocking back on my heels, hoping to convince him I am, in fact, totally foxed.

Fitzgerald shakes his head in dismay. "Let me see if I can perhaps put her mind at rest."

"Thank you."

His head tilts, and he waits, silent, while I wait, confused. "The question?"

"Oh, yes, the question." Damn it. "Yes, the question." What is the blasted question? For Christ's sake, I will kill her at this rate, so what does it matter if my little sister is ruined?

"Yes, the question. And make it good, Melrose, so I may return to my bed at least satisfied I was awoken for a worthy reason."

"Thirteen!" I blurt, something coming to me, something I have actually wondered myself but never thought to ask.

"Thirteen, what?"

"There is no number thirteen Belmore Square," I say, turning and going to the door, passing Fitzgerald's baffled-looking butler. I open it and motion to the beautiful square, where the finest properties circle the lush, colorful square gardens that are contained by shiny gilded railings. "One through to fourteen, but you miss number thirteen and I…" I hesitate. "Clara has often wondered why, and now she has piqued my curiosity too." I face him with a smile, quite proud of myself for thinking so quickly, especially when I am quite top heavy. I'm even prouder when I find Fitzgerald smiling broadly. I believe I may have dug myself, and Clara, out of this little hole.

"I was wondering when someone might ask."

"You were?"

"Yes, albeit I never expected it to be in the middle of the night." He comes to me and looks proudly out at his square. "There are a few reasons, if you must know."

"Oh?" I look out on the square too, admiring it with Fitzgerald.

"I'm rather religious, Melrose," he says. "And a tad superstitious, I suppose, so, you see, I omitted the number thirteen for fear of cursing it. Judus Iscariot was the thirteenth guest at the Last Supper and went on to kill Jesus Christ. Also, Loki, who was notoriously terrible and suspected to be the root of all evil in the world, was the thirteenth god to arrive at the party in Valhalla, destabilizing the twelve gods who were rather enjoying themselves up until his entrance." He smiles. "Add to that the fact that two houses on my previous projects have burned down, I decided to eliminate the number from my life."

"Those houses—"

"Were both number thirteen."

"Bloody hell."

"Indeed. Thankfully, they stood empty at the time. Perhaps it is foolish, but I would rather not have the deaths of anyone playing on my conscience."

"Seems reasonable."

"I agree."

"Great. Then I must be going." I still need to find my wayward sister. "Thank you, Fitzgerald. Do sleep well." I march down the steps, surely leaving behind a quite perplexed man staring at me. I hear the door close and stop on the cobbles, casting a beady eye across the square, wondering where on earth she could be. "The stables," I say to myself. "Of course, the stables." I pivot fast.

And crash into something. It yelps, and I realize some*thing* is, in fact, some*one*. "I do apolo—" I am bombarded from all directions by the most inexplicable shocks that render me quite stunned, but I still manage, out of instinct, I suppose, to lift my hands and hold on to the person, stopping them from falling flat on their face.

There is no yelp this time, but a…whimper.

The shocks I felt sizzle under my skin, heating it, and I look down and come face-to-face with a mass of dark blonde hair. Her face is buried in my chest. Or squished. Or flattened. My God, her scent is quite intoxicating. Honeysuckle. It reminds me of our home in the country. The smell is as bold as she is.

We remain quite still, the pair of us, my fingers clawed into the bare skin of her upper arms between the end of her gloves at her elbows and the start of her cap sleeves. Creamy, soft, warm flesh. I find, and it is quite out of my control, my nose dropping to the top of her head and inhaling, taking a huge hit of that scent. An overdose, I am sure, for I am dizzy. Never before has a woman made me dizzy with pleasure, least of all when fully clothed. Blood starts to pump in all places, and I shift from one boot to the other, willing it to pipe down, but when her bosom pushes subtly into my chest, even with my smart new velvet jacket between us, my attempts fail miserably. My God, I am on fire. Burning.

And then so very quickly, I am stone cold, my hands dropping her and moving back. "Are you hell-bent on being ruined?" I ask, running a stressed hand through my hair.

Taya's eyes dart, her mouth opening and closing rapidly, as if she's struggling for words. And then she finds some. "Get your dirty hands off of me," she seethes. "Or, I swear it, I will scream so loud, Scotland will hear me."

Somewhat dazed and very confused, I stare at her fierce expression. "What?"

"I am not interested in your advances, Mr. Melrose, so please do stay away or I will set my brothers on you." Spinning, she pushes her shoulders back and walks away, leaving me standing like a gormless fool on the cobbles, wondering what the hell just happened. Advances? Brothers? She is stark raving mad!

I go after her, outraged, stamping along behind her, chasing her heels, my fury building. "You are insane, woman," I say, looking at her arms swinging to match her stride, her hands clasping the skirt of her dress to hold it up, making it swoosh dramatically. "I would never waste my affections on you."

She snorts. "You make it sound as if you are fussy, and we all know that not to be true if you entertain the likes of Lady Dare."

What on earth? "How the hell do you know that?" It is out before I can think to stop it, when I should have taken a moment to consider denying it. But, my God, she's infuriating. Twists my brain. Sends me crazy!

"I overheard a conversation between your mother and my lovely new sister-in-law."

She did? She has a habit of eavesdropping. And whyever would Mama and Eliza be discussing my love life? I will be having a very stern word with them. Wait. I don't have a love life. "Jealous?" I ask, with a lack of anything else to say in my defense, but it appears that one word has quite an impact, and Taya stops and gasps, her nostrils flaring angrily. I smirk dirtily, satisfied.

"Absolutely not!"

"Are you quite sure about that?"

"*Quite* sure," she grates, before shoving me in my chest, making me grunt a little with surprise, and marches on.

I narrow my eyes on her back. "You should not be out alone at this hour." I bark, an annoying streak of concern emerging. No hour at all, actually, but something tells me Taya Winters is not one for rules.

"Everyone is too drunk to notice my absence. One brother is tending to his new wife and the other has paid a visit to Gladstone's."

Oh? Not Kentstone's, the less respectable gentleman's club? That surprises me. I would have expected Sampson Winters to be quite the rogue. Regardless, back to the matter at hand. I may find Taya annoying, for many reasons, but I do not wish harm upon her, so I shall do the right thing and escort her home, despite it being highly inappropriate, and hope we are not spotted alone. I would have guessed Taya Winters cares not for being ruined, if I hadn't heard with my own ears her concern for the family name. So what on earth is she doing wandering out alone at night and placing herself in the company of a man without a chaperone?

Taya turns sharply into the gardens, and I do not contest her as it is probably a good idea to keep in the shadows to avoid being seen. So I follow, watching her unruly hair bounce across her back, the glossy waves shimmering when the moonlight catches the shiny strands. I have never met anyone so self-righteous in my life. She condemns Lady Dare, and yet she behaves just as inappropriately. She really is deluded. My eyes drop to the bunched fists around the material of her dress, seeing, even in the darkness, that her knuckles are white. She releases her dress but keeps up her march, letting the material drag across the ground behind her. Mistake. My boot steps on a trailing piece of fabric, jarring her, and she stumbles backward.

"My God!" she gasps, my arms rising speedily to catch her,

and, annoyingly, but it is something I have come to expect, sparks fly around the square on contact. *My God indeed.*

She's laid across my arm, her fists now clenching the front of my new coat, screwing it up, but I cannot say I am all too bothered about that in this moment, as I stare into her wide green eyes. I see the lump in her throat from her swallow. See her wet her lips before they part. Hear the sound of her dragging in air. Or is that me? Compelled and quite out of my mind, I'm sure, my mouth starts lowering of its own volition to hers, her lips like a truly powerful magnet.

But a noise snaps me out of the moment and Taya shoots out of my arms, leaving them feeling quite empty. "Damn it," she curses, quite unladylike, it must be said, as she looks past me. And then she's off again, darting down the path to the center of the gardens. I frown and look back, seeing her brother, Sampson Winters, walking with quite some sway into Belmore Square, singing to himself. I laugh under my breath and wander back out to greet him, knowing his infuriating sister will be quite safe hiding in a bush in the gardens for now.

"Evening, my lord," I say, crossing the cobbles toward the youngest of Taya's brothers, the Earl of Chester.

"Melrose," he chants, undoubtedly too loudly for this hour. "Or should I call you brother now?"

"Melrose will do." Because if Sampson Winters was to call me brother, Taya Winters might like to, too, and that would be most unfortunate. "And how was Gladstone's this eve?"

"I wouldn't know, for I was not there."

"Oh?" I say, frowning. "I thought…" I catch my tongue in time, as something else comes to me. "Ohhhhh," I breathe. "Kentstone's?" The mention of the seedy club where ladies of the night hang around and blue ruin will, indeed, ruin you, makes me wince. It's as I thought. He's far more suited to Kentstone's than the stuffiness of Gladstone's.

Sampson Winters grins, and I am sure I do not appreciate

it. What does he know about me and Kentstone's? I am about to ask, but he enlightens me before I can. "I heard quite an amusing tale about a certain rescue of a certain drunken man from the rooms of Kentstone's some weeks ago. That's you by the way. The drunken man."

"I gathered," I say quietly. "What is it with you Winterses listening to conversations you should not be listening to?"

"We Winterses?" he asks, interested.

I am unsure as to whether or not I like Sampson Winters. He is far too cocksure. "I walked myself out of Kentstone's," I say, making that clear. It was the rest of the journey I didn't contend with all too well. Or remember, for that matter. I suppose I should be grateful for Eliza's intervention that evening. And Johnny's assistance, because as strong minded as my sister is, she is slight and would never have held me up all the way home on her own.

Sampson laughs. "Good evening to you, Melrose."

I stuff my hands in my pockets wishing I could also stuff something in his mouth to shut him the hell up. "Good evening to you." I hope he walks through the gardens and finds Taya hiding in the bushes. I hope he thoroughly scolds her too. Which reminds me...

Clara.

I wander off toward the stables, looking back, seeing Sampson staggering from one side of the path to the other, making his journey, I'm sure, especially long. But rather than exit on the side where number one Belmore Square is, his home, he diverts, heading down the right-hand side. *Where the hell is he going?* I sigh and turn back to ensure Taya gets home safely. Surely that is Sampson's responsibility? Of course it is, but I cannot tell him I know of her whereabouts without rousing suspicion. So instead of alerting Sampson, I watch as he approaches a house and knocks at the door. "Oh good God," I whisper, watching as the door opens, revealing Scarlett Dare in quite an outrageous sheer chemise. Her blonde hair, that is usually so polished and perfect in public, is spilling over her shoulders. She smiles suggestively at Sampson, reaches for his jacket, fists it, and hauls him into her home. Scarlett Dare. Oh, Scarlett Dare. When her husband died, he left her rich and free too, and with that liberty came nonconformity. I can attest to that, for I have stepped into number six Belmore Square where Lady Dare resides, and I have experienced that nonconformity. Only on a couple of occasions, I must add. Or was it three? Regardless, my brief encounters with her came to an abrupt stop when I discovered, only recently, mind you, that she threatened to expose Eliza as being ruined. She might be a smooth seductress, but her integrity is somewhat cracked. It appears to be a consistent problem with the women I have become involved with in London, and a reminder of easier, more carefree days in the countryside. The ironmonger's daughter was not so ruthless. Neither was the butcher's daughter. Nor the farmer's or baker's. Where is these women's integrity? Their ambitions beyond bending a man to their will?

I expect whips and restraints await Sampson Winters this evening. "Lucky devil," I say without thought, making myself start. I can only conclude that my lack of action these past few weeks is contributing to my pathetic thoughts. I should like to be entertained by Scarlett Dare about as much as I should like to be tortured. I look around, as if searching for witnesses to my slip-up.

And I find one.

"Lucky?"

I roll my eyes. She looks to be over her earlier fluster. Good. So am I. "Are you still here?" I pick up my feet and walk onward, deciding I'm done trying to stop her being ruined or murdered. She clearly has a death wish.

Reckless. Unmanageable.

"Go home, Taya," I say tiredly, exhausted by this evening. By the whole day, in fact. Not only have I had my plans derailed by my ambitious sister, I have been forced to endure the silver tongue of Taya Winters.

And her sparkling beauty.

And heavenly scent.

Forbidden!

"Oohhh Fraaaank," a young, sweet voice sings.

I look up at a window of our house, seeing Clara in much the same position that I saw her in earlier when she was also spying on me. Basically, with a front row seat to all of my pathetic shows. The relief I feel that I have found her is lost amid my growing annoyance. "Go to bed," I demand as she looks between Taya and me. "This minute, or so help me God…"

She grins, infuriatingly smug, and pulls the window down, and, without looking at Taya, I walk on, exhausted. But stop. Think. "Bugger it all," I mumble, turning back, keeping my eyes low, and taking the top of her arm. "Home," I order.

"I can walk myself," she protests, stumbling along beside me, her spare hand trying to pry my fingers from her flesh.

"Not fast enough, and I should like to get to bed." I need to rise in the morning with a clear head and revise my plan now that I have learned of the unfortunate fact that my beloved sister Eliza has postponed her travels.

"Anyone ever tell you what a terrible gentleman you are?"

"Never, perhaps because to everyone else I am the perfect gentleman."

"So it is just me that is lucky enough to have to endure your winning personality."

"Apparently so."

"Lucky devil," she whispers.

"Jealous?"

She snorts, disgusted. "You're nothing but a rake, Frank Melrose, and as I have said before, I am not partial to rakes."

She's full of the devil. "If you find me so repulsive, my lady, then staying away from me should not be a problem for you, should it?"

"Not at all."

"Good. I'm glad we've got that matter resolved."

We make it to the gate outside number one, and I open the creaky little thing and push her through it, looking up when their butler, Hercules, opens the door. He shakes his head in dismay. *I get it, my friend. I do.* "Good evening," I say, nodding to him and scowling at Taya, before turning and heading home, fighting to get this funny buzzing feeling on my skin whenever she is close under control. It makes no sense to me. It's quite frustrating.

Chapter 5

The next morning at a most unfortunate early hour, I stroll into the dining room as I fasten the buttons of my new gray velvet jacket. The table is partially laid, courtesy of our trusted butler Dalton, who never ceases to amaze me with his uncanny ability to know exactly who needs what and when, such as now. I have risen precisely seventy-five minutes earlier than my usual nine o'clock, and, somehow, Dalton has a fresh pot of coffee awaiting me.

I pour myself a cup and wander to the window, feeling somewhat melancholy as I note the screaming silence. The emptiness. Other than coffee on the table upon my arrival to the dining room, I would also usually find the eldest of my sisters, Eliza. Not today.

My attention is captured by movement on the other side of the square. "Lord above." I lower my coffee from my lips as I watch Sampson Winters slip out of number six Belmore Square, otherwise known as Scarlett Dare's home. Or, not so widely known, as her place of work. Whatever we are to call it. He stayed all night? I wince, thinking he must be rather...sore. I should have known she would get her claws into Sampson Winters. He has looks and a cheeky, happy-go-lucky charm about him, the exact opposite of his older brother, Johnny, who has always been quite brooding and serious. Eliza has loosened him up somewhat, it must be said, but he remains quite a foreboding fellow for the most part. I hum, looking back at the empty table. I do not like this. I put my coffee down and leave the dining room.

"Sir?" Dalton calls.

"I shall not be needing breakfast this morn," I say over my shoulder, swinging the door open and breathing in a new day. The sun is shining, the morning breeze light and fresh.

I cut through the gardens, admiring the blooms as I go, and exit the other side opposite number one Belmore square. I carefully pluck a rose from the bush that edges the gilded gate and wander across the cobbles, open the creaky gate, and present myself at the front door, knocking, and I make it quite a long knock, one that's determined and firm.

Hercules answers with a frown. "Morning," I say, slipping past him before I am invited inside. "I am here to visit with my sister." I follow my feet to where I know the dining room to be and burst through the double doors on a smile.

It falls when I find no one around the beautifully dressed table, not a muffin or china cup out of place. What on earth is going on? I turn to Hercules. "Where is my sister?"

"I believe she is still asleep, Mr. Melrose."

"But it is past eight. She is always, without fail, unless she is ill, of course, up past eight." Oh God, is she ill? I inhale quickly. With child? Oh, pray do tell me she is with child. That would be the answer to my problem, and I could get on with things without upsetting anyone.

Hercules clears his throat, and his eyes drop to the polished wooden floor. "I think perhaps His Grace had a very late night."

"It was only past midnight," I say over a laugh. "Has the man no endurance?"

"Very late to sleep, sir, not to bed."

I jerk and step back, as though a lightning bolt has hit me. God, no, I cannot bear to think it, but…"Eliza was in no fit state to…" I fade off, not quite believing I am speaking such words, and to the Winterses' butler! "Never mind."

"Perhaps a coffee while you wait, sir?"

"No, no, it is fine. I have coffee on my own table ready to drink, and it is not far home now, is it?"

"I would love some coffee, please, Hercules."

Another bolt of lightning hits me, that voice the cause. I hardly want to look past the Winterses' butler to where it came from. Hardly. But, God damn it, I cannot stop myself. My scowl is fierce as I divert my eyes to the stairs, where Taya Winters is standing looking all wild and fresh-faced, in a white chemise with the tie loose, revealing the smooth, sun-kissed skin of her decolletage.

Such a pleasing sight. It is such a shame she is most irritating. And forbidden.

"I will get some," Hercules says, snapping me from my staring episode.

"Thank you," she replies, taking the steps and approaching, her green eyes glued to my blue ones, her walk more of a saunter, her smile so small it is hardly visible. But it's there. Oh, it is there. "Good morning to you, Mr. Melrose."

"Good morning, my lady," I reply, my voice gruff. "I trust you slept well."

"I did indeed sleep well." She stops before me, her chin lifting to keep her eyes on mine. "And you?"

"Very well."

"Very good."

"Very good," I mimic, my eyes moving to her lips.

"Tell me," she says, her lips moving slowly as she plucks the rose from my grasp and takes it to her nose, smelling the bud. "How am I to avoid you if you show up in my house on a morning?"

I blink and frown, stepping back. "I…" My throat closes as my eyes absorb the skin around her neck. "I…" Jesus Christ, what is wrong with me? "I'm here to visit with my sister."

Taya moves past me, and her arm brushes the sleeve of my jacket. "She and my brother are sound asleep after what I can only conclude was a rather exhausting night consummating their vows."

I balk at her in horror as she takes a chair at the end of the table. "Please do spare me the details."

"As you wish," she says, resting the rose down and helping herself to a muffin, tearing off a piece and slipping it past her lips. Damn my eyes, they watch as she slowly chews.

"I do wish," I murmur, transfixed. I swear it, she is some kind of witch, casting spells upon me, making me think inappropriate thoughts and say inappropriate words. *She is off limits, Frank.*

"Wish for what?"

"For…" I shake my head. "Nothing."

On a nonchalant shrug, she pulls some paper from nowhere and picks up a pencil from the table, and I watch, fascinated, as her head tilts from one side to the other, her lips pouting, as she considers the paper, just like she did in the carriage from the church. What is on the paper? I take a step forward, stretching my neck, desperate to catch a glimpse of what is holding her attention, making her ponder so carefully.

"Frank!" Eliza shrieks, making me jump. She tackles me from the side, taking me in quite a firm hug, too firm, really; I am struggling to breathe, but it is appreciated all the same, as without Eliza I was struggling to stand. "What are you doing here?" She breaks away and looks me up and down, and I know what is coming before she has thought it herself.

"Yes, another new jacket," I confirm, rolling my eyes. All right, I have become somewhat fond of a new jacket or ten. In fact, I think I shall pop in to see Mr. Jenkins later today and buy another, perhaps in a paler blue to match my eyes, as I am yet to add that color to my fine, expansive collection. "And I am here because, tragic as it is, I found myself feeling quite lonely at breakfast this morning." I look down Eliza's body, grateful she thought to make herself decent, unlike some people around here. I turn a disapproving look to Taya Winters, finding her watching me closely, with no expression at all, folding the piece of paper as she does, smiling, but I cannot fathom if it is genuine or not. Whatever, I am not here to ponder the complicated behaviors of Taya Winters.

I return my attention to Eliza, my sweet, smart, now married, Eliza. "I brought this for you," I say, lifting an…empty hand.

"What?"

"Oh, that is odd," I say, trying to cast my mind back to the moment I lost the rose.

"Are you looking for this, Mr. Melrose?"

I turn and find Taya spinning the stem of the rose between her fingers, and she is chewing again. Slowly again, and this smile is definitely knowing. What kicks does she get out of taunting me? I hope she pricks a finger on a thor—

"Ouch!" Taya yelps, dropping the rose and hissing as she inspects her finger, where a drop of blood is beading. "Idiot."

I do not know if she is speaking of me or herself. I expect me. Nonetheless, I take no pleasure from a lady in distress, so I swallow my pride, feeling rather awful for wishing this, and go to her, pulling a chair up and taking her hand.

"What are you doing?" she asks as I take a napkin and dab at the pad of her finger to clear the blood so I can see exactly what I am dealing with.

I squint, getting closer, trying to see if the thorn has broken off, or if it is still intact, but, suddenly, her hand is not in mine any more, Taya having wrenched it away.

"I can take care of it myself, thank you."

Something tells me she is not thankful at all. "Have it your way."

"I will." She scowls at her finger and pops it in her mouth, and I find myself shifting on the chair, forcing myself to look away.

Unfortunately, I discover Eliza's interested eyes jumping between Taya and me. "What?" I ask, uncomfortable.

"Were you two in here alone before I arrived?"

"No," I say quickly.

"No," Taya blurts, both of us looking at Hercules, who is placing a bowl of sugar lumps on the table. He shakes his head mildly to himself before leaving. I have no idea why I am breaking out in a sweat. Eliza is a fine one to judge when it comes to the rules around here, for I know for certain she shared company with her husband unchaperoned before he was, indeed, her husband. But isn't that the point? He is now her husband.

"All right," Eliza says, coming to the table and pouring a coffee before taking it and leaving.

"Where are you going?" I ask, standing.

"I'm taking a coffee to my husband in our bed."

I recoil. I'm pretty sure that's not standard husband and wife practice. "But I came all this way to have breakfast with you."

"All the way across the square, Frank? Oh, please. Hercules," she calls, going on her way. "Please do keep an eye on them." She tosses a knowing, warning look back at me, and I snort my thoughts.

Taya stands. Oh good, she's leaving.

"Bugger it to hell!" she yells, making me flinch, lifting her finger into the air, where it proceeds to drip all over the fine rug beneath our feet. Such a shame. It looks expensive, probably imported too, from India or somewhere equally exotic, I expect.

And we can't have that now, can we?

I sigh, take her wrist, and pull her down into the chair, muttering something about everyone being ruined for one reason or another, anyway, and she does not fight me. In fact, she is rather quiet, and when I look up, I notice her green eyes look a little glazed. Oh dear, is she crying? Noticing I have noticed, she roughly wipes her face with her free hand and drops her eyes to her lap.

"Are you all right?" I ask softly, not liking the sight or her like this. Not at all.

"I am fine."

She is not fine. Neither am I, it would seem, for the vision of her not looking her usual confident, vibrant self is quite perturbing. "Taya?" I say quietly, still holding her hand, her finger now dripping blood all over my breeches. Oddly, it doesn't cost me a thought, as I stare into her glassy eyes when she looks up at me. All breath seems to leave my lungs and breathing becomes awfully tricky. Look at her. God, just look at her, wildly beautiful and spirited. I ache to kiss her. To touch those lips with mine.

I clear my throat and go back to her finger. "I'm sure I can dig it out," I say through my clogged throat.

"What with, a spoon?"

I look up at her, finding her smiling. I roll my eyes. "Very funny." I return to her finger. Make conversation, if only to distract myself from what I am doing. It's easier said than done. I have never found myself needing to make conversation with a lady. "What book are you reading?" I blurt, frowning to myself.

"You assume that because I am a lady, all I have to do is read literature, play harp, and look pretty?"

I feel myself blush, scowling down at her finger.

"Then you are a typical man, aren't you, Mr. Melrose. Not just a rake but a pig."

I gasp, outraged. "I am not a pig. Ask my sister."

She laughs a little. "But a rake?"

"Is that a concern of yours?"

"I suppose not."

"Well, then that is the end of that." I shrug. "And what of your future?"

"What of it?"

"I am sure His Grace wishes to marry you off to some fine gentleman."

She snorts. "No thank you."

I smile. We'll see about that. "And how are you finding London?"

"If you must know, boring. I was happy in the countryside." She looks a little wistful as I look up at her. "It's not the same here without Papa."

I'm not sure I like sadness and vulnerability on Taya Winters. "I am very sorry about what happened to him."

"Thank you."

I rip my eyes from hers and focus on her finger. Her skin against mine.

She clears her throat. "And when may we be blessed with this secret story of yours, Frank?" she asks, and I smile.

"And when may I see whatever it is you're penciling?"

Her head tilts, her teeth nibbling her bottom lip, thinking. "You will think it is terrible."

"What is terrible?"

"What is on the paper."

She wants to show me. "I'm quite certain I won't. And how do you know if you do not share?" Has she shared with anyone? Anyone at all? Something tells me no.

Clearly nervous, Taya reaches for the paper with her good hand and places it before us, and I look down. My God, I did not expect that. I am staring at a drawing, a fine drawing, of my sister and the Duke standing in the church. It's…incredible.

"Taya, that is wonderful," I breathe, taking in every detail, for there is much, even down to the reflections on the gold buttons of Johnny's jacket. "You are a fine artist."

"You really think so?"

Do I *think* so? "It is proven beyond all doubt," I say over a small laugh, motioning to the tatty paper. She smiles, proud, and, Lord help me, it is life. My God, she is wonderfully tempting, maddeningly alluring, infuriatingly annoying, and…I must kiss her. I simply must!

She swallows. "Have I stopped breathing?"

"Pardon me?"

"Bleeding!" she blurts. "Have I stopped bleeding?"

I look down at her finger. She has not. I swallow and take her hand, lifting it to my mouth, and slip her injured finger past my lips, sucking the pad in between circling the tip of my tongue across her flesh, feeling for the thorn. My body sings, my lungs shrink, and Taya visibly shakes before me, clenching her eyes closed. I find the thorn. Suck. Spit it out.

"Taya?" I say, my eyes drawn to her mouth, moving closer and closer and closer. I reach for the table to steady myself, certain my pounding heart might knock me from the chair.

Crash!

The sound of breaking bone china rings out, startling us from our rapture, and we both jerk, gasp, and start to shake. I am disoriented, completely befuddled, and when I find Taya shaking before me, I realize she is too.

I hear pounding footsteps, not just one set, maybe three or four. *Shit.* I shake myself to life, check a still-dazed Taya is stable on her chair, and scan the tablecloth. There's only one thing for it. I grab a corner and yank, creating another deafening crash of bone china. It's sacrilege, I know, but I know not what else to do.

"What's going on?" Johnny appears at the doorway looking quite indecent in his undergarments and a bare chest, his eyes jumping from a silent and still Taya to, what I expect, but hope not, a rather guilty-looking me.

"Small accident," I say, as I edge my way to the door, quite sure I should leave before I succumb to this madness. "I do apologize."

"For what?" he asks, watching Taya closely for a few uncomfortable moments as I will her to find that smart mouth of hers and fool her brother into believing…anything! Anything so he does not murder me, because I am pretty sure he looks capable. I am not a coward, be sure of that, but I would rather not take on the notorious Duke of Chester, because...well, he is family now, and it would upset Eliza greatly if we were at odds.

Johnny eventually makes his way to where his sister sits and motions to her chest. "Fasten it," he orders shortly, making Taya reach for the loose string of her chemise and tie it, albeit with shaky hands, and I know Johnny notices because his mood seems to darken some more.

Time for me to leave. "For the damage, please do send the bill." I make haste, but get intercepted by my dear sister, who does not look so dear right now.

"What did you do?" she hisses.

"Nothing!"

"I do not believe you. Need I remind you that Taya isn't only a lady, officially, I might add, she is also my sister-in-law."

I laugh. She is no lady. *She's a goddess.* "Since when did you become so self-righteous? Need I remind *you* that Winters is a duke, and you had no title." What am I saying? I need to sew my mouth shut. "Oh, never mind, we are having a discussion about something that needs no discussing. Nothing happened. The end."

"You cannot play games with her, Frank. She is not just another lady for you to have fun with, she is my husband's little sister!"

Play games? This isn't a game. No. It's more like a bloody nightmare. "Good day to you, sister." I walk on, avoiding Eliza's eyes, for she knows me too well, and only when the door closes behind me do I breathe easy, having to reach for the wall to steady myself.

There must not be a repeat. I will surely end up dead, killed by my shiny new brother-in-law.

A GENTLEMAN NEVER TELLS

What on earth is she trying to do to me?
What am I doing to myself?
Stay away!
Good God, I need to work more than I ever appreciated, not only to scratch this insatiable itch, but to keep myself busy.

Chapter 6

The dining room is still empty when I arrive home, and with my appetite vanished, at least my appetite for food, I go to Father's study. A copy of today's edition of *The London Times* is on the desk awaiting me. I drop to the chair and pull it over, unfolding it and finding the headline. It's as much as I can do not to slam it shut and stamp all over it when I see today's catchy, enticing string of words meant to lure the reader in. For Christ's sake, she got married yesterday. How did she also manage to get her story to the printworks in time for today's edition?

Two Dukes at War—Pistols at Dawn

Of course, Eliza's tactic works, and before I can think better of it, I'm reading the full article on the next page, and I am most perturbed, if only because I know the whole damn story already because I have had it straight from the horse's mouth. That horse being my delightful new brother-in-law. And there you have the magic of Eliza Melrose. Damn it, I can't be mad with her. She's too bloody good at this.

I shut the paper and slap it down on the desk, quite heavy-handed, before pulling over the figures for last week's sales, mulling over the numbers. I cannot deny, and I would never, for I am not a fool, that Eliza's storytelling talent, her way with words, has indeed catapulted the number skyward, and we now sit pretty at a more than respectable fifteen thousand copies per day. "But it can be more," I say to myself, knowing that once this story is told, numbers will drop, and we need them to climb if we are to become national. Or even global. Just imagine…

I sit back in my chair, my fingers laced and resting on my velvet jacket, my mind racing.

Taya Winters.

"Oh hell," I mutter, getting up and pacing, pulling the piece of paper from my inside pocket and reading what I have written once again. Distraction. Where has the horsewoman come from, what is her purpose, her story? Who is she? These are all questions I plan on finding answers to, as well as wowing the ton with the utterly preposterous notion of a highwaywoman. Preposterous but true. At least, I bloody hope so, or else this story is simply a story like all others. Ordinary.

But I wasn't seeing things, I'm certain of it, and Eliza confirmed my suspicions. Fluttery lashes. Dainty hands. A smaller frame than her fellow riders. Of course, it could be a man of slight build, but…those lashes. I rest my hand on my chest when my heart yells its presence, smiling. It has been weeks since my encounter with the highwaymen. I don't lack motivation, but I must find more inspiration if I am to continue my story and keep myself busy writing.

I hum, sitting back down, but flinch when the door swings open. The Duke stands on the threshold of my father's study looking quite menacing, but at least now he is fully dressed in quite a lovely claret velvet jacket. I admire it for a few moments as Dalton hurries up behind the Duke and announces him. I smile and wave him off as Johnny closes the door and wanders toward the fireplace.

"Your Grace," I say, neglecting to rise from my chair to greet him.

"Melrose," he replies flatly and quite unfriendly-like, cluing me in that this isn't, unfortunately, an impromptu visit for a pleasant chat.

"Please take a seat," I say.

"I'd rather stand if it's all the same to you."

"Makes no difference to me."

"Oh, it would," Winters says. "I have a much better swing while standing."

I recoil. "Now let us not get excited, Your Grace. And would you mind enlightening me as to why you might want to swing at me?"

He comes to the desk and slaps his hands on the edge of the wood, leaning over, getting his face close to mine. Johnny Winters is a notoriously handsome man. Foreboding, yes, but darkly handsome. Not today. Today he is simply menacing. "Stay away from my little sister."

My brain is telling me to agree, no question, but my ego, my stupid, foolish ego says instead, "Or else?" and Johnny Winters takes on a rather frightening stance, one that tells me he may very well launch himself across this desk and strangle me. I am not a man who likes to be told what to do. I am also not an idiot. "Rest assured, I have absolutely no desire to be anywhere near your sister," I say, deciding to appease him, if only for an easy life.

"Why, what's wrong with her?" he asks, insulted.

Oh, for the love of God. What does he want from me? "What's right with her?" I reply on a sardonic laugh, and then I'm quickly up from my chair and on the other side of my father's study when he lunges, threatening, snarling like a wolf. "All right," I say, getting a strange thrill out of seeing my sister's husband looking as murderous as everyone once thought him to be. It's no wonder, really, that he earned such a reputation.

"I will kill you," he says quietly, almost on a hiss, "If you so much as breathe in her direction."

"Kill me?" I ask, my head tilted. "I think my sister might have something to say about that."

"Not if I make it look like an accident."

I recoil. This is ridiculous. I have better things to do than play this silly game of clash of the egos.

"Her virtue is precious," he goes on. "She must not be ruined, do you hear me? I will not have a rake like you tarnishing her."

"Well." I laugh lightly, thoroughly insulted, making Johnny snarl. My ego is somewhat dented. Everyone seems quite keen on pointing out my shortcomings, and by *everyone*, I mean Johnny and his sister. "Are you saying, Your Grace, that I am not good enough for Taya?"

"That is exactly what I am saying."

"Don't hold back now, will you?" I pull my jacket in, daring to step closer to the fireplace, therefore closer to my temperamental brother-in-law. "I thought you of all people would be an advocate for true love." What the hell am I saying? "Not that I am in love, of course. I'm merely pointing out that to judge and—" I wave a hand in the air, searching for the right words, hopefully words that will not get me killed. "—put people in boxes according to status is rather hypocritical. My sister held no title before you…you…" *Choose your words wisely, Frank!* "…wowed her with your gentlemanly charm."

Johnny rolls his eyes. "Taya is my little sister."

"As Eliza is mine," I reply, cocking my head, wondering when I became such a daredevil. There is no question, I should stay as far away from Taya Winters as possible, I do not refute that, but I simply cannot help putting the Duke in his place. "I believe I gave you my wholehearted support when you came to me with your whole woeful story."

"Woeful?"

"Tragic."

"It matters not. Taya is not available, especially not to you."

And there he goes again. *Especially not to me.* I might not have a title, but at least I am not disgraced. "She's nineteen!" I laugh. *Shut the hell up, Frank!*

"And I have not officially launched her into society."

"Will you ever?"

"That is my prerogative."

"Indeed, it is," I say, going to the door, looking back. "Your Grace, if it pleases you to hear me say it, be assured, I have no interest in your sister. Now, I have my day to be getting on with." I exit the study, leaving the Duke behind.

"Very well," he calls after me.

"Send word to the stables, please, Dalton, to have my horse ready in an hour." Let us get back to business. Will today be the day the highwaymen show their faces again? Will I have it confirmed beyond all doubt that my suspicions are correct?

That thrill. The addictive one—it glides down my spine at the very thought. Because it could be quite the disaster if I publish the first part of this story and I am wrong. What an anticlimax that would be!

Up and down I have trotted, for at least an hour now, and there has been no sight nor sound. In what world does a man pray to be ambushed by thieves? By two o'clock, I have had enough and resign myself to purchasing that new jacket in pale blue to match my eyes.

As I am tying Figaro up outside Mr. Jenkins's shop on Jermyn Street, I see a familiar curricle rumbling along the cobbles. I follow its path, seeing old Viscount Millingdale at the reins, his new, young wife, Lizzy Fallow, seated beside him, on their way to his bank, I expect.

Lizzy spots me, and her back visibly straightens as they pass at quite some speed. I would feel sorry for her…if she wasn't a status-hungry, shallow flirt. Thank the heavens I dodged *that* bullet. In true gentlemanly style, I smile and tip my hat.

Then I step inside Mr. Jenkins's. I am surprised to find Sampson Winters here, standing at the back of the shop while

Jenkins measures his inside seam. "I apologize for appearing so blunt," Mr. Jenkins says as he peeks at his tape measure, "but I must insist on payment up front."

"Up front?" Sampson asks. "We are respectable noblemen, Jenkins. Good for the money."

"Mr. Brummell, as I thought, was respectable too. He's had dozens of jackets and trousers made with promises of payment for months now, and I am yet to see even a penny."

"Well, that really is most unfortunate," Sampson says, as my eyebrows arch in surprise. Brummell is quite the character, a respected one, just as Jenkins said. I was not aware he had fallen on hard times. Sampson spots me by the door. "Ah, Melrose," he sings, his cheeky smile as cheeky as ever. I must be honest, I'm wondering how he has the energy to be standing after his night-long encounter with Scarlett Dare.

"Afternoon to you, Winters," I say, taking in the black velvet jacket he's sporting. I like it. I have one. "Shopping for pleasure or an occasion?"

"I only subscribe to pleasure," he says, grinning. Good grief, does he know his brother has entertained Lady Dare? Me? All men? He is new to the neighborhood, or, at least, he's new to the *new* Belmore Square and its new residents since Fitzgerald built the houses around the Winters residence and they were snapped up by some of England's finest families.

"A friendly word of advice, if I may?" I say, as Jenkins wanders off into the back room of his shop, his tape measure around his neck.

Sampson Winters is still grinning as he looks at me, fiddling with the cravat Jenkins has left hanging around his neck. "You may."

"Lady Dare."

"What about her?"

Yes, what about her? And what advice do I think I can offer in that regard? He's a grown man, and I am no longer interested in the pleasure to be had there. "She's a very lovely lady." I smile and reach for a roll of pale blue fabric.

"Indeed she is," he replies, sounding all too curious.

I think perhaps I will return another time to purchase my new coat, as I am feeling a trifle stifled. "Good day to you." I turn and take the handle of the door, but I do not get a chance to open it, for someone bursts through, knocking me back a few staggered paces.

I stare at her. I just stare, as if I have been placed under a spell. "My lady," I say, my throat thick as I vehemently try to fight off the shakes.

"Mr. Melrose." She nods, swallows, her gaze moving past me. I turn and see Sampson with eyebrows higher than the ceiling.

"Excuse me," I say courteously, moving toward the door and taking the handle again, keen to escape the thick atmosphere.

It flies open again and Lizzy Fallow appears with her husband, the old Viscount. "Mr. Melrose," she breathes.

I quickly find my poise. "My lady." I dip past them quickly and leave the shop, taking in the fresh air, regulating my breathing as best I can, really rather worried, for I cannot seem to control myself in the presence of Taya Winters and that is a serious problem.

She enthralls me. Bloody typical, isn't it, that the one woman who truly captivates me is forbidden. What a mess.

I pace toward my horse, planning on a trip to Gladstone's so I may lose myself in some blue ruin, but when I see Scarlett Dare, who is stepping down from a coach, spot me and smile in that seductive, enticing way that she does, I quickly divert, abandoning my horse and escaping down an alleyway. Never would I have dreamed I would be avoiding women. Never! And yet here I am skulking down some dirty alleyway to escape the disingenuous clutches of Lizzy Fallow, the tempting seductions of Scarlett Dare, and the magical powers of Taya Winters.

I do not have time for this! I've spent most of my adult life pursuing women. Now I feel like I'm spending all my time avoiding them.

"The highwaymen!" someone screeches in the distance.

I come to an abrupt halt, my ears pricking up, as well as my heartbeat, when I hear the distinct, thunderous sound of horses' hooves pounding the ground. "My God," I breathe, turning on my heels and running back out of the alleyway. I notice a commotion in the distance, people jumping out of the way, horses becoming agitated. One rider even falls from his horse when it starts to buck and kick. There are a few screams, some gentlemen yelling, and then I see them at the top of the promenade. Three horsemen—two on black stallions and one on a white one, charging toward us. It must be an innate something stupid in me that refuses to allow my legs to function when faced with wild horses. *Or wild women.* I am frozen. My eyes pass across all three riders, all standing in the saddle, all cloaked in brown leather with hats upon their heads and scarves covering their faces. Two of the riders are significantly larger than the other, only substantiating my suspicions. *Or my hopes.* I will my legs to life and wander into the middle of the road, watching as the horses stampede toward me, and I am mesmerized as I follow their path. They coast past at quite some speed. My skin prickles, my heart pounds. Now *this* feeling is not forbidden, and I must feed it, nurture it, for it is sure to do me no harm.

Enough is enough. I cannot hold back any longer.

I must tell this story.

Chapter 7

When I burst into Father's study, I find him at his desk.

With Eliza.

"Sister," I say, slowly closing the door. "Whatever are you doing here?"

She rests some papers down on her knee, no doubt the next chapter in the tale of her disgraced husband's tragic story, and smiles brightly at me. I refuse to ask myself why she appears to be so happy, but, then again, I suppose one of them needs to be, as her husband is quite a conundrum. I never know whether he is about to blacken my daylights or laugh and haul me in for a manly hug. "Frank," she replies, her head tilted as I regard her carefully. She's glowing, her cheeks pink, her skin radiant.

I join them at the desk, my father smiling fondly at us both. I cannot deny it, it is wholly wonderful to see him looking so light and free since the removal of Lymington from both our business and personal lives. "Papa," I say, nodding as I lower myself to the chair, giving Eliza a curious eye to match the one cast upon me. "Might we discuss business?"

"Oh?" he says.

"Oh?" Eliza mimics, making me smile. She is very aware of the story I am itching to tell.

"I believe I have the next big st—"

"Burt!" Mama shrieks, bursting into his study, pulling all of our attention her way. "Those highwaymen stole Frank's coins and left him for dead! He's disappeared, nowhere to be seen, and I fear he is in shock! Perhaps disoriented, or maybe he's lost his memory from the trauma and cannot find his way home."

"Oh, for the love of God," I breathe, sliding down my chair.

"Oh?" Mama says, finding me. "There you are." She flounces over, running her eyes all over me, while Eliza laughs and my father rolls his eyes.

"Really, Florence, we have no need to embellish the drama, now, do we?"

She pouts on a small smile. "I am merely maintaining the momentum."

"No need, dear. We sold over fifteen thousand copies yesterday."

"Wonderful!"

"In fact, Eliza and I were just discussing purchasing another machine to keep up with demand."

"You were?" I blurt.

"We were," Eliza confirms, struggling to hide her smile.

This is utterly absurd. "Without me? Did Eliza at some point grow a tackle and not tell me?" I ask, forgetting myself for a moment. I pay for it as well. My sister marches over and gives me a close-up of her disgusted expression. "I didn't mean that," I admit, exasperated. "But…" But, what? I have no defense. I have hardly earned the privilege of being taken seriously in business. Eliza has. So she must appreciate this urge in me. It is really quite something, this feeling, this desperation, to indulge the imaginations of the ton. Or is it simply an urge to indulge my own imagination?

"Francis Melrose!" Mama snaps, smacking me across the head. "We do not use such language."

"No, not these days, eh, Mama? Not now we are who we are with what we have. For the love of everything, when did you become so high in the instep?"

"Yes, and those lovely coats you sport each day are a part of what we have." Eliza raises a brow, and I scowl in return.

"So the new machine," I say. This might not be such a terribly bad thing. At least I will be suitably prepared for the inevitable extra load of copies we may need to print when I release my own story.

"Johnny has it in hand," Eliza smiles brightly.

"Yes," Papa confirms. "His Grace is in talks with the German manufacturer, who, understandably, has asked for proof of Johnny's father's invention." Ah. The invention—a small but significant part that made it possible to produce those wonderful revolutionary and obscenely expensive steam printing machines. Without them, our business would be limping along like the rest of the newspapers. That rat Lymington claimed the invention and sold it to the Germans. His crimes know no bounds.

"Excellent," I agree. Now to broach the matter on my mind. "Papa," I say, reaching into my inside pocket, feeling Eliza's eyes on me. "As I said yesterday, I should like to start writing a—"

"I have not seen Clara today." Papa frowns.

"What?"

"Clara." He stands, and I look out the corner of my eye to Eliza, as she looks out the corner of her eye to me. She shakes her head. I shake mine. Neither of us have seen her.

"She isn't with Governess?" I ask, trying to sound casual.

"No," Mama says. "Quite unfortunately, she broke out in a hideous rash which I fear is contagious." She whirls round. "Emma! Emma, have you seen Clara?" She breezes out and Papa follows.

"It must be your turn to find our wayward sister," I say to my sister, as Papa goes after Mama and my opportunity to plead my case goes too. *God damn it.*

"I am busy, Frank." Eliza leaves the office, and I go after her.

"I think our readers are ready for something new, sister."

She whirls around, shocked. "But I am yet to conclude my story."

"Perhaps it is time."

"So I might make way for you?"

"Yes."

"No." She marches on, and I follow, chasing her heels.

"Eliza, come now, let us be reasonable."

"You be reasonable, Frank. You have always basked in the glory of my words. Allow me to enjoy this newfound sense of pride."

"I do not want to bask in the glory of your words, Eliza. I should like to bask in the glory of mine. After all, you said they were rather good. Isn't this best for the business?"

"Since when have you cared about the family business?"

I skid to a stop, injured. My God, everyone is being so very brutal with their opinions on Frank Melrose this week. I cease chasing her. If there is one thing I know about Eliza Melrose, she is a stubborn mare. "I have always cared about business," I say to myself. Although, admittedly, it has been a while since I paid a visit to the printworks.

So, on that thought, I find a hackney coach and give the jarvey instructions to take me there, where I find Grant, who was recently promoted to oversee the workers on the factory floor. He's a round man, with rosy cheeks and a charming twinkle in his eye, and has been working for Papa for many years. "Mr. Melrose," he chimes, dropping a sack of something to the ground and dusting off his hands before approaching me. "What a lovely surprise."

"Good day to you, Grant," I say, casting my eye around the printworks, where men at every turn are run ragged trying to keep up with the speed of the printer, and the noise is piercing.

"Her Grace paid a visit just yesterday morning. We are honored—two Melroses in two days!"

"Eliza was here?" On her wedding day? My eyes narrow. Her commitment knows no bounds.

"Yes, she wanted to be sure her story wasn't interrupted."

Grant starts to wander the factory floor, and I follow, as hot as a pig on a spit.

"How very thorough of her," I muse, amused. *Obsessed*.

"Indeed, Mr. Melrose. Our new editor-in-chief is taking her role very seriously."

I recoil. editor-in-chief? "Who is the new editor-in-chief?" I ask. And why don't I know?

Grant stops, looking back at me, apparently oblivious to my shock if his big grin is a measure to trust. "Why, Her Grace, sir. Your father sent word only yesterday. A wedding gift, I believe."

What?

I stare at him, probably looking like a surprised goldfish. "My younger sister is the new editor-in-chief?" Poor Grant suddenly registers my disposition, and he knows not where to look or what to say.

I do not believe this. I never dreamt I would begrudge my sister's ambitions. I also never dreamt my own ambitions, albeit delayed in coming forth, would suffer as a consequence. "Good day to you, Grant." I tip my hat, he tips his in return, and I walk out of the printworks, feeling an incredible sense of hurt.

No one thought to tell me this news?

Chapter 8

I stew all the way home, muttering and cursing under my breath, having numerous full-blown and quite heated discussions with my father in my mind. I triumph in every single one of them.

As my Hackney coach is rounding the corner into Belmore Square, I see our family coach bumping across the cobbles, heading out on the other side. "Follow that coach," I yell to the jarvey, prompting him to look back to see in which direction I am pointing, and to which coach, as there are a fair many of them on the square. I lean out to keep my eye on Papa. "Can't you go any faster?"

"On these cobbles, sir? I'll lose my wheels."

Bugger it, I could run faster. "This is a—" I'm suddenly catapulted forward when the jarvey yanks on the reins, stopping the horse quite abruptly. "Fuck!" I hit the front section of the coach with so much force, I am sure I hear the wood crack. Then I fall to the floor in a crumpled heap.

"Apologies, sir, a lady stepped out in front of me."

I wince and curse my way up, propping myself against the side, looking out as I rub at my sore head. Lady Rose wanders casually across the road, oblivious to the chaos she has caused, the feathers of her hat swaying in long, slow waves to match her slow pace. "Take your time," I yell, making sure the old deaf wench hears me. Of course, that then means she stops and delays me further. "Get out of my way!"

"I beg your pardon?" she splutters.

God help me. I smile through my teeth. "I said, I hope you're having a lovely day."

"Splendid." She gets going again, at a much slower pace, which is an achievement because she was already traveling like a snail. She eventually makes it to the gardens and the jarvey orders the horse onward. I settle in my seat and work to compose myself and cool my temper, for presenting myself and my grievance to Papa with anything less than full control would be quite foolish. I must appear reasonable.

Our family coach comes to a stop outside Gladstone's and Papa enters. I slip the jarvey a few coins, tell him I am done with his services, and follow Papa into the gentleman's club.

I find him at a table in the corner going over some papers. "Papa?"

He looks over his glasses. "Frank, what are you doing here?" He drops his spectacles on the wood as I take a seat. "How has your day been?"

I laugh to myself. I am beginning to wish I had never bothered to rise on this morn, for my day has been quite intolerable from the moment I woke and has gotten progressively worse. I have so many grievances at the moment, I do not know where to begin! "Enlightening." I am, apparently, a rake and a disappointment. I suppose I only have myself to blame.

"How so?"

I suddenly know where to begin. "I paid a visit to the printworks early this afternoon." I definitely notice a slight falter in my father's soft smile. "Eliza? Editor-in-chief, Papa?"

"Oh, that."

"You didn't think to tell me?"

"Since when do you care about the running of our family business?"

Ouch. "Since now."

"You want to be editor-in-chief?" he asks, almost laughing.

Again, ouch. "Why is that so amusing, Father?"

"Frank, son, you have expressed very little desire to manage our business, even less desire to write. I hired Porter, God rest his soul, because of that. Now you're telling me you want to? What's changed?"

How do I explain this? "There was an incident, Papa."

"An incident?" He appears very worried. "What kind of incident?"

"An encounter." I frown to myself. "With…someone."

"Who?"

"The highwayman. Or woman."

His eyes widen. "Woman? You think the highwayman is a woman?"

I look around nervously for listening ears. It would be tragic if the rumors were to break and ruin my story. "Well, one of them. I think." I'm sure, but I can't say with confidence that I would put my life on it. "I'm still investigating." Doesn't it speak volumes that my sister has not shared this with my father? Is she feeling threatened? I am not like other men she has faced, she knows that. I do not wish to take anything away from her. But I should also like some energy and excitement for myself. She should be thrilled that I have found this…this…this… whatever we are to call it.

"Oh my," my father muses, and then he smiles. "You've been sparked."

"Pardon me?"

"Sparked. It happened to me, and it happened to your sister. My spark came when Mrs. Jones—she was the washer woman back home—was accused of being a witch!" He sits forward in his chair. "I felt compelled to prove it was utter claptrap. I swear, Frank, my boy, my hand couldn't keep up with my brain. I wrote, I researched, it consumed me!" He smiles wistfully. "Eliza's spark was the butcher boy who was accused of stealing. Your sister knew it not to be true and set on a mission to prove his innocence and therefore save his hand."

I smile, remembering it well. "Then, yes, I suppose we are to call it my spark." And what a thrilling feeling it is, to be sparked. Except I have no outlet, and the urge to share is becoming too much.

"So it is time to find you a wife."

My mouth drops open. Wait. When did I mention anything about a wife? Two Scotches are placed on the table, and I look at the lady server like she might have the answer I'm looking for. Of course, she does not. "Pardon me?" I say to Papa.

"For you to settle down."

"What?" Settle down? With one woman? "I have to be married to be taken seriously?"

"Marriage is a sign of commitment, my boy. Maturity." He cocks a brow, and I move back in my chair, not liking this in the least bit. "Are you a devoted dandy or a devoted businessman, Frank?"

"A—"

"You think your mother and I are oblivious to your reckless pursuits? I cannot very well enforce marriage upon your sisters and not my son now, can I?"

"Enforce?" I blurt. "You tried and failed, Papa," I remind him. "I believe you wanted Eliza to marry that drip Frederick Lymington."

"Well, yes, but she married a duke instead, so all is well."

"A disgraced duke," I laugh. My God, why did I open my big mouth?

"You have had your fun. I am not proposing an arranged marriage, Frank. You can marry whomsoever you so wish, within reason of course."

"Yes, within reason, I know that, Papa." I spent plenty of time talking Eliza around to that. Alas, she still went and fell in love with a duke who was thought to have murdered his entire family. That is, until they all showed up in Belmore Square a few weeks ago. And I am currently ensuring Clara stays away from a highly inappropriate stable boy. So, yes, I know about suitability. I just never anticipated Papa would land it at *my* feet, too. His daughters, yes. But his son? I should be focused on running the family business, and I will; I realize that now. Finally. With a little kick up the arse by a horsewoman and her horse. Literally.

"So, is there anyone who springs to mind?" he asks, taking his Scotch and relaxing back in his chair.

"No one at all," I laugh, though it is not in amusement. Yes, a drink. Good idea. I reach for mine and down it in one fell swoop.

"What about Esther Hamsley?"

"What?" I say, just as my empty glass hits the table. "Papa, she is on her fifth season and looks about as friendly as an injured cat."

"She is from good stock. If you want me to take you seriously, Frank, show me you can be serious."

I cannot believe I have talked my way into this. I have to marry if I am to claim my right as Papa's heir? It doesn't seem fair. "And what about my story?" I ask as he calls for a refill.

"You can publish your story. We have ten pages now, Frank."

"Right," I sigh.

Papa's shoulders drop and his hand rubs into the line on his head. "Eliza has earned it, Francis. I cannot recant because you, after all this time, have suddenly found your passion for what I have built." Because Eliza found it first. Appreciated it first. "You haven't proven yourself!"

I cannot argue with that, for he is right. And if I am to be truthful with myself, I have always found Papa's business, especially since we moved to London, to be somewhat of an unwanted pressure. I rather enjoyed the manual labor I was responsible for on the fields back home. *Home.* No, the countryside is not home anymore. Belmore Square is home, and I've been quite happy being ignorant and leaving Eliza to fill the pages of *The*

London Times while I bought new coats, pretended to work, and delighted the ladies. But now? Now I have been sparked. Now, I see there is more to life than fine threads and female flesh.

"I'm very sorry, Frank, but you must be patient and allow Eliza the time she deserves to thrive."

I wedge my elbow into the arm of the chair and rest my heavy head upon it. I am not disputing that she does, indeed, deserve to thrive. "I have ambitions too, Papa."

"Lying with as many women as possible does not count as ambitions, Frank," he snaps, and I recoil, aggrieved. Father shakes his head, finishing his Scotch and ordering yet another, while I sit and lick my wounds, injured.

"You cannot claim to be reformed and expect to claim the front page, not to mention all the responsibility," he goes on, calmer. "As with all things in life, Frank, in order to receive respect and trust, one must prove oneself worthy."

"And by marrying a disgraced duke, Eliza proved herself worthy, did she?" I grumble, seizing my Scotch and knocking it back, knowing I am being unfair. She's worked her way to this. I have shagged my way to nothing.

"Don't be bitter, son. I have worked so very hard, been through quite an upset to get us to this point. Our newspaper is the biggest in London! After everything that's happened, I need confidence, Frank. If we are to go national in the future, I need someone dependable at the helm."

Dependable.

He leans forward. "And since we're talking honestly, I must tell you His Grace came to me with a great concern."

"And what is that?"

"You will stay away from Lady Taya Winters. I mean it, Frank. Your rakish ways must not extend to the Duke's sister. We rely on him for the machines we buy, Frank. We would be at a loss without them if he were to withdraw them."

"You've bought those machines fair and square."

"Indeed, but he can most certainly withdraw the small part that his father invented that is needed to make them operate."

I snort. "He would never do such a thing, Papa. It would greatly upset Eliza if the Duke were to sabotage the business she so cherishes."

"Let him not give us reason, son."

I look away, as if hiding the desire in my eyes. I have not indulged in a woman for weeks. I wish I could tell him that. I have, however, fought to resist one. "Thank you for your confidence and trust, Papa." I bow in respect when I feel very little in this moment, and leave him behind to go seek solace in something more *me* than, apparently, running a business or being trusted by one's own family.

"Frank," he calls on a tired sigh. "Come on, let us not be at odds."

I raise my chin and keep on my way, leaving Gladstone's and standing on the steps for a few moments. I breathe in the air, my eyes falling onto a concealed entrance across the road. "Bugger it," I say, pacing over and slipping inside Kentstone's. After all, being a rake is, according to my father, my sister, and Taya Winters too, all I am good for. It would be a mighty shame to disappoint them.

The harem of naked women roaming the rooms of the secret, lurid club were somewhat intimidating the first time I encountered them. Loud, brash, unashamedly brazen. Now, they are a welcome distraction. I flash one particularly attractive dark-haired beauty with unusually pearly white teeth a smile as I slump into a chair—she's new here, I'm sure of it, for I do not recall her and I'm certain that bright smile could not be missed, not even in the dim, smoky rooms of Kentstone's. In fact, she illuminates the place. And yet…I feel nothing. No urge. No thrill.

Am I broken?

"Drink, sir?" she asks, pushing her chest out subtly, her lips red, her nipples a lovely shade of pink.

"Gin," I say, relaxing back in my chair. "And then why don't you come take a seat?" I pat my lap, and she smiles.

"Looks comfortable."

"Oh, it is."

Her head tilts, her perfectly arched eyebrows arching further. I watch her the entire time she's away from me, the sway of her bottom, the jiggle of her breasts, the bounce of her dark locks when she walks. She is quite the siren. I cannot take my eyes off her. Perhaps all is not lost. Perhaps I can muster some desire from somewhere—get that highwaywoman out of my head, since I can't tell that story yet, and Taya Winters, since I can't *ever* scratch that itch.

She places my drink down carefully, but rather than take a seat on my lap, she lowers herself to another chair.

"What is your name?" I ask as I claim my gin.

"Ruby."

My drink pauses at my mouth, and I take her in carefully, admiring, noting a mole above her lip. "Suits you."

"Thank you. And yours?"

"Patrick."

She nods and crosses one partially bare leg over the other. "Now we have the tiresome chore of formalities out of our way, would you like to divulge your requirements?"

I hum to myself, thinking Ruby is rather polite and well-spoken for a cyprian. Too posh, to be honest, and I am somewhat intrigued by it. I lean forward in my seat. "Tell me a little about yourself, Ruby." I surprise myself. Since when have I desired conversation?

She cannot conceal her recoil. "Men do not usually come to talk, Patrick." She, too, leans forward. "Ten shillings for my tongue, my mouth, my hand, and my hole."

I blink rapidly, caught off guard by her brazenness, which doesn't suit her, but very much suits the rooms of Kentstone's, and, with the greatest of confidence, I suspect it is a ploy to convince me that she does, in fact, belong here. "Which hole?" I retort stoically, and she inhales, telling me all I need to know. She absolutely does not belong here.

In somewhat of a fluster and ignoring my lurid question, she quickly gets up, places herself on my lap, and kisses me hard, her breasts compressed against my front. And still, I feel absolutely nothing. But I see plenty in my darkness. Dark blonde hair, green eyes, flushed cheeks.

Jesus.

I am about to pull away when Ruby jumps up off my lap quite abruptly. "Have a nice evening," she says, hurrying away, leaving me frowning at her as she goes. She approaches a large man with award-worthy mutton chops and a belly that makes his jacket bulge at the buttons, straining them. He's a serious fellow, who does not even crack a smile when approached by the vivacious, wildly attractive Ruby.

I sip my drink as I watch, interested, as the man plonks himself in a chair and Ruby perches on his lap, stroking at his body, for there is much to stroke at, while he, quite absentmindedly, squeezes one of her breasts from time to time. How…odd.

I've worked my way through a few gins when the man stands and declares, in a loud, booming voice for the whole of Kentstone's to hear, that he is using the water closet. He leaves, and Ruby remains exactly where she is, despite there being plenty of other men around for her to please and earn some extra shillings—it's surprising what one of these cyprians can achieve in just a few seconds, be sure of that—so I am left to conclude that the big, serious-looking fellow is extremely plump in the pocket and will make it worth her while to remain by his side all evening. Good for her.

Besides, I don't really want to be here, so I get up, dip in my pocket, and pull out a shilling, wandering over to Ruby, who now, strangely, or perhaps not so strangely, will not look at me.

I hold out the coin, and she peeks out the corner of her eye to me. "For the kiss."

She waves me off. "The kiss was free."

"I've never known anyone to give anything away for free, especially around these parts." I slip the coin onto the table, and she whips it back up and hands it back to me.

"I must insist."

I frown. "You won't take my money?"

"No, because you did not enjoy the kiss."

I withdraw, embarrassed. "It's nothing personal," I rush to say. "You are a very pretty lady. It's just…well, I'm feeling a little off lately, if you mus—"

"Oh bugger," she whispers. "Please, Patrick. He is in a foul mood after being hijacked by the highwaymen en route into London."

What?

I accept the coin, not particularly liking her apparent distress, and slip it back into my pocket. "Thank you, anyway," I say quietly.

"What is this?"

I turn and find the fat man looking between Ruby and me, his beady eyes accusing.

"My apologies," I say, bowing my head out of thought for Ruby, not for this oaf. If I knew she would be safe from his wrath, I'd put him in his place before I leave. "I did not realize the charming Ruby here was claimed."

"Well, she is."

"Indeed. Can I buy you a drink?" I ask.

"No, I am busy." He drops back into the chair and Ruby is soon back on his fat lap. What a heathen. Ruby is frightened of him, and that irritates me. I hope the highwaymen took every penny from him, although something tells me it would not dent his pockets, which I have concluded are as fat as he is.

"Then I shall bid you farewell," I say, backing away, Ruby

looking at me like I might be mad, and the heathen not looking at me at all.

"Another drink, sir?" Another cyprian asks.

"No, silly me," I say, tapping my forehead, as if I am reprimanding my brain. "I forgot, I must get back to my investigations. Those highwaymen aren't going to be caught while I sit around in gentleman's clubs drowning in blue ruin and tempting women, now, are they?" I nod my head. "Good evening to you."

I turn, take two paces, and halt when I hear a low, rumbling voice demanding me to wait. *Got him.* "Yes," I say, slowly pivoting to face him.

"Highwaymen, you say?"

"Indeed. I hear they're on the loose. They must be stopped."

"They must." Suddenly, he shoves Ruby off his lap and points to a chair. "Sit," he orders. "Let me buy you a drink."

I need no more alcohol, be sure of that, but for the sake of my mission, I take a seat and order one more.

"Your name?" he asks, trying to lean closer, but his big belly hinders him, his buttons pulling so much, they look like they could ping off at any moment and possibly take one of my eyes out. So I sit back.

"Melrose," I answer. "Frank Melrose." I peek at Ruby when I feel her surprised eyes on me.

"Melrose, you say? Of *The London Times*?"

"That is correct. And you are...?"

"Byron Fleming."

I inhale. I know that name. "Of Fleming Transportation?"

"That's me."

"Boats?"

"Indeed. And carriages, of course. One hundred of them. I have a fleet of fifty boats, Melrose, that deliver whatever you so desire anywhere on the four thousand miles of canals that stretch through England." He nods, happy. Anything I so desire? How about newspapers? "I am also working closely with a man who is adamant we'll all be traveling by rail very soon, which, of course, will extend my reach and be far more efficient."

"Interesting."

He nods to himself and holds his glass out for Ruby to fill. "Tell me about these highwaymen."

I catch Ruby shaking her head, either begging me not to rat her out or not quite believing I've lied about my name. It's probably a bit of both, but the former is of particular concern to me, for I expect she is fearful of Fleming's fists. I would like to see him try on *my* watch.

"You sound quite interested."

"My coach was ambushed yesterday on the common. I was informed that Hampstead Heath has become quite dangerous, but to avoid it would have put an extra day on my journey and I did not have time for that."

"I am running a report imminently on their activities and will soon discover the faces and names behind those high scarves and low hats."

"And how, may I ask, do you propose to do that? From what I have heard and now experienced, they are quite elusive and work rather fast."

And mysterious. "I have my ways," I muse. "I expect it will be a rather popular piece."

"I for one would be most curious to discover the identity of the men who took my purse. Not that I was terrified, you must understand."

"Of course." I smile. "I expect it would take much more to have a strapping man such as yourself trembling in your boots."

Fleming huffs his agreement and throws back his drink. "You must keep me informed of your progress and notify me immediately upon your discovery of who they are. Bring them to me."

Oh, I will. If I get something in return. "So, you're in transportation, you say?"

"That's what I said."

"Perhaps there is an opportunity for us both here, Mr. Fleming."

"Elaborate, Melrose, and be quick about it. I have more Scotch to drink and a woman to hump."

I inwardly wince. And highwaymen to exact revenge on, for I have not known Fleming for all that long, but it is obvious he is a self-important man who holds a grudge. "As I was saying, I expect this story to be vastly popular. I can handle the volume of printing, meet demand, but I am looking for the means to deliver the story far and wide."

His bushy eyebrow quirks. "You want access to my means of transportation?"

"It will be worth your while." Fleming, while quite arrogant, is a businessman, and he's useful to *The London Times*.

"Tell me how."

"Revenge is sweet, Mr. Fleming, but plump pockets are sweeter. With your transportation, I can take *The London Times* national, perhaps even global."

"You bring me the highwaymen, I might consider it."

How did I become a vigilante? "I'm no Bow Street Runner, Mr. Fleming, I am merely a businessman and heir to *The London Times*."

He leans forward, and I lean back as a result, just in case one of those buttons pings off. "I became a rich man because I make calculated business decisions. How many copies do you sell?"

"At best, fifteen thousand."

"And one assumes the quality of the content dictates the demand."

"Of course."

"And you think your story on the highwaymen will help."

"Absolutely. I'll even credit you with their capture. Free advertisement for your business, too." Going national in the future? I smile, imagining Papa's face.

"Sell twenty thousand and we'll talk again."

Twenty? "That's nearly one edition for every person who lives in Coventry, Fleming. One for every thirtieth person who resides here in London." How ridiculous! Any one of our newspapers is read dozens of times by different people. Seven bloody pence per copy is the reason why, God damn taxes.

"It is not worth my while otherwise." He takes more Scotch, and I sink more gin, feeling the pressure. Of course, I have every faith in myself and the story. But…twenty thousand? We will need another two machines, not one! I pout, thinking, my mind, which is becoming increasingly foggy, beginning to ache too, as I try to concoct a plan to get my story in the pages. I am certain I can achieve those numbers. Certain! But how if not given the opportunity? I need my story out there to not only sate this newfound and quite unquenchable drive in me, but also to advance the business. I am wounded by my father's lack of confidence in me, but, I accept I am without the substantiated evidence to prove his concerns are misplaced.

I slump further into my chair, ignoring Fleming in the next seat, who has invited Ruby back onto his lap for a fondle. And I certainly do not want to marry in order to prove my devotion to sensibility. Good grief, how did this happen?

"How might I keep in contact with you?" I ask without looking at him.

"I will be staying with my cousin in Belmore Square," he answers in between squeezes of Ruby's breasts.

"Your cousin lives in Belmore Square?"

"That's what I said, Melrose. Simpson's the name."

"The ship builder?"

"You know of him?" he asks, still focused on the two creamy mounds of plump flesh within his grasp.

"I too live in Belmore Square." This is fate. It has to be.

"Then I suppose we will be seeing a lot of each other, either there or here." He turns a grin my way, one I can't say I appreciate, and suddenly being here in Kentstone's feels even more wrong. I am better than this seediness. The Melrose name is better than this.

"I look forward to doing business with you, Fleming," I say confidently. I am going to make this happen, just as soon as I have appealed to my new brother-in-law's softer nature. That's my solution. Him.

Problem is, I don't think the Duke has a softer side. At least, not with anyone other than his new wife, and I highly doubt I can get into her good books, for she will certainly be suspicious of my motives. Rightly so. But this story will not be fresh forever, and men like Fleming don't come along every day.

Papa wants to make the newspaper national? I can make that happen. And best of all, I don't have to get married to do it.

Chapter 9

I am, unfortunately, far drunker than I planned to be, but the chatter went on after Fleming had finished fondling Ruby, who is quite possibly more a bluestocking than a cyprian, for she often, if only momentarily, forgot herself and spoke with too much knowledge and with a good tongue.

What would Fleming say, I wonder, if I were to tell him that I suspect one of the highwaymen to be a female? I smile at the thought of his outraged face as I wobble down the steps of Kentstone's onto the street and look up and down for a Hackney coach, finding the cobbles empty, the street quiet. Well, I think, as I start wandering toward Piccadilly, at least I am able to walk without assistance.

The time alone offers me the perfect opportunity to mull over the events of the day. Get married? I laugh out loud as I wobble around the corner and, most unwelcomed, Taya Winters's face pops into my mind's eye and brings my amusement to a sharp end. Yes, quite a day, which ended with a strong dose of Fleming's utter vulgarity and started with a strong dose of Taya Winters's *charms*. My God, resisting her will kill me, I'm sure of it, but resist her I must. Not resisting her will have me killed. The urge to kiss her. The taste of her fingertip in my mouth. The way she gazed at me. *Would it be a terribly bad idea?*

Yes!

No.

Yes, yes, yes.

No, no, no.

Jesus, yes.

I must be drunker than I thought to think such pathetic thoughts, perhaps the fresh air assisting there. I must get the deal with Fleming underway so that I may become too busy to let my mind wander to Taya Winters. It's a good plan, and one I must stick to.

I smile as I turn onto Belmore Square, but it drops when I lose my footing and stumble into the road, narrowly escaping being run down by a carriage that is traveling at quite a remarkable, and, I might add, unacceptable speed. "Watch it!" I yell, righting my staggering body, the blue ruin not helping. "Idiot," I grumble, watching the coach leave the square. "Someone needs to impose speed limits ar—" Something catches my eye, disappearing into the gardens, a cloaked being moving too fast, up to no good. "Who goes there?" I call, cautious, hearing the sound of footsteps. Light footsteps. If I am not mistaken, the light footsteps of a female. I follow the sound, making it into the gardens, and stop, looking around the darkness, listening carefully. I hear a bush rustle, and then see movement in my peripheral vision. I dart my eyes that way, just catching sight of a figure. A figure in dark breeches and a dark jacket.

And a hat.

I inhale. "Hey!" I yell, going after it, dipping and weaving my way through the bushes and shrubs, stopping every now and then to listen, to watch. Another rustle, another flash of movement to my left. My neck cracks when I snap my head that way, just seeing the waft of some dark locks. "Show yourself," I call, following, my heart as frantic as my pace. I eventually find my way to the edge of the gardens and stumble out onto the road, turning on the spot, searching for her. *Her!* It was a female, her frame, her footsteps, her hair.

Then I hear the distant sound of hooves hitting the cobbles, and I wait, bracing myself, the trampling of the ground growing closer, and then out of the darkness, from nowhere, it would seem, a white stallion comes charging toward me, and I am useless, motionless, my eyes set upon the rider who is standing in the saddle, bent over low. I cannot see her eyes, but I can feel them on me, daring me not to move. I *cannot* move. It is not bravery, but rather simply being mesmerized.

And when the horse sprints past, I am spun on the spot on a gasp from me, and one from her. A gasp too high in pitch to belong to a man. I gather myself, straightening, and watch as the horse races out of the square, and I don't move until the echo of its hooves is no more. "Hell," I breathe to myself, scrubbing a hand down my face, looking around me, as if the darkness might offer an explanation. What was she doing here?

"Frank?"

I look over my shoulder and see Lady Dare approaching with her maid, and quite a vision she is in a blue satin gown, her hair an elaborate pile of precisely placed ringlets.

"My lady," I murmur, scanning the square again, wondering what on earth just happened.

"Lost something?"

"Yes, my mind, apparently."

"Pardon me?"

"Nothing." I shake my head and move out of the way of any potential carriages that might come this way. "Good evening to you, Scarlett."

"Oh, we remain on first name terms, do we?" She pouts, a grin breaking. "How delightful. Care to escort me home?"

"A generous offer, I'm sure," I reply, smiling insincerely. "But regrettably I must decline."

"We must not live with regrets, Frank."

"Indeed."

"Then I suppose I ought to call upon alternative company."

"I suppose you should," I whisper, looking back in the direction in which the horse and its rider fled. What, I must ask, was she doing around here? Off her horse?

One might think I am being threatened. Warned.

But why?

Chapter 10

I was totally foxed by the time I made it to my bed, having sunk another few Scotches to try and tame my wild imagination, so when Clara bursts into my room at the crack of dawn and yanks the covers from my body, I am most perturbed. "Bugger off," I mutter groggily, pulling them back.

"I will not." She once again removes the bedsheets, and this time dumps them on the floor at the bottom of my bed so as to make it as inconvenient as possible for me to retrieve them. I am, in all honesty, surprised she is in here making a nuisance of herself. Has she forgotten I am on her case and will—*I will, damn it*—pull her back into line.

"I forbid you to see the stable boy," I snap.

"The Duke is here," she says, evading my statement.

I recoil and do a terrible job of hiding it. Christ, has Taya folded under the pressure of her brother's bad mood and exposed our secret? Did she confess that we nearly kissed? That I was a whisper away from ruining her? "And what of it?" I ask, tentative, mentally wondering if I should be climbing out of the window before my sister's new, unpredictable, and, frankly, frightening husband tracks me down to my room and murders me in my bed.

Clara smiles. "Eliza is with child."

"What?"

"Yes! She's skipped her courses! I heard it with my own ears."

I am out of my bed faster than a fox running from the hounds, dashing bare-chested down the stairs to Papa's study,

where I find the Duke sitting comfortably in a chair opposite Papa, who looks, and it shouldn't be a surprise given the
ungodly early hour, most sleepy.

"Frank?" Papa questions, taking in my half-naked form as
Dalton follows me in and sets a tray on the table between them.
"Are you all right?"

"Did you forget to dress?" the Duke asks.

"Your Grace." I ignore both of their questions and casually
help myself to some coffee. "I've just heard the good news," I say.

"Frank!" Clara yells, and I turn to see her in the doorway,
positively raging.

"Clara, what have I told you about eavesdropping?" Papa says
on a sigh, rubbing at his tired eyes.

"Not to do it," she mutters, throwing me a cutting glare that
is totally wasted on me.

Mama appears, guiding Clara away. "Come on now, dear.
You must perfect your piano piece. Papa is most anxious to
hear it!"

The door closes, and I turn to my lovely brother-in-law. "Is
it true?"

"It is true," Johnny confirms.

"Then she must take to her bed immediately," I declare, starting to pace the rug, my mind spinning. "This is wonderful news!"
The *best* news. I couldn't ask for better news, for Eliza will now
be busy being with child and realigning her priorities so that
the Duke's offspring may arrive safe and healthy. "Congratulations, Your Grace." I smile and raise my coffee cup.

Johnny shakes his head, and I think it might be in exasperation, perhaps for me, I cannot be sure. "Most perturbingly,
your sister, my beautiful, ambitious, duchess, does not parade
enthusiasm as infectious as your fine self, Melrose."

"She is not happy?" I ask. "How can that be? She is to provide
a boy heir and perhaps many more little lords and ladies for you
to enjoy." *And keep her busy.*

"Unfortunately, it has come as a shock to Eliza, though I know not why when..." His Grace fades off and shifts uncomfortably in his seat, glancing at Papa nervously. It is ridiculous, if you ask me, for him to act with supposed honor. We all know Eliza was indulged by the Duke's *charms* before she was leg-shackled. "She is most shocked," he says simply, sinking further into his seat, looking like a beaten man. I have always admired my sister's free will, nurtured it to an extent, and perhaps taken advantage of it when the time called for it, but... oh, she cannot let her ambitions cause unrest in her marriage. The Duke, despite being an oaf at times, is a good man, and he makes a fine husband who has his priorities in good order.

"Where is she?" I ask. "I should like to speak with her." Perhaps, in a lovingly, brotherly way I know I am capable of because my sister is oh so dear to me, I can bring her around and she may be happy about this, because, naturally, it is a happy occasion!

"She has resorted to barricading herself in our room to avoid words of reason." Johnny takes some coffee and sips, and, for he surely looks like he needs it, I ponder offering him something harder. I feel pity for him. He looks very strange.

"Rest assured, I will fix this," I say, placing my coffee down and leaving the house, my destination and purpose my only focus, therefore I cannot say I pay too much attention to the odd looks coming at me from the staff or the residents who are up and about at this early hour as I cross through the gardens of the square. Naturally, I cast my eyes over the bushes as I go, reliving last night, the energy and thrill of the chase, of possibly catching a glimpse of her face. I stop at a rather large laurel bush, my eyes set on something entwined around the thick, green leaves. Reaching forward, I pluck the hair and pull the long strand free, watching as it wafts in the light morning breeze. Dark, long. I release it from my grasp and watch it float away. I had momentarily wondered if I had dreamt the whole thing. Or imagined it. I was certainly drunk enough. But that hair…

She was here, in Belmore Square. And again I ask myself why. Oh, the mystery!

I shake myself back to life, cross the cobbles to number one, pass through the creaky gate, march up the path, take the gold lion's head door knocker, and give it a good whack. Hercules answers, looking surprised. "I must see my sister," I declare, entering without invitation. "Where will I find her?"

"Top of the stairs, third door on the right, Mr. Melrose," he answers without hesitation or question, telling me Hercules here is most pleased I have arrived. I take the stairs and put myself outside the door, taking the knob and turning. The door does not shift even an inch, so I knock gently. "Eliza, it is I, Frank."

Silence.

"Come now, sister, we are all very worried."

"Go away!"

I recoil and pout, thinking that was rather uncalled for. "Eliza, be reas—"

"What on earth are you doing here at this ungodly hour?"

I whirl round and find Taya Winters behind me looking beautifully sleepy and disheveled in a pair of calf-clingers and a sheer chemise. *Lord have mercy on my soul.* I remind myself of everything I reminded myself of many times before—she is forbidden, I'll die, it'll ruin the family name, the business. All of that, of course, annoyingly, for it does not help matters, also reminds me of that brief almost-kiss. I must ignore her. For both of our sakes. Or be rude. Make her hate me. "Me being here is of no concern to you."

Her expression is fierce. "Except it's my house, you fool."

Fool. She is, of course, correct. On both counts. I turn back toward the door and knock once again. "Eliza, please, let me in." I look out the corner of my eye, feeling her getting closer, and I inhale, pressing myself into the wood of the door, effectively taking myself out of reach of Taya as she passes. Except, she still somehow manages to brush my back with her shoulder, and I swallow repeatedly, trying to dampen down my heating blood. *Please, please, sister, let me in!* I watch Taya tread on light feet down the hallway, her long, wild dark blonde hair swishing across the top of her backside. I am transfixed, my eyes rooted to the curve of her waist. She has a piece of paper in her hand. What is she penciling now?

As soon as she is out of what is apparently a trigger range, I sigh, relax and rest my back against the door, scrubbing a hand down my face. "Lord, help m…bugger it!" I'm suddenly free-falling backward, landing on my back with a grunt, and Eliza appears above me, her face a map of curiosity.

"What's wrong?" she asks, assessing my flustered state.

What's wrong? With me? She doesn't want to know. Besides, my wrongs are not the reason I am here. "Nothing is wrong," I mutter, wincing at the stab of pain in my elbow. Today started so well—the news of my sister with child the best wake-up, but it has soon deteriorated. *Her* fault.

I pout up at Eliza, though she will know the truth of why, and her shoulders drop. "Come now," she breathes, exasperated by me. I completely understand, for I am most exasperated with myself, too. She offers her hands for me to take and hauls me to my feet on a grunt that is, in my humble opinion, a bit over the top; I am not so big I might warrant such oomph. Her husband, on the other hand, is quite a lump of a man—tall, sturdy, and imposing with it. My more athletic frame pales in comparison, but, make no mistake, I would certainly hold my own if we did get to a point of violence. The Duke might bring fat fists and a few extra pounds, but I will bring speed and agility. I frown at my loose thoughts. Why I am thinking such things I do not know—I never plan on so much as looking at Taya again, so the

Duke, or his brother Sampson, will have no cause to attempt to murder me.

"What are you doing here?" Eliza asks as she walks me to the bed and sits me down on the mattress.

"I have come to talk some sense into you." Ironic, really, isn't it, that I am to talk some sense into Eliza?

"You look troubled," she says, pouting, doing a fine job of ignoring my answer. "Perhaps some tea will help." She starts to turn, but, quite harshly, if unintentionally, I seize her wrist to stop her.

"I do not need tea." Some Scotch, though? "You are with child," I say, making sure she knows I am privy to the situation. Not that it should be a situation, of course, since she is married. "This is cause for celebration, Eliza, not melancholy. Whyever do you appear so grim?"

With shoulders that look too heavy for her slight frame, she faces me again. Her pointed expression is evidence of her disposition, and I fear I'm about to cop a swing or a whip of her smart tongue.

"Please do not hit me," I say, pouting like I used to do when I had upset her and was fearful of her temper. "One female's black book is enough to be in."

"What?"

Oh bugger. I scratch around for something to say, to divert my sister before she fathoms what has occurred or can press me to confess, but, because of the pressure I expect, and perhaps because of the expectant, knowing look pinned to me in this moment, I find nothing. Not one thing.

"Frank," Eliza says slowly, making me drop my eyes to my knees like a naughty little boy who has been caught red-handed misbehaving. "What have you done?"

I laugh on the inside. She does not want to know. I look at the rumpled bedsheets beneath my breeches, hiding my guilty face, and it occurs to me, too late, perhaps, that I am sitting on my sister's and her husband's bed, and I care not to know what has happened beneath the sheets. Not my sister. No, I refuse to believe it, but, stupid idiot that I am, I remind myself why I am here. She's with child.

So, yes, back to the matter at hand.

I get up from the bed and start roaming the room. "Do not change the subject, sister. You are with child, and it is a joyous thing."

"But of course you would think that," she hisses. "It means you can take my place and reclaim your name as writer of the finest stories, except this time, I suppose, you might actually write them yourself!"

"You wound me." I place a hand over my heart as if it is aching. "I want what is best for you." I truly do, even if me being here isn't completely selfless. "Are you telling me you do not want this baby because you want to continue working? What? Forever? Why would you get married, especially to a duke who will be eager to continue his dukedom and produce heirs, if you long to write forevermore?"

"I love him." She dumps herself on the bed. "And I *do* wish to give His Grace children, many, if he so desires, but we agreed that I would enjoy the wonders that writing affords me, and now I can claim my words for myself, I find, quite unexpectedly, or not so, perhaps, that it is quite habit-forming, Frank! The praise, the awe, the hunger for more."

I can relate and am yet to release my story, so yes, I recognize her plight and my heart goes out to my sister. Always so energetic and passionate, sometimes about things that should not require her energy or passion. "You must take care of yourself. You can write again, just as soon as the baby is born." I know she has no desire to mingle with the lords and ladies, to frequent the parties and be seen showcasing her new status. Rank means nothing to Eliza, even though she is nearing the very top of the status tree. She is not and never will be high in the instep. "I'm sure His Grace will have an army of staff to take care of your children and teach them all that you could possibly desire to fill their little minds with. And with their mother's genes?" They will be little geniuses!

Eliza gets up and comes to me, her clenched fists pushing into my chest. "That's just it, Frank. Everything I want my children to know, I should like to teach them myself. I do not want them to have a governess. I should like to nurse them myself and enjoy raising our children with their father to help me. And Mama and Lady Winters too."

I smile softly. She wants to eat her cake and have her cake. Do all of those things but work too.

"But I wanted to wait at least a year," she says quietly. "I have only just begun to truly enjoy the thrill of journalism, and I am yet to finish my story too."

"The Fates have other ideas for you, Eliza." Taking her hands where they remain on my chest, I lift each one to my mouth in turn and kiss her knuckles. I must say, I have always abhorred seeing sadness and despair on Eliza. Now more than ever. "How about we compromise?"

"How so?"

"I keep the pages of the newspaper warm for you while you grow in belly. You can remain editor-in-chief, if you so wish. I will merely hold the fort while you're busy being fat."

She swats my arm, and I smile. "Papa told you of his gift?"

"No, Grant told me when I visited the printworks. It was a shock, I confess, and just because I am disappointed for myself does not mean I am not delighted for you."

Eliza appears to soften everywhere, from her face to her body. "Really?"

"But of course! You really do need to stop seeing me as you do all other men who have and still do question your strengths." If there are any, they must be brainless idiots. "But the fact of the matter is, Eliza, you married a duke and times may change, but men will *never* be able to bear heirs. It is a matter of science, not politics."

She laughs lightly, looking down at her flat tummy. "I suppose you are right. And will your focus on work keep you busy?" Her eyebrows lift, and mine lower with a scowl.

"And what is that supposed to mean?"

"It means, will you take your eyes off the ample new female flesh that's within your grasp?"

I scoff. "You speak as if I am an out-of-control rake, Eliza. And if you must know, I have not so much as sniffed a woman for some weeks."

"I don't believe it."

She shouldn't because it's not technically true. A strong waft of honeysuckle overcomes me and I find myself holding my breath to avoid it until my lungs scream for air. "You should believe it," I say on my exhale. "I have seen the drive in you, Eliza. And I always wondered where it came from. I realize now. You had passion for your stories and how you told them."

"You're really rather captured by these highwaymen who might not be men, aren't you?"

I shrug, appearing nonchalant. "A little, I suppose. But not only that, I saw Papa build everything up and watched as it was very nearly taken away—everything he had worked so hard for, the business, our name. It must be protected, and, frankly, I feel quite guilty for not doing more sooner, instead of seeking more instant, unrewarding gratification."

"So you will be married?"

"He's spoken with you on matters of marriage?" I ask, shocked.

"I would love nothing more than to see you settled down, Frank. Happy!"

"I am happy," I laugh. "I do not need to be married to achieve that."

"But your rakish ways will be no more."

"That is quite a promise to make." I pull a hand through my

hair, starting to sweat. Am I expected to make a vow of celibacy in order to be taken seriously? Surely not!

"All right, promise not that, but you will promise me that you will stay away from Lady Taya."

"Taya?" I snort, sounding wholly disgusted, when on the inside I am really rather alarmed.

"You do not find her desirable?"

I hate lying to my sister. "Not at all."

She laughs. "Are you blind?"

"No, I am not."

"Are you sure? Really sure?"

"Yes, I am quite sure."

"So you can see that you are naked?"

"What are you blathering on about?"

"This," Eliza says, motioning down my body, and I frown as I glance down to my chest. My *naked* chest.

"Oh," I breathe.

"What is it with us Melroses dashing around the square in a state of undress?" Eliza smiles, and I join her, taking her in a hug. "We must keep up momentum in sales, Frank. We have another machine to pay for now."

I laugh under my breath. "No pressure," I whisper. But I am confident. All of the ingredients are there, I just have to put them together.

"I want your word, Frank. No more inappropriate dalliances with unsuitable ladies. We have a name to protect. Scandal to avoid. I am a duchess now, and after everything Johnny and his family have been through, I cannot bear thinking that I might bring disgrace to their family name, not when they have only just repaired what was broken."

"I understand," I say, and it is not with reluctance.

"I rather love my brother and should like to keep him."

I stare at the draperies, humming my agreement. "I am focused on work, I assure you."

"You'd better be."

"Is that a threat?"

"Yes, it is. I have worked hard and I am about to hand the reins to my rake of a brother who has always preferred to hold a woman rather than a pen. Papa isn't getting any younger, you know. He should not be stressed."

I flinch. She is right, of course. Always right. I have spent too long with my priorities askew, and I would like nothing less than to see Papa looking so forlorn and broken again, when he thought all was lost. When he was backed into a corner by Lymington and his blackmail. This isn't only about sating this reborn desire to write, the spark. It is about continuing Father's legacy. "You have my word. Now, come with me as I wish for you to make friends with His Grace." I have no doubt my intervention on this matter will be received with gratitude, and, hopefully, if the Duke was to ever discover that I very nearly ruined his sister, he might spare me my life and perhaps only break one leg. "Come," I say, breaking our hug. "Let me take you to your husband."

"Where is he?" Eliza asks, pulling on a coat.

"With Papa in his study."

"Oh, wonderful. Papa knows?"

"It is not Papa you should be worrying about, but our crafty little sister."

"Oh no, the whole square will know. And what of the stable boy, Frank? Good grief, Clara is heading for trouble." Indeed. It is not only I who can bring disgrace to this family.

"I can't say I enjoy this," I admit. "But even I can appreciate this is an unsuitable match. We have no choice but to order his return to the countryside before their friendship is discovered, but I fear I do not carry enough clout to make such demands."

"No, but Johnny does." Eliza pouts. "Such a shame, it is. He is a sweet boy, but even I am worried for Clara's dreams, for they are certainly more impossible than mine ever were."

"She is sixteen, Eliza," I remind her. "This is calf-love. She knows not of true love."

"And you do?"

"No, and I have never claimed to." I reach for my jacket to pull it in, frowning. I look down at my bare chest.

"I see you still haven't found your clothes." Taya appears from another room fastening the button of her coat dress.

I puff my chest out and smile my brightest smile. "You are welcome."

She snorts and barges past me.

"Have a wonderful day," I call, earning myself a jab in my naked ribs from Eliza. "Owww."

"Must you rile her?"

If I am to avoid kissing her, then yes. "No," I breathe, walking Eliza down the stairs.

"Stay away," she warns. "That, too, is part of our deal."

"That is not a problem," I reply, sounding surer than I should.

Chapter 11

The moment we pass through the door, Mama is pouncing on my poor, helpless sister like a lion, smothering her in her affections. Of course, Florence Melrose will be flaunting this news with the greatest of pride, for not only is her daughter now a duchess, but her grandson will one day be a duke. I smile to myself. My nephew will be a duke. Who would have thought? "Wonderful news!" Mama sings, cupping Eliza's cheeks with both hands, scanning her face. "My God, you are glowing already!"

"Mama, please," Eliza breathes, taking her hands and releasing them from her face. "If I am glowing it is merely because I am roasting hot." She blows out air, flapping the front of her coat. "Are the fires raging?"

"No, the fires have not been lit for weeks, my darling, not since the weather improved." Mama's delight transforms into worry. "You are not running a fever, are you?" Her hand slaps onto Eliza's forehead.

"No, I feel well enough, just very hot."

"Oh, good. His Grace is in the study with your father." Mama opens the way to Papa and Johnny, her shining, excited eyes on Eliza, gazing at her fondly. "You will cherish every moment of your condition just as I did, Eliza. It is a joyous time, full of wonder and excitement, but, of course, you must not get stressed or overdo it."

"See," I pipe up. "Mama is right."

Eliza turns her tired eyes onto me. "I will stuff an orange in your mouth, Frank, be sure of it."

"All right." I hold up my hands in surrender. Is this impudence, I wonder, because she is angered about stepping aside, or is it purely a baby-related thing? My God, women are complicated creatures.

"Now let us get this over with," Eliza says, as she marches to the door, pushes it open rather abruptly, and stands on the threshold.

"Come, Mama," I say, gently taking her elbow and following my sister.

"Eliza," Johnny breathes, standing from his chair, looking like a beaten man. I know not what he has said to incite such an extreme reaction, but right there on the spot, Eliza bursts into tears.

"It was not supposed to happen so quickly!" she cries, her shoulders jerking violently.

Papa looks surprised. "Then perhaps a chastity belt might have been a good idea."

"And I know not if I am prepared to be a mother!" Her hands cover her face as she cries rivers of tears into them. "I wanted you to myself for a time, and now I shall be fat and exhausted, and you may not desire me anymore."

My eyes widen, and I cast a look across to Papa, who is, as I expected, looking wholly uncomfortable. "All right," he says, suddenly finding life in his tired bones. "I think it is time for me to depart."

"It is sensible, I suppose," Eliza goes on, ignoring our father's discomfort, "as Frank has made me realize, to slow down until the babe is born and I have nursed him to one year."

Johnny smiles and goes to Eliza, taking her hands. "You make me a very happy husband, my duchess, when you are reasonable."

"Don't get used to it."

He laughs and hauls her into him, and I smile, not because I am finally being blessed with the opportunity I so need, but because I definitely caught Eliza's soft, loving smile before her face was buried in the Duke's big chest.

"Wonderful!" Mama sings, blocking Papa before he can leave his study. "Burt, we will be grandparents!"

"Yes, Flo, that we will be." Papa looks across to me and nods sharply, an acknowledgment as such. *Do not let him down.* He need not worry, I will not. I just pray he doesn't bring up that small matter of marriage again.

Papa puts an arm around Mama's shoulder, leading her out. "Come, Grandmama, us old boots should get some breakfast."

Her laugh is high-pitched, thrilled, and utterly wonderful, and I watch with a certain fondness as they leave, feeling the love all around me.

"So, sister dearest, I thought perhaps you could release the rest of your story without delay," I say, taking a seat at Papa's desk. "Readers will be most perturbed should they have to wait until the babe is born and you have nursed it to one year."

"If you refer to my son as an *it* again, Melrose, I won't think twice about dismembering you." Johnny raises an eyebrow in warning.

"Son?" Eliza questions.

"It will be a boy," the Duke assures her, losing the sharp warning in his eyes as he regards my sister's flat tummy. "I am certain of it."

"Right." The amount of mawkishness happening is overcoming. "Back to the matter at hand."

"Little Lord."

I frown. "What?"

"You must call my unborn child a little lord because that, Melrose, is what he is."

"Of course," I exhale my tiredness. How could I forget? "Little Lord it is." I smile mildly, and the Duke growls.

"And what is your plan?" Eliza asks. "You must tell me."

"To expand," I say.

"So soon? How?"

"My plan is still in the making," I say, taking the tops of her arms and planting a kiss on her forehead. "Now go expect your child and enjoy." I leave her and walk with quite some bounce out of the study but stop at the doorway, something coming to me. I turn and find the Duke. "I have a favor to ask of you."

"Oh?"

I close the door so it is just my sister, her husband, and I, blocking out Mama and Papa, for I should not like them to know of this little problem and cause them untold stress, but also to limit the potential of our crafty little sister overhearing, or, more appropriately, eavesdropping. So I lower my voice too. "Eliza and I have decided we must intervene."

"With what?" the Duke asks.

"Clara and the stable boy."

"Oh, that."

"Yes, that."

"And what would you have me do?"

"We," Eliza says quietly, looking at me, her eyes telling me to let her handle it. I am absolutely all right with that. "Frank and I, that is, think it is best to ensure Clara cannot see Benjamin anymore, for she will not listen to our pleas."

"Send him away," the Duke states. "It is the only way."

"I'm glad you agree." I nod, and Eliza closes her eyes. I can see she is having a hard time of this too, but she knows as well as I do that it is for the best. As I have said and thought numerous times, this is merely calf-love, nothing more.

"I will speak with Fitzgerald," Johnny says.

I nod and leave, going up to my bedroom and finding my piece, reading it again, chewing my lip, quite satisfied, if only because my suspicions about one of the highwaymen being a woman are nearly certainly confirmed, before dressing and getting on my way to the printworks.

Chapter 12

The next day, the rest of Eliza's story about the Winters family was published and London went positively daft for it. Naturally, I was more than proud of her for capturing the imaginations of the masses. Naturally, too, I felt immense pressure when I was kindly informed by Grant that sales broke records, topping an incredible, and quite unbelievable, sixteen thousand! It is a great starting point for me, but, of course, it sent the printworks into a blind panic and the employees were asked to work through the night to accommodate demand, for which they were compensated handsomely. This also, of course, meant Johnny had to pull his finger out and get us that new machine pronto, which he did within just two days.

"To sixteen thousand!" Papa sings, pouring champagne for all. "I cannot believe it!" With the help of Dalton, he fills everyone's hand with a glass. "To Eliza!"

"To Eliza," we all sing, toasting and sinking our drinks, smiles all around; but mine, inevitably, falls when I catch the eye of Taya Winters. I quickly look away, but before I can walk away, avoid her, she is approaching, and I am a frozen form of a man.

"Congratulations," she says, and I hold my breath, blocking off my sense of smell. I nod and smile my thanks. "I hear you have quite a story to launch with."

And where did she hear that? I turn curious eyes onto her, always curious, just as she lifts the glass to her lips and sips. Slowly. "Yes," I all but whisper.

"Is that the paper I found on the floor of the carriage? The one you always carry in your pocket?"

"Perhaps."

"How thrilling." She looks truly excited for me, and I am thrown. We're supposed to be hating each other. It's so much easier than this...this...this...what? "And what is the story about?"

Lust. It is just lust, as I have felt it time and again before. I cannot risk my life as well as the family fortune for lust. But love? I blink and look away, catching the eye of Sampson Winters, who appears all too interested. "It was very lovely talking to you."

"We've hardly talked."

"It's for the best," I murmur, wandering over to Papa, breathing easy once again when I have put some space between us.

"The machine is up and running, Frank. I do so hope it has not been a waste, for your sister has set quite a bar."

I laugh nervously. "No pressure, huh?" I say once again, catching a wicked glint in Eliza's eye.

"None at all," she muses, all too casually for my liking, flicking some nonexistent lint from her dress too. "Sixteen thousand. Can you believe it?"

I know she wants me to succeed, as I did her, so, really, these games are a bit pointless. Nevertheless, I shall continue to play, if only to entertain my sister while she is busy growing in belly. Who am I to remove *all* fun from her life? Besides, I believe I should appreciate how brilliant she is, because Fleming insisted that twenty thousand copies was the magic number, and my darling sister has boosted the chances of me meeting that target.

"I have delivered my story to Grant, and it shall be printed tomorrow." I nod, raise my glass, and drink.

"Excellent." Papa toasts with me.

"Tha—" I am cut short by an almighty wail and a door slamming.

"Good heavens," Mama cries, leaving the drawing room to go investigate the commotion. My eyes instinctively move to Johnny, and he nods, telling me I am suspecting right. "Clara," Mama calls. "What has happened?"

"I hate him!" she yells, bursting into the room, now with Mama chasing her.

"Hate who?"

Clara's finger comes up and points at me. "Him! I hate him!"

I deflate, loathing the guilty feeling creeping up on me. "Clara, I—"

"Don't!"

"What's going on?" Papa demands.

Clara, obviously remembering herself and where she is, backs down, much to my relief, for I would hate to further her dismay and be forced into sharing the unfortunate situation with our parents. Her little nostrils flare. "I just hate him."

I wince, not relishing the thought of anyone hating me, especially one of my sisters, as Eliza moves to my side and rubs my arm reassuringly and Clara marches away.

"Well," Mama says, blinking back her shock. "I don't know what's gotten into her!"

"Me either," I murmur, shaking my head, wondering what that deep-rooted sense of guilt is all about. The stable boy wouldn't be good enough for Clara even if our address wasn't Belmore Square. I go to the table and top up my champagne, feeling parched.

"So I am not the only person around here who hates you," Taya says, joining me, holding out her glass for me to fill.

I stare at it for a time, holding the bottle and my now full glass. To be hated isn't a very pleasant feeling. I look up at Taya. Her small, smug smile drops when she sees what I expect is sadness in my eyes. "I must be going," I say, clearing my throat and setting the bottle and glass down. "Good day to you." I leave the house, put on my hat, and march across the square, each hit of my boots on the cobbles knocking her out of my head.

I reach number five and give the knocker two solid thwacks. Mr. Simpson's butler pulls the door open. "Mr. Melrose," he says, nodding his respect. "How may I help you?"

"I'm looking for Fleming, actually. I don't suppose he is here, is he?"

"Yes, I am." Fleming appears behind the butler, struggling to fasten the gold buttons of his jacket. "Let us walk to my carriage. I am late for a business meeting at…" He hesitates and glances around. "Kentstone's," he whispers.

A business meeting? Not at Kentstone's, I can be sure of that. The only business that happens at Kentstone's is of a seedy nature. "I believe we are on course," I say as we take the steps down from Mr. Simpson's house, but before we reach the bottom, Fleming stops suddenly and throws his arm out, stopping me too.

"She's quite a sort, that one, isn't she?"

I frown and follow his line of sight, seeing Scarlett Dare breezing across the square. I don't answer. "So, as I was say—"

"And that one over there." He nods across the square, and I see Lizzy Fallow being escorted by Millingdale, or, more to the point, her escorting him, for the old goat can hardly walk.

"Yes, indeed, now, if we could get back to—"

"And that one, lord have mercy on my soul, would I like to bend her over."

I sigh and follow Fleming's line of sight to…*Oh no*. What is that heat in my veins? "I suggest," I say, seething, but my voice strong and warning, "you refrain from having such lurid thoughts immediately, or I'll blacken your daylights." Shocked by my own outburst, I stare at Lady Taya Winters, who is rushing across the square, her loose hair wafting delightfully all over the place. She looks…distressed.

"Excuse me?" Fleming coughs his surprise.

"Said her brother to me when I had my eye on her," I quickly add, shaking my head, reminding myself that this man is a means to an end, however vulgar he is. "He's quite an animal, her brother."

Fleming snorts. "I'd like to hear him warn *me* away."

"You really wouldn't," I murmur, loving the thought of the wayward Duke pummeling this letch to death.

"Pardon?"

"Nothing." I start walking again, and Fleming follows. "As I was saying, I believe we are on course to striking a very lucrative deal. Just yesterday we sold sixteen thousand copies."

Fleming pulls his fat body up into his carriage. "I heard your sister penned every article you ever put your name to."

"Well, not all, but a fair many, yes."

"But not now? Because, Melrose, I assure you, I have no interest in working with a woman. They're good for only one thing, and it isn't business."

My God, he is disgusting. I feel as though I am selling my soul to the devil, just by talking to him, let alone doing business with the beast. But, I remind myself, national. Global!

"Eliza is now married and with child."

He nods, happy about that. "Twenty thousand. We'll talk then. And the highwaymen, too." His lip curls and he roughly wipes at his massive nose. "Onwards!" He slumps back in his seat and the carriage pulls away, leaving me feeling the pressure once more. Twenty thousand. Jesus, he's right. Eliza has built her following. Nurtured it. Politics and religious claptrap have come second to the promises of entertainment from a compelling tale of betrayal, murder, and scandal. I am starting from scratch and have the added burden of a new machine to pay for. Not to mention, I don't appear to be anywhere close to actually discovering who the highwaymen are.

Perturbed, I pull at my velvet jacket, my nervous sweat quite real.

Chapter 13

But the next day, much to my surprise, although I would never admit it, we sell another sixteen thousand copies! I would have put it down to the reader expecting more of the Winters family's tragic story, but Eliza made it quite clear that the end had come. I read her final piece myself to be sure, and I smiled when she signed it off with the exciting announcement of the next day's front page news.

I mean, and I'm not too reserved to admit it, my headline was really quite genius, and it obviously had the desired effect.

ENGLISH ROSE OR ENGLISH ROGUE?

THE HIGHWAYWOMAN RUNS AMOK IN LONDON

Yes, you read that right. A woman! I myself can confirm...

And the next day, as I ride through the royal parks on my way to the printworks, everywhere I look there are people reading *The London Times*, their faces buried in the pages, eager for every word they can get, every piece of information.

At the very least, two dozen men ask me as I trot through the crowds if I have any inkling as to the identity of the highwaywoman, but I merely smile, feeding their curiosity, for it will surely lead to better sales tomorrow, too. Another dozen snort their doubts, insisting I must be mistaken, and I confidently assure them I am not.

"You must have been terrified," Lady Blythe says as I pass.

No, I was mesmerized. "I barely lived to tell the tale."

"She was violent?"

No, she was captivating. "She wielded a pistol with the greatest of confidence."

"You write with passion, Mr. Melrose, and your words are quite catchy, even if I do say so myself." She smiles demurely.

"Such a compliment from an establish, talented novelist, I'm sure," I say, nodding my respect.

"Oh, be sure of that. I always knew Florence's son was a handsome fellow, but such a talent too? My housemaid's son sweeps the floors at your printworks, and he told her the machines are running at full pace, day and night! Your father must be very proud of you and Her Grace." She goes back to the article. "Perhaps you might offer me some inspiration for my next novel, Mr. Melrose."

I smile, kicking my horse to encourage it into a trot, seeing Fleming in the distance, and, pleasingly, he too has his face buried in the pages of *The London Times.* "Morning, Fleming."

He looks up and slams the paper closed. "I was robbed by a woman?" he hisses.

"Indeed you were, Fleming, indeed you were."

"You will bring her to me."

"Oh, I will," I assure him quietly, sounding and appearing confident, but Fleming here has, annoyingly, taken me away from the accolades and thrill for a moment and reminded me that I have only enough words for perhaps another few editions, and I am far from close to discovering who she is. My heart pumps. Adrenaline, I'm sure. "I shall furnish you, along with everyone else, with the information as it unfolds."

"Good to hear. And what do you propose after she is captured and revealed, Melrose, and we strike a deal on my transportation means? What stories do you have up your sleeve then?"

"Oh, her capture is just the beginning, Fleming." Then we get into the whys and wherefores, not to mention the trial. That is, *if* she can be caught. She is playing a very risky game, I must admit. Perhaps she is a thrill seeker. One of those arrogant criminals that takes pleasure from taking risks.

I hum. Her arrogance may be the end of her.

I met Papa and we rode together to the printworks on horseback, chatting about business and stories. It was pleasant, as was the fact he neglected to mention anything about marriage. I think I might be off the hook for the time being, so long as I can maintain this momentum. Prove I do not need to be wed to demonstrate commitment.

Grant shows us the new machine at work, and Papa agrees to pay rises for all the staff. "Wait," he says, appearing to consider something quite carefully as he turns toward me. "What do you think, Frank?" he asks. "Two shillings a week per worker?"

"Perhaps a little tight, Papa. We have more than doubled the workload in recent weeks."

"You are right, of course. Five shillings it is. That'll please your sister," he says as he removes his hat. "And what of this?" He motions to a table that is stacked high with paper.

"Those are the requests for advertising space in *The London Times*," Grant tells us as I start to sift through the piles. "Requests have multiplied tenfold."

"What do you say, Frank?" Papa asks, coming over. "We cannot possibly accommodate such volumes."

"Readers wish to be informed and entertained," I say, starting to pace. "We can increase the pages to accommodate a mere fraction of these requests, but, should we take that route, we must employ more journalists to balance the advertisements with news. We are down two contributors, what with Porter dead and Eliza with child, and we cannot fill all the pages, Papa, so we should think to replace them without delay as a priority. To exceed that, not to mention the extra printing costs and weight for distribution, I fear would be counterproductive, at least for now." I do not need to add any more financial pressure on myself, not until I have more material to work with and have exceeded twenty thousand copies. But as soon as I have secured a deal with Fleming for distribution nationwide and can take advantage of readers further afield, it will take the pressure off and it will be full steam ahead. "Now, I think I would recommend ensuring the workers are suitably incentivized to meet our current demand, and then perhaps we reevaluate in the near future." I nod to myself and turn to Papa, who looks adorably stunned.

"Yes, yes, I agree." He blinks rapidly and appears to shake himself back into the room. "Grant, see to it that the workers are happy." He pats my shoulder. "And the story, Frank, such great writing. I was compelled myself. Now keep up the good work." Papa leaves and I exhale, hoping to God that I can keep up the good work, and leave Grant, walking back to my horse. To keep up the good work, I must have something to work with, and there's been no sight nor sound of the highwaymen for some days.

I spend the evening at Gladstone's mulling over my predicament. Lord above, I may have scared her away. She may have, along with thousands of other people, although I expect she stole a copy rather than paid for one, read the report, and decided it was too risky hanging around London waiting to be caught, revealed, and subsequently hanged. A distressed sweat dampens my brow, the pressures of running a business, a newspaper, hitting me, not for the first time, with significant force. I look down at the Scotch in my hand. I cannot fail. I cannot let my family down. Tomorrow is a new day, and it must not be wasted with a hangover.

I nod to myself, finish my drink, and leave, walking home, humming to myself as I do. I turn onto Belmore Square and come to a stop by the entrance to the gardens, looking up at our house. I can see shadows in the drawing room, the candlelight making the partygoers' silhouettes flicker and jump; the sound of laughter and chatter is muffled but still loud. I climb the steps and enter. The voices get louder, voices I recognize—Lady Wisteria, Lady Blythe, Lady Tillsbury, and then the gentlemen, laughing raucously with Papa. The gathering sounds far from finished, but I am without the energy to join them, so I slip into Papa's study for a nightcap and a few quiet moments alone before I take to my bed. I close the door gently and go to the sideboard where Papa keeps his decanter of Scotch.

"Good evening, Mr. Melrose."

I still and stare at the crystal cut glass in my hand, my shoulders lifting slightly at the sound of her voice, as if I am tense and I know not why. It is ridiculous. "My lady." I brave facing her, and I am nearly as ruined as any blue ruin could ever ruin me. She's sitting by the fireplace with a book on her lap.

She holds it up. "Her Grace brought me in here to show me this. It is a book about my family. She read it when she saw a painting being carried into our home before she and my brother became"—she pauses for thought, for the most appropriate words she can find—"aquainted."

It's laughable. "So you do read books?" I say like a gormless fool, and she smiles, her cheeks filling with blood.

"Well, I suppose it is part of what a lady should do." She places it to one side and collects a newspaper. "I must say, your story, it's..." She pauses once again for thought, and I step forward, interested to know what she thinks. "It is quite enthralling."

"Is that a compliment?"

"Perhaps," she answers, nonchalant, or trying to be. "I particularly enjoyed the part where you state..." Looking at the ceiling, she hums. "How did it read? Oh, yes." She looks at me with eyes full of excitement, and I am taken aback by it. *"My heart raced surely as fast as the steed that I was nose-to-nose with could run."*

"It was certainly thrilling." *Like the thought of kissing you.*

"Not frightening?" she asks, watching me closely as my shoulders, of their own volition, roll back, making me stand taller.

"And that, yes." *Again, like the thought of kissing you.*

"I thought as much," she whispers, her eyes falling to my lips. "Because I am certain if I were face-to-face with a highwayman, I would be terrified."

"It was a woman. A highway*woman*."

"Of course." She blinks and returns her eyes to the newspaper. "It is refreshing to read something that does not rouse memories. I found it very difficult, you see, to read your sister's story." She frowns. "Or *our* story." She looks at me and smiles. "I love your story, Frank."

She is an unconventional sort, unruly in dress, hair, and personality. And all the more beautiful for it. And, obviously, she is so very deeply distressed by what happened to her family, though she tries to put on a brave face. Perhaps her snarky way is a defense mechanism.

I flinch and quickly turn away, if only to escape the blinding glow Taya is radiating, painfully accepting what I have ignorantly refused to accept for some weeks since Taya Winters returned to Belmore Square and dazzled me. I am not only attracted to her, but completely and utterly enamored of her. God damn me, I think she is possibly the most beautiful creature I have ever laid my eyes upon, and I have laid my eyes upon many a beautiful woman. But just as quickly as I accept that hard truth, I also accept that my infatuation matters not. Not only am I without a title, as Taya kindly informed me herself, I cannot let my family down. Any dalliances with Taya Winters would surely cause untold scandal for the Winters family, and very likely end the Melroses and our business. But, by God, she is most tempting, and I am fast losing my willpower to resist her.

"I should like some privacy," I say, alarmed by my thoughts, as I walk to the door and pull it open. "If you don't mind." She loves my story. I didn't think my desire for her could be any stronger. Lord have mercy on my soul, this could be an even more unfortunate situation if I allow it. I must not allow it! *Focus, focus, focus.*

"Of course, my apologies."

I frown as she stands and approaches, having an internal battle, my head and heart at war. My head is commending her for her sensible, adult approach. My heart is begging her to challenge my coarseness.

"One more thing," she says, stopping just short of the doorway.

I do not look at her. "And what is that?"

"I have drawn something. After reading your story, I was quite inspired. I must at least thank you for that." She holds up a piece of worn paper, and I accept, staring down at the pencil drawing of a white stallion standing nose-to-nose with...me. It is exceptional. The detail, the shading. I look at this picture she has drawn and feel exactly as I felt on that day.

Mesmerized.

What a talent she is. Talented and beautiful with plenty of sass.

"Good day to you, Mr. Melrose."

I quickly slam the door, and Taya jolts, but her eyes remain on the wood, her body still.

The sounds of Mama's and Papa's soirée register behind me, but it does not prompt me to do what is right. What I *should* do. On the lumpiest of swallows, I search for some words. *Any* words. In fact, I am struggling somewhat awfully to speak at all. So instead, I take one step and place my body in front of hers. Her hands shoot up and fist my jacket, and I inhale sharply, looking down at the back of Taya's head. She cannot look at me. I can feel her heart pounding, punching into my chest. The heat of our bodies so close getting hotter by the second. I recall each time she has touched me, whether fleeting or not. The exhilaration.

Christ, I must not bow to this insanity, for it will surely be most disastrous. I need respect and recognition. I need Papa to see I am serious about the family business, that I am worthy of the responsibility. To give in to this madness would be to risk my plan, and my plan is not to continue my rakish ways, but to step up and be serious. To ensure the family business not only survives, but goes from strength to strength.

But then Taya slowly lifts her face and I have her eyes, and all of my reasoning is lost amid a wave of complete and utter awe. My God, such beauty is most certainly dangerous to men. Her eyes dart across my face and land on my lips, and I for sure know if she moves in for a kiss, I will not be able to resist. I will not be able to deny myself the certain pleasure of it.

She comes toward me, and as a result of that small move, all kinds of big things happen in my breeches, the rubbing of her body in such a sensitive place quite unbearable. "Good lord," I breathe, inhaling, seeing her pink, wet tongue trace her bottom lip, and when her mouth delicately brushes mine, I am gone, no longer here in the study, but floating. No longer fearful of the repercussions, but excited to be inside her, my body hardening…everywhere. I fall deeply into our kiss, my hands going to her back and holding her, pulling her closer, as our mouths move, our tongues dance, and our bodies sing.

You are a rake, Francis.

It is time to settle down.

Are you a businessman or a dandy?

No! "Hell," I gasp as I step back and release her from my hold, but not before ensuring she is safely standing, of course, albeit on wobbly legs and looking somewhat dazed. I am with her, totally befogged. "We must not," I say, refusing to look at her, my eyes and head low, not only to avoid facing Taya for fear of caving to the connection, but ashamed I have been so weak. "Your brothers will marry you well. I cannot be responsible for ruining your prospects." I will certainly lose my mind if I have to spend another moment with her, so I hurry out and rush up the stairs. "Bloody hell," I breathe, raking a hand through my hair as I fall into my bedroom. I drop to the bed and fall to my back, frowning when something in my hand registers. I hold it up. The drawing, more crumpled now than before, after being held in my fist. I sit up and smooth out the paper and stare at the sketch. It is exceptionally good. And I didn't even tell her so. *I should have told her!* I *want* to tell her.

I hear a sound outside and hurry to my window, looking down onto the square. My heart sinks when I see her perched on the bottom step, her head in her hands. She is upset? Not… regretful? Perhaps that is why she is upset, because she is regretful. "Oh, Taya Winters," I whisper, making the glass fog before me. "You beautiful, confusing creature." I leave my bedroom and walk with purpose and grit back down to the front door and swing it open, ready to…do what? Kiss her again? Embrace her? Talk to her? Explain why I left so abruptly after such a beautiful, consuming kiss? Tell her I think her drawing is wonderful?

It matters not.

She is gone.

Chapter 14

A fortnight later, I am feeling the pressure more acutely, for my words have run dry, being stretched to their limit, and I am without anything to continue feeding the insatiable thirst of the ton with news of robberies or encounters involving the highwaywoman. It is as I thought. She has disappeared to avoid being caught. *Damn it.* I have scared her away!

Sales have dropped and I am far off the twenty thousand required for Fleming to entertain any business deal. I am also far off delivering him, or the curious members of the ton, for that matter, the identity of the highwaywoman. Frankly, I'm in a bit of a tricky situation, for the business now has more overheads; we could not possibly withdraw the promised pay rises, as it would certainly cause anarchy, and Grant has warned me we are on the cusp of reporting losses. I'm hiding all of this from Papa, I do not wish to trouble him, and neither do I wish to see everything he has built destroyed.

What a mess. And damn that highwaywoman for teasing me and then disappearing! Hasn't she got purses to steal? People to scare?

As I wander into the dining room, I find Clara, as I have each morning, looking as forlorn as ever, chewing her way through a bread roll. She peeks up, blessing me with a look that could turn me to stone, and returns to her breakfast. I sigh, accepting of her silent treatment, and pull out a chair next to her, but the moment my backside meets the seat, she gets up and rounds the table, taking a chair on the other side, far away from me.

I help myself to coffee, watching her, thinking she is looking a little skinny, her rounded jaw sharper, and her eyes, no doubt, have lost a little of the fire that once burned in their depths. To think this girl was bursting with joy at the news we were moving to London from the countryside. "Clara, I—"

"Do not talk to me, Frank." She slams her bread roll down on the table.

"It was an impossible situation," I go on, trying to appeal to her reasonable side, if at all she has one, which I'm wondering more often these days if she does. Then again, I think, what woman has? The stable boy, for Christ's sake. "You are sixteen, Cla—"

"Nearly seventeen! It is not fair, Frank. God knows what nitwit I'll be paired with when the time comes."

"I'm sure Mama will make sure he's a very nice nitwit. A suitable nitwit."

"But a nitwit nevertheless. Did you know Mama is rumored to be favored by all to become a patron of that Almack place? She'll have me in there every week! I'll run away, Frank, I swear it."

I roll my eyes and get a sugar lump thrown at me for my trouble. I remember Eliza promising to do just the same when Papa was trying to marry her off to Frederick Lymington. Now, he most definitely was a nitwit, but, I admit, a rather endearing one who was at the mercy of his father's control. Poor chap. I do hope he's found happiness with his first love in Cornwall. He acted out of honor for his father. He can be forgiven that.

I drink my coffee and stand, rounding the table and taking Clara's shoulders, dipping and kissing her cheek. "You are loved, Clara. We only want what is best for you. A man who will look after you and provide for you." I squeeze her shoulders. "I will see to it that Mama allows me to take charge of the situation when the time comes, so you need not worry about being paired with any nitwits." Like our Eliza, Clara needs a man with a bit of oomph. A man who can handle her fire. What is it with all these women full of fire that I am surrounded by? Surely I am set to be burned. "I must go. I have business to deal with." *And a highwaywoman to coax out of hiding.*

As I leave Clara sulking into her coffee and head for the stables, I once again mull over the notion that the mysterious highwaywoman has read my story. It's the only explanation for her, as well as her partners, lying low. To be captured or even revealed would lead to her being hanged, and that would be most unfortunate. For her, of course. For me, I would have the greatest of stories and a deal with Fleming. I must be patient. That is all well and good, but sales are decreasing by the day and I'm feeling enormous pressure to maintain what my father and sister have built. Lord above, to lose the family fortunes? I break out in a sweat as I slip a boot into the stirrup and haul myself into the saddle.

I cannot say I am enjoying this side of being a businessman, I think, as I kick Figaro onward.

First job of the day is a meeting with Grant, who kindly informs me that only one of our outrageously expensive printing machines is in use again now, due to a further decrease in sales yesterday. *Oh joy.*

I reaffirm the need to keep this information from Papa for fear of distressing him. He has pretty much left me to run the business after a remarkable start, and I am running it into the ground.

"Someone must have *something* of interest to report," I say, dropping into a chair in Grant's office and scratching through the piles of papers. "Something other than the political and censored nonsense we must spew around the endless advertisements." My hands fall onto a piece of paper with a name I recognize. "What's this?" I ask, starting to read it as Grant comes over to see what I have found.

"Oh, yes, we received news of that just yesterday, Mr. Melrose, although much of it is unsubstantiated."

"Perhaps, but I know Mr. Brummell to be in debt, as I heard it with my own ears from a man to whom he owes quite a substantial amount." Interesting. "So rumor has it he's fled the country?" I muse, nodding. It's a shamefully underwhelming headline for tomorrow's edition, but Mr. Brummell, who also happens to be the Prince Regent's closest friend, could owe much more than that he owes the tailor on Jermyn Street, and probably does. It is a matter of national service to enlighten the public, I think. Yes, it is, and while it is quite underwhelming for a headline, it does mean, with the absence of Mr. Brummell, the top spot as London's finest dandy is available. I smile to myself. "Run it," I say, handing the paper to Grant. "It'll give me breathing space to get more material to continue my story."

"Sir, I think that may put us in the Prince Regent's black books, as I know Brummell to be a very good friend of his."

I scoff. "If the Prince liked him that much, Grant, he would have paid off his debts and saved him the potential humiliation of having to flee Lon..." I trail off, something coming to me, something quite inconceivable.

"Mr. Melrose?" Grant says. "Are you all right?"

"You know, Grant, I think I am." I look at him, my mind spinning. "The Prince Regent hasn't paid off Brummell's debts because he has been drawing the bustle too freely and he too is cleaned out." The Prince is a notorious party-goer, lavishing money on endless soirées and luxuries. It has been rumored for some time that he is spending more than he has. I grab a pen and start adding more words to the paper before handing it back to Grant. He reads it, and his eyes get progressively wider.

"Mr. Melrose, must I remind you the *The London Times* is the Prince's favored read?"

"You need not, Grant. It is common knowledge, as was his friendship with that snake of a business partner Lymington, who censored most political and religious reports in our newspaper to suit the agenda of the Prince, and I am sure he was compensated for that. But Lymington no longer has an interest in our newspaper, and I am not about to roll over and have my belly tickled by the Prince. What has he ever given us in return for supporting his leadership? It certainly isn't money, for he has none! No, we shall print what we like, and I should like to inform the public that their regent is in quite deep, for it is the taxpayer's money funding his lavish lifestyle, and we are taxpayers, Grant, as are our readers who have been hit with quite an eyewatering tax most recently on their choice of read." To think the Prince passed the newspaper tax bill—the nerve! And he expects us to continue dancing to his tune? Never. "Run it," I say again, getting up and leaving, feeling quite relieved to have found something to buy me some time.

NOT A PENNY TO RUB BETWEEN THEM

As I pass through the gilded gates of the royal park, I wonder to myself, on a smile, I admit, whether I will be permitted to ride here after tomorrow's headline is released. To speak ill of the Prince might also find me without an invitation to any of the parties he can't afford to throw. "Such a shame," I muse, ambling along at a leisurely pace, admiring the never-ending stretch of rich green grass and trees bursting with fat leaves. I see Mama in the distance chatting with Lady Blythe and Lady Tillsbury. "Good afternoon, ladies," I say as I reach them. "Whatever are you plotting now?"

Mama laughs, loud and high enough to makes one's ears bleed. "Oh, Francis. We were just discussing the Prince's party tomorrow eve."

Another lavish affair that the Prince cannot afford to hold. Marvelous. "Or what to wear, yes?" I cock a wry smile at them.

"Perhaps," Lady Blythe says coyly.

"Am I coming?" I ask.

"Of course, he invited you personally!" Mama's hand hits her chest, her eyes bright. He invited me personally, did he? I laugh under my breath. Call me suspicious, but could the Prince be trying to keep me sweet? "How handsome you look today," Mama goes on, looking out the corner of her eye to Lady Blythe and Lady Tillsbury, her lioness senses obviously tingling, telling her some hungry eyes are on her cub. "I cannot wait for you to find a young, fresh bride." With her tongue in her cheek, Mama coughs and snaps her two friends from their daydreams—her two not so young and perhaps not the freshest friends. "Let us continue, ladies," she says, motioning them on. "I have much to share about tomorrow's edition."

She does? That's odd, because I have not shared anything about tomorrow's edition. She's merely enticing them away, distancing the claws, and, perhaps, maybe, probably, removing temptation from me. She need not worry; I am a changed man. I frown and shift in my saddle. Yes, a reformed man, but even a reformed man needs a release. My breeches are becoming tighter by the day. I may have to take matters into my own hands. Literally.

"Good day to you, Melrose," Fleming calls, approaching on his horse, which, I must say, I feel incredibly sorry for. He looks like a sad old struggling donkey that's weighed down with too many saddlebags. "Do you have any news for me?"

"No news," I say, giving Figaro a subtle kick, moving him on faster. He's asked every day, but until numbers start moving back in the right direction, I will be avoiding in-depth talks with Fleming.

"The offer won't stand forever, Melrose. I'm leaving for Scotland next week, so pull your finger out."

I wince. "You'll get your name and twenty thousand copies," I assure him, and probably myself too, while throwing a little prayer up to the sky. When I drop my eyes again, I find myself in the path of a black stallion, and quite a handsome one at that, with an enviable muscled physique and a glossy mane. And upon his back, the cheeky, charming Sampson Winters, a man, I'm sure, who could give the most rakish of rakes a run for their money. I admire his green velvet jacket, a purchase from Mr. Jenkins, I'm sure, for I had my eye on that green material myself. "Good day to you, my lord," I say.

"And to you, Melrose." He pulls his horse to a slow stop. "I just saw your father."

"Gladstone's?" I ask, thinking I may join him.

"No, he was creeping through the back door of Lady Dare's."

I balk at Winters, astounded. What? Is there a man in the land that Scarlett Dare has *not* gotten her claws into? *Fuck.* I find myself in quite the muddle with not any words coming to me that I might use to defend my father. Christ, the last thing we need are those kinds of rumors spreading, even if they are not rumors. Of course, it is commonplace for a man to take a mistress, more common than not, but, actually, I prided myself on having parents that had that rare and precious thing called true love. In fact, deep down, it rather inspired me, and I know it did Eliza. I have, I concede, had many dalliances with many women, but every encounter has lacked wonder. There has been excitement, yes. Charging blood, yes. Anticipation, yes. But never, not once, has there been awe. I should like to experience that one day, for I can only imagine it would heighten all of the pleasures of attraction.

You've had it, Frank, and you scarcely touched her lips!

I push that thought away as Sampson regards me closely, and I continue to scratch around in my brain for the right words. I find not one, so, instead, I decide to talk to Sampson man-to-man. "My father is a good man, Winters."

"That I know."

"I can only imagine he's having a momentary lapse in sanity. I would ask you kindly to withhold this information, for I fear it would upset my mother greatly to learn of his indiscretions."

Sampson nods mildly, appearing to think very carefully. "You have my word."

"Thank you," I say, somewhat surprised.

"You, like me, Melrose, wish to protect the females in your life."

"Indeed, I do," I reply quietly, wondering if there is a backward threat woven in there somewhere. Undoubtedly. My mind is suddenly awash with memories. My nose bombarded by the scent of honeysuckle. My skin heats. Just thinking about her! My God, I'm in trouble. I blink, swallow, and look away, worried Sampson may see all of my sins in my eyes.

"Perhaps one day you might compensate me for my discretion," he goes on.

"What did you have in mind?" I ask, as Figaro starts treading on the spot, sensing, I expect, my growing anxiousness.

"Nothing yet, but perchance there may be something in the future that may require your prudence."

I nod, kicking my horse on. "Have a good day, my lord." I clip-clop on, greeting everyone I pass as they throw compliments my way, feeding my ego but also reminding me that I am all out of words where the infamous highwaywoman is concerned. And Papa? What am I to do with that?

"Oh no," I whisper, another problem finding me. Taya is up ahead, and when I feel my lungs shrink, for she certainly leaves me breathless, I know I should turn Figaro around and leave the royal park.

Except I do not.

Because I am an idiot.

I pull Figaro to a stop and narrow my eyes at myself, fighting back the memory of our brief kiss. She is sitting by a tree, a piece of paper on her lap, a graphite pencil in her hand. She's drawing again. What this time? Damn my curiosity! The neckline of her dress is low—too low if you ask me; I am surprised her brothers permitted her to leave the house—and her hair unconventionally loose, as always, the sun making the strands glisten brightly as the light breeze whips it around her face. She reaches up and catches a tendril, pushing it off her cheek. My God. My eyes drift down to her pink lips as she nibbles at a corner, contemplating what she has drawn. "If you wore a bonnet, or even secured your hair, you would not have the problem of hair whipping your face and getting in your way."

She stills for a moment, then glances up. "I like my hair whipping my face. It's wild. Free."

I like her wild, free hair whipping her face too. I throw my leg over and jump down from my horse, and I pay no mind to it, either. "You are alone?" I ask, looking around.

"You know me, Mr. Melrose," she says, getting to her feet.

"Do I?" I tilt my head, curious of the odd feeling in my stomach. Nerves? Yes, it must be. I'm nervous.

"If you're lucky."

I laugh under my breath at her blatant cheekiness as I tie my horse to the tree. *If I'm lucky.* I think our kiss means we know each other rather well already. "Why did you cry?" It is out before I can stop it, my desire to know overwhelming, making my mouth pour out words I perhaps shouldn't.

Her face falters, albeit briefly, before she quickly corrects it. "I did not—"

"I saw you, my lady. On the steps, your face in your hands." I inhale as she stares at me, and I make a point not to break the contact. I know I am on dangerous ground, and yet I am unable to control these urges where Taya Winters is concerned. All other women, yes, but Taya?

"I was crying because I felt deep regret for what happened, and I was quite worried of the repercussions."

I swallow and nod. "You need not be worried," I say, finally breaking the eye contact before it breaks *me.* "I give you my word, and my word is my honor, no one will ever know, because I too am full of regret." I am mentally darkening my own daylights over and over for being such an idiot. Regret? That kiss was like nothing I have experienced before, or ever likely will again. How could I regret it? "Good day to you, my lady." I untie Figaro and walk on.

"Wait," she calls, making me stop and turn. She's coming at me, not quite running, but definitely faster than a walk, and I lean back on my heels, wary. "I have something I must share."

"What is that?" *Kiss me again! Draw for me again! Talk to me, tell me you love my story!*

"Mr. Casper," she says. "He was ambushed just this morning on Hampstead Heath."

What? "He was robbed? By the highwaymen?"

"That is what I said, didn't I? He paid a visit to His Grace this morning."

"Why?"

"My brother has been consulting with Mr. Casper about many of my father's inventions that he never ensured were legally protected before...before..." She drops her eyes, flinching "...before he was murdered by that monster Lymington." She appears to shake herself out of her reverie.

"Are you all right?" If we were alone, I would be sure to take her in a hug, for she looks like she needs one.

Her smile is small, but I can tell she appreciates my condolences. "Papa was the most wonderfully chaotic man."

"I have heard he was a very good man too."

"Oh, he was." She laughs, and, I swear it, the oddest feeling flutters through my belly at the sight and sound. "He was quite the character." Then she sighs, and with the loss of her laughter comes an air of sadness that flattens the pleasant feeling within me and replaces it with something not so appealing. *What is happening?* "Anyway," she goes on, correcting herself, smiling mildly once again, but this one does not touch her eyes. "His Grace would like to ensure my father's inventions are protected to avoid any more crooks like Lymington coming along and stealing them. Mr. Casper was quite shaken when he arrived, and Johnny was forced to feed him some Scotch to calm his frayed nerves."

"Go on," I say, gesturing with my hands. "Tell me more."

"That's all I know." She shrugs. "I don't make a habit of eavesdropping."

I give her a tired look. "Oh, please."

"I don't," she says over another laugh that sends me somewhat dizzy. Jesus Lord above, that sound. The vision. I study her for a few moments, as she watches me also, her smile mild as she brushes some hair from her face. I must find Mr. Casper. But… I look down at her hand, where the paper rests in her grasp. "What are you drawing today, my lady?"

She looks down, her face alive and bright and light. "Well, Mr. Melrose, I read the newspaper each day eagerly along with the rest of the ton, hoping for more news on the highwaymen—"

"Woman."

"Woman," she corrects. "But the past while, the pages of *The London Times* have been absent of your marvelous words, so I have had no inspiration." She holds up her paper. "So I was forced to draw Lady Rose."

My eyes land on the picture, and laughter rises up from my toes and bursts out of me. "My God, she will have you hanged." I chuckle, bracing a hand on my knee to hold myself up.

"Shhhh," Taya giggles, and I stop laughing immediately, the sound sending me quite dizzy. She tucks the paper away in the low neckline of her dress, and my eyes rest on the smooth, peachy flesh.

"I must find Mr. Casper," I blurt out, untying Figaro and marching away, furiously fighting off these odd sensations overcoming me, controlling me.

"Are you blind, Frank?" Taya calls, making me look back over my shoulder. "He is a mere fifty yards away."

"He is?" I ask. "Where?" I scan the many people congregating in the park and spot him chatting with Lord Hamsley and Mr. Simpson. Oh no, I bet Casper is sharing his story right now! I must intercept and get the exclusive.

I tie Figaro back up to a tree, pull in my jacket, and hurry over. "Mr. Casper," I say. "May I have a brief word?"

"Of course, Melrose," he replies, smiling through a frown. "Is everything all right?"

"In private," I add when he makes no attempt to move away from Hamsley and Simpson.

"Oh?"

"Let us promenade." I smile and motion forward. "After you."

Casper leads and I follow, and we're soon walking side by side. "Oh Melrose," Lord Hamsley yells at my back. "Your father and I have been discussing the rather exciting prospect of your engagement to my daughter, Esther. She is quite a catch."

Jesus. I do not turn around. Papa is in no position to be discussing such a thing, especially now. "Is he still offering money to marry his daughter off?" I ask, and Casper laughs. "How humiliating." Esther Hamsley is no beauty, be sure of that, but she is also not a wench. She is, as I would put it, quite plain, I suppose. As for her personality, I could not comment, for she hardly breathes a word to anyone in public. Shy? Socially awkward? If only she would smile, I'm certain it would brighten her face. I shake my head. I am being distracted by trivial matters. I am not getting married, and definitely not to Esther Hamsley.

"Now, I am terribly sorry to pry, for I am sure you are quite disturbed and remain shaken, but, you see, I am so very curious."

"About what?"

"Well," I laugh, a little confused. Isn't it obvious? "About your encounter with the highwaymen."

Casper stops abruptly and glances around, suddenly most fidgety. "How do you know of that?" he asks, increasing my confusion.

"Well…" I fade off when I catch Taya beyond Mr. Casper making a sign that cannot be mistaken for anything other than *I will kill you if you tell on me!* "Um, well," I laugh, scratching around in my mind for an answer as I disintegrate under the threat of her stare. "I, ummm…" Taya starts making unfathomable symbols with her hands, and I am damned if I can decipher them. Is she wiggling something imaginary? Her hand is jiggling, moving from side to side over and over. She's pretending to write. "I am a journalist, Casper," I say, tilting my head as Taya visibly deflates and rolls her eyes, at my being slow, I expect. "It is my job to know of all things." I return my attention to him before I lose my focus and start admiring again how wonderfully wild she looks today. What's amiss here, with Casper? Is he embarrassed? I know not, but I suppose this might mean that he has not been sharing his encounter with anyone. Anyone except Johnny, of course. "I expect it was a terrifying ordeal."

He laughs but quickly corrects himself. "Yes, quite."

"I have encountered them myself."

"Yes, I read your report."

"Indeed."

"Indeed," he agrees, getting us walking again, both of us with our hands behind our back, casual, waiting for the other to speak. "So, if you have encountered them, then you must be privy."

"To what?" I ask.

"The thrill!" He practically bursts before my eyes. "My God, Melrose, one flutter of her eyelashes and I was ready to hand my coin purse over. I was mesmerized. Mesmerized, I tell you! I couldn't see her smile, but I could tell it was there, right in her eyes. She was enjoying herself."

"And the other two?" I ask. "They were there?"

"Yes, one guarded each way."

"On black horses?"

"Yes, and she on a white one." He comes closer. "You must not tell a soul."

I laugh. "Mr. Casper, I am a journalist."

He stops, looking at me in horror. "I must insist you refrain, Melrose. I am a respected businessman. I would be a laughing-stock if anyone were to find out I offered my money on a plate. And my wife! She cannot know I dreamt of those eyes last night, or that I have had the most outrageous thoughts to ride out to the common once again if only to feel so spellbound."

"Dreams?" My God, that horseman is a witch! And, clearly, I am not alone in my pathetic behavior. She's dazzling us all!

His head goes into his hands. "Please, you will ruin me."

I breathe out heavily. "I have no desire to ruin you, Casper." He is a decent fellow, after all, and he does a fine job for me and the business in all matters of a legal nature. "I propose this," I say, moving in a little closer. "I will run my story, but I will omit the name of the victim."

"You will?"

"Yes, for you, Casper, I will." Surely it'll only add more intrigue, everyone wondering who has fallen victim to the highwaywoman now. "Now, can you tell me any more? Height? Features? Did she speak, laugh, did you see her hand when she took your coin purse?"

He looks momentarily stunned by my barrage of questions. "No," he says simply, looking past me. "She was covered, and she wore gloves. Oh, there is Mrs. Casper. I must go." He dashes off and joins his wife, and I hum, thoughtful, my next headline writing itself.

"Well?" Taya asks, joining me. "Is it worthy of the pages of your fine newspaper?"

I turn a nonchalant expression onto her. "Meh."

Now, it is Taya's turn to roll her eyes, and it is adorable. "Do not act as if this is not valuable news to you, Frank Melrose."

"Fine," I relent.

She looks all too pleased with herself. "And how might you repay me for this lead?"

"Excuse me?" I ask, recoiling, my mind instantly ambushed with a million ways in which I could repay her, and none of it involving gold. God help me, I must remember I am a dead man if I so much as smile at Taya Winters. And I have already done a lot more than smile at her. *Don't ask. Don't ask.* Oh, hell, living is overrated. "What do you want?" I whisper, inhaling as I do, watching as her lips part and she swallows.

She doesn't answer.

It's probably a good thing for both of us.

"I should be going before we are seen alone together." She nods, smiles...

And I fall a little harder.

"Goodbye, my lady," I say quietly, watching her pivot and float away.

Chapter 15

I changed my mind and decided, after not very much consideration, to shelve the story on the Prince's financial ruin and instead run with the story of Casper's ambush.

SHE WILL STEAL YOUR MONEY... AND YOUR HEART

I am reclined, comfortable, and smiling in Papa's chair, reading my article while sipping coffee, and what an article it is, even if I do say so myself.

But my reading is disturbed when the door of Papa's study opens and Mama appears, looking glorious in a red dress that will surely be the talk of the square the moment she steps out for her daily promenade in the royal park, which, I know, is her plan. "Mama, you look beautiful." I smile and stand, approaching and giving her a peck on the cheek. How Papa could desire to seek attention elsewhere when he has the vibrant and dazzling Florence Melrose at home, I do not know, but I am becoming worried about the situation. How might I approach this?

"Thank you. I have a busy day." Oh good, perhaps she won't notice Papa's absence. "I am to walk with Eliza and Clara, then I will meet Lady Blythe and Lady Tillsbury at the new teashop up in Berkeley Square, and then I must collect my new dress and hat."

"Emma cannot collect your dress and hat?"

Mother's shoulders drop. "I'm afraid I must report to you

that Emma has left our employment and returned to the countryside."

I wince on the inside. But of course, Emma, Mama's maid, is the stable boy's mother. "That's a shame."

"Yes, something about her son being relieved of his duties with Mr. Fitzgerald."

"Then we must get you a new pair of hands," I declare, going back to the desk and dipping the quill. "I shall write an advertisement for tomorrow's edition this minute."

"Very well. Where is your father, anyway? I haven't seen him much these past few days."

"Probably with Grant," I say quickly. "We have two machines now, Mama, and the printworks is busier than ever."

"Well, that is good news." Picking up the bottom of her dress, she breezes out. "Clara," she calls. "Come now, we must go."

I slump back down in my chair, exhaling heavily. Enough is enough. I must find Papa and talk some sense into him before Mama discovers his betrayal.

Eighteen thousand! It is a record, possibly a world record. I make a trip across town to find Papa with no success, so decide to visit Fleming at Kentstone's to update him on the progress of sales, but as I am trotting down St. James's Street, I see our family carriage up ahead, another following it.

I pull the reins of my horse and lift a hand for the jarvey to stop. "Papa?" I say, dipping to see inside the carriage.

"Ah, Frank." He smiles, but it is nervous. "You will not believe the news I have!" He slips out of the carriage and rubs his belly. "First, I must have a drink, for I surely need one." He's off across the cobbles, marching on, his target Gladstone's, and, I must agree, he really does look like he needs a drink.

"Papa, wait," I call, sliding down from Figaro and securing him to the nearest gas lantern. "Hey," I call to a boy across the street with armfuls of loaves. "Watch my horse." I throw him a shilling, and the loaves tumble from his arms to catch it. "There's another for you when I get back." I hurry after Papa and enter Gladstone's, seeing Casper, Fallow, and Millingdale all seated around a table laughing while sinking Scotch, and in the corner, the Prince Regent placing bets he cannot afford.

I find Papa in another corner, a drink being poured for him, and he looks alarmingly ashen. "What is it, Papa? Should I call for a doctor?"

"I have had quite a shock, Frank," he says, taking his glass and drinking his Scotch back in one fell swoop. "Quite the shock, I tell you." He looks at me, and I withdraw, worried. He taps his glass, and it is full once again, but I suspect it won't be for long. "I encountered the highwaymen." He throws back his second Scotch.

"What?" I whisper. "Are you hurt? Did they rob you?" Where did this happen? And when? Was it in London? Outside? On the common or Hampstead Heath? A million questions run amok in my mind as I stare at Papa, who once again taps his glass for a refill.

"I am all right," he says, smiling his reassurance. "Just a little shaken." He laughs. "It was quite unfortunate, really."

"I'd say so too, Papa." Is he drunk?

"No, no, you misunderstand."

I do? Because he's looking all too happy about being robbed. I'm confused. "What happened?"

"I was on my way home, Frank, when I saw a carriage in the distance. I recognized it. It was Lady Rose. The wheel of her carriage came right off after hitting a rock, and she was stranded, so, of course, despite our family being at odds with the old hag, I stopped to offer my assistance, for she is still a lady, after all." Another drink, and this time I join him, nodding to the server to pour and taking the glass, anticipation killing me.

"Where was this?"

"Just on the other side of town in a small clearing just before the inn on Hunter's Lane. Anyway, I st—"

"What were you doing on the other side of town?"

"That is a story for another day." He waves off my question with ease, and, naturally, given he's been spied entering Scarlett Dare's abode, I'm suspicious. "So, as I was saying, I stopped and assessed the wheel, and concluded very quickly that there was little I could do, so I helped Lady Rose into my carriage, and we got on our way. We had gone just a few meters when I felt the vibrations on the ground, and when I poked my head out of the window to investigate the noise, I saw them, two black stallions and a white one!"

My blood starts to pound with excitement, and I know it is wholly inappropriate given we are discussing the mugging of my poor, terrified father. "And …?"

"And they were coming right at us."

"And …?"

"And, Lord, Frank, I was truly terrified, but, of course, Lady Rose was more terrified, screaming like an angry fox being chased by the hounds, begging me not to let them take her money, for she had a lot on her person."

"And …?"

"And, well, I could hardly stop them, could I? But I didn't need to, because, you see, one of the riders on the black stallion pulled down his scarf, smiled, winked, and Lady Rose handed it right on over on a breathless whisper of gratitude."

"What?"

"Yes," he laughs, falling back in his chair, appearing to have lost his shock and found hysteria. "She was in a trance, I tell you, Frank."

This sounds so familiar, for I know what it feels like to be in a trance, as does Casper. "And he didn't take *your* purse?"

"No," he says over a chuckle. "He obviously assumed I was

Lady Rose's manservant and thought I did not have one, so I got off scot-free!"

"My God," I whisper, my mind racing.

"Yes!" Papa laughs. "They are dazzling their victims into handing over their money."

"Or putting them under a spell," I muse, taking more drink. "The female hasn't shown her face." I turn to Papa. "But you said the man, or one of them, he removed his scarf?"

"Yes, right there in front of us with not a care in the world."

"Very bold," I say, thoughtful. "And what did he look like?"

"I couldn't tell you. His face was a mess of hair. It was dark. His eyes pale."

"Pale?"

"Yes. Pale gray eyes. Almost silver. And they twinkled madly."

I stand. "I must visit with Lady Rose and get her account, too."

"I doubt very much she will admit to being hypnotized into giving up some of her fortune."

"Probably not, but I have a very reliable source who can confirm my claims." I smile widely, and Papa shakes his head in what I expect is exasperation, but also a little pride.

"You will most certainly gain an enemy if you run this story, Frank."

"Oh, please, Papa. That old witch has been mean to each one of us. It's nothing more than she deserves."

"Granted. I expect she would have dropped her pantaloons too, should he have demanded it."

I laugh and visibly shudder, as does Papa. "Must dash—I have a story to write for tomorrow's edition and a countess to question."

"Yes, yes, you go." He shoos me away. "I must say, I look forward to reading my own newspaper each day since my children are quite the talented journalists. It is a waste not to have these stories reach further afield."

"I'm working on it, Papa, I assure you."

"Oh?"

"That is a story for another day." I tilt my head, and Papa smiles, seeming to miss my hint.

"I can't wait to see what else you have up your sleeve."

I cringe at the room, my eyes falling to the corner where the Prince is laughing like a frenzied fool, drinking gin like it is a race and throwing coins on the table that are quickly claimed by others. He's losing his bets, getting further into debt. Every coin that hits that table is the taxpayers' money. I might gain quite a few enemies. "It'll be sure to cause a frantic scramble to get a copy."

"That's my boy," Papa says, and I smile, but it's hesitant. "Happy writing."

Chapter 16

LOCK UP YOUR PURSES…AND YOUR WIVES

"I did no such thing!" the countess shrieks the next evening, glaring at me in horror, her face under the glow of candlelight really rather frightening. "I was robbed! Threatened with a… a…a…a…"

"A…?"

"A pistol!"

"Oh?" I say, brushing my chin with the side of my index finger. "Because my source said you were threatened with a dashing smile and nothing more."

Nostrils flaring, the countess waggles an intimidating finger at me. "We both know the source you speak of is your father, Frank Melrose, and he is lying!"

The poor old dear, she is terrified of being a laughingstock, of the ton knowing she lost a large amount of money because she gave it away to a handsome crook. "He's an eyewitness, my lady, and a reliable one at that." I stand. "Anything further to add?" I cannot express my enjoyment in this moment. Perhaps Lady Rose might think twice about looking down her nose at my family in future. As it turns out, money doesn't always make you the most powerful, or, at least, before half of it was stolen, but owning a newspaper does.

"I will have the Prince hang you!"

"I cannot be hanged for telling the truth, my lady." Which is my only saving grace, since the Prince will very likely want to string me up too once the story of his debts breaks. "Good evening." I smile and leave, pulling in my jacket and breathing in the night-time air. It has been a most productive day and it is about to get even more productive. My hand is itching to write. How amusing, I think, as I am taking the steps up to my house, that a night of writing fills me with excitement, where spending a night with a female once did.

I reach for the doorknob, and Mama bursts out in an emerald-green gown and nearly knocks me back down the steps.

"Frank!" she shrieks, making my ears bleed. "There you are! And where is your father, for the love of God? We will be late."

"Late for what?" I ask, searching my mind.

She balks at me, like I am stupid. "The Prince's party."

I groan under my breath. How could I have forgotten? "Oh, yes, of course. Well, I suppose I ought to make an effort, since I expect I will be banished come the morrow." Mama's face is a mass of confusion as I pass her. "I shall ready myself now."

"And your father?" she asks my back as I take the stairs, my face screwing up, pained.

"I expect he—"

"I am here, Flo, worry not." Papa's voice lifts the weight from my shoulders.

"Ah, Burt! There you are."

I turn and see Mama fussing over his gray jacket, and I smile at the sight of my parents together, Papa regarding his wife fondly as she pokes and prods at him. Tonight, I shall speak with Papa and talk some sense into him, I swear it, if it is the last thing I do.

"You are changing, yes?" Mama says, as Papa takes her fussing hands and returns them to her dress.

"Yes, dear, I am changing. What would you have me wear?"

"I thought your brown velvet jacket would complement my dress perfectly."

He looks down at her green frock. "Yes, and if I put you on my shoulders, we shall look like a tree."

"Oh, do stop."

He comes up the stairs, giving me a tired expression that I know he won't dare share with Mama. "And how was your meeting, son?"

"As we both expected."

"Meeting?" Mama says. "What meeting, and with whom?"

"Frank's meeting with Lady Rose about her being half rescued by Papa but then ambushed by the highwaymen," Clara says all too casually from the entrance to the drawing room while she fastens the tie on her bonnet. Her face looks like a slapped backside.

"How do you know about that?" I ask.

"Ah!" Mama sings. "Another journalist in the making. Aren't we lucky, Burt, to have such studious children?"

"Quite blessed," Papa laughs, while I keep my questioning eyes on the youngest of my sisters.

"And what were you doing rescuing that old wench?" Mama asks. "You should have left her for the wild boars to snack on."

"You are truly awful sometimes, Florence Melrose."

"Shhhh," she whispers, giggling before flouncing into the drawing room. "Some wine, please, Dalton," she says. "Now will everyone please get ready, or we will be late, and a respected lady of the ton, that is I, by the way, cannot be late for such an event."

"Yes, Mama," I sigh.

"Yes, dear," Papa breathes, smiling at me fondly for a few moments.

"What?" I ask. "What is it?"

"I am proud of you, son." He reaches for my face and gives it a light, loving tap. "I just wanted you to know that."

I smile, but it's hesitant. "This is all rather out of the blue, Papa. Is something the matter?"

"No, nothing is the matter. You have stepped up and proven I can depend on you. I see great things for us ahead, my boy. Great things." And with that, he turns and climbs the rest of the stairs.

"Great things," I say, following. "I agree, Papa."

Admittedly, the Prince's parties are always events one does look forward to. The glamour, the drink, the food, and the music, but in the name of public favor, I shall happily forgo my place amid the masses of riches. Besides, I cannot abide how flaming long it takes merely to get inside, the line of carriages stretching from the palace back to Belmore Square, I'm sure of it, and crawling along at an inconceivably slow pace. "It shall be time to leave the moment we arrive," I grumble. "I could walk faster, I swear."

"One cannot be seen arriving on foot, Frank," Mama says, tutting.

One absolutely could be seen arriving on foot, and one wouldn't care, but one should not like to embarrass my mother. "Ah, finally," I say as a footman opens the door. I leave the carriage first, followed by Papa, who helps Mama down. I hold my hand out to Clara, who raises her nose and, most revoltingly, but not unexpectedly, ignores me, huffing and barging past me.

"I see she's still as delightful as ever," Eliza says, joining me in watching our sister stomp away. I dip so she can reach my cheek when she leans up to kiss me. "How are you, my favorite brother?"

I cock my arm for her to link and walk us toward the grand hall. "I am your only brother," I point out.

"Not true. I have Sampson now, too."

Why does that annoy me? "How are you feeling?"

"Exhausted, if you must know." Her violet eyes, now she mentions it, do look a little glazed. "I do not expect I could lift a quill to write even if I wanted to." She smiles. That looks tired too. Is this normal, I wonder? "I do, however, have the energy to read, and I am being kept most entertained by your words, Frank." I return her weak smile, touched, but more worried.

I stop us walking and turn to her, thinking perhaps she would be grateful of my physical support because she looks fit to crumple to the ground. "Eliza, you look terrible."

"Why thank you. I love you, too." Her hand circles her tummy. "I cannot deny it, I feel plain awful."

"Why are you here?" I ask, irked.

"Because she is a stubborn thing who does not listen to her husband." The Duke appears, looking grim and impatient. "I am taking you home." He claims her from me, and I do not argue.

"I am all right," she insists, shrugging him off. "You big oaf."

"I have told you many times, Eliza, where you are concerned, I do not mind being an oaf." And with that, he scoops her up and carries her toward the Winters family's carriage, where Lady Wisteria is stepping down. She shakes her head in delighted despair and joins me.

"Good evening, my lady," I say, bowing my head.

"It's the first trimester, you see," Lady Wisteria Winters says, waving for Mama to come join us when she sees her looking on, concerned. "She cannot keep any food in her belly."

"She vomited in the bushes in the royal park this morn," Mama says, and Clara starts laughing, earning a dark glare from Mama, who links arms with Lady Wisteria Winters and walks onward.

"Stop being such a brat," I warn Clara.

"Bugger off." She pivots and stomps off, and I am left alone for all of a second before I sense another presence.

"Good eve to you, Mr. Melrose," Taya says quietly.

I look to the heavens for strength before I face her. "Good eve, my la—" The words get all caught up in my mouth when the impact of her hits me, for she looks like nothing I have seen before, in a soft pink tiered gown and gloves to match that just cover her elbows. Her dark blonde hair is unconventionally piled high upon her head, and her neck, my God, her long, smooth neck, is draped in the most ornate, beautiful diamond piece. I clear my throat. "Good eve, my lady."

"Is it?" she asks, brushing herself down, looking as uncomfortable as I am beginning to feel with the space in my breeches shrinking by the second.

"You look…" I blink, clearing my throat, stuck for words.

"Cat got your tongue?"

"More a lion, I think," I admit. "I hate to tell you, Taya Winters, but you look absolutely sublime this evening."

Her lips press into a straight line, and it is obvious that she is restraining a smile. "You look awful," she says.

"Of course I do." I pull in my jacket and gesture the way. "After you, my lady."

She nods and starts an unhurried walk, and I link my hands behind my back, perhaps to restrain them from grabbing and ravishing her, falling into a slow stride beside her, not too far away from her mother ahead to cause concern, but far enough so that we may not be heard. I am very glad no one was there to witness that moment of awe, because I am certain there was nothing I could have done to hide it.

"I loved your piece today," she says, keeping her eyes forward.

"Did it inspire you?" I ask lightly, smiling down at her.

She laughs delicately, and I inhale and look away, reining myself in. I cannot enjoy this woman's company. I must not. It's an odd feeling, odd but pleasurable, to want to have conversation with a lady. "Oh yes, it did."

"I'm glad." I want to see whatever it is I have inspired her to draw.

"Would you like to see it?"

"Yes," I breathe out the word, and she eagerly pulls out a piece of paper, handing it to me. I smile down at the picture of an oversized horse and a small man with hearts in his eyes staring at it. I chuckle. "It actually looks very much like Mr. Casper. Though, I must say, your depiction rather implies he is enthralled by the horse."

"Should it imply otherwise?"

"Well, yes." I frown at myself. "He's obviously enthralled by the rider."

Her face falls. "Oh." She takes back the paper and stares down at it for a time. "And what about you?" she asks. "Are you enthralled by the rider?"

Oh hell. "No," I laugh, awkward, and step back, not at all liking her wide, hopeful, doe eyes. "I'm merely fascinated." I motion for us to keep walking before we find ourselves alone and attract attention. "Why would you ask such a thing?" *You're on dangerous ground, Frank.*

"Curiosity, I suppose. You write about her with such passion."

"Are you jealous?" *Shut up, Frank!*

Taya's chin lifts high in a move to demonstrate sureness, but her teeth sinking down onto her bottom lip and her eyes dropping betray her. She is. She's jealous. *Oh dear.* "Don't be ridiculous." She peeks up at me, her lips almost blue from the force of them pressing together, but not in impatience, no. It is undoubtedly to stop her from confessing that she really is jealous. *Very dangerous ground, Frank.* Her lips twitch, and the memory of me tasting them comes flooding back, and when she peeks up at me and her green eyes fall down to my mouth, I know, I just know, she is recalling that moment of exquisite pleasure too.

I find my pace slowing until I come to a gradual stop, my eyes unable to move from her face, taking in every perfect inch of it. The distant sound of the orchestra seems to fade in this moment as we regard each other, until all that remains are the thuds of our heartbeats and our heavy breathing. That kiss. The forbidden, beautiful kiss. Oh, to have that again. I ache for it. Positively ache for it.

I blink and jerk, and the noise and bustle of chatter and laughter pour back into the room with us, and when my tunnel vision clears, I find Taya is gazing at me, looking as concerned as I am feeling, for it was all too easy to forget myself when placed under her spell. "I should like to proposition you," she says, and I give her a stunned look.

"Pardon me?" I say, getting us moving again, circling the room behind our mothers, now a little further away than is probably acceptable, so I increase my pace and rely on Taya to follow my lead.

"You really are full of yourself, Frank Melrose. I speak of business."

"What of it?"

"I should like the opportunity to work with *The London Times*."

No way. "I must respectfully decline."

"Respectfully?"

"Indeed."

"You would not hire me?"

It would be hell. I cannot promise I would be able to keep my hands to myself. I would be utterly stupid to invite temptation, but, naturally, I cannot divulge that. "We are not hiring."

"Well, that is fine, because I am not asking for a job."

"Then what in God's name are you asking for?" I am not sure I should have asked that question.

"I should like to work on a freelance basis."

"Pardon me?"

"Drawing for your best stories."

"What?"

"Imagine," she whispers. "If your readers also had drawings to build the picture along with your words."

I stare at her, my mouth agape. My God, that is a genius idea. Genius! I hardly want to admit it, for I fear to accept her offer may be my downfall.

"Well?" she asks, excited.

I nod, mute, my eyes once again being drawn to those lovely plump rosy lips.

"I must say, I am parched," she says quietly.

Me too.

"Frank?"

"I will fetch you a drink!" I blurt urgently, jerking out of my trance.

"Very kind of you, Mr. Melrose. I would avoid the far corner as there are a few flies buzzing around over there, and I suspect they'll be in your ear should you get too close."

I frown and look to the far corner, seeing Scarlett Dare and, not too far away, Lizzy Fallow. "Have you been eavesdropping again?" I ask.

"Not at all."

I highly doubt that. "It is your bro—" I stop abruptly before I drop Sampson in it and reveal to Taya that she is worrying about the wrong man. "I'll get that drink." I hurry off and get my mouth under control, as well as my thoughts, seeing the Prince lording it up by the champagne table, laughing like he has not a care in the world. I don't suppose he has when all his guests are funding his lifestyle. And to think they're all here thanking him for his hospitality, being grateful for the invite? I snort and take two glasses of champagne, looking around for Clara, who I find within safe proximity to Mama, although looking pretty deadly.

"And who might that be for?" Sampson asks, appearing as if from nowhere.

"You." I thrust the champagne into his hand and smile my sincerest smile. "There's a fly over there who should like to see you."

He looks over his shoulder to the corner, where Lady Dare is floating, sipping, and smiling this way. "Or perhaps she should like to buzz around your father."

I stare at him in disbelief. Why would he say such things,

especially in public, especially in the palace? "I trust you are being discreet in that regard."

"Of course." He bows, smiling. "I trust you are keeping a safe distance from my sister."

"I am," I answer confidently, hoping, praying, Sampson did not see me with Taya.

"So my eyes were playing tricks on me, were they?"

Shit. "I assure you, my lord, I have no interest in your sister."

"I hope you are a man of your word, Melrose, for I would hate for anyone to find out your father has been paying visits to a certain house in Belmore Square."

"You're blackmailing me?"

"It's only blackmail if you're guilty."

"Then it is a very good job I am not, wouldn't you agree?" *The nerve!*

Sampson hums and backs away, and I notice the endless women giving him eyes. I hate to admit it, but I am jealous, but only because he is not being exhausted by the challenge of keeping his control. Good grief, if ever I needed another reason to keep my hands off the enchanting Taya Winters, I just got it.

"Where's my drink?" Taya asks, prompting me to swiftly step away from her and check for Sampson's whereabouts. He is gone. Thank heavens. I look down at my empty hand. "To fetch you a drink might lead to gossip about my intentions."

She looks at me, confused. "What?"

"Good evening." I quickly divert my eyes from hers and hurry away, my exhaustion taking on another level, and because I am an idiot of the highest quality, but a desperate one at that, desperate for some respite from this madness, I approach Mr. Hamsley and ask for his permission to dance with Season Five Esther. Anything to convince Sampson that there is no need for blackmail. Of course, Lord Hamsley is most grateful, and Esther, bless her, is most stunned. "You look very lovely," I say, following the lead of everyone else on the floor dancing the minuet.

"Um, thank you, I suppose," she says, looking like a startled fox who has come face to face with a hound. "I know not how to dance, Mr. Melrose."

"I am not a professional myself, so we should be fine. I grant you permission to stamp on my toes should I be so clumsy to step on yours."

She chuckles, and it is a sweet sound, but the last thing I want is for Esther to think there is anything more to this dance than a dance. "Tell me, Esther, are you fussy?"

"Excuse me?"

"Season Five."

Her cheeks take on a rather vivid shade of crimson. "You need not remind me. I am very aware that I am here enduring yet another year of indulgent, narrow-minded humans."

I balk, taken aback by her frankness. "Why would you not get married and be done with it, then there would be no need for you to endure such atrocities."

"I am without the inclination, or looks too it would seem, to dazzle a potential husband."

For the first time, I look at Esther closely, and for the first time I see her smile. She is not an unsightly lady, not by any means. Perhaps, as I previously thought, a little plain, but she is quite attractive, and she seems to be holding a conversation with me rather well. "You are very pretty, Esther, be sure of that fact." Her blush increases, and I turn us so we begin working our way down the middle of the grand hall again. "I believe our fathers have been plotting," I go on.

"Yes, they have."

"And how do you feel about that?"

"Awful."

"Are you saying you're not attracted to me?"

"Correct."

I smirk. "Are you blind?"

She laughs lightly, and the sound is sweet. "I can see perfectly well, Mr. Melrose, which is why I know your interests are directed elsewhere."

Oh? "With whom?"

"Taya Winters."

I jolt, shocked, my eyes widening, and I scramble through my mind for the right words to convince Esther she is incorrect. "Then perhaps it is a good job I am dancing with you so I may squash that rumor."

"Is it a rumor, though, Mr. Melrose?"

I eye Esther, my lips pursed, and she smiles, small and knowing. "You have too much time on your hands if you are to make assumptions like that based on...what?" I think it best not to give her an opportunity to answer that, so I quickly go on. "So let us inspire the men to come calling, shall we, and then you may dazzle them with smart conversation like you have dazzled me?" I smile brightly, as does Esther. "Now laugh."

"What?"

"I said, laugh. Laugh like you are having the most wonderful time with me, and I assure you, eligible bachelors are sure to be most interested."

"They will?"

"They will, Esther, if you would only smile and reveal what you have shown me. Smart *and* pretty? Oh, what a triumph!"

Her lips twitch, and I silently will her to break the stoic Esther Hamsley that everyone has come to know and judge.

"Go on," I whisper. "And be careful not to crack your face."

And with that, she bursts into fits of laughter, and the sweet sound fills the room, lighting up the space along with her face, and I am most gratified by the sight and sound, as well as the attention it has captured from every corner of the ballroom. I nod to myself, satisfied with a good day's work, and when I am tapped on the shoulder, I grin down at Esther, whose eyes have widened further. "I believe we have our first candidate for the affections of Esther Hamsley," I say, breaking away and facing whoever it may be trying to move in on my dancing partner.

"Can I help you?" I ask the young man, who I guess is not far off my age, perhaps a smidgeon older, with jet black hair and the darkest of eyes. Quite a handsome fellow, I must say.

"If I may," he motions to Esther, whose cheeks, and it's quite adorable, are getting pinker by the second.

I appear to consider his request for a few moments, torn, as though I am perturbed to be having my dance cut short. "I believe that is the lady's decision." I turn to Esther and tilt my head, looking most anxious for her answer.

She clears her throat, blinks a few times, straightens her shoulders, and looks at the young man. "Ummm…yes… I would be delighted." She flashes her newfound smile once again. "I suppose."

"Oh, fiddlesticks," I mutter, holding out my hand to my challenger. "You won fair and square, my friend. Enjoy, she is quite a vision and most enchanting."

He nods. I move away, happy with myself, ready to find some more champagne and have a quiet, stern word with myself, for not only has Esther Hamsley observed me behaving oddly around Taya Winters, but so has Clara, and both of her brothers have warned me away, so I am obviously failing in my endeavors to act in a non-peculiar way.

I help myself to champagne and sip as I watch many couples circle the floor, the sight a dizzying swish of colors and smiles. "You are such a social climber," Clara remarks, breaking away from Mama, who is engrossed in conversation with Lady Blythe and Lady Tillsbury, and joining me on the edge of the dancing area. "I mean, Esther Hamsley?" She helps herself to some champagne and I swiftly remove it.

"She is rather sweet, if you must know."

"I hardly recognize you these days."

"I hardly recognize myself," I muse, feeling eyes on me, but refraining from looking to confirm whose they are, for she will certainly place me under her spell again and I must keep my wits about me. I must.

Damn it.

To know she is there and not steal the opportunity to admire her? Impossible.

My eyes drift to my left, and, God save my soul, I'm flung into an abyss of pleasurable reminiscences: our skin when it has touched, our lips when they met, our tongues when they have swirled.

"Frank!"

I jump out of my skin and find Clara glaring at me. "I will never forgive you," she says with a strong voice. "Ever, do you hear me?"

"I think I need a drink."

Clara's nose wrinkles as she scowls. "You have one."

"I do?" I look down at my hand. "Oh, I do." I think I must need some sense to go with my drink. "Stay with Mama," I order, leaving Clara to go in search of that sense, thinking, if I am lucky, I might find it outside with a shot of fresh air. I finish my champagne and collect two more, walking with pace and focus toward the exit. I pass Lizzy Fallow, whose eyes follow my path from where she stands at the side of her decrepit husband, and then Lady Dare, who is having a conversation with Mr. Fitzgerald but watching me leave.

I make it outside and take a moment to inhale the cool, fresh air, taking some much-needed deep breaths, feeling as if I have broken free of the danger zone and can breathe easy again. I drink one of my glasses and throw it in a nearby bush, then wander down the middle of the lawn, where trees line the sides, every blade of grass is equal in length, and the moonlight bounces off the statue at the very end. The sound of the party is now distant, and I am, for the first time this evening, relaxed, now I have left temptation behind.

I walk to the very end of the lawn, which I am certain must be a whole mile, until I am at the top of a wide set of stone steps that lead down to a maze, the walls high, with climbing plants blanketing them, making it not only private and secluded, but pretty too.

"What a night," I say on an exhale, dropping to my backside on the top step, grateful for the peace and quiet; it is a needed opportunity to get myself back on the right track, for the wrong track will certainly lead me to terrible places.

Like a grave.

Or our family being banished.

I laugh to myself, rubbing at my face with my spare hand and taking more champagne, my relief to be free of the suffocating palace lost when I consider the rest of my life, because I am quite certain Taya Winters is not going anywhere soon. So I must endure this torture for eternity. I begin to sweat. Or, at the very least, until her brothers marry her off to some high-ranking gentleman and she might leave London for a country estate. "Over my dead body," I say without thought, jerking. "Oh hell." I rest my forehead in my palm, feeling all too queasy, not just at the thought of Taya in the arms of another man. Will he appreciate her fire? Her drawings? Her blinding beauty?

Naturally, I pray he does, for to think she might be unhappy and unfulfilled is most perturbing. As is the thought of another man having her. And yet, there are a million reasons why I may not have her, and again I circle to my earlier thoughts. Is this infatuation simply because she is strictly forbidden? I should give myself some credit. No, it is not that. It is because she smiles and makes me tingle. It is because she talks and my ears beg for more of her words. It is because she touches me and my body comes alive.

I am in trouble.

Perhaps it is I who should leave London. *Come on, Frank, you are stronger than this temptation.* I toast that thought and sip more of my drink, but my glass freezes at my lips when the hairs on the back of my neck stand on end, my skin prickling all over, my stupid damn heart throbbing. And there is my problem. The effect she has on me is uncontrollable. Overwhelming.

Wonderful.

How is it that I can sense her so acutely?

"Taya," I say, not looking over my shoulder, for it will increase the risk of me succumbing to her allure. "I must insist you return to the palace."

"Insist all you like, Frank Melrose."

I see the skirt of her gown in my peripheral vision as I lower my glass, gulping, silently begging her to leave, go, and remove the temptation from my reach. "Why do you insist on torturing me so?"

"I am here in a professional capacity, I assure you." She lowers herself beside me and pats down the puffs of her skirt, looking at me out of the corner of her eye. "You torture only yourself."

I release a light huff of laughter. "You should not be here at all, whether in a professional capacity or not." I look over my shoulder, to the palace that seems so very far away. "If either of your brothers were to discover us alone, your prospects will be ruined forever." And my mama will be heartbroken when the tale of my father's escapades break.

"Let them be ruined."

I look at her as though she is mad. "What is it with young women these days caring not for their futures or wellbeing?"

"Perhaps the world is changing, and it might soon be tolerable for ladies to behave like heedless rakes too."

I cough, shocked. "You really are mad."

"Better than suffocated, though, yes?"

"Are you suffocated?"

"No, I am not. Fortunately, I come from a family who care not for social expectation, only for happiness, so your being concerned about ruining me is a tremendous waste of your time and energy."

I am laughing again, but this time it's a good belly laugh. "Oh, Taya, why do you say words we both know not to be true. Are you forgetting that I have been warned off by both of your ape brothers?"

"Oh, not at all. But what you neglect to understand, Frank, is that they have not warned you away because they fear my prospects being ruined."

What? "Then why, my lady, have your brothers threatened me should I so much as sniff you?"

"Well, simply because they think I can do better, of course."

I nearly choke on my tongue. "Excuse me?"

"They thi—"

"Yes, I heard you just fine, thank you, I just cannot believe you have been so frank."

"Frankness, Frank, is important in life, don't you think?"

Be that as it may…they don't think I am good enough? Why does that sting? Granted, I have had my fair share of dalliances, with many women, but I have abstained from female company for quite some weeks. It is a record; I'll have them know. I am omitting the kiss Taya and I shared, naturally. "They don't think I am good enough?" I mutter. "That is rather rich, coming from both of them." Alas, the Winters brothers may be many undesirable things, but they have titles, and a title is, more often than not, a pass to immunity.

"You'll get over it," Taya says, nudging my shoulder playfully, making my champagne splash up the glass. "Besides, you looked to be having a rather lovely time with Esther Hamsley."

I look at her tiredly. "Jealous?"

"Yes, if you must know." She takes her hands and places them behind her, leaning back, looking up at the sky on a smile I am

JODI ELLEN MALPAS

sure I will soon want to wipe off her face with a kiss. "This is classified information, Mr. Melrose."

"Your jealousy?"

She drops her head, looking at me with a small smile, and the moonlight hits her eyes, making sparkles explode from their green depths. Something inside of me explodes too. "No, the information I am about to share that I overheard at the party."

"Oh."

"Are you worthy?" she whispers.

"I am worthy," I say quietly, my body naturally edging closer, her lips getting nearer, the magnet stronger, my heart faster, my veins hotter. "Do you consider me worthy?"

"I suppose I do," she says huskily, her eyes jumping from mine to my lips, back and forth, as I come closer and closer. I can smell her. Honeysuckle.

"You completely beguile me, Taya Winters."

"I do?" she whispers, her voice rough.

"Oh, you do." Our lips brush, and my body folds under the pleasure, an animalistic, low, gravelly growl erupting, as she whimpers, pushing herself nearer, opening up to me. That is it; I give in. I cannot resist her, and I cannot deny myself this flurry of renewed sensations devastating every nerve ending. I must have her. I must!

I get closer, squashing the space between our bodies, feeling the heat creep across my skin, my tongue dipping lightly into her mouth, wet and warm, and the softness of her breasts compressed against my chest. "Taya, we must stop," I say for the sake of it, as if it is my duty to express my half-hearted thoughts. "Before we are discovered."

My words only seem to encourage her, her lips pressing harder to mine, her chest too, her tongue getting firmer in my mouth, the swirls faster, her moans louder, and I am a slave to it. My mind is lost, and I am certain it will never be found, as I take her in my arms and melt into her completely, moving a palm to her bare nape and holding her securely, feeling her trembles sinking into me.

"Frank," she gasps, her hands clawing at my brand-new velvet jacket, surely crinkling it, possibly even shredding it, but I do not give a damn. She could tear it from my body, for all I care. In fact, I hope she does.

"Don't speak, Taya," I order gently, softly kissing my way across her lips and plunging back inside her mouth with my tongue. "This moment needs no words."

She breaks away, taking in air urgently, as do I, breathless and mindless from that kiss, and looks at me with drowsy eyes. "I want my first time lying with a man to be special, not a clumsy, fast affair."

"Oh, God, yes." And my lips are on hers again, kissing her to death, taking everything I can get and wanting so much more. Special. She wants her first time to be special, as it should be, and here on the steps in the gardens of the palace is not the time nor the place, but I do not think I can wait.

I must.

I will not take her like an animal. I will take her gently and lovingly and make it so she may never forget it. *Or me.*

I flinch at that thought and deepen my kiss, my hand taking on a mind of its own and feeling down the bust of her dress to her breast. I groan at the feel of her soft flesh filling my palm and ache for more. *Not here!* I am doing myself no favors, I know, but I find myself quite addicted to this feeling.

Stop!

I wrench myself away, gasping for air, feeling as though I have run for miles and miles. "We must postpone this until a more convenient time and place."

"Must we?" she says, moving in again, trying to kiss me, but, and it takes all of my strength and willpower, I decline.

"We must." I put some space between our bodies and rake a hand through my hair, blowing out my cheeks. "Jesus." I am buzzing from my head to my toes. "You are quite a surprise, Taya Winters." I smile and risk a quick stroke of the creamy skin of her cheek, and she nuzzles into my hand. "I have a plan," I say, standing abruptly. I wince when my breeches, which are tighter than usual, squish me in a place a man should never wish to be squished. "Lord above." I instinctively place a hand there, hissing, and when I look down at Taya, her wide eyes are set right there on my hand.

"Control yourself," I tease, reaching down and pulling her to her feet. "Can you stand alone?"

"Can you?"

I wrinkle my nose, and I cannot help it, so I kiss her again, unable to resist.

"The plan?" she asks around my mouth.

"Oh, yes, the plan." I pull away, step back, and pace, if only to keep her at a distance. "You will inform your mother that you are unwell and should like to leave."

"That shouldn't be too tricky, for she is privy to my distaste of parties such as these."

"Good. Very good. You will get a carriage back to Belmore Square, where I will be waiting for you in the gardens."

"And how might you escape the party?"

"Don't worry your pretty little head about that."

"And what happens once I find you?"

I stop pacing and face her. "You want details?"

"Yes, I want explicit details."

"Oh, my glorious Taya, you are not ready for explicit details, my love." I move in and take her in my arms, breathing every bit of her into me, for I am certain she is life. "But I shall give them to you."

"Please do," she begs quietly, gazing up at me, so much longing in her eyes.

I smile, my thumb dragging across her lips, and I kiss her chastely. "Once I have you in private," I whisper, letting my lips brush hers too, gentle and soft, "you will tell me what you over-heard at the party."

"Oh," she whispers, looking guilty.

"You didn't hear a thing, did you?" She was trying to entice me in, and, God help me, it worked. I reach for her backside.

Her gasp is endearing, and I chuckle. "You only want me for my eavesdropping abilities."

I reach for her backside and give it a cheeky squeeze, making her eyes go all round. It is a novelty to see the quick-mouthed, smart-arsed Taya Winters taken aback, if I am honest, and I plan to make it happen more often. "Now go," I order, taking her shoulders and turning her back toward the palace. "I will follow you in shortly so as not to rouse suspicion."

She starts walking, and I relax back on my heels, watching her, my hands linked behind my back. I am certain if I could see her legs beneath her beautiful dress, I would see them shaking. They're not the only things that will be shaking soon.

Every inch of her and every inch of me.

And, I know it, the earth too.

Chapter 17

Escaping the party was far more difficult than it should have been. Suddenly, and disconcertingly, everyone had something to say, no one more than Mama, who wanted to pick my brain about my impromptu dance with Esther Hamsley. Apparently, our little twirl around the floor was the talk of the party.

After having my ear chewed off and working to convince Mama that it was merely a friendly dance—we don't want her getting too carried away, now, do we?—I made my excuses, something about a breaking story that needed to be written and taken to the printworks immediately, and left with haste, anticipation killing me.

I quickly calculate that I am a good twenty minutes behind Taya now, twenty minutes too long, and I like not the thought of her hanging around in the gardens of Belmore Square alone, regardless of the fact that she appears to hang around in the dead of night alone a lot. The family carriage is not going to get me to her as quickly as I would like.

I see a curricle speeding toward the palace, the owner up from his seat looking like he's having a whale of a time on his two-wheeled fancy means of transportation. The curricle skids to a stop, the horse neighs and stamps the ground, as aggressively as his owner drove, and a man, broad in shoulder, tall in height, and pointed in face, with a black mop of hair and mutton chops that would be the envy of many men far and wide, except for me, for I am not a fan, steps down and twirls his stick, looking important and aloof as he scans the palace.

I am in action before I can think better of it, approaching and bowing. "Sir."

"Lord Gayton," he declares, swanning past me without even so much as looking at me, leaving this supposed footman to take care of his impressive curricle.

"You're welcome," I say, hopping up and taking the reins, a new excitement finding me, to join the excitement I feel to get to Taya. I have always fancied myself owning a curricle, and I think I rather suit one. I take a seat, flip the reins, and I am off, racing away from the palace at an alarming but thrilling speed.

I must get myself one of these, I think, as I near Belmore Square, my journey time being cut by more than half, I'm sure, making up for the time I have lost being grilled by Mama. I leave the stolen vehicle around the back of Belmore Square, ensure the horse is secure in a stable with hay and water, and hurry to the gardens, navigating my way to the middle, but when I arrive there, slightly out of breath, there is no sign of her. "Taya?" I call quietly, my vocal cords straining terribly as a result of fighting back my urge to yell her name, panic getting the better of me. "Where are you?" Lord, I do so hope I didn't pass her en route, for it is a distinct possibility. I remember not one minute of the journey from the palace.

"I am here."

I whirl around and find her emerging from a bush, and to see her alone brings relief to my thrumming heart. She is, quite simply, the most beautiful rose amid some rather extraordinary roses. A vision.

How foolish I have been, to pretend I could resist her.

"Frank?" she says, her voice meek and unsure, and it does not suit her. "Are you all right?"

"Am I all right?" I repeat quietly. Am I, for I am somewhat befogged by the clattering of my heart? What is this I feel, as I stand here staring at Taya? Anticipation? It must be, for I simply have to kiss her again, so I do, going to her and taking her face in my palms, scanning every inch of her before pressing my lips to hers again and breathing every little bit of her into me, my shoulders rising, my tongue exploring, my ears soaking up the peaceful sounds of her whimpers. It would be too easy to get carried away here in the gardens of Belmore Square. I must be wise and controlled.

I slow our kiss and leave her lips, closing my eyes and resting my forehead on hers. "I am all right," I assure her. "Come, before we are spotted and find ourselves the subject of Belmore's latest scandal." One last chaste kiss before I claim her hand and lead her toward our house, my eyes watchful, my ears alert, as I try to decide my best, least risky option for getting Taya to my bedroom. I discount the back entrance, for Dalton or Cook will surely be disturbed and venture from their rooms to investigate. I dismiss any windows, despite knowing Taya would be perfectly capable of scaling a drainpipe or two. "The front door it is, then," I say to myself, leading Taya up the steps.

"You're going to walk me right on into your house?" she whispers, sounding alarmed.

"Yes, I am." I open the door quietly and listen carefully for a few seconds before I bundle her inside, checking the square quickly too before closing the door. "Wasn't so hard, was—"

"Mr. Melrose?" I hear Dalton call from downstairs. "I was just retiring to my room." The sound of his feet hitting the steps fills the space, along with the renewed anxious pounds of my heart.

"Frank!" Taya hisses, falling into a panic too. "What must we do?"

"Would you like me to fetch you anything before I do so?" Dalton adds, sounding closer, just around the corner, in fact, about to appear at any moment and catch me trying to sneak a woman into my room, and not just any woman.

"Bugger it," I mutter, grabbing Taya's hand and practically dragging her up the stairs behind me. "It is all right, Dalton,"

I yell back. I reach the top, haul Taya up the final few steps, and shove her into my room, slamming the door. "I'm quite exhausted and ready to fall into my bed." I put myself at the top of the stairs and try to appear steady in my breathing instead of as strained as I feel, at the same time smiling while I stretch on a yawn. Dalton appears, and, as expected, he's frowning. I pat at my mouth. "Good night to you, Dalton," I nod and back away, opening the door to my room and edging inside, quietly closing it. Being underhanded is exhausting. How did Eliza manage to maintain such escapades when she was sneaking around seeing the Duke? I rest my forehead on the wood and take a moment. A moment that is, apparently, too long.

Taya clears her throat, and I look back over my shoulder, trying not to think about how I might get her out later but instead appreciating what is before me. Anticipation returns, and the anxious beats of my heart change to thrilling throbs, as I watch her closely standing at the end of my bed. As much as she looks delightful, a beauty in her pink gown and perfectly pinned hair, she is by far more beautiful in her wild state. On that thought, I wander over slowly, delighting in the slight shifting of her body, her chest rising and falling, her eyes wide and full of wonder. I cannot wait to get my hands all over her. I reach for her face and push a loose tress away, and her eyes follow my move, her shoulders rising as she breathes in deeply. I am imagining her gorgeous golden locks splayed across the pillows of my bed. Her sun-kissed skin against the white sheets.

My knuckles brush over her cheek, and her eyes close, robbing me of the sparkle. "Open your eyes, Taya," I order gently, kissing her cheek. "I do not want you to miss a moment of this." She convulses, and when I pull away, her eyes are wide open. I smile my approval and unbutton my jacket, shrugging it off and letting it drop to the floor. "We'll start with undressing your hair," I whisper, reaching for her head and feeling gently around for the pins holding it in place. One by one, I remove them, dropping each one to the floor, watching, happy, as her long dark blonde hair tumbles down in sections, framing her face, the loose curls wild and glossy. When I am done, I slide my fingers onto her head and massage her scalp, and she moans, her head falling back on her neck, but her eyes, as instructed, and because, I hope, she is unable to rip her stare away from me, either, remain wide open. "Feel good?" I ask, and she nods as best she can. "Now let me undress those lips," I say, taking her mouth firmly but slowly.

"You have," she says around my kiss, breathless, "on numerous occasions, already removed my lip stain, Frank."

"Are you objecting?"

"Not at all." Her hands grab my shoulders, her short, neat nails sinking into my flesh through the material of my shirt. "I would never."

"I am glad." I pull away, panting in her face. "And now for this fancy frock."

She inhales fast, swallows hard. "And what of *your* clothes?"

"What of them?" I ask, my tone teasing.

"Well, I am not an expert, as you well know, but I am certain of it that both parties are usually undressed to partake in such an act."

I hitch an interested brow. "Such an act?"

"Whatever we are to call it." Her nose wrinkles. "You will remove your clothes, yes?"

"Or I might make *you* do it."

Her eyes widen momentarily before she corrects it. "I might oblige."

I laugh, and it is a lost, joyous sound. "Why thank you."

"Welcome. Now, can we get on with this?"

She's nervous, God love her. But I know I would do well not to point that out. "Are you impatient, my lady?" I ask instead.

"For you, yes, I am most impatient."

"So to torture you would be cruel, would it?"

"Most cruel." She fists my shirt on the shoulders and brings her face close to mine. "You are not a cruel man, Frank Melrose."

"No, but I am an indulgent one, and I should like to indulge in you, so you will be patient, my lady, for the wait will be worth it."

She pulls me in for another kiss, and I am taken aback by her hunger, if delighted too, but…I take her hands and detach them, breaking away from her body.

"You must wait," I say, releasing her and turning her around, gathering up her hair and draping it over her shoulder down her front, giving me access to the back of her dress, where a million buttons greet me. I pout, my nose wrinkling. "How attached are you to this dress?" I ask.

She looks back, her chin on her shoulder, her smile small and knowing. "Do you like it?" she asks.

"It's a beautiful dress, it must be said."

"But…?"

"I think I will favor what is beneath it." I grab the material with two hands and yank, and the silk buttons ping off, scattering far and wide around my room. Her corset is revealed, a cream affair that's laced expertly. *My God*. There will be no yanking that. I let the dress fall to the floor, pull a ribbon, and the tie unravels until her corset falls apart, and I have her back. The bare, beautiful, creamy skin of her back. "Oh, Taya," I whisper, as she lifts her arms, and the corset joins the dress on the floor. I have to take a moment, blinking to clear my vision, my eyes journeying the length of her spine to the top of her bottom. I shake my head in wonder and step back to get a broader view. "Just stay there a minute," I say, my voice gruff. "Just, please, stay there and let me absorb this vision."

"You do not want me to turn around?"

"I need to gather myself before that, Taya, for what I am staring at now is already too much." Or not enough. I take my hand to my face and scrub down my cheeks, my mind a mess of thoughts, as my chest constricts and I push away every warning I've had and every promise I have made, both to myself and to others, where this woman is concerned.

"Are you done?"

"No, I am not." I don't think I will ever be done admiring her. I drop my eyes over the two firm peaks of her backside and down her shapely legs until I am met with the masses of material of her dress. I step in, take her hips, and lift her, kicking the dress and corset aside and setting her down again, frowning when her hands come up to her breasts. She turns around, her eyes low. "What did I say, Taya?" I ask, and she looks up. "Don't hide yourself from me. Not your eyes, not your breasts. Remove your hands."

They fall to her side.

"Better."

Jesus Christ, she is curvy, full in bosom, shapely in leg, tiny in waist, and wide in hips. Perfect, childbearing hips, I think, but the thought jars me.

"Frank, what is wrong?" she asks, covering herself again.

I scowl at myself and reach for her arms, taking them back down. "Nothing is wrong," I assure her. "Nothing." I lower to my knees before her until I am face-to-face with the triangle of hair at the apex of her thighs. I lean in and kiss her just north, and that alone has her folding and crying out. I can see her skin vibrating, and when her hands find my head and hold it, for support, I expect, I feel those vibrations too. I lick across her tummy, my eyes closing in bliss.

"Frank," she whispers. "Please."

"I like hearing you beg." I nip at her flesh, looking up at her, satisfied to see her eyes are open and she is watching me. I lock our stares and trace a line up the inside of her thigh until I'm brushing the edge of her entrance. "Beg," I order.

"Please," she croaks, convulsing when I push my fingers into her, every greedy muscle inside her grabbing on and tightening.

So tight. Blood rushes south and starts to pound, and I withdraw and push forward again, circling slowly. "I'm preparing you, Taya," I tell her. "So it will not be so painful."

"It will hurt?" she gasps, twitching.

"Perhaps just a little, but it will pass and then you will feel the pleasure, I promise you."

"All right," she breathes, her body loosening as I thrust my fingers, placing kisses across her tummy as she tugs at my hair.

"My God," she says, starting to roll her hips onto my mouth.

"You've experienced nothing yet," I assure her, removing my fingers and rising to my feet, stepping back and leaving her to recover while I undress before her. "Nothing."

She bites her lip and watches with intent as I pull my cravat loose and toss it aside. Then my waistcoat is gone. My shirt pulled over my head. Her eyes widen, and I smile. "Nothing," I repeat, taking her hands and placing them on my chest, my mouth moving into her neck and sucking her, biting her, kissing her, as her palms stroke across my torso. I kick off my boots. "My breeches," I whisper in her ear, feeling her shudder. "Take them off."

Her hands shake against me as she clumsily pushes them over the swell of my backside with my undergarments. My cock springs free, keen to escape, and stands to attention, dripping with need.

"Oh God," she whispers, mesmerized by the sight, but before I can give her too much time to panic, I circle an arm around her waist and take her to my bed, lowering her to the end and kneeling before her. I collect my cravat.

"What are you doing?" she asks as I thread it through my hands, my eyes spoiled for choice, not knowing where to look—her face, her bosom, her legs, to name but a few, for everything before me, every tiny piece of her, is glorious, and I am enthralled by it all.

"Making your first time an experience you'll never forget." I settle for her lips. I have never seen lips so pink, so plump, so utterly kissable, and an overwhelming urge comes over me, one that is unfathomable.

I must not let another man taste those lips.

Whatever is my mind rambling on about? I shake my head and my inappropriate thoughts away and lean up, taking my cravat to her eyes. Her lips part ever so slightly, making it nearly impossible to resist plunging my tongue inside her mouth again. "You said I must keep my eyes open," she says, sounding breathless with anticipation. "That I must not hide myself from you, and yet you hide yourself from me."

"You will feel me."

At that, her hands lift to my naked chest and touch gently as I, with shaky hands, tie my cravat, securing it, not too tightly, but enough so it may not slip down her face. "I feel you," she whispers, padding her fingertips softly across my skin.

And, God, do I feel her. "Do you feel this, Taya?" I ask, stroking down her cheek. She nods, just a little, her feeling hands continuing on their journey across my chest. "This?" I move my touch to her thighs, stroking, and then dip, placing a delicate kiss on the edge of her patch of hair.

"Yes," she whispers.

"And…" I walk my fingers up her stomach to her breast and pinch her nipple. "This?"

"Oh God," she cries, her back arching violently. "Please, Frank, I feel like I could burst."

"And you will," I assure her, cupping her nape and pulling her mouth onto mine, taking myself in my hold and stroking myself, my kiss becoming harder, my body tenser. I had planned to seduce her for a long while, to make this last all night, but my body has other ideas. It matters not. There will be plenty more opportunities.

So I get to my feet, bringing Taya with me, and lay her down, climbing on top of her. "Are you ready?" I ask, taking a small break from her mouth to get her answer.

"I am ready."

I inhale and lift my hips, bucking when I feel the heat of her desire skim the tip of my arousal. "Jesus," I hiss, clenching my eyes closed, my nostrils flaring, as I attempt with everything I have to get a hold of myself or I'll spill my seed before even being inside of her, and that would be most tragic. And a waste.

What the buggery hell? A waste?

Good grief, I can only assume this need and want are sending me crazy, for I am having the most pathetic thoughts. There is nothing left for it. I swivel my hips and gently push my way inside her on a broken groan, the tautness eyewatering but marvelous in equal measure.

"Frank!" she yelps, making me instantly still, breathing heavy, her nails scratching at my back brutally.

"Taya!" I yell in reply, gritting my teeth and tensing my back, every sense alive and sensitive, so sensitive I can hardly tolerate it. I blow out my cheeks, feeling her squeeze around me. "Taya, you must stop that."

"I cannot!"

More teeth gritting. More air leaving me. Now, too, my eyes cross, and my face turns up toward the ceiling briefly before my head drops, the energy needed to hold myself up too much. I open my eyes and find her neck, and I watch as it swells over and over on her constant swallows. I dip and kiss it, then her chin, her cheek, her mouth. And I roll my hips. I swear, I have never felt a pleasure like it. Never. I have lain with many women, some I'm certain were virgins, but none of them, not one, had me at sixes and sevens like this. I cannot fathom why Taya Winters has had this confounding impact on me. I cannot, but I wish to the gods that someone could elucidate so I might comprehend how I should handle this unexpected situation I have come to find myself in.

I stare down at her. Why, I wonder, have I covered her beautiful eyes?

The answer scares me. It truly scares me. But still, I reach up and push the material away, and she blinks rapidly as I take her hands and lift them above her head while I wait for her to find her focus and, more importantly, find *me*. When she does, something kicks inside of me, something profound and significant. Except I don't know what it is or what it means.

Or, perhaps, I simply do not want to acknowledge it.

"Taya," I whisper, kissing her as I roll and thrust, slow and concise, ensuring we both feel every tiny movement, for it is exquisite.

"Frank," she breathes in return, her tongue seeming to find its flow from mine with ease, and I marvel at how good a kisser she is. "I have never felt anything like this."

"Me either," I admit.

Her mouth stops suddenly, and as a result, my pumping does too, and I frown, pulling back. She looks as confused as I feel. "But, Frank, you have done this many times, with many women, I am sure."

"You are right." I nuzzle our noses and resume with my drives, showering her face with kisses, long and short ones, deep and chaste ones. "But you, my lady, are quite another experience."

"I am?"

I jerk, the blood starting to rage down below. "God, you are!"

"Oh!" She jacks up off the bed. "What is that? What is happening?"

I say nothing, unable to speak, and maintain my pace and pressure, thrilling in the signs that she is on the brink with me.

"Frank!" she yelps, grappling at my back. "Oh my God!"

It hits me like a charging stallion, and I yell, releasing Taya's mouth and throwing my head back, my body contorting, bending...breaking. "Jesus!" She squeezes me so hard, and I relish the pressure, feeling my seed being drawn out by the constrictions of her internal muscles. "My God," she breathes, going lax beneath me.

"Indeed." I am but a useless pile of man, unable to even roll off her. "I must be heavy," I say into her neck, smelling the salty scent of sex and sweat. It is delightful, I must tell you, so delightful my tongue leaves my mouth of its own volition and licks some of it up, and I release her wrists and slide my fingers through hers, clenching our hands together.

"I am fine," she pants. "Very fine, in fact."

"Very, very fine?"

"Yes, I am, but please refrain from allowing your ego to swell."

I grin and bite my way up to her face. "What about *your* ego?"

"I do not have an ego, Frank Melrose."

"Oh, my sweet lady, you most certainly do." I kiss her nose. "How are you feeling?"

"I feel the most content I have since…" She fades off, frowning.

"Go on," I prompt.

"Since Papa was alive and thrilling me with his perfectly crazy mind." She smiles sadly. "I do so miss him."

"I'm sorry," I say once again, and it feels wholly inadequate. "Tell me about him."

"Really?"

"Yes, really."

"Oh." Her forehead creases a fraction, her smile unsure. "All right. Well, while he worked on his inventions, I would draw him. He loved that. Would pull all kinds of silly faces. I know I have my brothers and my mother, but…"

I offer a small smile, which again feels inadequate. How I would love to remove all of her heartache and sorrow. I know I cannot. Ease it? The Duke is quite an irate man, and Sampson, I'm sure, jokes his way through his grief, but how does Taya deal with the loss? I sense, like her eldest brother, there is anger. A need to repel the ton. Break rules. I wince when I consider how disappointed her father would be with her now. Damn me, but I could not help myself. I have never been so charmed.

I slide out of her on a hiss, and I am at a loss without the feel of her warmth swathing me. "Come here," I order gently, rolling onto my back and inviting her in to my side. She comes with ease, and I smile to myself, closing my eyes and exhaling.

"We will rest for a moment and then I shall see to it that you get home."

"All right," she replies sleepily, starting to caress my stomach, her strokes making me sleepier. "Frank?"

"Yes, Taya?"

"I quite like you."

"I quite like you too," I say, pulling her in further to me and blindly kissing her hair. "Probably a little too much, if you want the truth of it."

"What does that mean?"

I don't answer her.

She knows.

Chapter 18

I wake up to a new day, and I am smiling. Yes, I am smiling, and it is quite a smile indeed, stretching from one side of my face to the other. I am very warm, too, warm and cozy, and I have absolutely no desire to rise and get on with my day.

"Frank!" I hear Mama shriek, the distance between us not at all lessening the piercing sound. I flinch. "Frank, where are you?"

"Where the bloody hell do you think I could possibly be at this hour?" I mumble to myself, even though I have no idea what hour it is. I shake my head to myself and start the challenging task of encouraging my muscles to wake up and sit me up, but with only one tiny move, something tickles my nose and I sneeze, jolting.

"Oh my heavens," a small, sleepy voice says, making me freeze where I am, startled, my eyes dropping to my chest, where a mass of wild dark blonde hair greets me.

"Oh no," I whisper, as Taya scrambles to sit up, her face awash with alarm as she faces me, the sheets pulled up over her torso.

"I dozed off!" she blurts, her eyes, despite the troubling situation, still managing to get a good look at my bare chest. I'm delighted, of course, but now is not the time to be egotistical.

"Frank!" Mama yells.

Now is *definitely* not the time.

Taya gasps, her attention turning to the door, beyond which the sound of my mother's thumping footsteps are getting closer. There is nothing left for it. I seize Taya and shove her under the sheets, trying my damn hardest to position my body on its side so as to conceal the lump behind me, and I do it just in time for Mama to fly through the door like a bullet.

"She's gone!" she says, her hands finding her face. "I have searched high and low, and she is not here, Frank!"

"Who is not here?" I ask.

"Clara! She told Papa and me that she was leaving with you last night."

"What?" I'm up out of my bed in a heartbeat, making my efforts to hide Taya a complete waste of my time. "She did…" I fade off and my brain, which may be slightly sleepy at the moment but still functioning, thank goodness, stops me in the nick of time before I give Mama news that will surely heighten her worry, for to confirm Clara was not with me yesterday evening will turn her into anxious wreck, and she is quite dramatic already. "I'm sure I can locate her, Mama," I say, approaching, frowning when Mama steps back. "You know our Clara; she is not happy unless she is up to no good."

"Where are your bed clothes, Francis Melrose?" Mama asks, her eyes wide.

I look down to my naked form. *Bugger it!* Forgetting I'm supposed to be hiding someone, I reach back and seize the bedsheets, pulling them off the bed to cover myself. And in the process, of course, I reveal what is in my bed.

Taya yelps and grapples to win back the sheets. "Oh God," I blurt.

"My goodness!" Mama shrieks, swinging away from us to face the door. And then she is silent, and I suspect it is because she knows not what to say.

"This is a problem of my own making, Mama."

"Whatever happened to being reformed?" she shrieks at the door, and thank God she is, because I fear if she were to see me rolling my eyes in this moment, she might well dress me down with some stern words. *Taya Winters is what happened.* I look over my shoulder to Taya, who has since found my shirt and slipped it on to cover herself. My God, she looks incredible there in my bed, all disheveled and flushed. My mouth slowly curves.

"You must marry her," Mama declares, finding it in herself to face us.

"What?"

"You heard me, Frank Melrose."

I laugh, and it is quite hysterical. "Let us not be hasty, Mama." Married?

Mama's face suddenly blanches. "Clara," she whispers, her original distress coming back to her as she looks past me to Taya, shaking her head to herself as she does. "I will wait outside for you, if you would care to dress and meet me there." She leaves, and I face Taya.

"Well, this is all rather unfortunate, isn't it?"

"Terribly unfortunate," she says with a tight jaw, standing abruptly from the bed and practically ripping off my shirt, leaving her naked as the day she was born. She is shaking like a jelly, her entire body vibrating. "You are an ass, Frank Melrose." She swipes up her clothes and pulls them on with heavy hands, her face tight, while I stand like a fool in the middle of my room watching her dress, confused by the animosity pouring from her.

"You think I'm an ass?" I ask.

"Yes, I do."

I recoil. Well, her opinion certainly did change quickly. I was a god last night. "I suppose that is your privilege."

"You are right. Now, if you don't mind, I will be leaving." She breezes past me, her chin high, and I reach to stop her but get smacked away.

"Taya, be reasonable. This situation needs some careful consideration. You can't very well go storming out in your clothes from yesterday evening in broad daylight. The whole square will be talking." She surely isn't *that* bold and uncaring of society's opinion.

"Fear not; I am quite capable of getting myself out of this little scrape that I have come to find myself in."

Or walk into willingly, I think to myself. Scrape? She makes it sound like an unfortunate happening. Regardless, I am sure she is right, for if Taya Winters is anything, she is resourceful. "Then at least leave by the servants' entrance at the back."

She huffs and pulls the door open, and Mama stops in her pacing outside. "Mrs. Melrose," Taya says, nodding her respect, as does Mother.

"My lady."

"Where might I find the back exit?"

"The kitchens," Mama says, following Taya with her eyes as she walks on and takes the stairs.

"Thank you."

I frown as I watch her lifting her dress and taking the stairs, wondering what has gotten into her, but I do not get long to ponder that. Mama is soon shrieking her distress again. "One missing daughter and a philandering son," she says. "My God, we will be ruined."

I am exasperated. Truly. "Mama, please," I beg. "I thought you had passed the point of caring." I turn and collect my breeches from the rug and wave them at Mama, prompting her to turn and give me some privacy to dress.

"It is a matter of decency, Frank. One must refrain from having dalliances with the sister of your sister's husband."

"So it is all right for me to have dalliances with other females?"

"You were twirling Esther Hamsley around the floor last night!"

I sigh, pulling on my breeches and shirt, and I get a waft of honeysuckle as I do. Lord above, I can smell her all over my clothes. All over *me*. "Esther Hamsley and I are—"

"Oh Frank," she cries. "I am but a sniff away from being elected a patroness, and I need *not* any of my children's shenanigans hampering that."

And there we have the truth of it. I am disappointed. "I don't know why you are so invested." I drop to the end of the bed and pull my boots on. "Almack's is little more than a meat market where snobbish mamas of the ton go to procure suitors for their offspring. Why would you want a part of that, Mama? It is beneath you."

Outraged, she swings around. "I have considered this greatly, if you must know. Has it escaped your notice that your sister is now a duchess, and one with child at that, and you and your father are running the family business?"

"That has not escaped my notice."

"And what of me?" she asks, and I am taken aback by it, I must admit. "What am I to do while you are all being busy? Clara will soon come of age, marry a man who I'm sure will thrill her, and then what will become of me? I have raised my children and I have done a fine job, if I do say so myself, albeit they are somewhat insolent and disobedient from time to time."

I pout to myself, thinking perhaps now isn't the right time to tell her that Clara may have already found a stable boy that thrills her. I doubt Mama's tolerance falls to such a level. Or that Papa is hardly running the business with me at the moment. What a mess.

I am about to offer reassurance of some kind when she moves toward me, eyeing me in a way I do not like. With suspicion. "How long has this been going on?"

"Forget about that. It is not important." I go to Mama. "It is not the end of the world if you do not get elected as a patroness, Mama. And be assured, our family name and business will not be ruined."

"Perhaps it is not the end of the world," she shrugs. "But it is something to do, you see, Frank. Papa is so busy, as are you. I need something to fill my time, and since I enjoy the company of Lady Blythe and Lady Tillsbury, and they, apparently, are rather fond of me, it seems like an obvious pursuit."

I flinch. *Papa is busy.* "If it makes you happy," I say, kissing her forehead.

"Clara!"

I flinch and Mama jumps from my arms.

"Where could she be, Frank? We must find her before Papa rises and Governess arrives."

"I will find her," I assure Mama. "She is probably sulking somewhere."

"Whatever is she sulking about?"

"Nothing."

"Francis, are you hiding something from me?"

"Of course not." I had planned on writing my next piece this morning about our lovely Lady Rose, since I was otherwise engaged yesterday evening, but it shall have to wait. I grab a jacket and leave my panicked mother behind. I'm hiding far too much, I think to myself as I descend the stairs. And what of Taya's ill temper? What changed so suddenly? Is she regretful? Is her rebelliousness all a front and she's somehow between yesterday eve and this morn realized the gravity of the repercussions? "God knows," I sigh as I make it outside and gaze around the square, wondering where to start in my search for Clara. I am distracted by a commotion across the road outside the former residence of the Lymingtons. I see two men negotiating an impressive, dark wooden cabinet up the steps to the front door.

"Good morn to you, Mr. Melrose." Lizzy Fallow appears, smiling coyly.

"What is happening there?" I ask her.

"New residents."

"Oh?"

"The Earl of Pembrokeshire, Lord Gayton, the Countess, and their son, Eric." She rounds the back of me and comes to a stop beside me, looking across the square with me.

"You're rather well versed in the details," I reply, taking one step away from her.

"Owners of the *London Chronicle*."

"What?" I ask, thinking the name rings a bell, and then a man emerges from the house. "Oh bloody hell." The same man whose curricle I *borrowed* last night. "I have to go," I say, slipping away rather hastily, rounding the corner and heading in the direction of the stables where I left the horse and curricle, but much to my dismay, there is no curricle, and the horse I put safely in the stable is nowhere to be seen. "Kip," I call.

"Yes, sir?" He appears with arms full of hay, his orange hair long and scruffy, the freckles splattering his cheeks prominent.

"Where is the horse that was in this stable?"

He frowns. "Sir?" he questions, looking at me as if I may be going mad. "That stable is reserved for hay."

We have been robbed! And I cannot tell a soul. "Of course." *God damn it.* "How long will it take you to prepare my horse?"

"Not long at all, sir." The hay is released from his hold and he's getting to it immediately.

"Thank you, Kip." I start to wander, wondering how I handle this additional problem. Another problem of my own making, but, regrettably, me stealing my business rival's mode of transportation is not my biggest problem in this moment. Where the hell has Clara gotten to, I ask myself? The answer comes to me like a bolt of lightning. "Bugger it all," I mutter, raking a hand through my hair and looking up, coming face-to-face with—

"You're the footman who relieved me of my curricle yesterday eve at the palace."

"Ah," I back up, my brain not working nearly fast enough to tell me what to do. And there was me thinking he paid no attention to me. "I can explain."

"Who are you?" he asks, anger breaking his expression.

I will not be telling him *that*, for a feud between us would add to my already growing stress. "Mr. Melrose," Kip calls, and I shrink.

"Melrose?" Gayton asks. "Part of *The London Times* Melroses?"

"The one and only," I say, my ego getting the better of me. "Would love to stay and chat." I quickly jump on my horse and gallop away, hearing Gayton yelling after me, demanding to know where his curricle is. God damn it, I will surely be required to compensate him, and not only for the curricle. It will cost an arm and a leg! I break out of Belmore Square and canter toward the edge of London. It has been twelve hours since I last saw my wayward little sister. It is a head start, but she is on foot, and I am on horseback. I expect I will catch up with her within a few hours.

Nethertheless, I do not have time for this.

Chapter 19

But twelve hours later, there has been no sight of Clara and I am less irritated and more worried. I am forced to stop at an inn, for my horse is weary and in need of water and I could do with something to eat myself, and perhaps a few hours' rest.

I slide down off Figaro, feeling awfully stiff, and tie him up by a trough, before dragging my tired body to the inn, stretching on a groan as I go. "Can I help you, sir?" a woman asks as the door closes behind me.

"I need a room for the night. Some supper and some ale." I toss a few coins down and find a table, taking a needed seat and glancing around, seeing many men slurping from tankers, being raucous. I smile, memories of our past life in the countryside coming back to me, the times when Mama used to come and drag me out by my ear if I failed to make it home for dinner on time. The times when, on the odd occasion, Eliza used to make it to the inn before Mama and warn me she was on her way. The times when a lusty, busty female would bat her lashes at me, and, somehow, we would end up rolling around in the hay or grass. Less pressured times.

I jump when a jug of ale slams on the table, followed by some bread and a bowl of brown slop, which I'm pretty certain will be delicious. "Thank you," I say, tucking in, my stomach growling to be filled. I am right. It is delicious slop, and I work my way through it fast, mopping up every last drop of stock with the bread and downing the ale. I am suitably full, and more than that, feeling even more exhausted. I stand, planning on getting just a few hours until dawn breaks and I can get on my way again.

I nearly make it to the rickety wooden staircase in the corner when I am stopped by the sight of some familiar lusty lashes being fluttered my way from the female behind the bar. Familiar, not because I know her, but because I know how this will play out. Her smile is suggestive. Her bosom big. Her curves attractive. But, and it is a shocker to me, I am uninterested.

Too consumed by the vision of another female, one who is, according to her foul mood this morning, not speaking to me. I'm still wondering why. Last night was really rather pleasant. Unexpectedly so, and while it pains me to admit that it was wholly wonderful, I must, if only to honor my conscience. I am quite taken by the lovely, reckless, wild Lady Taya. But her title is not the only reason I must abstain. Abstain and pray whispers of our encounter do not make it to the ears of… anyone. My livelihood depends on it, as do my legs. Not to mention our business and reputation. And Papa's! I cannot be responsible for our downfall. Never. So the fact I am in Lady Taya's black books, even if I have no idea why, is probably of benefit to us both.

I take the stairs and push my way into the last room on the right, stopping and gazing around at the drab, grubby space. It is a stark contrast to the luxury that I'm afforded these days.

I kick off my boots and drop to the bed. It isn't long before I am dozing off with vivid memories of last night: Taya Winters, her wild hair, long lashes, and whimpers of pleasure invading my dreams. It's a nice change, to be honest, from my usual dreams of a white stallion and mysterious horsewoman.

I wake with a start. It is light, and I jump up in a panic, stuff my feet into my boots, and hurry downstairs, getting an unpleasant waft of stale ale as I weave through the tables to the door and burst out into the fresh morning air. There are a few locals out and about, telling me it is not as early as I should have liked to rise. I mount my horse and get going, trotting through the village, and I am about to break into a gallop when something catches my eye.

"What the devil?" I whisper, pulling the reins of my horse and slowing him to a stop. The curricle I borrowed from that Gayton man is sitting by the roadside with a broken wheel and no horse. I frown and am about to slip down from Figaro when I remind myself of my mission, and it is not to locate and return the curricle I stole yesterday evening. I must locate my sister first, and then perhaps I will return and deal with the curricle, although how I might get it back to Belmore Square with a broken wheel and missing horse will prove a challenge. It is one thing after another these days.

I am about to start on my way again, wondering who could have possibly stolen it, when I hear a familiar voice. I pull my horse to a stop and frown at thin air, listening.

"Blast it all to hell!"

I look over my shoulder and balk. "Clara?"

She whirls round fast and looks up at me on Figaro. "Oh, this is perfect," she grumbles and deflates before my eyes. "What the hell are you doing here?"

"Me?" I blurt, dumbfounded.

"Yes, you."

"I'm flaming well looking for you!"

"Well, you need not bother. I have run away." She turns back toward the broken curricle, her hands planted on her hips as she inspects the knackered wheel.

Furious, I get down from my horse and march over. To think it was Clara who stole the horse and curricle? She will be the death of me, I swear it. "I don't know why you are standing there looking at it like you might be able to fix it." I can see it is beyond repair. "And where is the flaming horse?"

"It bolted," she snaps, throwing a hand out at the wheel. "I hit a ditch and it startled the horse."

"Great," I mutter, rubbing at my wrinkled forehead. "How the hell am I going to explain this?"

"Explain what?" she asks.

"This curricle belongs to the Earl of Pembrokeshire, who also happens to be the owner of *The Chronicle*. Not only have you stolen it, you've buggered the bloody thing up and lost his horse."

"You stole it first." Her nose lifts in an act of pride she has no right to parade. "And I did not crash it. It is obviously of poor workmanship if it cannot stand the test of a few bumps in the road. You…" She shakes her head, as if disappointed. "…Pretending you were a footman? Shame on you, Frank Melrose."

She was there? Heard me? "You stowed away from the palace?" I ask, finally finding my voice.

"Where did you need to be in such a hurry that you would risk your life by stealing a horse and curricle?"

I freeze, my brain not working nearly fast enough to spill my reasons, and she smiles. It is wide and smug and everything I despise about both of my sisters, for it means they have me in a fix. I have nothing. Absolutely nothing. "Shut up." I look around me, searching for any means of transport to get us home. "Your little adventure is over."

"I beg to differ," she snorts, stomping away. "I will walk if I must."

"Oh no." I catch up with her and snake an arm around her stomach, lifting her from her feet and carrying her back as she kicks and screams like a petulant child. "Enough!" I yell, getting a few hits in my shins from the heels of her boots. "We can do this the easy way, or the hard way."

"The hard way!" she yells, her arms and legs flailing. "I hate you!"

"You might be disappointed to hear, sister, but your hatred of me is the least of my worries at the moment." I plant her down and wave a finger in her face. "You will do as you are damn well told. I am yet to decide whether I will tell Mama and Papa of your bid for freedom, so you will do well to remember that."

"I care not who you tell." She slaps my hands away, and I wonder, not for the first time, how I came to be so unfortunate as to have not one, but two insolent, defiant sisters.

I take a deep breath, reminding myself that there is a certain way in which the Melrose females must be handled, and making demands of them is not the way. Reasoning with them, however, is. I need to get home and write an article, for the love of God. I have a business to run! Readers to please. *A woman to tame.*

I frown to myself.

"Clara," I breathe. "You realize you will drop dead on the spot if you so much as kiss a man before you are wed, don't you?"

Her eye roll is impressive. "Oh, please, brother. You tried that nonsense with Eliza, and I know it to be true that she did a lot more than kiss the Duke before they were wed, and she was still breathing last time I checked, was she not?"

"Eliza's antics prior to the Duke making an offer are not certain."

"God, you're an idiot."

Damn my smart siblings. "OK, you may not die," I relent, "but you will become seriously ill. Don't you remember that rather nasty bout of influenza that Eliza suffered only a month or two ago?"

She frowns. "Yes. She was taken to her bed for a week."

"That is correct. I know it to be true that she kissed the Duke only the day before." I do not know it to be true at all, but I must do what I can to resolve this problem that, this time, is *not* of my making.

She inhales and withdraws. "Mama was forced to call the doctor."

I nod.

"Eliza sweated like a pig for days and could not stop vomiting."

I nod again. I shall surely go to hell. I realize this tall tale has a short lifespan, but so long as it's long enough to get her home and caged.

Clara pouts, contemplating that, and then fixes the filthiest look onto me, so filthy, in fact, it could melt me here where I stand. "You talk rubbish. I am not gullible, Frank." She smacks my arm. "Now go home. I have important matters to deal with."

I laugh loudly, and she kicks the broken wheel in a temper and growls under her breath. "I hate you, Frank Melrose."

So we are back to hating, are we? I breathe out heavily and reevaluate my approach, for I am currently going around in circles. "Tell me, my dear, sweet sister, what do you—"

Clara gasps, her scowl falling and a smile rising. "Benjamin!" she shrieks.

"What?" I ask, following her sparkling eyes to the stables not too far away. There I find the one and only stable boy, standing stock-still looking somewhat, and expectedly, I suppose, struck.

"Clara?" he questions.

"Yes, it is I!"

"What are you doing here?"

"What are you doing here," she asks, "for this is miles from your home?"

"It was the closest village in which I could find work."

My head swings back and forth between the young pair, so much so, my neck starts to ache. This is a disaster. I had a chance, albeit slight, of getting her home, even if I was forced to manhandle her. Now? This is most unfortunate.

Clara steps toward him, but Benjamin remains where he is, and then Clara stops, and I look past her to see a young girl emerging from the stables, pulling at the neckline of her dress, hay in her hair, looking downright disheveled. Oh boy. I have rolled around in enough hay with females to know what I am looking at now. *The little scoundrel.*

I peek at Clara, seeing her nostrils are flaring dangerously, and that tells me she is well aware of the situation we are faced with. "I hope you catch the flu and die a hot, painful death!" She runs to my horse, jumps on, and kicks it hard, making it break into a gallop, then a canter.

"Clara!" I yell, watching her getting farther and farther away. "Bugger it all!" I scan around me for a horse, any horse, preferably with a saddle, but I find none. I growl and run around the corner. "Yes!" I jump up onto the back of the black stallion and kick it hard, trying not to pay too much attention to the fact that I am, yet again, stealing another horse, a crime that could see me hanged. How the hell do I get myself into these situations? I race out and see the stable boy up ahead. I cannot help it. I stop, swing my leg out, kicking him accurately in his chops, before racing away in pursuit of my sister.

Clara is an experienced rider, our childhood in the countryside an advantage, so it is no surprise that she has gained some distance, but, lucky for me, I have stolen quite a speedy steed, and I have caught up to her in no time. I take no pleasure in the tears streaming down her cheeks. None at all. I should have kicked the little brute harder. "Clara, stop," I yell over the pounding of hooves.

"Go away!"

"Clara, please, you will injure yourself traveling at such speed!"

"Good!"

"You will injure me."

"Good!"

I flinch, stung, despite knowing she wishes no such thing. I am left with one option, a crafty—and dangerous—one at that, but I am desperate, and I will be pained if she takes a tumble from my horse and breaks a bone. I slow, bellow a yell, and then, like a prize idiot, throw myself off the horse.

I land on the ground with a thwack, flinching, a piercing pain searing my shoulder. "Bloody hell," I bark, coughing, getting a nose, mouth, and eyes full of dust. That didn't exactly go to plan. "Frank!"

I wince as I peek up, seeing Clara galloping back toward me. It is a relief. How annoyed I would be if I had thrown myself from my horse and broken something for nothing. She hops down before my horse has stopped fully and runs to me, dropping to her knees and assessing me.

"Don't die," she pleads. "I beg you do not die. I love you, Frank! I do, I love you!"

"I am all right," I assure her, though I seriously doubt that, if the pain in my shoulder is a measure. I hold it and sit up with Clara's help, wondering what in God's name I was thinking. I shake my head in despair at myself and look at my baby sister, hating her wet-stained cheeks and sad eyes. "You should listen to your brother, Clara, for I have your best interests at heart, and I only ever want to avoid your hurt."

Her lip wobbles and she lunges for me, hugging me fiercely. The pain, I swear, is excruciating, but her hug, however, is wonderful. She has been so absent for so long. I am only sorry in this moment that her affections were wasted on that pathetic urchin. "Come now," I say, encouraging her from my chest. "We must get home before Mama and Papa send out a search party."

"Oh, Frank, please do not tell them." Her blue eyes are beseeching, but I do not know how I can avoid it.

"What would you have me say?"

"I was at the library."

I laugh, hissing when my jerking body jars my shoulder. "The library was not open when Mama burst into my room at the crack of dawn after she'd found you missing from your bed."

"I was at the stables."

"You haven't been at the stables once since we moved to

Belmore Square. At least, not the Melrose stables, but perhaps the Fitzgeralds'."

"Do not speak of it," she warns, her voice strong but tight.

"As you wish," I relent, struggling to my feet. "I will think of a story to explain your absence from your bed this morn, but, Clara, you will be indebted to me for a long time."

"Yes, yes, I know." She stands too and dusts herself off.

I rub at my arm and wonder…what now? I am no doctor, but I am certain I cannot remain on horseback with only one hand to hold on to the reins, especially at any speed. I will be forced to trot, and that will take us days to get back to London. "We need a carriage," I say.

"We do not. I can ride perfectly well. You can be my passenger."

I laugh, but not in humor. "Absolutely not, and if you know what is good for you, you will not defy me on this."

"What about what is good for you?"

"I know exactly what is good for me, and it is to eliminate all women from my life, for they are a constant source of distress."

"You're so dramatic."

I ignore her and look up when I hear the telltale signs of hooves. "Yes," I sing, seeing a post chaise heading this way, its yellow paintwork glowing under the morning sun. "Perfect." I wave at the post boy who's seated upon the front left horse of the four, calling for him to stop.

"Do you have passengers?" I ask, craning my head to see if there is any luggage strapped to the roof or any servants riding on the bench on the back. There is neither, a promising sign.

"No, sir, we are to collect Mr. Green from the next village and take him to Oxford."

"I will pay double for you to take us back to London."

"Two and thruppenny a mile," the boy says, and I scarcely conceal my glare. He is trying to fiddle me, the little scoundrel! That is way over the going rate. Alas, I am not in a position to tell him to bugger off.

But, still, I am a businessman. "Two shilling and not a penny more."

"Hop on board," he says, smiling.

"We must bring the horse too," I tell him, nodding for Clara to tie Figaro to the side of the yellow boulder. I look around for the black stallion I stole, seeing it nowhere in sight. It's unfortunate, but I do not have the time to find it and return it to its rightful owner, whoever that may be.

We board and settle in the seat, and Clara looks at me with sorry eyes as I rub my shoulder. She isn't to know that I only have myself to blame. To throw oneself from their horse? How stupid! "We should take the short cut," I say, surprising myself.

"Hampstead Heath?" Clara blurts. "Are you positively insane, Frank? Good grief, we'll be robbed and murdered."

"One hopes," I say quietly, making her eyes widen somewhat. "Well, robbed, at least. Hopefully we can talk our way out of being murdered." Poor Clara looks like she's seen a ghost. "Oh, relax," I say, smiling, getting comfortable in my seat. "I'm sure we'll avoid a brush with death." Or perhaps, thrillingly, we won't. "My shoulder is bloody killing me, and I need to see a doctor without delay."

I don't see disbelief on my little sister often. It's a novelty. "You are…" she mutters. "You are insane, Frank," she hisses, leaning close. "Hampstead Heath is said to be the most dangerous place in England."

"I know."

"So why the buggery hell are we taking that shortcut?"

"I told you, my arm is killing me and I need some pain relief."

"We'll stop at the next village and find you some Scotch."

"I'm not drinking."

"Why do you lie?" she asks, endearingly exasperated. "Are you saying you are going to get me killed by a deadly highwayman to save yourself a little pain?"

"A little? I'm in agony here, Clara."

She prods me in the shoulder and I wince, but quickly realize it is not a very good demonstration of exactly how much pain I'm claiming to be suffering.

"Arhhhhh," I yell, trying to fix that.

"You want another story," she says accusingly. "Pray tell me your logic, because I am struggling somewhat."

"You are not going to be killed," I assure her, resigning my-self to indulging her and at the same time reassuring her. "The highwaymen are not murderers, Clara. They're thieves. Quite charming ones, too. Lords and ladies who have encountered them merely claim terror to save their egos."

"Why would they do that?"

"Because most of them willingly hand over their gold."

She laughs. "Oh, please."

"It is true," I say quietly, wondering, not for the first time, why the highwayman left Papa untouched. Papa thought perhaps he considered him beneath Lady Rose, but he was dressed in his fine threads that day, and he always has a healthy sum on money on his person. I'm skeptical.

Quite some hours later, the landscape becomes more rugged, and I conclude quite quickly that the lack of horses trampling the ground, leaving the grass and bushes to grow undisturbed, is the reason why. I cannot deny, my heart is pounding in my chest as I scan the overgrowth, the tall bushes, the perfect place for highwaymen to hide. Are they hiding now, waiting in the dense wilderness for their prey?

"You should have to pay the coachman danger money," Clara grumbles as I scan our surroundings, shaking the coins I have about my person. "What in the devil's name are you doing?" she blurts in horror. "Good God, you're enticing them."

Come on, give me something, I think to myself, watching the planes of land, tingles of excitement engulfing me. "I am of the op…" My words fade, and I poke my head out of the carriage when I hear a familiar sound. "Did you hear that?" I ask. The sound of hooves pounding the ground. "Stop the carriage!" I yell, and Clara shoots forward in her seat abruptly on a yelp, forcing me to save her before she flies headfirst into the wood.

"What the hell, Frank?!"

I gasp when a horse comes up alongside the carriage. "What on earth?" I whisper as the Duke of Chester flanks us.

"What in heaven's name are you doing on Hampstead Heath," he asks, slowing his horse to keep with the speed of the carriage.

"Is that Johnny?" Clara asks, going to the window and sticking her head out. "Great," she sighs. "If the highwaymen don't bludgeon us, the Duke will."

"Don't be ridiculous," I snap. "We have already established that our sister's husband is not a murderer."

"Oh, Frank, please do not tell him I ran away. He will tell Eliza and Eliza will tell Mama and Mama will tell Papa."

"What else am I to say? We're hardly here for a pleasant countryside jaunt, and my bloody shoulder is broken." I get out of the carriage as soon as it comes to a stop, hissing in pain as I do, and approach my brother-in-law, who looks as forbidding as he always does.

"What are you doing, Frank?" he asks, his jaw pulsing in anger. He swings a long leg over his horse and stealthily dismounts.

"I believe you already know, Your Grace." Let us not beat around the bush. I am sure Mama has gone to Eliza and wailed her worry, and, in turn, Eliza, the smart thing that she is, has figured out exactly where Clara has disappeared to and sent Johnny to track us down. I highly expect she tried to come herself, and I highly expect there were some stern words spoken between the newly married couple when Johnny refused to allow it.

Johnny looks to the coach where Clara is looking out the

window, appearing as ashamed as she should. "Clara?" he asks, obviously waiting for a show of remorse. I do not think he needs me to tell him that he will not get one. Her mouth is firmly shut. Until it isn't.

"Frank's trying to entice the highwaymen," she blurts with urgency, jumping down from the carriage and swinging an arm out toward me. That's it. I will kill her, I swear it. After everything I have just endured for her?

The Duke's eyes widen as one would expect. "I cannot bel…" He pauses, seeming to gather his patience. "Get back in that carriage and back to London before I…I…" Another pause for breath. "I shall escort you home."

"She's telling Banbury tales." I throw Clara a dark, warning look. "To distract us from her crimes."

"What is it with Melrose women?" the Duke asks, his eyes turning onto my sister, his stance loosening.

"You have a nerve." Clara stomps over to him, and her hands land on her hips. "Just because you are married to my sister, do not think you can speak to me in such a way." She scowls. "Your Grace."

He rolls his eyes and shows the sky his palms. "I find your sisters quite exasperating."

"Don't we all," I muse, thoughtful, my mouth pouting in contemplation.

The Duke opens his mouth to speak, probably to agree, but the sound of a horse interrupts him. I gasp and whirl around, seeing three horsemen on the horizon, the stampede heading this way.

"My God," I murmur, noticing the Duke looking somewhat pale in complexion, matching Clara, I expect. "Are you all right?" I ask. It is quite a stupid question when a gang of criminals is racing toward us.

"This is far from ideal," Johnny says, pulling a pistol from his breeches, and Clara's hands immediately lift into the air. "Get in the carriage." He takes her arm and leads her to the carriage, and she does not object, her feet working fast to keep up with the Duke's long strides. I see the post boy jump down from his horse and start running away as Johnny slams the door and faces me.

"I am impressed," I admit, thinking perhaps my new brother-in-law has learned a thing or two about handling Melrose women since he started courting Eliza. I need to get myself a pistol.

"You will let me deal with this," he says. "If you want to come out alive."

"I rather do," I murmur, looking toward the charging horse-men, anticipation whirling in my stomach. I most certainly want to come out alive. *So I can pen the story.*

"They are very dangerous men."

"Men," I muse. And there is no evidence to suggest they are dangerous, only the tall tales of the ton. "Have you not been reading the newspaper lately, Winters?"

"Yes, I have."

"Then you will know they are not all men."

"It is but a myth."

"I can assure you otherwise, for I have seen with my own eyes."

"God damn you, Melrose." The Duke marches off and mounts his horse quite gracefully for such a big fellow, and in such a frantic situation too. "If you get me killed, the Duchess will certainly murder you with her bare hands."

"Oh for pity's sake, no one is getting killed." I go to Figaro but stop when I hear what I fear is the sound of a pistol being prepared to be fired. I look back and see the Duke aiming it at me.

"You will stay with your sister."

The man is controlling in the extreme. "Eliza won't be best pleased to hear you have held me at gunpoint."

"I'll take my chances." He trots off leisurely toward the band of horsemen, and I watch in interest, wondering what the hell he's going to do. Hand over his gold? I smile. The Duke would never. So perhaps he will threaten them. Threaten them and they will never return. My story will be no more. All of my plans will be ruined.

Oh no.

I watch with bated breath as he is circled by the horsemen, and he holds something out to one of them, and then tosses it into one of their hands. His money? So I was wrong. Bugger, he will surely want reimbursing.

"I am never listening to you again, Frank," Clara yells from the carriage. "You are a danger unto oneself."

"Oh, do shut up, Clara. You're like a fly buzzing in my ear." I start marching toward the Duke, determined.

"What are you doing?" Clara asks, hanging out of the window of the yellow boulder.

"Getting my story." And just then, the rider on the white stallion trots over to the Duke…and punches him square in the face. I flinch, gritting my teeth.

"Oh my," Clara breathes. "You're in for it now."

The Duke wipes his nose and spends a few moments gathering himself, until, eventually, he breaks away and trots back toward us. "At least you still have your life," I say, assessing his face, seeing just a small scuff on his cheekbone. "And, respectfully, it would have been a lot worse had one of the two gentlemen planted you one on the face."

"Shut up, Melrose," he growls. "Did you steal their horse?"
Oh shit.

Laughter breaks out behind me, Clara the source, and we both turn dark glares her way.

"I didn't know it was their horse," I say, wishing Clara would shut the hell up before I shut her up myself.

"Jesus Christ, Frank, do you have a death wish?"

No, just a wish to know the identity of them. In fact, I would pass up the men. I care not for them. I want the woman.

"Fear not," the Duke sighs, exasperated. "I will explain to them."

"Explain what?" I ask.

"That you're a blithering idiot."

"I will explain myself," I declare, pulling in my jacket with my good arm and passing the Duke, wondering if I am brave or stupid. "I don't know what the fuss is all about; he's clearly found the beast." My eyes home in on the white stallion and the rider upon it, my heartrate increasing as I get closer, the Duke yelling at me to stop. *Never.*

I make it to them, and I am soon surrounded. Intimidated. I can't see her face, but I'm pretty sure she's scowling at me. Then, quite unexpectedly, she kicks me with some strength in the chest, and I fly back and land on my arse, jarring my shoulder further. I yelp in pain, feeling the whole damn thing pop out of the socket. "Christ alive!" I holler, my eyes watering, my breath held, my body tense, all in an attempt to stem the pain. Naturally, I get no apologies. "Are you not going to reveal yourselves to me?" I ask, sounding cockier than I should. My request has the desired effect, and the man whose horse I stole pulls his scarf down, revealing quite the hairy face, as Papa said. But still very handsome. Even I, as a man, can admit to it. It is no wonder Lady Rose handed her purse over without protest. His gray eyes sparkle like stars. "Your name?" I ask, knowing I am pushing my luck.

He smiles and looks past me, as Johnny joins us, slipping down from his horse and helping me to my feet. "You will get us all killed," he snaps, guiding me away, but, of course, I cannot fight him when my shoulder is screaming in pain. I quickly get a last glimpse of the white horse and its rider, seeing a few strands of her dark hair are loose and dangling. She's either getting careless or she simply does not care. I expect it's the latter, which defies the point of her hiding herself. But, I must admit, the mystery is thrilling.

The horseman whose face I can see yells, and they are soon all cantering off at top speed.

"What have you done?" Johnny asks, looking at my arm, which is hanging lifelessly from my shoulder joint.

"Better than death, I suppose."

He grunts and leads me back to the carriage, and my next headline is born.

IT IS DEFINITELY A WOMAN FOR SHE HITS LIKE A GIRL

A gentleman never tells, but he doesn't mind telling you this...

Chapter 20

My shoulder aches, but the doctor assured me it would ease off in no time, right after he'd yanked it back into place and sent me through the roof in agony. Mama was so relieved to have Clara home and was so busy fussing over me, she seemed to forget what had brought us to my shoulder being put out of joint and Clara wailing like her heart has been broken. I locked myself away in the study for hours, first writing about my encounter on the heath for it was fresh in my mind (and in my shoulder) before moving on and penning the details of Lady Rose's encounter.

I smile as I read over the headline the next morning in Papa's study, opening the front page and admiring the double-page spread. It's glorious. But if it were to have drawings? I pout to myself, thinking perhaps Lady Taya's mood is an indication that she no longer wishes to work with me. It's probably for the best.

For the best.

What is for the best? Who decides what is for the best? Because it cannot be for the best that I feel this awful ache in my stomach.

I continue reading my story, an attempt to distract myself from the ache, I suppose, where I detail not only my encounter, but Lady Rose's too. It's a masterpiece, even if I do say so myself. A risk to blend the two stories and make one juicier tale rather than two separate tales, but the bigger the risk...

I reach up to my chest where she planted a precise kick, falling into thought. Black hair. Long lashes.

The door opens and Dalton appears. "His Grace the Duke of Chester," he declares, backing out as Johnny paces in, looking no less irritated than yesterday. He slaps a copy of today's *London Times* on the desk. "You must stop with this ludicrous obsession before you get yourself killed."

I blink rapidly, as Dalton appears yet again. "Her Grace the Duchess of Chester," he announces, edging out again as Eliza breezes in and frowns at her husband. "Why are you here?"

"Trying to talk some sense into your gormless brother."

"Gormless?" I ask, outraged. I am many things, but gormless is not one of those things.

"Stupid. Idiotic. Foolish." He waves a hand flippantly. "Whatever you wish to be called."

"I'm trying to solve a mystery. The whole of London wants to know who's on that horse."

"I don't!" Johnny barks. "And I certainly do not want to be chasing you out to Hampstead Heath to save your skin."

"Then don't," I reply, kicking my feet up onto the desk. "And you hardly saved my skin."

I get scowled at, and it is a mighty scowl, before he growls and leaves, muttering something about murdering me himself. I look at Eliza, who looks torn between going after him, or pressing me for information, for I know she is as intrigued as I. "How are you feeling?" I ask, nodding at her belly, prompting her to hold it.

"I would be better if you and my husband were not at odds. What were you doing on Hampstead Heath, anyway, Frank?"

I frown, somewhat confused. She knows what I was doing, and that is why she sent Johnny. "I was saving our sis—"

Dalton enters again. "The Countess of Somerset." And quickly exits, getting himself out of the way of Lady Rose, who marches in swinging an umbrella, her face ravaged.

"Lady Rose," I sing, removing my feet from the desk and standing. I am not looking at Eliza, but I sense her smile, which means she too has read today's article, in which Lady Rose and her brush with the highwaymen is detailed in full.

"I demand you remove it from sale!"

Dalton, once again, enters the study. "Another visitor, sir," he says, his tone droll, as Grant presents himself, removing his hat and bowing to the ladies in the room.

"You are here with news, I expect," I ask him, and he nods.

"Yes, Mr. Melrose. Twenty-two thousand, sir."

"Twenty-two, you say?"

"Twenty-two thousand?" Papa blurts as he meanders in, his face sporting a satisfying expression of extreme pleasure.

"Twenty-two?" Mama breathes, following him.

"I believe that is what Grant said." I look at him, thoroughly enjoying myself, as Lady Rose seethes where she stands, looking about ready to shove that umbrella somewhere I expect it would be most painful.

"That is correct, sir," Grant confirms. "Twenty-two and three-hundred, to be precise."

My grin widens. "How delightful."

"I'm sure," Lady Rose hisses through puckered lips.

"Delightful indeed!" Mama sings, clapping her hands.

"Well, would you believe it?" Papa breathes.

"Believe it, Papa," I say, daring to approach Lady Rose. "Readers are quite enthralled." I do believe I would be wise to keep my distance, and just as I think that, she launches at me with her umbrella, at quite some speed for an old dragon, it must be said, and clobbers me on the arm with a solid, accurate swing of it. My *injured* arm. I grit my teeth, my shoulder flaring with pain.

"You will go to hell, Frank Melrose."

"Now, now, Lady Rose, don't be like that," I say, wishing she'd bugger off. "You are but one of many who will fall victim to his charms. There is really no need for all of this embarrassment."

"I am not a victim, neither am I embarrassed! I was robbed! Terrified!"

"As is every member of the ton when they come within a meter of your ravaged face," Mama says quietly, and I snigger.

"What did you say?"

"Nothing, my lady." Mama smiles. "Now, if you wouldn't mind, my family and I have luncheon to eat."

She huffs, puffs, and whirls round, stomping her way out.

"What a dreadful woman," I breathe, rubbing my throbbing arm.

"Twenty-two thousand, my boy!" Papa sings, smacking my shoulder, making me yelp. "Oh, bugger it, I do apologize, Frank."

"Well done, brother." Eliza leans up on her tiptoes and kisses my cheek. "I am truly thrilled for you."

"For us," I say. "This is a family business, after all." Not that Eliza is financially dependent on us anymore, of course, but still. She'll always be a part of the family business. "We may need His Grace to source another machine."

"Wonderful. Now, I have a luncheon with Lady Blythe and Lady Tillsbury." Mama leaves, and everyone, one by one, follows, leaving me to take a moment.

Twenty-two. Incredible! I smile, but it wavers when I recall the other part of Fleming's deal. I have no idea how I can make *that* happen—how I can acquire the identity of the criminal wreaking havoc on the ton.

Dalton enters, looking truly exasperated. "Lady Taya, sir," he says on the deepest of sighs.

Oh? I feel my back lengthen, my shoulders pushing back. It is as though my body, instinctually, it seems, for I did not instruct it, may be bracing itself for her. "I'm popular today, eh, Dalton?" I say, my busy mind now pondering something else. Why is she here? The last time I saw her, she was not talking to me. Because I ruined her? But she wanted it.

"Indeed you are, Mr. Melrose." He moves back and makes way for Taya. "Indeed you are."

She remains on the threshold of the study, appearing reluctant to enter, her eyes low. "My lady," I say quietly, certain I do not like her disposition.

"Mr. Melrose," she says quietly, avoiding my eyes.

"Are you all right?"

"I am fine." She clears her throat and looks up at me. Her eyes suggest otherwise, for they are glazed with tears that look ready to fall, but knowing Taya Winters, I am certain she will never allow it.

"Are you really?"

Her chin lifts. "I am here to say goodbye."

My heart drops like a rock into my stomach. "Where are you going?"

"It matters not, only that I am leaving."

"Leaving Belmore Square? Leaving London?"

"England."

I recoil. It is unstoppable and perturbing. "What?"

"I'm going to Paris."

She's leaving the country? That feels a trifle drastic. Assuming, and I am very aware that I should not assume anything when it comes to Taya Winters, it is me she is trying to escape.

"I believe you heard me just fine," she says, her voice tight.

"You believe right, but what I cannot fathom, my lady, is why? You have not mentioned a desire to travel before."

"Do you think I should have?"

"Do *you* think you should have?"

"No."

"Then why are you here now?"

Her mouth snaps closed, she withdraws, and her face hovers between annoyance and hurt. I wait. I wait a good many seconds for an answer, but I get nothing, so I continue, for apparently I have plenty to say. "And I do so hate being the bearer of bad news, my lady, but I highly doubt that your brothers, or your mother, either, for that matter, would permit such a reckless endeavor." I certainly do not approve myself. A female cannot clear off out of the country without a chaperone. I won't hear of it.

"Fear not, Mr. Melrose. My brother, Sampson, will accompany me to the port. He is quite well-traveled, as you know. My second cousin on my mother's side will meet me in France."

This is ridiculous. Why did she even come to tell me this? Because it feels remarkably like an attempt to injure me. It is working. Worse than that, I have just comprehended, perhaps because I am faced with the possibility of her leaving, and I say *possibility* because I will go to great lengths to prevent it, that I will miss her. I will miss her arrogance. Her words. Her smart mouth. Her smiles. Her drawings. God damn me, I will miss her, and I like not the thought of a day without her or…a kiss from her.

"You have to help me out here, Taya," I say, starting to pace. It is either pace or touch her, grab her, and I know that to be a terrible idea. "Correct me if I am wrong, but by my mind, and I thought by yours too, until, at least, you left my bed, that our night was…" How does one put it? "Extraordinary," I say, looking at her. I realize it was her first time and she has not one other lover to compare it to, but surely she wasn't disappointed? My stomach turns at the very thought. What a waste, I think, if that is the case. She will have been ruined for nothing.

"It was average," she shrugs.

I laugh, because she is really rather hilarious. "How the bloody hell would you know? I was your first."

"Do not mock me, Frank Melrose."

"I am not mocking you, I am stating a valid point."

"Actually, your point is moot. Regardless of how extraordinary the night was, it was, however, just one night, and as you have kindly stated, with the utmost sureness, while laughing, I might add, that is all I should expect."

I am so confused. I said that? "Ta—" And I realize…*Come, Mama, let us not be hasty.* It is what I said when Mother demanded I marry her. *Oh, Taya.*

She pivots and takes the door handle, and I am across the room fast, wedging a hand into the wood to prevent her opening it, gritting my teeth when the damn pain sears my damn shoulder for the tenth damn time today.

I look down at her dark blonde waves just under my chin. Smell the honeysuckle. And there, I can say with utter sureness, is the issue. She's injured. Hurt. "They were words spoken under pressure, Taya." But there is not a hope in hell's chance of us ever being together—her brothers will never allow it.

"It matters not," she says to the door. "It was a mistake. You should return to your obsession."

I frown. My obsession is her. "What?"

"Your story, Frank. Your obsession."

My God, she is so *so* mistaken. I no longer dream of the wild white horse. I dream of her. I have thrown myself into work for many reasons, and one of those reasons was distraction. Yes, I am enthralled by the criminals and their escapades. My heart thunders at the thought of the highwaywoman. My blood pumps. It's an incredible feeling. And all of that happens when I am with Taya. Except it's more potent. Stronger. More thrilling.

Impossible but amazing.

"Well," I breathe down on her, my eyes narrowing a little as they observe the slight trembling of her shoulders. "Then I suppose this is farewell."

"I suppose it is."

My eyes move to the doorknob, where her hand trembles too. *Oh, Lady Taya, how you frustrate me.* "If I was sharp-eyed, and unfortunately for you, I am, I might observe the quivering of your body under my closeness." I whisper and hear her inhale subtly. "Is it a challenge, I ask you, to be close to me, my lady?"

"Stop it," she breathes, her breath strangled. "I beg you."

"Why?" I ask, every part of me tingling in response to her closeness too. We are reactive, us two. Together, we are reactive to one another, and, my God, it is utterly overwhelming. Unstoppable. "Afraid you may succumb to the power and prove I am right?"

"Right about what?"

"That our night together was the most incredible night. For both of us."

"And what of the other nights you have shared with plenty of other women?"

"A gentleman never tells," I whisper. "But with you"—I dip and place my lips on her bare shoulder—"it was like nothing I have ever been blessed to experience before." I kiss my way to her neck, inhaling her scent, her need, her want. "I must have it again."

She moans, her body folding, her head tilting to give me better access to her skin. "And if I were to refuse?"

I smile against her flesh, lick it, bite it, suck it, feeling her shake. "I dare you to try."

She whimpers and spins around, throwing her arms over my shoulders and pulling me onto her mouth, kissing me frantically. What a pointless few minutes we have just wasted. "I no longer want to try and resist you," she says around my mouth, her pace and vigor relentless. "For it is exhausting."

I lift her from her feet and carry her to the desk, placing her on the edge and take her to her back, feeling her legs and all the material of her skirt wrap around me, as I try to reason with myself. This is not the time or the place! God be damned, anyone could walk in at any moment. I pray they don't. *Please don't, for I will certainly go mad if I do not have her again.* And as if he has heard my prayers and wants to stamp all over them, Johnny's booming voice interupts me.

"Where is he?" he bellows, and I shoot up, breathless, disoriented. "I swear, I will kill him."

I stare down at Taya, who looks as dazed as I expect I do, but despite my muddle, I manage to comprehend something. Something rather worrying. "Jesus Christ, they are sending you away." I quickly pull her up from the desk. "Your brothers are sending you away to keep you away from me, aren't they?"

"Sampson was waiting for me when I left here the other morning. We argued. I suppose he told Johnny and he has assumed…"

"But the Duke was just here," I say. "Demanding I halt in my endeavors to discover who the highwaywoman is." He was also at Hampstead with me, and he murmured not one word about Taya.

"I suppose he and Sampson have only just seen each other. Sampson is not an early riser, and Johnny was out on his horse before nine. Why do you so desperately want to know who she is, anyway?" she asks, sounding…jealous? She *is* jealous.

I smile, enchanted. "She is merely part of a business deal I have with a charming fellow called Fleming."

"Oh, I see. That is all?"

"Yes, that is all."

"Melrose!" The Duke's booming voice echoes around the house, sounding closer.

"Oh bloody hell." I wipe my lips while observing how pink and swollen Taya's are. "Did you tell them where you were?"

"Of course not!"

"Then we must deny it."

"Naturally."

Natural. Is it? I pause for thought. Perhaps I shouldn't since time, it would seem, is not on my side.

"Melrose!" Johnny yells, the thuds of his boots getting closer.

"You must hide," I say, taking her arm and leading her to the masses of taffeta drapes that frame the window and placing her behind, arranging the material to ensure it disguises her body behind it. "And keep quiet." I hurry to my desk, slump down into the chair, and collect my paper, settling in and wiping the panic from my face, a moment before the door flies open and Johnny appears, his stance wide, on the threshold of the study. I look over my paper casually, eyebrows high. "Did you miss me?"

He scowls, casting a suspecting eye around the study, his chest puffy. "You're alone."

"Very observant of you." I fold the paper and place it down, all so calmly, I really have no idea how I'm achieving such nonchalance. "Why, is your matter one of a private nature?"

"Yes." He steps in, slams the door, and levels me with quite the frightening glare. "You will stay away."

"From whom?"

"Do not play games with me, Melrose. You may be my wife's brother, but I will not think twice about snapping you in two."

"A little extreme, don't you think? What am I supposedly guilty of to warrant such a ferocious threat?"

"You know fine well."

"Do I?" Yes, deny, deflect, lie. Whatever it takes. At least, until I fathom how to deal with this because I have tried to resist her and I'm failing miserably.

"Listen to me, Melrose," Johnny goes on. "My family has been through hell and back to find us back here in Belmore Square working to earn the respect and recognition of society. Taya will marry, and she will marry suitably. I will not have you interfering."

He is a bloody hypocrite. Since when has Johnny Winters cared for the opinion of the ton? "I assume this shift in concern of social opinion is a recent development in your personality?" I say.

"Concentrate on doing what you assured Eliza you would do, Melrose. Business."

I laugh. "Just earlier you told me to stop pursuing the high-waymen." What else will he demand I do or do not do?

He snarls. "I forbid you to so much as look Taya's way, for if I get sight or sound of her tears again, I will end you. I will withdraw all machinery. Ensure Eliza and your father know you cannot be trusted. Do you hear me?" He storms out, slamming the door with brute force behind him.

Her tears?

I hear her emerge from behind the drapes. "You were crying? When?"

"They were tears of frustration."

Tears are tears. And I caused them. *God damn me.*

The Duke is right. I could destroy everything around me, lose our business, but more important than that, and I would not forgive myself for it, I could hurt Taya. Ruin her prospects.

What have I done?

But it is salvageable. Mama would never breathe a word, I just know it. "You should leave," I say, going to my desk, doing my damn best not to look at her.

"I suppose I should," she replies in a voice too resolute. "Since my brother's concerns are valid."

I nod, pick up a quill, dip it in ink, and start writing nothing in particular.

"Goodbye, Frank," she says in a voice that reeks finality, which is undoubtedly a good thing. She has come to realize, as have I, with a little nudge from my friendly brother-in-law, of course, that the flirtations between us should have only ever been that. Harmless fun.

"Goodbye," I say in a strong, aloof tone, further insulting her.

The door closes, and I glance up to an empty room.

It matches my eternally empty heart.

I took a while—five hours, if you require specifics—sitting at my desk gathering myself. When I finally drag my heavy, defeated body up, it is early evening. I have missed breakfast, luncheon, and dinner. It matters not, for my appetite is as low as my mood. I cannot fathom this consistent, aching, irritating pain in my chest.

Back to business, I remind myself, where everything is going to plan. I must see Fleming and share the good news, as well as reassure him that the identity we all so want will soon be revealed, I am sure of it.

Papa is crossing the cobbles when I step out into the low sunshine, and my heart sinks further. "Where are you off to?" I ask as casually as I can muster.

He slows to a stop, and it takes an uncomfortably long time for him to face me. It doesn't bode well at all.

I inhale and find the courage I need to end this charade, taking the steps down to him while also checking the vicinity for listening ears. I lower my voice. "Papa, what were you doing going into Lady Dare's house?"

Papa smiles. He just smiles, and I am thrown. "Oh, Belmore Square," he sighs. "Nothing can be hidden around here, can it?"

I hope so, I think, as I look at him, confused.

"Dear boy, I am preparing a story."

"What?"

"Yes, I am writing a story about the ruin of the Duke of Devon, who squandered his fortunes on gambling and then swindled the Countess of Cambridge to pay his debts. Lady Dare, I recently discovered, is niece of the countess. That was where I had been the day we were ambushed by the highwaymen."

"Oh, thank God." I slap a palm on my chest. "I thought… Never mind what I thought."

"What did you think?" Mama says, coming down the steps and joining us. "That your father was being tied up and whipped in that harlot's whipping house? Why, that's my job, Francis."

I gape, and Papa laughs.

"I think I will be going," I say over a cough, heading toward the stables.

"Frank," Mama calls, chasing me down.

I know what's coming. "It was a mistake, Mama," I assure her. "A terrible mistake."

"So it will not happen again?"

"I assure you."

"And I am the only person privy to your inappropriate escapades?"

"You're the only one who knows it for certain, yes."

She nods, thinking for a moment. "For the best, I'm sure."

"Indeed."

"She is a sweet girl. I would be most troubled if she was to be hurt."

"Of course," I say quietly, carrying on my way.

Because I am only capable of pleasuring or hurting.

Not loving.

Chapter 21

I push my way through the door into the dim, smoky club, and order a Scotch, casting my eyes around the space. I don't see Fleming, but I do see Ruby. I lift my drink in greeting and lower myself to a comfortable chair by the fireplace as she wanders over, her red lips shining in the hazy light, her dark hair off her face this eve. "Good evening," I say, respectfully keeping my eyes on her face rather than her half-exposed chest.

"Mr. Melrose." She nods. "I would offer a drink, but you already have one."

"I do. Where is Fleming?"

She looks over her shoulder to the entrance, as if she is wary of his arrival. "I expect he will be here imminently."

"What are you to him, Ruby?" I ask outright, my curiosity getting the better of me.

Her head tilts, her smile small. "His whore, of course, Mr. Melrose."

I laugh under my breath as I take a sip of my Scotch. Ruby is pretending to be a whore. That much is clear, but what I want to know is why. She is an intelligent woman who has let her well-spoken tongue slip a few times too often.

My eyes fall to the top of her arm, and I spy a collection of bruises. She sees my direction of sight and covers the area with a palm, and I can't avoid it—I am angry. So very angry. "Ruby, I do not mind having him—"

"Melrose," Fleming booms, appearing behind her. "I trust you are here with the news I want."

"I am," I say, my eyes narrowing as I kick a foot up onto my knee, relaxing back, giving Ruby a look to suggest I am not done. "Today we have exceeded twenty thousand."

"Very good."

"Let us discuss the distribution," I go on. "Perhaps in private," I add, looking at Ruby, who starts to walk away but is stopped by Fleming's fat fingers wrapped around her wrist. Tightly.

"Nonsense." He wedges himself into a chair and yanks Ruby down onto his lap with unwarranted force. "Go on."

I inhale some restraint, reminding myself that Fleming is a necessary evil. At least, for me. But for Ruby? What is her story, I think again, for surely she does not need to sustain this treatment? "With another printing machine on the fleet," I say, turning my eyes onto Fleming. "I anticipate we can double to forty thousand in a few short months. I will hire the best journalists to fill the pages, too, send them further afield to obtain breaking news from all over the country."

"Let us not get ahead of ourselves," Fleming says, flicking one of Ruby's nipples so her chest concaves. It is painful, I see the discomfort fleetingly on her face, but she smiles at him anyway. "The name of the culprit who robbed me, what is it?" he asks.

I shift, uncomfortable. "I am not privy to that information just yet," I say. "But be assured, I am very close."

"Very close isn't close enough." Suddenly, he stands, setting Ruby on her feet. "The deal was twenty thousand and the identity of the highwaywoman." His roving eye drifts down Ruby's front, and I come over all queasy on her behalf. Then his fat finger rises and the pad rests on her breastbone. "Bring me a drink," he orders, wobbling off to one of the quieter rooms at the back.

"God damn it," I breathe, sagging in my chair. I told him I am very close. It may have been an embellishment. I need those distribution channels! It's all well and good printing in excess of twenty thousand copies of *The London Times*, but it's bloody pointless if we cannot sell them. We need further reach. God knows how long it will take me to discover the identity of the highwaywoman. I have machines to pay for in the meantime, and they are not cheap.

"I will leave you in peace," Ruby says, moving away.

"Wait," I call, making her stop and look back. Her bruises glow at me. "You do not have to go."

"Your concern is misplaced."

"How so?"

"I am here because I deserve to be."

"What? You speak rubbish."

"He ruined me, Mr. Melrose, and my family disowned me."

I recoil, shocked, but also not, for I suspected there was more to Ruby than meets the eye. "You were important enough to be ruined?" I ask, and she smiles, giving me my answer. "What was your name, Ruby?" Her lips press into a straight line, as if she is desperate to tell me.

"My name is Ruby, Mr. Melrose." She steps closer. "I will say one thing to you, sir."

"And what is that?"

She looks around, nervous and wary. "He has no intention of meeting your deal."

"What?" I step back. "Why?"

"Because he cannot. He is on the verge of financial ruin, Mr. Melrose. He simply wants the identity of the highwaymen so he may stop them ruining him completely."

"How have they ruined him?"

"Because they have ambushed every one of his carriages in the past year, and word is spreading throughout the upper classes who pay for his services that he cannot be trusted, for many of them have had priceless family heirlooms stolen, jewels and gold. Not to mention, his boats are old, dilapidated, and sinking one by one as he has not the funds to repair or replace them while his services cannot be trusted." She smiles and wanders off, leaving too many blanks to be filled. Old, sinking boats? Almost all of his carriages? Call me suspicious, but this sounds like a personal vendetta.

And my intrigue and interest just multiplied. As has my worry. Without Fleming's support, I could be on the verge of financial ruin myself. Lord above, I have machines to be paid for, salaries to pay, and now I'm faced with the prospect of these highwaymen ruining that?

I must find them and stop them so that Fleming's reputation can be reinstated, his boats repaired, and our business arrangement does not go down the pan. I must also tread very carefully. I knew Fleming was a shifty sort, but to try and trick me? My incentives have changed. My determination has grown.

I need to rethink my plan.

And I definitely need to get Ruby away from that heathen.

Chapter 22

The next morning, Papa is singing his way around the house while Mama laughs and follows, asking whatever has gotten into him. "Life, Flo, life! Life has gotten into me." He seizes her and starts to twirl her around the dining room while Clara and I watch, me worried and guilty, Clara frowning.

"No, really," Clara says, leaning toward me. "What has gotten into him?"

"He is happy. Let him be." I set my coffee cup down and stand. "I must be going," I declare. "To collect my new coat and deal with business." Although how exactly I am dealing with it I do not yet know.

"Have a good day, my darling," Mama calls mid-twirl.

"I will." I leave and step out into Belmore Square, taking in a new day. It is rather dull and quite cloudy, not dissimilar to my mood, Ruby's news hitting hard. Between that and the knowledge that Taya has left, I'm feeling thoroughly dejected.

I take the steps down to the cobbles and wander toward the gardens to cut through, and when I arrive at the Winters residence, I knock once and stand back, waiting for Hercules to answer my call. When he does, I am certain I see him sag, as if my arrival is a burden. "I am here to see Her Grace the Duchess of Chester," I declare, in case Hercules may have assumed I was here for someone other than my sister, because, of course, I am not. Because she's left the country.

"Please," he says, standing back and letting me pass. The door closes behind me and I take in the impressive, expansive hallway once again. "This way, sir." Hercules passes me and leads on toward the dining room. "I have just set out some fresh coffee."

"What are you doing here?"

I stop and look up the stairs, seeing Sampson descending, fixing the buttons of his tailored jacket. I could ask the same question. Wasn't he leaving? With Taya? "I am here to visit with the Duchess."

"Her Grace is in bed," Sampson says.

Worry grabs me. "Why, what is wrong with her?"

He makes it to the bottom of the stairs and rakes a hand through his wavy hair. "She isn't coping all too well with this first stage."

"Do not worry." Wisteria appears at the top of the stairs, too, smiling softly as she pushes a pin into her hair. "The doctor has visited this morning and assured us it is merely her body adjusting to her condition. She is exhausted and queasy. I know the feeling well. You children present challenges from the moment we discover you are growing inside our bellies."

"Lady Wisteria," I say, bowing my head as she floats down the stairs.

"Good morning, Mr. Melrose." She collects her hat and shawl from Hercules and passes them to Sampson to help her. "I am to meet with your mother for luncheon with Lady Tillsbury and Lady Blythe."

"How lovely."

"It is. Lady Blythe should like our opinions on her new story. Something heartbreaking, I expect, as all love stories are." She looks at me in a way I am uncertain of.

"All?" I ask, feeling as though she is saying something without saying something.

"Well, most. Eliza has asked for you to go up to their room for she is without the energy she needs to join you in the dining room. Come, Sampson, you can escort me." Hercules opens the door for her, and she nods her goodbye before floating out with Sampson trailing her, standing tall, as if guarding his mother.

"May I?" I ask, motioning up the stairs.

Hercules nods, and I climb the steps, running over Lady Wisteria's words, or more the way she was looking at me as she spoke those words.

Heartbreaking, like all love stories are.

Is Lady Wisteria alluding to her daughter? Is she heartbroken? I reach up and press my fist into my chest, scowling at the persistent, downright annoying ache, as my nose is invaded by the sweet scent of honeysuckle. *She's still here?* I try vehemently to shut off all of my senses, hurrying along the corridor to where I know Eliza's room to be. I knock and pray for a speedy permission to enter.

"Come in."

I exhale and push my way through the door, relieved beyond relieved. "Whatever is the matter?" Eliza asks from the bed. "You look troubled."

"I have been worried," I say, assessing her on the mattress, looking, frankly, pasty and sallow. "How are you feeling, sister, for you look plain awful?"

"Thank you. And, yes, if you must know, I feel plain awful, too," she mumbles grumpily. "So bloody rotten, Frank, and feeling like this is making me all the more annoyed about being with child. I did not bargain for this."

I pout. "Come now, sister. It is a glorious thing we must celebrate."

"Celebrate feeling like death? Yes, that makes perfect sense."

I decide perhaps a distraction would be best. "Where is His Grace?"

"Probably searching for a new wife who will give him less earache."

Well, that worked less well than I'd hoped. I smile and go to the bed, perching on the edge and taking her hand. "You and I both know that is not possible." He adores her, moaning or not. "It will pass."

"When," she sighs, squeezing my hand. "I am exhausted by feeling exhausted."

"I have news," I declare, going back to my plan of distracting. Also, I need a second opinion, and Eliza is my natural confidante.

"Oh?" Her eyes light up. Good. "What? What is it?"

"I met a man recently. Fleming is his name. We struck a deal that could launch the newspaper to new heights. He owns a haulage business, you see, and could expand our reach considerably."

"Oh? How exciting!"

"It was, yes."

"Was?"

"It appears Fleming has pulled the wool over my eyes."

"How so?"

"Well, you see, the day I met him, he had been ambushed by the highwaymen on his journey into London. They took his money and his ego."

"Oh, how terrible!"

"Indeed." It is not terrible. It appears Fleming is the kind of man who deserves to be robbed. "I expressed an interest in partnering with him to further our reach, and he expressed an interest in the identity of the highwaymen."

"Or women."

I shrug. "We struck a deal. If I hit the twenty thousand copies sold and brought him the identity of the highwaymen—"

"Or women."

I nod. "Then he would partner with us to take *The London Times* national, possibly global."

"Oh my."

"Yes. Except just last night, I learned something about Mr. Fleming that leads me to believe he may not be genuine with his offer and is perhaps tricking me to get what it is he wants."

"No."

"Yes, I'm afraid so, and that, Eliza, has increased the stakes, for we have invested heavily in new machinery and staff, and I must justify that investment."

"So now your curiosity regarding their identity has become more a necessity."

"Indeed."

"Well then, you'd better get on with things, Frank."

I laugh. Yes, get on with it. How simple. Sometimes, we over-think, and suddenly what is simple feels so very complicated. *Get on with it.* It. I stand, kissing her forehead. "Be well, sister."

She snorts. "I feel as though I might never feel well again. Be sure to keep me updated, Frank."

"I will," I assure her, leaving Eliza's bedroom and closing the door quietly behind me. "Get on with it," I say to myself, taking the stairs, stopping when I hear something.

Sobs.

I frown and reverse my steps, pushing my way into Eliza's room. She looks up at me. No tears. "What did you forget?" she asks.

My mind. "I forgot to tell you how much I appreciate you." I smile, ignoring her surprise, and close the door behind me.

I know I should leave this minute, go before I do something stupid, but as is the way with Taya Winters, I am drawn to her. I creep down the hallway and the sobs become louder and louder. It truly pains me, to hear her cry. Truly.

I reach the door and lift a hand to knock, but my fist does not meet the wood, my mind yelling at me to leave now. Leave before I enter and get us both into trouble. Leave now before I increase the risk of our previous dalliances being discovered and Taya being ruined forever. Leave before I ruin...*everything*. I drop my hand and back away, sense finding me, but then the door swings open and she appears, and I am without the breath I need to speak. Without the sense I need to turn and run. But the ache in my chest? It lifts for the first time since I sent her away from my study.

Our gazes are stuck, our breathing is so very loud, as we both fight the pull. The temptation. The forbidden. "I don't care if you hurt me," she says suddenly. "It cannot hurt any more than this excruciating pain that I feel right now."

Oh no. Oh no, no, no, she must not say things like that. I swallow. "I thought you were leaving."

"Sampson has some business to deal with before we can go."

"Oh." God, the pull of her is getting stronger. Harder to fight. "I must go, Taya."

"Then go."

I wrestle with my mind and my body. Stare at her. Will my legs to walk away. I cannot. God help me, I cannot. "Oh, hell." I lunge forward and kiss her hungrily, blindly pushing the door closed behind me, and we stagger around her room, our kiss clumsy and chaotic, her whimpers loud. "Shhhh," I order, breaking our lips and placing a hand over her mouth. "Eliza is but a few yards away."

Taya reaches for my hand and pulls it down, her green eyes so full of life and energy. It is surely a sight to behold. One I will remember forever, for it is the moment I admit to myself that I am in love with her. My God, how did this happen?

"Taya, you must understand." As I must remind myself, too. "I made a promise to your brothers, you see. To Eliza, too, that I would abstain from—"

"Me?"

"I do believe your name was mentioned during the warning delivered, yes."

"I am but a conquest?"

"N—"

"Because, if so, Frank, I believe you have already conquered, which raises the question why you have me in your arms now."

"Do you honestly think your brothers would give me their blessing?"

"You only need Johnny's, for he is the eldest."

"Well, I must say, that fills me with hope."

She rolls her eyes in the most condescending of ways, and I cannot say I appreciate it. "It is a moot point, anyway, because I require no blessing, not from Johnny nor from Sampson."

"Moot? Me being murdered is a moot point?"

She laughs. "Oh Frank, they will not murder you. What are you, a coward?"

"No, but I can't very well look after you if I am dead."

Her lips are quickly on mine again, shutting me up, and I feel wholly unstable, as if my legs could give way. I suppose I should get used to it, if I am to lose them imminently anyway.

So, with our debate apparently finished, of which the conclusion is obviously we are both at peace with my impending loss of limbs, I succumb to the desire overcoming me and return Taya's kiss with equal hunger. Equal desperation. Equal passion. Lord above, she tastes like the finest of wines, one which I could gorge on for eternity. I am not prepared to settle for that one time. It's made me insatiable. It's teased me. It's intensified the desire and anticipation, because now I know what to expect. Now I know that I am about to burn with pleasure in the best possible way. I cannot resist her.

I coax her mouth open with my hard kiss, grabbing the material of her dress and pushing it from her shoulders until she's forced to release me so I can get it off. Get access to her body. I've lost my mind and I do not care for the repercussions in this moment, when she is kissing me as if I am life.

Lost.

"Damn it," I curse, ripping myself away. "This could ruin our business. Our families."

"There must be a way," she pants.

A way. Yes, there must be. I am incapable of thinking of a

way right now, but there must be a way. It would be a travesty if we could not be together. I take her mouth again, desperate, frustrated, and walk her back to the mattress, full of a new purpose, and it is an odd but quite lovely feeling. One that is unstoppable and pure. Flutters in my belly. Awe. To think that any other man might have this with her is quite…unthinkable. I dip and kiss her nipple, and she whimpers. I moan my approval. The air is sizzling as I scoop her up into my arms, laying her down gently. She doesn't take her eyes off me, and it is gratification incarnate, making all of my guilt and worries slip away, and I let it, unprepared to allow anything to stop me. Not my conscience, not my sister, not my work, and not her brothers. I will fight for her, for this, because my life without her feels somehow inconsequential.

I stand at the end of the bed and strip down under her watchful eyes, and I am surprisingly slow considering how desperate I am to be inside of her again. But her watching me so intently, so full of wonder, eases the burden of waiting. I go lax, enraptured by the sight of her, my eyes making a slow journey across her skin, soaking up every tiny piece of her. My mind is taking mental pictures of her and locking them away tightly, and I cannot bring myself to fathom why I am doing that.

"Are you ready for me again, my lady?" I mumble, looking down between her thighs. I start to shake a little, swallowing hard. My hand rests on the inside of her thigh and pushes them wide, encouraging her to open up to me. She's weeping. It's bloody glorious. I take her foot and lift it to my mouth, licking the instep.

"Frank!" she cries, her back snapping into an arch, her creamy, plump breasts jutting up, her arms shooting above her head, her eyes closing.

"Tell me where you feel it the most."

"Here." Her hand drifts down her belly to the patch of hair

framing her special place. My eyes root there, watching her fingers hover on the edge.

"Pleasure yourself, Taya," I order, reaching for my pulsing flesh and grasping it on a hiss.

"What?"

"Stroke yourself."

"Oh God."

"Do it."

"I can't!"

"Do it!"

She growls and sinks her fingers into her waiting pussy as I start to work myself, my knees shaking, struggling to hold myself upright. But I must, for the view is sublime, like nothing I have seen before. Her long, firm, glorious body stretched out before me, her wild blonde hair splaying over the sheets, her nipples like stones, her face the picture of pleasure. "Oh my God," she whispers, her voice alone drenched in desire, enough to make me spill my seed already.

My eyes are spoiled for choice, not knowing what before me to appreciate the most. There's too much. I settle on her fingers moving slowly between her legs, exhaling my wonder as I settle her foot on my shoulder, circling her slender ankle to hold it there. My forehead is wet, my body tight and strung, and my gaze drifts to my working hand too.

"Talk to me, my lady. Tell me what you want."

"You," she whispers, pulling my stare to her face. Her eyes are now open, and she is studying me with fascination as I work a few slow strokes across my flesh. A glimmer of my seed beads at the tip, and I lick my lips. "Watch." I whisper, circling my wet head across her flesh. She cries out, her body arching violently. "Watch, Taya."

I stare at her with building anticipation, moaning as I rub against her, spreading the wetness far and wide. "Frank!"

"Just watch," I affirm, and her eyes drop to between her

legs, seeing my erection held firmly in my grasp as I rub into her.

"Say it," I order.

"Say what?"

"Say it," I grate, blood rushing to the tip.

She bites her lip and bucks, her body starting to vibrate. "What would you have me say?" she asks, her voice strong but strained. I smile at her coyness.

"I would have you tell me that you love me."

"What?" she yelps. "That's rather cocksure, Frank Melrose."

I laugh on the inside, knock her hand out of the way, and swivel my hips, diving deeply inside of her, prompting the most satisfying yelp of shock. I watch as her hands grapple at the sheets and clench, desperate to hold on to something. "Cocksure enough, my lady?" I ask, retreating and plunging forward.

"My God." Her back bows, her skin glistening and wet.

My face strains with the unrelenting pleasure consuming me. "Well?" I know not why I feel the need to talk, but the words are coming and I cannot stop them. I want to hear her say it, because validation is everything if I am to do what needs to be done.

I release her leg from my shoulder and let my body drop to hers while keeping us connected, her internal muscles keeping a tight hold of me inside of her. I nuzzle her face, kissing my way across her cheek until I am at her mouth, indulging in the sweetness once again, just for a moment, her hips rolling with mine, creating the most exquisite pleasure. I slide my hands up her arms until our fingers are laced and I find the will to break our kiss, making her lift her head to try and maintain the connection. No. I must see her. I must look into her eyes when she peaks. And when she says the words I want to hear.

I breathe in her face, labored and needy, scanning every inch of her. Her green eyes are glimmering brightly, full of want and desperation. If I'm not looking into the eyes of a woman in love, I will give up now. "I want this to be slow."

She moans loudly, but her eyes never move from mine.

"Are you going to say it?" Lowering my mouth to her shoulder, I kiss it gently, sending a million bolts of pleasure stampeding into my groin.

Tormented whimpers come thick and fast, her core convulsing wildly, screaming for more. "Frank, I beg you."

I look up at her, finding her eyes are wild with want. "Tell me how badly you want me."

"Frank!"

"Tell me, Taya." I withdraw and wipe the slippery head of my cock from side to side across her sodden flesh tactically. She stifles a yell, beginning to lose her mind. "I need to hear how badly you want me. Tell me and you can have me."

"I want you!" she pants, sweat pouring from her brow. "Frank, I want you. More than anything I've ever wanted."

My jaw tightens as I level up and advance, entering her on a long puff of air. I choke, falling to my forearms, my eyes on hers. I'm shaking terribly.

"Are you all right?" she asks, bringing her hands to my shoulders and holding me.

I swallow, gathering myself. "I am all right." *Except for dying from pleasure.* I swivel and grind deeply, withdrawing and driving forward again. She sucks in air and holds it, as I find a meticulous pace.

Our bodies move like they know each other soul-deep, have mastered the art of each other, our eyes never moving. Her fingers dig into my shoulders, her cheeks balloon. Her hand slides onto my neck and pulls me down to her mouth, and I uphold my rhythm, circling my hips onto her, kissing her like there will be no more kisses. Fighting off the notion that there might not be—her brothers are an obstacle, as is society's expectations—is harder than I want to admit, because that would be facing our reality. I am not supposed to have her. She is a lady, born to marry a lord or duke. I'm taking something that I am not entitled to.

"God dammit," I growl, frustrated. My pace speeds up, dousing my tormented conscience with a pleasure like no other, and Taya moans. "There it is," I murmur, swallowing down her groans, sinking my teeth into her bottom lip, as the pleasure takes over.

"I can feel it," she breathes, as I seize the telltale pressure, locking it down. "Faster!"

"Bugger!" I pick up my pace and thrust in and out, our gentle lovemaking turning manic as we both search for release. I jack myself up on my arms to find more leverage, my face dripping, my heart about to burst out of my chest from the strain it is under. Her eyes are wide with wonder. I can feel myself expanding within her, and her muscles grip harder as a result. My head drops back, and I release a suppressed yell to the ceiling, stilling suddenly above her, as I jerk, convulse, choke, and explode. My vision fails me, along with my hearing, but I just detect her yelp followed by a low, strangled moan. My face twists as I retreat and slowly push forward, her legs lock around my waist, and she pulls me down, until our sweaty faces are touching, nose to nose. Our moans stretch out for an age until both of our bodies go lax and we're heaving against each other, trying to catch our breath. I feel totally overwhelmed, relieved that this was as intense as the first time we shared. Powerful, emotional, and mind-blanking. This isn't lust. This is so much more.

And terrifying.

She buries her nose into my neck and tightens her arms and legs around me, clinging on to me. It feels so very natural. My God, I am so in love. The feelings are new to me, as is this odd protection instinct I have developed. I should have resisted her, but my self-control vanishes at the sight of her.

"I love you, Frank," Taya whispers.

I smile, thrilled, and withdraw to find her eyes, but I am somewhat alarmed to see they are full of tears. Oh no. My happiness was short-lived, it would seem. "Taya, why do you cry?"

She swallows, her lip wobbling. "I am to leave at dawn once Sampson has seen to business."

The news is like a dagger to my heart, but I find myself nodding even though I am mentally swearing that I won't allow it.

I have not yet had the time to consider how I stop Sampson taking her away from London, away from *me*, but I will, you mark my words. If His Grace, the Duke of Chester, can have my sister, a female with no title, albeit beautiful and intelligent, then he would be a hypocrite to forbid mine and Taya's love, and I will happily point that out to him. *Again.* Except this time, he will listen.

"Johnny is right, Frank," she says quietly, pulling my eyes to her. *What?* If she thinks that, then why is she here? "It is reckless and unwise to pursue outlaws."

I exhale, smiling. She's worried about me. It's quite endearing. "I'm afraid I have little choice, my love."

"Why?"

"Well, you see, remember I told you about a business deal?"

"I do."

"I must discover the identity of the highwaywoman as it is part of a deal I have in motion with a rather unpleasant man called Fleming that will take *The London Times* national."

"Oh, I see," she says quietly. "That is very unfortunate."

"Indeed, for our business will be ruined without the deal." I reach over and drop a kiss on her sweet lips before I push myself up, peeling our bodies apart, and slowly lift my hips, slipping free of her on a hiss. I roll to my back beside her and stare at the ceiling, one arm splayed over my head, my other resting on my pumping stomach, my knee bent, my foot wedged into the mattress. How do I approach all of this? Business, Taya? How do I achieve what both Taya and I wish for without ruining everything or getting myself killed? First, I will talk to her brother. Reason with him. Beg him, if I have to. I drop my head to find her. We are in love. He has to listen to me. I reach over and kiss her lips chastely and stand, dressing, full of fortitude. "I must go; I have work to do." A very tough job indeed, and I have limited time in which to do it. Time is of the essence. "You will deny any suggestion that we may have been intimate." If I am to stand any chance of winning her, I must act with honor and integrity. Or, at least, appear to.

I pull on my boots and make haste to the door. "Goodbye," I call back, hurrying to Eliza's room and bursting in unannounced. She looks me up and down on an extremely heavy brow. "You're still here?"

"Where will I find your husband?"

"What have you done, Frank?"

"Answer me, Eliza," I hiss, feeling the pressure. It could take me all night to track him down. I imagine it'll take me even longer to convince him that my intentions are honorable.

"He was to have drinks at Gladstone's." She looks at the carriage clock on the mantelpiece. "But he was due to meet the owner of the printer manufacturer to celebrate their official partnership at seven o'clock."

I, too, glance at the clock. Fifteen minutes past six o'clock. "Bugger it all to hell," I mutter, closing the door and hurrying through the house. I break out onto the square and jog to the main road, searching for a hackney carriage. Typical in an emergency, there is not one to be seen, and it will take Kip far too long to saddle up Figaro, so I continue my jog toward Gladstone's, people jumping from my charging path on yelps and gasps as I go.

Chapter 23

I am not a born athlete, I can be sure of that, despite having the frame of one. I cut through the royal park, seeing Mama walking with her friends and Lady Wisteria, and they stop as I race past, watching with alarm as I go. "Frank?" Mama calls, her voice caught up in the breeze whooshing past my ears.

"Can't stop, Mama," I yell back, starting to get quite out of breath. By the time I reach the edge of the royal park, I am disturbingly weary, and I am forced to take a breather, my hands braced on my knees to hold me up.

"In a rush?"

I look up and find Esther Hamsley sitting sidesaddle on a chestnut-colored horse. She appears quite smiley, looks prettier than I am used to, and she is definitely carrying an air of confidence that I have never seen on her before. "Indeed I am," I pant, trying to straighten.

"I must thank you, Mr. Melrose," she says, appearing to ignore my answer or exhausted form.

"Whatever for?"

"For dancing with me."

"Oh?" I answer quietly. Pray do tell me I have not won myself her affections and have to break the news that my heart belongs to another.

"Yes. Your interest certainly prompted the attention of many gentlemen."

"Oh…"

She grins, and it's impish. "Father has had three men call for me in the past two days!" She slips down from her horse.

Her declaration has me glancing around, looking for who may be chaperoning her. I spy her mother by a tree chatting with a few other ladies. "That's truly wonderful, really, it is, but I—"

"They are all very handsome, you know."

"I expect they a—"

"And wealthy too!"

"That's—"

"You know this is my fifth season, don't you, Mr. Melrose?"

My shoulders drop, and I simply cannot bring myself to rain on her parade. "I do know that, Miss Hamsley, and I know not why, for you are a very attractive female that many men should be queuing around Belmore Square to court."

She giggles, blushing profusely. "You aren't half as bad as they say, you know."

Who are they, and what are they saying? Need I ask? Probably not. Besides, I do not have time. "I'm very happy for you."

"Why thank you. I am very happy for myself too. You must let me repay you."

Ah. Now we are talking. "I have just the way in which you can do that."

"You do?"

"May I borrow your horse?"

"What?"

"I have an emergency, you see. I shall, of course, return it, fed, watered, and groomed."

"Oh, well." She looks between me and her mare. "I suppose—"

"Thank you." I grab the reins, place my foot in the stirrup, and haul myself up. "Good day to you, Miss Hamsley," I say, cracking the reins and breaking out in a canter, charging toward Gladstone's.

"Good luck!" she yells after me.

"I'm going to need it," I say, standing in the saddle, jerking the reins, quite sure this poor horse has not been working so hard and is used only to trotting around town with Esther Hamsley sitting sidesaddle.

By the time I make it to Gladstone's, it is fifteen minutes to seven o'clock. I leave the horse with a boy, slipping him a few shillings to ensure it is looked after while I'm gone and given plenty of water.

As I approach the entrance, I rake a hand through my hair and straighten out my jacket, as if my appearance might sway the Duke's mood or decision when I confess my love for Taya. I enter and spot him in the corner with Sampson, just the two of them sitting at a table, leaning in, whispering. Business. And what "business" might that be? It is a stupid question, I know it. Taya is the business. They are plotting what is to be done with her once they have forced her away from London, away from *me*. I blow out my cheeks, my task appearing more mammoth by the second. I need a drink. Perhaps a few. Yes, a little Dutch courage before I face the grizzly Winters bears. I find a table in the corner, out of sight of the brothers, but where I can simply crane my head to see them while I drink some courage. I order a gin and it is soon before me. It is also soon gone. "Another," I say, peeking around the corner, mentally planning my speech. Another gin arrives and another is sunk. "One more," I say, reaching for some coins. Another gin is poured, and I drink it in one fell swoop again. Enough, or I will be slurring my pleas for some blessings and mercy, and slow in ducking should either of them swing at me.

So I stand, taking one last long encouraging breath, but when I step around the corner, they are gone. "What?" I search the room, seeing no sign of the Duke or Sampson. "Damn it!" I curse, hurrying to the door and bursting out onto the street. I search, up and down the street, the daylight fading rapidly. They are nowhere to be seen. I circle on the spot, my head in my hands, damning myself to hell for wasting time trying to build that courage. Eliza did not say where he was meeting the owner of the printing machine manufacturer, so I know not where to even begin my search. "Evening," a female voice says, a voice I recognize.

I scowl at the night-time air before me, contemplating ignoring her and walking on, but, God dammit, she is a lady and she is out alone. I may not like her, but my conscience, regrettably, would not allow me to sleep at night should anything happen to her.

I face Lizzy Fallow. "Lady Millingdale, what are you doing out alone at this hour?"

"Have no fear, Frank; I slipped out undetected. The advantages, I suppose, of having an elderly husband." She saunters over, and I step back, wary. "Oh come on," she coos. "Don't you miss our intimacies?"

"No, I absolutely do not."

She keeps coming at me, and I keep moving back.

"Liz—"

She throws herself at me and kisses me like a desperate woman, and I am completely taken aback. Caught off guard. Just standing there in a state of stunned silence while she shoves her tongue down my throat. What in God's name is she doing? I raise my hands to push her away, but the sound of a horse neighing fills the street, and she dives away of her own accord, looking around, flustered, while I blink rapidly, at a loss for words. Then she runs off, disappearing into the darkness. She is mad. And that kiss? I roughly wipe at my mouth, feeling tarnished. I felt nothing. No warmth, no tingles, no energy, no passion. Nothing.

Which makes me all the more certain I am taking the right course of action. I must find the Duke. Make my pleas. Ask for his blessing and mercy. Convince him not to revoke the machinery that helps us run our business. I cross the road toward where I left Esther Hamsley's mare, but I am just shy of the street, passing an alleyway, when I hear familiar voices. I freeze and listen. The Duke. And…I frown. "Fleming?" I whisper to myself, daring a peek around the bricks to confirm it. I am right. There, halfway down the alleyway, by the back entrance to Kentstone's, are Winters and Fleming. I was not privy to their acquaintance.

"Go to hell," Fleming spits, marching off.

All right, so they are not friendly. Very hostile, in fact, if the Duke's heaving form is a measure. He looks toward me, and I shoot back around the corner. What in God's name is going on? I know not, but I have a very unnerving feeling in my stomach.

I hear the sound of his boots hitting the cobbles, and on instinct and instinct alone, for I must establish why Fleming has ordered the Duke to hell, I jog across the road and dip down another alley, concealing myself in the shadows. Winters emerges from the alley, and I watch as he peers left and right a few times, and then he stalks off, anger pouring from him in droves.

My mind a fog of questions, I turn and start pacing to think.

And come nose-to-nose with a white horse. I inhale, freeze. My eyes travel up the head, the body, until I am staring at the rider's scarf pulled high up, their hat sitting low, casting a shadow across their face, making their eyes impossible to see, even with the benefit of moonlight. The horse pads, and I exhale as a gloved hand is extended toward me. Without thought or hesitation, I reach for my coin purse and hold it out slowly, extending the time the rider must wait.

"I am but a poor nobody," I say, searching, hoping, praying for a glimpse of her face, anything to tell me who she is.

She doesn't speak, just takes the velvet pouch and tosses it aside.

There's a few moments' silence, and though I cannot see her eyes, I feel the burn of them. An accusing burn. Then she kicks her horse, and it rises up on its back legs, forcing me to stagger back and fall to the ground. My backside hits the cobbles hard, and I wince, but I make fast work of collecting myself, getting back to my feet.

She cracks the reins again, but the alleyway is narrow, and the horse struggles to turn, so she resorts to coming at me. Straight at me. I am standing in the middle of her path, and I will not move. I won't! What is this madness? "Come on, come on," I chant to myself, wondering if I have lost my mind. Definitely.

I remain steadfast, and when the horse is within reach, I turn with it as it passes and grab the reins, bracing myself to be hauled along and perhaps dragged to my death. "Flaming hell!" I roar, my shoulder jarring violently, being pulled right back out of the socket.

But still, I do not let go, and my tenacity (and pain) pays off. The horse yells, bucks, and tosses the rider from its back, and she hits the ground with a harsh crack and a high-pitched yelp.

I release the horse, crashing to the ground beside her, but before I can instruct my good arm to reach for her and capture her in my arms, she's up and running away, the horse bolting in the opposite direction. "No!" I bellow, jumping up. I look down at my lifeless arm, grit my teeth, take hold of a nearby meat hook, and yank against it, coughing when it pops back into place. "Fuck!" I choke, heaving, about ready to throw up. But...I look up and see her getting farther away. "Oh no," I say, running after her as fast as my agonizing shoulder will allow, which isn't fast enough. But she has a limp, hampering her, too, and I start to gain on her. She looks back. Starts to grab the rubbish that has been discarded in the alleyway, throwing back boxes and fruit crates, anything she can lay her hands on to slow me. Too bad for her, this is as close as I have gotten, and will probably ever get, to ending this mystery. I must confirm my suspicions! I am within reach, and I swoop out my arm, grabbing her brown jacket, and tackle her to the ground. I take no pleasure in the sound of another pained yelp from her.

I wrestle with her, and boy, does she put up a fight, thrashing her arms and legs, her hat getting lost in the fight, her dark hair coming loose, flying everywhere. Our exhausted breaths drench the air, her grunts, my grunts, her hisses, my hisses. Neither of us are prepared to give up, but I am stronger, far stronger, and I eventually get her onto her back and straddle her waist, pinning her arms down above her head.

"My God, woman," I pant, my damn shoulder screaming, a few cuts and scrapes stinging too. Aware she has lost, she accepts and settles, at my mercy, her chest swelling violently as she fights to catch her breath with me. I stare down at her long dark hair, as I transfer her wrists into my one good hold. I reach for a lock, twirling it between my fingers. Coarse. So coarse. And I frown as a familiar scent invades my nose.

My eyes dart to hers, now that I can see them.

Long lashes.

Green eyes.

I exhale sharply and yank her scarf down. "My God," I breathe, scrambling back, shock overcoming me. "Taya?" What the hell? Am I dreaming? Having a nightmare? I blink rapidly, perhaps hoping the vision before me might morph into someone else, but when I open my eyes again, I am still staring at the woman I love.

She stands, reaching up to her head, and pulls the dark wig of horse hair off, revealing her mane of beautiful, wild blonde hair.

"I…what…can…" I shake my head and get to my feet, my mind completely tangled.

"Hello, Frank."

My mind is full of plenty of words and questions, but I cannot seem to string them together and get them out of my mouth. "You?" This doesn't make any sense. None at all. Why would she, a lady, the daughter of a duke, wreak havoc on the ton? Why would she rob her own people? Risk certain death if her identity is discovered?

"Yes," she says, simply, flicking her hair out of her face, wincing and feeling at her neck, massaging her nape. "Me."

My mouth falls open, and one of my million questions, when my brain chooses to enlighten me on them, is answered. "My God, you used me," I say, a hurt like I have never experienced before overcoming me. She made me fall in love with her to protect herself, so that I may never be able to reveal who she is.

"I suppose I did." She breathes in deeply, nibbling her bottom lip.

Johnny is right. It is reckless to pursue outlaws.

My heart feels like it splits straight down the middle. "I cannot believe I have been so stupid."

"You must understand, Frank, that—"

I raise a hand to silence her, unable to find any words. My pain multiplies. I came here to plead to her emotionless brother for his blessing, and the whole time she was using me? She told me she loved me. My God, does she have a heart? Anger rises, and if I don't walk away now, I might regret my words. But my mouth doesn't appear to get the message. "I cannot bear so much as to look at you." I point a finger at her, outraged, and feeling so very foolish. My God, I bet she wasn't even a virgin. I have been completely hoodwinked. "You are, without a doubt, the worst kind of harlot, and I have had plenty of those in my time, I assure you."

Her face drops. It's an insult, to be honest.

I look at her with all the contempt I feel, my hurt getting the better of me. I absolutely do not hate her, but I am at a loss. Feeling robbed and cheated. For the first time in my adult life, I have opened my heart, and now I am ruined forever, for I will never be so gullible and open ever again. Ever! I turn and march away, yelling at myself for the small sense of guilt I feel when I catch a glimpse of her pained expression.

No.

I am done. Finished.

Chapter 24

I stared at the ceiling all night. I tried not to relive every moment I had with Taya, assessing it carefully, searching for signs that I missed along the way that she was playing me. I can't find any, but I know they must be there. I was just too distracted by desire, and now I am too exhausted to devote the time and attention needed to dig deep enough to find them. I want to never think about her again, and after this sleepless night, I will not.

I pick my way through breakfast the next morning, smiling sporadically when I sense Mama looking at me. I need to pull myself together before they sense my despondency and ask whatever the matter is with me. I could never explain, and, in truth, I never want anyone to ever know that I have been so pathetic. Fooled.

"What is the matter, brother?" Clara says on a whisper from beside me.

"It is nothing you must worry your pretty little head with," I say, patting her hand where it is on the table. "Grown-up problems."

She rolls her eyes, snatching her hand away, insulted. "You forget, brother, I have experienced heartbreak, so I am privy to the signs. Why does everyone around here insist on treating me like a foolish halfwit?"

I recoil. "I'd rather like to think I am treating you like an innocent, because that is what you are."

She snorts. "I assure—"

"Do not say it," I order harshly, fearful of what she might share. "Whatever it is you were to say, do not say it, for I cannot promise I will not hunt that lying little idiot down and end him."

She grins. "I love how protective you are."

"It's my job."

"That's very sweet."

"You're welcome."

"I would go and see Eliza, if I were you."

"Why?"

"Because she, like me, is not stupid." She comes closer. "Everyone knows you are in love with Taya Winters."

What? *Oh no. No, no, no.* "I can assure you, Clara, I am not in love with Taya Winters."

"Oh, do be quiet, Frank," Mama chimes in, making my eyes turn quickly onto her.

"I do not love anyone."

"If you say so," she sings.

My mother's easy chirpiness confuses me. "Why are you so smiley?" I ask. "You were about to burst a blood vessel just the other morning when…" I peek at Clara out the corner of my eye. Her eyebrows are high. "When…" Bugger it all, when what?

"When she found Taya Winters in your bed?" Clara says, casual and smug.

My jaw plummets to the table. How the hell does she know? She had run away!

Clara shrugs and pops a piece of bread in her mouth. "I heard Mama discussing the matter with Eliza."

I point my incredulous glare to Mama. She too shrugs, nonchalant. "I was shocked, be sure of that, Francis. Now I can see rather clearly that you are in love with her. Why else would you mope around like this?"

"See," Clara says. "Everyone knows."

I stand. "Please excuse me." I am not hanging around here to be scrutinized. I am not in love with her. How can any man love such a deceitful, disingenuous woman? God, I sure do have a habit of picking them. But not anymore. I shall be focusing on business for the foreseeable future.

But, of course, now especially, it isn't that simple, for my plans and potential deal with Fleming have been squashed in light of who the highwaywoman actually is. I groan, annoyed I still feel hurt for being played. I cannot see Eliza, for I refuse to step foot in the Winters residence.

God, I'm such an idiot. Has Taya left the country yet? Is Johnny home?

Can I see him and trust myself not to bark my demand to know what he was discussing with Fleming that caused such a hostile farewell?

So many questions...

I need to walk. Walk off this distress, so I leave the house and pace toward the main road, but when I stop to cross, I see a familiar carriage rumbling past, Sampson riding his horse alongside it, and I lose my breath, seeing her in the window. She does not look at me, her attention pointed forward defiantly. It is undoubtedly a good thing. My heart pounds. It annoys me.

Liar.

Cheat.

But you still love her, Frank.

I pick up my feet and walk to the royal park to hopefully clear my head of all these irritating thoughts so that I may clear my mind and concentrate on solving my business problem.

Alas, by noon, I have walked the park in circles and still not found a resolution. God damn it, I'm buggered.

"Frank!" Clara comes running down the path toward me, alone, and I look beyond her for who may be chaperoning her. "Yes, I am alone, but it is an emergency."

My heart starts to gallop, and all the possible dreaded scenarios run circles through my head. Mama? Papa? Eliza, is she all right? The baby? "What is it, Clara? You must tell me at once."

She slows to a stop before me, huffing and puffing. "Eliza has sent for you."

"Why?"

"I know not, except that she said I must find you at once." She takes my arm and starts hauling me out of the royal park. "Come, I have been promised five shillings to deliver you."

"I am not a telegram, Clara."

"No, you are an idiot."

"Hey!" But I let her drag me, all the way to Eliza's house, where I am escorted to the drawing room, a most lavish space with velvet draperies and sumptuous chairs. I find my sister in her housecoat pacing in front of the fireplace.

"You are up," I say, pleased to see her on her feet.

She whirls around. "You must cease with your mission to uncover the identity of the highwaywoman," she blurts, knocking me back quite a few paces. "Immediately."

Oh. Why would she ask me that unless she knew who the highwaywoman really is? The fact of the matter is, she wouldn't. She knows. But how? I ponder that for a moment, and something slowly clicks into place. Eliza knew of my business deal with Fleming. She must have told the Duke, and he must have decided to go to Fleming and request he terminate his mission to discover the identity to protect Taya. Or, perhaps, and more likely, as to ask Fleming to cease in his mission may rouse suspicion, I expect the Duke instead requested he not enter into business with me at all. My God. Johnny and Sampson know Taya is the highwaywoman! They weren't sending her away because of me. They were sending her away because she is a danger unto herself! And are they still enforcing that?

But I highly doubt Johnny would tell Eliza, not to protect Taya, but to protect his wife from distress when she is so very weak.

God, my head aches.

How should one play this game? "Why must I stop?" I ask, pacing over to Eliza and helping her to a chair before she drops. "I have a story to finish, a name to reveal to the ton."

She looks up at me, nibbling her lip, obviously stuck for how to explain herself. I won't play the game with her anymore. Besides, I need to know how she knows if I am to fathom how I deal with this godawful mess.

I take a chair next to her and hold her hand. "I know, Eliza."

"Know what?"

"I know that Taya in the highwaywoman."

She bursts out laughing, holding her stomach, falling back in her chair, and what do I do? I sit back too, a tired look on my face, waiting for her to shut her mouth and stop treating me like I am the stupidest of idiots. She catches my affronted expression, stops laughing abruptly, and sags. "Fine, I cannot lie to you, brother."

"How do you know, Eliza?"

"How do *you* know?" she asks.

"I asked first."

"She came home yesterday evening in quite a frightful state. Cuts and bruises everywhere, crying!" she says, and I inwardly flinch. Crying? Obviously with pain from her injuries rather than, like me, pain of the damn heart. Because she can't possibly have a heart. "She claimed to have taken a fall from her horse, which, of course, was perfectly reasonable since, like me, Taya is quite the breaker of rules and doesn't ride sidesaddle at a snail's pace, but instead canters everywhere she goes. Anyway..." She waves a hand flippantly. "I helped clean her up with Lady Wisteria, and then got her comfortable in her bed. I was suspicious—there were a few funny looks being passed around the Winterses—but it was not my place to ask, and I highly doubted my enquiries would be met with honesty, so I chose to play stupid."

"You have plenty of practice."

She smiles and it is wholly sarcastic. "I learned from the best, of course." I roll my eyes and gesture for her to continue. "Yes, so," she goes on. "I went back to my room and heard Johnny and Sampson enter, so I got a glass and pushed it up against the wall to hear."

"You're dreadful."

"Shoot me," she quips. "I overheard Johnny and Sampson chastising her. My God, they were angry. And when they told her she can no longer ride with the highwaymen, can you imagine my face?"

I realize that is a rhetorical question but I nod, nonetheless.

"They told her they were sending her away, but she told them not to bother as she was leaving London, anyway, that she no longer wanted to be here."

So she's leaving voluntarily? Good. "Well, why would she want to be here?" I ask on a laugh. "With the risk of being hanged?"

"Hanged?" Eliza says, frowning. "Why, are you going to reveal her?" She rolls her eyes. I'm getting an awful lot of that today, far more than I should like. "Oh, please, Frank."

She is, of course, right, but I do not tell her so. I am angry, but I do not wish death upon Taya. I cannot reveal her identity to Fleming, of course I can't, and I also cannot ruin both of our families, for if Taya's identity were to be discovered, it would certainly end both the Melroses *and* the Winterses. What a mess this is. The deal with Fleming is in the dirt. I have a machine the business cannot afford to keep, and now I cannot finish my story if I want to have any chance of saving our family and my sister's, so sales will rapidly drop. I must face facts. I have failed, and I have let Papa and my family down. "I should reveal her," I mutter, if only for the state of my heart. Whyever would she ride with the highwaymen?

"Oh, Frank, how you frustrate me." Eliza smacks my bicep. "You love her, you fool!"

Why does everyone keep saying that? "I absolutely do not love her." My heart kicks, as if protesting my words. "I assure you." I wince when it squeezes again. "She is a criminal, Eliza, and she tricked me into fall…" My fingertips meet my forehead and try to rub away the pain that's growing there, too. Everywhere hurts, damn her!

"Tricked you into…?"

"I dislike Taya Winters more than I could ever explain."

"Oh, for God's sake. You're being a stubborn, proud coward."

"Take that back, Eliza Melrose."

"My name is Lady Eliza Winters, Duchess of Chester, and you will address me as such."

"Bugger off," I say over a laugh, making her stand again, outraged. "You are Eliza Melrose, always will be, so don't start brandishing your new title as if you are better than I."

She marches across the room to me, seeming to have found some energy. "I am better than you, Francis Melrose, who has no title, because I was not too pig-headed to admit that I had fallen in love." Her hands push into my chest and she shoves me out the door. "Do not come back until you've stopped being pathetic." The door slams in my face, and I blink a few times, stunned. I'm sure I have heard that women who are with child can be rather challenging, and it seems the rumors are true.

"Well, that was rather uncalled for," I say to the wood.

"What was?"

I look down the corridor and find Johnny. "Nothing." I am *not* telling him. "I think Her Grace is feeling a little brighter today." I make my way to the front door, eager to escape before I am interrogated again.

"You will do the right thing, Frank."

I stop, and it becomes so very obvious to me that Taya has shared the news of my recent enlightenment with her brother. Marvelous. Will he kill me to silence me? "What is that supposed to mean?" I ask, facing him.

"It means what I say."

"Tell me," I say. "Why did you not come straight to me and warn me off my mission to discover her identity rather than telling Fleming not to do business with me?"

"Because, like your tenacious sister, when you get your claws into a story, nothing can make you let go."

That is very true, but… "So you must have known, even if Fleming had withdrawn from our deal, I would not have given up."

"Of course. That is why I have sent her away. To protect her from the consequences of being exposed." He turns his back on me and walks away.

He thinks I would do that? "Your Grace," I call, and he stops at the drawing room, his hand on the doorknob. "You didn't send her away to keep her away from me."

"She would be more ruined by herself than any man could ruin her." He looks back, his face grave. "But, I will affirm, I would *never* have allowed it."

"You would never need to allow it, Your Grace. There was nothing to allow." Because she used me.

"Indeed," he mutters, entering the drawing room, and I immediately hear Eliza vent her annoyance at him, demanding answers, or so help her God.

"Be calm, my glorious Duchess, for you will cause yourself and the baby undue distress," he appeases her, sounding calmer than he ought to be.

She would be more ruined by herself than any man could ruin her.

The questions running amok in my mind multiply. As does the ache in my chest.

She's gone.

"Mr. Melrose?"

I turn and find Wisteria Winters on the bottom step of the staircase. "My lady," I say bowing my head, bracing myself for yet another altercation with another Winters.

She approaches, a wooden box in her hand, and holds it out to me. "You must have this," she says, peeking over her shoulder to the drawing room.

"What is it?"

She doesn't answer, but places it in my hand and leaves, floating away silently.

I look down at the box, scared, and slowly lift the lid. I see a brown scarf and snap it closed, wondering if this is some kind of cruel joke?

A memento? What am I to do with this box? This pain? The unanswered questions? I am not equipped to deal with any of this.

I need a drink. Or twenty.

Chapter 25

I sit up, feeling groggy after another heavy night of blue ruin trying to drown out certain memories. I scrub my hands down my face, feeling the emptiness within me more than ever. Days have passed. Papa is back seeing to business in my absence, and I am back to wasting my time in drink. But not women. No. I don't think I will ever touch a woman again.

I blow out my cheeks, wanting to crawl back under the covers and hide. My eyes fall to the chair in the corner where I placed Taya's box. I had planned on tossing it in the river. I couldn't. I get up and collect it, opening the lid again for the first time since Wisteria Winters gave it to me, my nostrils being invaded by the scent of honeysuckle.

I sit on the end of my bed and pull out the scarf, revealing a collection of coin purses underneath. Goodness, she kept them? And beneath the coin purses, a piece of paper. I unroll it and find a drawing. A drawing of a man holding a white horse by its reins, leading it and its rider, a female to be sure, toward a sunset. Me. Taya.

Freedom?

Freedom from grief. From hate. "What?" I whisper, turning the paper over to find some words. Each one breaks my heart more. Her anguish. Her grief. Her anger. It is all on this page, how she abhors all members of the ton. It may have been Lymington who murdered her father, but it was the rest of the ton who ran them out of town with judgments and cruelty. Every purse she stole and every ounce of terror she instilled in her victims was a little bit of payback. A little more peace for Taya.

I have no doubt, her mother has given me this box to try and make me understand. But why? And do I?

I can't be sure. But I do know one thing…

I swallow, closing my eyes, seeing her hurt expression as I poured my hateful words all over her. Words I truly didn't mean. I was acting out. Being defensive. Trying to curb my own pain by increasing hers.

True love, I know, is rare, for we live in a time when feelings of the heart come second to status and power. My experience of true love was a rare and precious thing, and I did not handle it with the delicacy it deserved, so it serves me right that Taya got up and walked out of town, taking my one and only chance of true love with her. I've let her down. I should have been helping her, not abandoning her.

"You are an idiot, Frank Melrose," I say, falling to my back on the bed. If I had just stopped for a moment and thought carefully instead of bellyaching over my ego being dented, perhaps I could have saved us both some hurt. I must fix this. But how? I wince. Being blind drunk certainly isn't helping. I'm still in agony. Still broken. And what of Fleming? He's called upon the house numerous times looking for me. Will he ever relent and give up on his mission to discover the identity of the highwaywoman? A very nasty pain in my chest develops at the thought. She would be hanged. I lose my breath. If she is ever discovered, ever found, she would be hanged.

Mama bursts into my room, her face taking on quite the damning scowl when she finds me looking, I expect, somewhat horrendous. "God help me, Frank Melrose, I did not raise my children to be pathetic."

"I know, Mama," I admit, feeling so, so foolish and guilty. "Sending her away wasn't the right thing to do."

She softens before my eyes. "And whom are you talking about, son?"

She knows, but she would like to hear the word. "Taya, Mama. I am talking about Taya. They should be protecting her, not banishing her."

"And why, may I ask, is that?"

"Because I love her," I say, startling myself. The words come without much thought, and Mama's expression takes on an edge of sadness.

"Then why, Frank, did you kiss Lizzy Fallow?" She shakes her head in disappointment and leaves, closing the door softly behind her.

"What?" I breathe, confused. "Kiss Li…" I inhale, memories of that night coming back to me, when Lizzy Fallow jumped on me. "Oh no. Oh, no, no, no." My head falls into my hands. "God dammit!" I yell, mortified. What have I done? If I could only understand why Taya was there that night. If I could only explain why I was there. I quickly dress and go downstairs. I enter the study, finding Papa at the desk, a quill in his hand. He looks up and smiles. "Son."

"Papa," I say, closing the door. "Might I have a word?"

He rests his quill down and sits back, getting comfortable. "What is it, Frank? I am very busy."

I scan his desk, where papers are strewn everywhere. "Yesterday's sales?"

"Eight thousand."

I wince.

"The Earl of Pembrokeshire has moved in across the square. Did you know that, Frank?"

"I knew that."

"He's biting at our heels, badgering the Duke for a printing machine." The distress on his face ages him ten years, and it is entirely my fault. Where does my stupidity end? "And what of his curricle? He claims you stole it."

Technically, yes. But Clara crashed it. "I did not realize it was his curricle."

"What has gotten into you, Frank? I was full of hope and then…what? What happened?"

Love. I sigh, rubbing at my forehead. I may not be able to have my love, but I can protect her. I can at least do that, and then perhaps she won't hate me, for she hates too many people and it must be draining. I could live with myself then, at least.

"Frank?" Papa says, and I look up at him. He recoils. "Are you all right? You look incredibly pale all of a sudden. Should I call a doctor?"

"A doctor cannot cure me, Papa." I say, my mind whirling so fast, information landing in it too quickly for me to piece everything together.

"What on earth are you talking about?"

"I am in love, Papa," I blurt, unable to control my mouth as well as my thoughts, it seems. "I am madly in love, and I have made a thorough mess of it."

"In love? Who are you…" He sits back in his chair. "Oh no."

"Oh yes," I say.

"Oh no, no…wait. Does your mother know about this?"

"I am afraid I cannot lie to you Papa. Yes, she does know, but I did not tell her, be sure of that, because, quite troublingly, I did not realize myself." I stand abruptly, my head still spinning. "I cannot save my heart, Papa, but I can save our business and hopefully the life of the woman I love." I motion to the quill in Papa's hand. "May I?"

He looks down, as if he's forgotten what he is holding, thinking, as if wondering if he should give it to me. "The life of the woman you love?"

"You should speak to Mama."

"Do you know what you are doing?"

"No."

Papa laughs, shaking his head. "Not many men who are in

love do, Frank." He passes the quill across the desk to me. "I trust you."

It's as if he knows that I need to hear those very words at this very moment. I dunk the quill in the inkwell, pull a piece of paper toward me, and start writing the story that will save my business, my family, Taya, and, I pray, my heart.

I wake for the first time in too long with a fresh head and clear mind. I send word to Kip to saddle my horse, wash and dress in my finest threads, and pull on my gloves that Dalton hands me. "Where are you going?" Mama asks.

"I am going to fix what I have broken," I say, leaving the house, determined. Hopeful.

Praying I don't bugger this up too.

First, I visit Eliza when I know her husband to be out for his morning ride, and, after she hears me out, she is more than helpful and very supportive of my plan. When I arrive at the stables, Figaro is ready and waiting for me. I take a leisurely trot to Kentstone's to reassure Fleming I will return with the news he is waiting for. Once again, I have to talk myself down from blackening his daylights when I see a fresh collection of bruises on Ruby's arms, but now, more than ever, I need Fleming, so I must battle with my morals for a little while longer.

I return to Figaro outside Kentstone's, take the bag from the saddlebag, and place it behind a nearby fruit crate before getting on my way to the palace for an audience with the party Prince. The party Prince whose dibs are not in tune. Totally broke and yet living quite the champagne lifestyle.

I am greeted by a footman who kindly takes Figaro to be fed and watered, and I straighten myself out. I must admit, I am feeling slightly uneasy, for I can only imagine how my proposal will be met. I am led into the palace, and I make a point of admiring it, something I have neglected to do on the many times I have been here as a partygoer, for I am quite sure I will not be invited back again.

"I present Mr. Melrose," the butler says, opening the way for me. I enter and find the Prince sprawled in a chair being fed grapes by an attractive woman drenched in pearls and stroking the Prince's head intermittently. It is not his queen, which comes as no surprise, since, apparently, they do not get along. Perhaps because they are as eccentric as each other.

I bow. "Your Majesty."

"Ah, Melrose." The Prince waves the woman off and stands, his soft, round body today encased in enough fur to keep London warm in the most brutal of winters. "Heston, get the man a drink."

"I am all right," I say, taking my hands behind my back. I am not here to socialize, after all. Some might consider me mad to decline, but I am here in a business capacity, and I wish to set the tone. Now, more than ever, with my highwaywoman story hanging in the balance, I need every piece of outrageous news I can get, and since our current serving monarch is as outrageous as they come, that, unfortunately for him, means he's at my mercy.

"I see," he muses, one eyebrow hitched, his painted face thoughtful as he considers me while blindly accepting the wine being offered. He takes a sip and waves a hand for the female to continue feeding him grapes.

"I see your queen is unavailable to serve you," I muse, giving the female a moment of my eyes.

Another wave sends her on her way, along with Heston, leaving the Prince and me alone to discuss business, which he has, wisely, decided he might not like anyone to hear.

"I hear you have been dealing with the scandal of your sister marrying the murdering Duke of Chester."

"As I understand it, it was, in fact, your friend Lymington who was responsible for the crimes you speak of." The Prince should find better friends. Lymington a murderer, Brummell a terrible gambler. Then again, the Prince is a terrible glutton with no regard for his people's money and what it is spent on, so I suppose they, in all of their immorality, should get along. "I also understand that it was proven beyond all doubt that Lymington murdered the Duke of Chester, so it raises the question why you would pardon him. Perhaps he paid you." That I know not to be true. "Or perhaps you owed him money and he wrote off your debt in return for your pardon." That I know is a definite possibility.

He hums, pushing his overweight body out of the chair and starting to walk and sip his wine. "You have a very vivid imagination, Melrose."

"Oh, yes, Your Majesty, I do. Be assured of that fact."

"Sit."

"Thank you, Your Majesty, but I am quite comfortable here." I remain where I am, by the door, for I expect I will be leaving very shortly, anyway, and should not waste time and energy accepting his invite to take the weight off my feet.

"Then might we get to the point so I can get on with my day?"

"Of course, Your Majesty." I reach into my pocket and pull out a piece of paper, setting it on a nearby table. He frowns and approaches, and his frown soon turns into a scowl as he picks it up and reads the article detailing his supposed debts. On a yell, he tosses it in the fire.

I smile. "There are tens of thousands more copies."

"I demand you to cease with the release of such a damning story."

"Why?"

"Because it is full of falsehoods!"

"I do believe your close friend Brummell is in quite some debt. I have sources to prove it."

"Who?"

"I'm afraid a gentleman never divulges such information, Your Majesty."

"And what of this nonsense you speak of?" He waves at the raging fire. "That I too, am in debt?"

"You're not? Oh, well, that can quite easily be cleared up by an audit of the Privy Purse and a chat with the keeper."

He snorts, his cheeks reddening with a building rage. "There will be no audit."

"All right." I shrug, backing away on a bow. "A pleasure, Your Majesty."

"I forbid you to print lies about me, Melrose!"

"I do not print lies, Your Majesty, only truths."

"Have it your way." He waves his glass of wine, and it splashes all over the oriental rug. "Seize him!"

The doors fly open immediately, and I am circled by eight footmen. "Oh, well, this is getting rather ugly, isn't it?" I muse, craning my head to get the Prince in my sights. He looks smug. *Idiot.* "I am afraid, Your Majesty, that the story has been passed and approved, and with word of my incarceration, it will be distributed far and wide. Did you know we have partnered with Fleming?" I smile brightly as his face drops. "A very lucrative deal indeed, it is." I am uncomfortable at how well I am lying. Perhaps it is because my life, quite literally, is depending on it. Or is it because my love's life does? Stupid question.

The guards back off with a wave of his hand. "What do you want, Melrose?"

"It is our duty as a media outlet to report on all manner of news to the people. I realize, Your Majesty, that censorship is the foundation on which your relationship with the media is built, smoke and mirrors, if you will, but..."

"But...?" he prompts, impatient.

"But, Your Majesty, I'm afraid that arrangement does not work for us anymore, and I need to renegotiate the terms of our deal." I stroll across to a chair and lower myself into it. "I think I will have that drink, after all. We can go over my proposal while we enjoy what I am certain will be the finest of wines."

I leave the palace rather relieved. The Prince was at Point Non Plus, so my offer should have been received with grace and appreciation. Except it was not. Of course it was not. The Prince is not only a glutton, but he is also an arrogant fool. Still, he is not what matters. Saving my business is what matters, as well as my family name. And, more important than all of that, Taya's life. I have to ensure that no one can *ever* discover that it was she who rained holy hell on the members of the ton—she and two others, who names I am yet to learn. My curiosity in that regard will not relent, but if I am to right my wrongs, I must force it into submission. It is a tricky situation to juggle, be sure of that, but, by God, I might have found a way.

After stopping off at the printworks to deliver the story to Grant, I head to Kentstone's to track down Fleming. His portly body is, as expected, wedged into a chair that should without question be double the size to accommodate him comfortably, and even then I think it would perhaps be a squeeze. Ruby is perched on his lap, and my eyes home in on her cheek, where a blemish has been poorly concealed with paint and powder. My teeth grit, my jaw clenching.

"Fleming," I all but growl. "A private word, if you will."

Ruby starts to lift from his lap, but he seizes her arm harshly and yanks her back down. She winces but tries to hide it. "I'm busy, Melrose," he grunts.

"Have it your way," I say, approaching, giving Ruby eyes to suggest she should move quickly, and she does, jumping off his lap, leaving the fat old pig grappling at thin air before him, struggling up from his seat, demanding she come back or so help her. I soon knock him back into his chair with a swift, accurate right hook.

He yelps and grabs his nose, stunned. "The deal is off!" he yells, his eyes watering something terrible.

"Then you won't want to know who has been raining holy hell all over London and beyond, stealing purses and merchandise," I say, settling in the chair.

"You know?" he asks, releasing his nose.

I smile.

"Who?" he demands. "God damn it, Melrose, who is it?"

I inhale, considering him for a moment, watching him watch me with impatience and curiosity. He is absolutely ravenous for this name. "Why, Fleming," I muse quietly. "It is you."

"What?"

I toss a paper on the table. "That is tomorrow's news." Fleming's name is splattered on the front, along with a very damning headline.

"What is this?" he asks.

"This is my newspaper telling the people of London and beyond that you are the highwayman. Or one of them."

He laughs, low and nervously. "You want this deal, do you not? You want my boats and carriages."

"Oh, you must mean the knackered boats and the carriages no one dare use because you are wholly reckless with their cargo and take shortcuts no sane businessman would take in order to save a few pennies."

His nostrils flare. "If I'm the highwayman, why would I hijack my own carriages?"

"Why, to steal your customer's cargo and sell it on, of course."

His face drops.

"Priceless paintings, diamonds, gold." For the first time, I wonder where all of that treasure is, because Taya most certainly was not stealing for the riches, only for the revenge.

"I will be hanged," he says on a mere whisper.

"Hopefully, yes."

"You must stop these lies."

"Oh, they are not lies." I pull Taya's scarf from my pocket. "I have proof, you see." I place it down and look at Ruby, who drops a box on the table. Fleming frowns and opens the lid, then gasps as he realizes what is inside.

"Is that…?"

"Every coin purse you have ever stolen?" I ask him. "Yes, indeed, that is correct."

"You must help me."

"Must I?" I look at Ruby. "Should I help him, Ruby?" She shrugs, nonchalant, and I sigh. "Fine, I will help you." Leaning in, I lower my voice. "You will sell your failing haulage business to me for, say, ten pounds?"

"That's ridiculous!"

"Perhaps, but still, I feel I am being rather generous." I slap ten pounds down. "The story will still print," I tell him. After all, I need a decoy if I am to 1) settle the curiosity of the ton and complete my story, and 2) kill the mystery and therefore save Taya from possible exposure.

"What? You can't do this!"

"Don't you worry, Fleming. I've had a little word with my friend, His Majesty, and he has agreed, very kindly, I think you'll agree, to spare you the rope in exchange for your cooperation. I'm nice like that, you see. And the Prince is rather fond of my newspaper—it's his favorite, don't you know—so he is rather excited about having it reach every corner of England so that his people may read about how wonderful he is from time to time." It's a small price to pay for the love of my life's life. "You will be banished to Scotland." His nostrils flare. "Or be hanged."

"You dirty, rotten scoundrel!"

"At least not a woman beater, Fleming." I look at Ruby, who inhales, draws back her arm, and extends her fist hard, punching him on his bulbous nose too. He yelps, and I flinch, thinking Ruby has quite the swing and any man would do well to avoid it. "And for ruining my lovely friend here, you shall compensate her generously." I'm sure all the money in the world will not compensate Ruby for having to suffer this pig, but she deserves a fresh start with the means to suit her lady status. "I do believe that is all our business concluded for today. I will have our lawyer draw up the papers." I push the money toward him. "Good evening to you, Fleming." I down the Scotch on the table, *his* Scotch, get up, and leave the club, and when I'm on the steps outside, I take in a deep breath, nodding to the two Bow Street Runners waiting for me. "He's in the far left hand corner." I start the walk home, passing Casper outside Gladstone's, nodding when he thanks me for my discretion.

My discretion and his desire to remain married are what made this plan possible.

Highway*woman*?

What highwaywoman?

Chapter 26

The next morning, the gasps of the ton, I'm sure, stretch as far as…well, Paris. I look out of the window, seeing *The London Times* in the hands of every resident in Belmore Square. "Twenty thousand copies dispatched, sir," Grant says from behind me. "I expect another print run will be required before sundown."

I smile. "Very good, Grant. See to it that all the staff are rewarded for their hard work."

"Yes, Mr. Melrose. Thank you."

I look down at my travel case, and then to the ticket in my hand that will sail me to Paris. To Taya. My stomach spins with anticipation, with excitement with…nerves. She might send me on my way. Laugh in my face.

But at least I will have tried. I will deal with her brothers after, if, indeed, I need to deal with them at all. Pain is a vice around my heart at the thought of Taya rejecting me. I don't think I will survive it.

I see Grant taking the steps down to the cobbles as the family coach pulls up outside, and I finish my coffee and dip to collect my bag, just as Clara bursts in unceremoniously, her mouth open ready to speak, but when she spots Dalton laying a new pot of coffee down, she snaps it shut and walks calmly and slowly to the table. "Good morning, Dalton."

"Miss Clara," he says, nodding, his eyebrows lifting. "Can I get you anything?"

"No, thank you." She smiles sweetly, and as soon as Dalton is gone, she turns wide eyes onto me. "The Duke is on his way."

"What? Why?" That is quite possibly the most ridiculous question I have ever asked. Of course he is coming to stop me from seeing through my plan. But how does he know? I haven't told a soul. No one! It matters not. It would take a rhinoceros to stop me. Unfortunately for me, my brother-in-law *is* a rhinoceros.

Mama bursts into the room too. "His Grace is coming, Frank!" She snatches up my bag and grabs the sleeve of my jacket. "Come, you can escape to Paris through the back door."

"How do you know I am going to Paris?"

"I saw the ticket."

"Mama!"

"Oh, do be quiet. It's wonderful!"

"And you told no one, am I right? So the Duke is coming to merely visit with us? Or to congratulate me for today's report in *The London Times*?"

"Ah, well, you see…"

"Oh, Mama."

"Lady Wisteria promised not to share!"

"Well, she obviously broke that promise."

Lady Wisteria bursts into the room, too, out of breath and quite red in the face. "I did not breathe a word."

"I neither," Eliza yells, following in behind her, the skirt of her dress pulled high to avoid tripping over it.

"Or me!" Clara sings.

"My God," I breathe, dropping to my chair. "So if none of you broke your vow, how the buggery hell does the Duke know?"

Eliza raises her hand, and I look at her. "He may have come by some words I have penned, a story, for you have inspired me, about a man who journeys the world to win back the love of his life." Her lips straighten, and my shoulders drop. I am, confusingly, caught between despair for me and joy for Eliza.

"You all make me want to throw up," Clara sighs as the front door bangs and everyone stills, throwing each other wary looks as the sound of boots pounds the wooden floor to the dining room.

"Oh my," Clara whispers, sitting herself down at the table and collecting a muffin, settling in for what I expect will be quite the show.

The Duke enters, heaving like an angry gorilla. Eliza pouts and folds her arms over her chest, as does Mama, as does Wisteria, three quite steely stares pointing the Duke's way.

"You may all leave," he grunts.

He gets shaking heads in return, from *all* of the women.

"Eliza, you should be in bed," he snaps, and I cringe. He is a brave man, it must be said.

"Would you like to change your tone, or am I to embarrass you in front of all these people?" she asks, unfolding her arms and motioning around the room.

His nostrils flare, he starts to pace, and I stand, rising slowly, needing to have a presence, my eyes following his strung body around our dining room, for what seems like hours. I haven't got time for this.

"For heaven's sake, man, will you speak?" I grate, my patience wearing thin. "I have somewhere I need to be."

"I forbid you to go."

"That is your hard luck now, isn't it?" I pick up my bag and walk past him. "Wish me luck," I quip, getting a chuckle from Clara, the little daredevil.

"Melrose," he warns.

"Pray do tell me what you would have done had I, or anyone else for that matter, tried to stop you from going to Eliza when she thought all hope was lost?"

He snarls.

"Indeed," I say.

"You do not deserve her."

"And you do? Deserve my sister, I mean?"

"No, that is the bloody point! But I will never hurt her, and I will protect her at all costs."

I raise my brows. "Yes, I know how that feels. Love of the richest kind, am I right? A sense of ill purpose without them? Yes, I feel that too. As though life is pretty damn pointless without them? Indeed." His eyes widen as comprehension dawns. "One day, Your Grace, you may thank me. You failed her. You should have protected her, not sent her away."

His body deflates, though he tries to conceal it, maintaining his glare.

"I will return with Taya," I go on. "And you will give us your blessing. I have cleared her name, already protected her. What did you do, I ask? What did you do, Your Grace?"

He winces.

"Perhaps if I can convince her to love me, I might also convince her to forgive you for your cruelty."

His head is now in his hands, shaking, and Eliza goes to him, placing a hand on his shoulder. He blindly seizes it, squeezing, his body inflating as he withdraws from his hiding place. "My God, what am I doing?" he whispers, looking at me. He levels me with serious, sincere eyes. "If you can persuade her to show me mercy, I will, of course, be indebted to you."

I nod and leave, but I cannot smile or be grateful for taming the beast. I still have the biggest challenge ahead of me.

Chapter 27

The barren land is endless, as is the journey. I doubt I have even made it halfway to the coast yet. My backside is numb, my thoughts circling, my self-hatred endless. Christ, how I wish I had not been such a pig-headed idiot. How I wish I had taken a moment to think properly about what I was faced with instead of barging in and blurting words I did not mean. How I hope it is not irreparable. How I wish Taya had confided in me! I look down at the drawing.

Now, crazy as it is, mad as it seems, the Winters brothers are the least of my worries, the smallest hurdle to clear. Now I have to convince Taya that I am a man of honor, and I will love her fiercely, like no other man could ever love her. That she was not a dalliance. That I would rather face lions—or her brothers—than be *without* her. Of course, I may be clutching at straws. She may well laugh at me and tell me I was a game, an added thrill in her mission to exact revenge on the ton.

Then I remember our night together. Our kisses, our laughs, our conversations. No one is that good an actor. They can't be.

And still, I am nervous.

I should throttle Lizzy Fallow. Throttle her! That horse neighing, the sound that jerked her off me, before I had come to my senses, got over the shock of her throwing herself into my arms, was Taya. She saw me kissing Lizzy Fallow. "God dammit," I mutter, jumping in my seat, flinching, when we hit a rock in the road. We have not seen another traveler for miles. Not one, not on horseback, not in a yellow boulder, a hackney carriage, nothing. It is not unusual for this route, mind you, for in my haste to get to Taya and repair the damage I have caused, I elected to travel the highway to shave at least a day off my journey time.

"Whoa!" the coachman yells, and the carriage jolts once again, but this time, concerningly, I suspect it is not as a result of a rock in the road. We start to slow.

"What is it?" I call, poking my head out of the window. A broken wheel? A lame horse?

It is neither.

"Hide your purse, Mr. Melrose," he calls back as we come to a standstill. "We are under attack."

I see the two horses charging toward us—both beautiful gray stallions—and my heart gallops along with them. "My God," I breathe, sitting back in my seat, a sweat coating my forehead. I reach for my cravat and pull at it. This is bloody typical, I think, as I frantically try to unravel my tangled thoughts, try to figure out what it is I must do, even though I have considered this scenario carefully. Hide? I slam my fist down on the seat, frustrated, but, in truth, I had anticipated the risk of taking this route, a renowned shortcut for the bravest of the wealthy. We got through Hampstead Heath unscathed, not a surprise since the highwaymen that rode those lands are no more, but I knew of the risk to continue on this dangerous route.

Which is why I brought a pistol along, because if I am robbed, I will have no choice but to turn back and return to Belmore Square.

Never.

I reach under my seat and pull it out. I will be dead before I must turn back. Dead! I step out of the carriage, keeping the pistol behind my back, and wait. Oddly, I am not fretful. No, I am more annoyed to be delayed on my journey to deal with this. The horses get closer, and are soon upon me, treading the uneven ground, their heads nodding, fighting the tension on the reins. I pull out my pistol and aim it at one horseman, then the other. "Not today," I say, catching the eye of one just before he looks away. My gun lowers, my gaze taking him in from top to toe, my forehead becoming heavy from my frown. He turns the horse away, jerks his head, a sign to the other rider, and kicks his horse into action, cantering away, his partner following.

"You certainly did tell them!" the coachman sings, laughing.

"What the devil?" I breathe, watching them go, the dirt being kicked up behind them hampering my view. I look at the carriage. The slow, bumpy carriage. Then to the two horses pulling it. I am working to release one of them, the strongest, fastest, before I can convince myself I am going crazy.

"Sir?" the coachman says, watching from his sitting post as I dismantle the leathers and hooks and create a makeshift set of reins.

"I will be back for you, I swear it," I say, hauling myself up onto the horse's naked back and yelling, breaking out at a hair-raising speed across the barren planes of land. I keep myself low, squinting to see ahead. I cannot see the horses, but I can see the dissipating clouds of dust they're leaving in their wake. "Come on," I yell, kicking the horse's rump as best I can. He responds beautifully, as if he senses my urgency, and I am soon gaining on the highwaymen. I see one of them look back, seeing me coming up behind. There is no way my horse will keep up this pace for much longer, and I am without all the tack I require to ride far. I have to end this chase.

Chase?

I laugh to myself. Has there ever been a member of high society turn the tables on any highwaymen? What is this madness I find myself in?

I draw closer, my stomach muscles aching somewhat terribly, and when my horse's nose is level with my target's thigh, I am about to start yelling, but his horse loses its footing momentarily. It is just a moment, but at this speed, a moment is all it takes. The rider yelps and is tossed from the back. "No," I roar, yanking at the reins to slow. I jump down and run back, breathless, worry overcoming me. The body—the dainty, fragile body—is in the dirt, sprawled and without a hint of life. "My God," I breathe, falling to my knees, my hands extending and retracting, not knowing what to do, to touch, move.

She is in Paris!

I must be going mad. I reach for the scarf hiding the rider and pull it down, praying I am mistaken. "No," I whisper when her beautiful face is revealed. "No, no, no!" Her eyes are closed, her body still, but, thank God, I can see her chest rising. She is breathing. "Taya," I say, feeling at her face, patting and dabbing everywhere. "Taya, open your eyes. Open!"

She does not.

My heart begins to slow, my damn eyes prickling with tears, as I watch her chest begin to slow, her breathing getting shallower by the second. "You must not die!" I yell. "Do you hear me? You must not, or, I swear it, I will never speak to you again." I take her shoulders and shake her. "Wake up!"

I look up and around, as though the empty land surrounding me for miles might be able to offer me some help. I see the other horseman approaching slowly, and though I cannot see his face in its entirety, I know it to be grave. "Is she breathing?" he asks, his voice rough.

"Hardly."

"You must get her to a doctor."

"How?" I yell. "It will take me days to get us back to London."

He jumps down from his horse and whistles, and Taya's horse trots to us. "I will ride with you," he says, coming to us. "With two of us, we can share the weight so the horses get respite from the weight of two. It will cut our journey time considerably."

I watch him as he dips and strokes Taya's cheek, pulling his scarf down as he does. It is the same handsome man. Ruggedly so. It is no wonder Lady Rose was mesmerized. But who he is or where the other highwayman is, for they always worked in a threesome, is not a priority. Taya's life is. I have not broken laws and framed men, albeit unscrupulous men, to save her, just for her to die on me now.

Chapter 28

It took twelve hours to get back to London, the unnamed high-wayman and I taking it in turns to carry Taya's lifeless body draped over the horse. I am truly thankful she is unconscious, for I know not how she would have sustained the wretched journey otherwise. I barely have myself, worry overcoming me, my heart relentlessly pounding with fear.

On the edge of town, we come to a stop, as I assess the best route to the stables without being seen. To be seen would be to blow apart the story I manufactured to save Taya and our names.

It is dawn, the streets quiet, but we cannot risk it. "We need a hackney carriage," I say, motioning to one not too far away, stationary on the cobbles, the jarvey probably taking a nap.

He nods and kicks his horse, leaving me to go and hire the coach. I frown. "We're hiring it, remember." I hear a gruff chuckle, and I look down at the back of my horse where Taya is draped. Guilt squeezes me. Why did I make chase? God damn me, why? Because I was scared that I would never see her again, but better not to see her than lose her to death. I clench my eyes closed and inhale. If I lose her, I will never survive it.

We get Taya carefully in the coach and attach our horses to the side, ordering the jarvey to take us to the stables at the back of Belmore Square. Her head rests on my lap, and I stroke her hair, realizing for the first time that she is without the dark wig that had me fooled for so long. She was too far from home to be recognized, so perhaps that is why she abandoned the disguise.

"I do not know what happened between you and the lady," the highwayman says, "and I do not wish to, but I will say this..." His eyes fall onto Taya's limp form. "If she dies, I will kill you."

"You need not worry; I will kill myself," I whisper, my gaze moving from her face to her chest constantly, to check her breathing and to check if her eyes show any signs of opening. Nothing.

We make it back to the stables and I scoop Taya into my arms, ordering the horseman to take a hessian sheet from the stable floor and lay it over her to conceal the clothes that are a giveaway. "I thank you for your help," I say, and he nods. "Truly, I am indebted to you. May I ask your name?"

He smiles, reaching for Taya's cheek and stroking it. "You can call me Alf."

"And how do you know Taya?"

His eyes lift to mine. "She saved my life." He laughs under his breath. "And then threatened to kill me if I did not teach her all I know."

"How to rob people?"

"Not just any people."

"The kind of people who damned her family."

"Indeed." *Revenge.* He gestures with a jerk of his head. "You should go before you are seen."

"And what of you? How will I get word to you?"

He smiles and pulls his scarf into place. "Take care of her, Melrose."

I nod, turning and carrying Taya out of the stables. I stop and look back. He is gone. I look down at Taya's sleeping face, dipping and kissing her soft lips, taking comfort from her warmth. "I love you," I whisper, my voice hoarse, my regret crippling. How I wish I had told her. I can only pray I will get the chance when she can hear me. See the sincerity in my eyes. The love.

I pick up my feet and walk on heavy legs through the gardens toward number one Belmore Square, the Winters residence. I do not have a chance to knock. The door flies open and Lady Wisteria lets out a pained whimper at the sight of her daughter in my arms. "Oh, my precious girl." She feels at her face, as Johnny comes racing down the stairs fighting his way into a jacket, looking like he's in a hurry to be somewhere.

He stops and looks Taya over, inhaling. "We just received word that she did not arrive in France."

Sampson appears too, looking as distressed as his brother when he sees Taya in my arms. "I watched her board the ship," he breathes, shaking his head.

"She went back to the commons." I pass Lady Wisteria, then Johnny, and make my way upstairs to her bedroom, letting myself in and laying her on the bed.

"I am not going to ask how you knew this was her room," Johnny says.

"I wouldn't if I were you," I reply, getting her head comfortable on the pillow. Red stains it immediately, and I flinch at the sight.

"Hercules, send for the doctor immediately," Lady Wisteria orders.

"Yes, my lady."

"And fetch us some warm water and cloths."

Johnny lowers himself to a chair in the corner as I unravel the hessian from around her. "What happened?"

"I was ambushed by two horsemen." I cast the sheet aside. "They didn't rob me but scarpered instead. I made chase, and she fell from her horse." I wince, hearing her precious, delicate body hitting the hard ground. "I would like to blame you, but I fear this is all my fault." I crouch, taking Taya's hand and clenching it in both of mine, desperate for her to open her eyes and see me. To hear my apologies. To feel my touch and my love.

"Frank?" Eliza's worried, questioning voice drifts into my foggy hearing, and I turn to see her blurred silhouette at the door in a nightgown. "Oh my heavens, what happened?"

I shake my head, unwilling and without the energy to speak the words again, for each time I do, the pain flares.

I will never forgive myself for this. Never.

I feel so lost. So helpless and guilty, just sitting by her bedside, waiting, hoping, praying for her to wake up. Her breathing has remained shallow and strained, her arm is braced, for the doctor discovered a broken bone, and her head is bandaged, the cut to the back deep and ragged, from a rock, I expect. I have washed and re-dressed the cut daily, and no one has tried to prevent me from doing so. I have to do *something*.

Not one minute passes by without me demanding she wake up, whether silently or out loud, as I place my lips on her hand, her face, anywhere, wishing she'd feel the warmth of my mouth and the love in my kiss.

"Wake up, I beg you," I say quietly, my throat thick with emotion. I know with each passing day, hope fades, but I refuse to accept it. What is the point of life, I ask myself, if I do not have someone to share it with? Everything I have achieved for the business will be inconsequential without Taya to marvel at my words, for she truly is the only opinion that I crave. And her drawings. The world must see her talent.

I feel a hand on my back and turn to see Mama behind me, a beef sandwich on a plate in her hand. "I am not hungry, Mama," I say, returning my attention to Taya, watching her eyes again, begging for a flicker of movement.

"My boy, what use are you to her if you are without the energy to look after her when she wakes?" She sets the plate on the cabinet and gives me another rub of my back, and I silently thank her for her optimism when I am lacking it myself. "Please, try, even just a bite."

I nod, and she leaves and, so utterly exhausted, my eyes dry, my head heavy, I rest my forehead on the mattress and clench Taya's hand in mine, closing my eyes and giving in to tiredness.

I dream of her. Of our laughter. Our intimacies. Our quarrels. I see her brown scarf covering her face, and her hat low. I see her remove it all to show herself to me. I see her talented hand drawing. Her beautiful face smiling. However I resisted her for as long as I did, I will never know. But now I feel as though it was time I did not have to waste.

"Frank," she says, and I hum, acknowledging her. "Frank, what are you doing here?"

"Looking after you," I whisper.

"Oh."

I smile at her easy acquiescence and settle again. But...

My eyes spring open, and I bolt upright. "Taya?" I ask, seeing her eyes closed, her face peaceful, her body still. And then movement. A flicker of her lids, and, God have mercy on my soul, I take her shoulders, shaking her a little.

"Ouch, God damn it, man."

I breathe out heavily, and I cannot deny it, perhaps on a small whimper, as she opens her eyes and scowls at me. I have never been so overjoyed to see her scowl. I love her scowl. I love her mouth. I love every little thing there is to love about Taya Winters. "You're alive." I take her in my arms as best I can around her broken arm and hug her to me fiercely. "I am never letting you out of my sight ever again. You may never ride a horse, at least not cross-saddle, and if you so much as think about hijacking any more coaches, I will tan your backside with a crop, I swear it." I pull away and see her blinking rapidly, and I cannot fathom why she looks so surprised.

"What happe—" She stops abruptly and frowns. "You kissed Lizzy Fallow."

What? Of all the things she could remember first, it is that? "No." I shake my head. "I will drag her here if I have to, and she will tell you the truth of it."

"What is the truth of it?"

"She jumped me, I swear it, Taya. Dived at me like a desperate harlot and caught me by complete surprise. I was about to shove her away and demand to know exactly what she thought she was doing, but then, of course, your presence became apparent, and she scarpered."

Her lips purse, like she's unsure if she believes me. Fine. I stand. "I will go fetch her this minute."

"No!" She seizes my arm and pulls me down. "It is not necessary."

"It is not?"

She shakes her head. "I was very mad, be sure of that." She winces, reaching for her head and feeling it.

"Leave it," I say, pulling her hand back to the bed.

"That night, I was there for you."

"What?"

"You needed my identity for Fleming, and of course I could not give you that, but I could give him another glimpse of me so as to nurture his interest. At least until I figured out how to get myself out of this mess. When I heard whispers of your story about the highwaymen, I had to stop you, but I knew not how. Then I read your story, and, God, it was so impassioned. And about me, Frank! I wanted to stop you, I wanted to encourage you. Draw for you." She hisses as her head lifts off the pillow, and I rush to ease her back down. "Why were you on the common so far from London?"

"I was on my way to Paris to find you and bring you home so that we may be together."

Her sleepy, heavy eyes widen. "What?"

"I solved our problems, Taya. All of them. I have saved the business, our families' names, and framed a most undesirable man for your crimes so that you may remain in London and be with me."

She looks a little taken aback.

"Anything for you, Taya. Anything."

Her smile is small but hesitant, her lip a little wobbly. "I…" She coughs, winces, and I wince at her pain too. "Is it very sore?"

I ask, wishing I could get rid of her pain as I have gotten rid of our problems.

"It aches. Everywhere aches." She breathes out and settles, closing her eyes again, already tired. "I want to spend all of my energy on love, Frank, not hate." Her eyes clench closed.

"Then love me," I whisper, silently begging her. "Because I truly, deeply love you, Taya," I say, and it feels so good. "Open your eyes, for me, my lady," I whisper. "So I may look into your beautiful green eyes when I tell you again." She swallows and slowly peels her eyes open. I swear it, I fall deeper still. "I have loved you from the moment I saw you."

"You have?"

"I'm certain of it," I lean up and give her a little kiss on the lips, soft and brief. "Can you forgive me for being such a fool?"

"Can you forgive me?"

"I already did."

"What of my brother?" she asks, worry finding her. "He will never allow it."

"Let me handle your brother."

"Oh? Are you sure that is wise, Frank? You—" I kiss her again, silencing her. "All right," she says around my mouth. "If you insist."

"I do." And I shall be insisting on many more things, too, just as soon as she is back to full health. "Now, as much as it pains me, I must leave you for just a moment." There is no time like the present. "I will be back with the doctor."

She nods and settles, and I reluctantly leave her to do what I must do, for I will not settle until I have seen to business.

I open the door and find Lady Wisteria with Eliza, and both shoot worried eyes my way. "She is awake," I say, and they both deflate, hands on their chests. "Where will I find His Grace?"

"His study," Lady Wisteria says quietly, reaching for Eliza's hand, her lips straight, worried but hopeful.

I nod, clear my throat, and take the stairs, my chin high, my resolve unwavering. "Be gentle with him, for he is riddled with guilt," she calls.

I do not answer. I knock the door and enter without waiting for instruction, and I find him by the fire in his chair, a glass of Scotch in his hand. He looks at me and stands, his face worried, while mine remains eternally impassive.

"You will do the right thing," I say quietly, and he exhales heavily, taking the mantelpiece for support.

Then he nods. "I will always be in your debt, Melrose."

"No need," I say, offering my hand. He looks at it for a moment, considering it, before he takes it and shakes, only very lightly. "The care of your sister is now in my hands, Your Grace."

"Of course."

"And I will marry her just as soon as she can walk down the aisle."

He breathes in, clearly struggling. But he nods.

"And she will be working with me at the newspaper."

He laughs under his breath. "Whatever you want, Melrose."

I nod, drop his hand, and turn, leaving to return to my love.

And I will never leave her again.

Epilogue

I feel a nudge in my side, and I look to see Johnny watching me, his eyes reassuring. Of course, he's only recently done this himself. Was he as consumed by nerves as I am? "I am all right," I say, swallowing hard and fixing my new jacket, a black velvet piece with gold buttons and trim. The smartest of the smart. Nothing but the best for my lady.

"I beg to differ," he muses.

"Your forehead is wet," Sampson says on a light laugh. "Are you regretting this?"

I swing a filthy look his way. "I know it might disappoint you both, but no, I am not regretting this." I am merely nervous with anticipation to see her. It is the end of the season, and this, our wedding, is the final occasion, the talk of the town.

My closest family stand behind me, and back in Belmore Square, the residents are waiting to congratulate us and drink all the champagne that Mama has stocked the drawing room with. Regrettably, we will be forced to join the celebrations, as Taya is not yet well enough to travel for our bridal tour. For that reason, her brother suggested we postpone the nuptials until next season. I cannot repeat what I replied while Sampson belly laughed, and Lady Wisteria smiled. The short, profanity-absent version is, basically, *never*.

So here we are in the same small church where Johnny and Eliza were married only weeks ago. Mama has married off two of her offspring in one season. She is setting records and earning quite the reputation as a steadfast, determined mama, who will fit right in as a Lady Patron of Almack's. Of course, neither my nor Eliza's choice of husband or wife were Mama or Papa's decision. We are the signs of a new era, I believe.

"Oh, finally," Sampson mutters, elbowing me in my side, and I glance up and follow his indication to look, clenching my lips together and slowly turning my eyes, bracing myself. I inhale at the sight of her, her hands joined loosely at the front of her ivory silk gown, her sleeves covering her thick bandage. Her hair is loose and wild, just as I love it, with a halo of flowers set upon her head.

"Good God," I whisper, dazzled by the sight of her. My lips part, and I shake my head in wonder. Her face is flawless as she walks to me, and when she arrives, her green, sparkling eyes blister my skin with her scorching gaze. I slowly lift my hand to her cheek and cup it, and she nuzzles into it. All of my nerves disappear, my heart steadying and my body starting to relax again. "I have never in my life seen such a beautiful vision."

Her smile. It is glorious. It is life. "Neither have I." She takes my hand, squeezes it, and turns us toward the clergyman, who has the Book of Common Prayer in his hands.

I cannot take my eyes off her as our vows are read, and I am prompted twice, for I am mesmerized, to accept the blessed ring to put upon Taya's finger. I turn to her, hold her hand, and look into her eyes. "With this ring I thee wed," I say quietly. "With my body I thee worship, and with all my worldly goods I thee endow." She blinks slowly, making her unfathomably long lashes flutter. "In the Name of the Father, and of the Son, and of the Holy Ghost. Amen."

Her lips twitch, and I beg them to stop, for holding myself back from claiming them is becoming distressing. I struggle through communion, fidget my way through the scriptures, will myself to get through the prayers, and as soon as the ceremony has ended, I hold her and walk us out of the church, our family following. I will pull her into a private space, win us just a moment for ourselves, so I can kiss my bride, my wife, and tell her, again, how much I adore her.

"I am desperate to taste you," I say urgently, quickening my pace, trying to put distance between us and our family behind us.

"As am I you," Taya whispers.

I look back and slow my urgent pace, having a stern word with myself, for I momentarily forgot in my desperation that she is still so very fragile. "Your arm."

"Is all right," she insists.

We break out of the church and come to an abrupt halt when we are met with raucous cheering and pellets of rice being hauled our way. "Oh bugger it," I mutter, and Taya chuckles. "I thought they were awaiting our arrival back at Belmore Square." This is the worst luck. "It isn't funny," I mumble. I might die soon if I do not get to kiss her. Truth be told, I want to do a lot more than that, but I am a reasonable man.

"Just smile and it will all be over very quickly."

"I highly doubt that." I slap on a smile and walk us through the crowds. "Have you seen the size of the cake Mama has baked?"

"I have not."

"It will take us a year to eat it, even with the help of every resident in Belmore Square."

"I love cake," Taya says, and I smile.

"And I love you."

"I hate cake," Taya mumbles, circling her belly with her hand, and I laugh, truly amused.

"That'll teach you for being a glutton." I take her plate and set it on the side, placing a glass of champagne in her hand. We have danced, indulged in the most wonderful wedding feast, and eaten enough cake to last us a lifetime. I look across the room to Mama, who is still pushing her creation on all the guests, insisting, if they have had some already, they have a second piece. And for those who have had a second piece, they must have a third. The damn thing nearly touched the ceiling when it was whole.

I gaze around and take in the celebrations. Papa is dancing with Lady Wisteria, Johnny is nursing Eliza and some cake, Sampson is…

I hum, watching the subtle flirtations between him and Lady Dare. "Do you think there is something going on?" Taya asks, looking in the same direction as me.

"Definitely not."

She laughs. "You men. Of course there is. That woman has worked her way through Belmore Square, including my husband and my brother."

I cringe, but I do not deny it.

"Sampson is fresh meat, but he'll soon get bored of her."

"Or she him," I muse, as Clara joins us. "How are you, sister?"

"I'm having the most wonderful time!" she sings.

"You are?" I ask, surprised.

She rolls her eyes. "Of course I'm not. I'm as bored as one could be. The only benefit I am taking from this, and Eliza's wedding too, of course, is that I may marry whom I choose when my time comes."

I laugh. "My dear, sweet sister." I put an arm around her shoulders and pull her close. "Have you missed the fact that Eliza's husband is a duke and my new wife is a lady?"

Her face drops. "Are you saying I may marry whom I chose so long as they bear a title, no matter if they are a suspected murderer or a highwaywoman?"

I feel my face blanch, and I dart my eyes around the room, looking for listening ears. "Clara!" I scold, and she shrugs, nonchalant.

"Bear the fact of my knowledge in mind, brother, when you come to force me into marriage." Her eyebrows jiggle as she dances off.

"The little…" I have not the right word for her, nothing effective enough for how I feel about the youngest of my sisters.

"Well, she certainly has you backed into a corner, doesn't she?"

She does. Thank God I have one more season to figure out how I may deal with her. Hopefully in that time, she will forget that my wife was a highwaywoman. "I am bored of pretending I am having a lovely time."

"Are you not?" Taya asks.

"No, because there are far better things we could be doing."

Her body tightens before my eyes. "Oh?"

"Do you think you can manage?" I ask, hopeful. It has been weeks since I have taken her. Weeks! It has been a backward blessing, I suppose, since her brother, the Duke, on agreeing to me having her hand, laid down one condition after dinner that eve. I must abstain until she is my wife. I had made a point of being insulted. The Duke had made a point of ensuring I knew that *he* knew of the difficulties in holding oneself back from something one thrives on, which only made me point out, gladly, that he should for that reason understand my plight.

Nevertheless, he upheld his condition, said something about it making him feel better for failing in his duties and honoring their father. It was with those words I knew I could not disobey his request, so when Taya tried to seduce me a few evenings later while I was bathing her—he never said I could not do that—I was tossed into a conflicting position, my body screaming for me to accept, my integrity forbidding it. So, as you can imagine, I was truly relieved and most thankful when Taya hissed in pain and relented to her body's refusal to cooperate. But now…?

I get her upstairs to her room and shut us inside and go straight to the window to draw the drapes. I freeze, my hands on the taffeta, ready to pull them across, when I see a horseman across the road.

Alf.

He's looking up at the window, and when he sees me, he

raises a hand, and I raise one in return, sure he will know Taya is fine. Sure he will have watched us be wed. Lifting his hat from his head, he bows, rests it back in place, and then yells, whipping the reins, and canters out of the square. I smile and silently wish him well as I close the drapes and turn toward Taya, pulling at my gold cravat as she begins to squirm and pant where she is. Oh, how I have been waiting for this. "I hear it is to be a beautiful sunset this evening," I say, and she stills. "Perhaps we should ride into it later."

Her smile is as blinding as the sun surely is. "I would love that."

"Me too," I agree, tearing off my new jacket carelessly and tossing it aside. "Tell me something." I approach the bed and she claims me with her good hand, yanking me down onto her.

"What?"

I am nose-to-nose with her, my senses being bombarded in every way. "Who were the highwaymen?"

She stills, looking me directly in the eye. "A lady never tells," she whispers huskily, pulling my mouth down to hers.

Acknowledgments

Thank you again to Orion for encouraging me into this whole new historical world. Belmore Square is fast becoming one of my most favorite places to be. The colorful characters, the scandal, the scenery. Frank has thoroughly delighted me with his escapades, and Taya was an absolute joy to create. The chemistry is unstoppable, the pleasure irresistible, the stakes high. Forbidden love is my favorite to write about, and Frank and Taya are most certainly forbidden.

I hope you've enjoyed their story.

JEM

Keep reading for an excerpt from

ONE
NIGHT
with the
DUKE

Chapter 1

The view from the drawing room window is not one that I am accustomed to. I don't see the rolling countryside and crops growing aplenty. My favorite mare, the blackberry bushes, the cowsheds.

The smell.

I sniff, getting a whiff of the new aroma. It isn't horse manure or grass, but instead an odd earthy smell. Bricks, mortar, and paint. It's the smell of our new house. A grand new house that sits beside many more impressive dwellings, looping the lush green gardens of Belmore Square, where a fountain, a few benches, and rosebushes are all closed in by cast-iron railings beyond the cobbled road. There's not a farmer to be seen for miles. Instead, here in London, we have affluent members of the ton strolling with no urgency, the fancy, gold-trimmed clothes of the gentlemen and the intricate lace-trimmed garments of the ladies providing an eclectic color palette I'm not used to. Top hats, canes, and carriages. Money leaks from every brick, cobble, and pruned bush. It's another world, one I am not entirely certain I can fit into. Or *want* to.

It's the start of a new season, and my very first. The politicians will do their work in Parliament and the businessmen will conduct business, while their wives update their wardrobes and plan their social calendars for the next few months. There will be parties galore, dinners, and gossip to be had. Now I am a part of the circles I had only ever heard of. Not dreamed about but *heard* of. Perhaps even dreaded. I can't say I'm all too keen on what I have experienced of London so far, and, worse, I am without the freedom I was once blessed with in our old life.

I grimace.

And I can hardly breathe in these fancy frocks.

On top of that, my inspiration is lacking, and I have absolutely nothing to write about, unless, of course, I should like to indulge in the unsubstantiated nonsense that Father's new business partner and financial backer, Lymington, Duke of Cornwall, thrives on. Which I don't, and it is a good thing, because I am not allowed to write for Father's newspaper in London.

I pout to myself, remembering the times I would take a story to Papa and he would sit in his chair by the fire smoking a cigarette, humming his interest. And his wry smile when he would say, every time, "You know, my dear Eliza, this is really rather good." Then he would dip, plant a kiss on my cheek, and send me on my way. The fact that each and every story I penned and that was printed in Papa's newspaper was credited to my brother, Frank, was a small price to pay. Recognition wasn't something I sought, even if, admittedly, I would have liked it. It was more the freedom to write what I desired and not what I thought people would want to read. I wrote factual, informative pieces meant to educate people with the truth.

Alas, now Father's newspaper only has space for censored news and advertisements, and Lymington doesn't mind reminding Father, at any opportunity and sometimes without opportunity, that it is his name and backing that allowed my parents to buy the final plot on Belmore Square and build this sprawling, beautiful cage.

I am surely not the only young lady around these parts that feels suffocated. Or perhaps I am. The residents here are a peculiar bunch of humans, who do not seem to care for the world, but rather their position in it. The men must be successful, wealthy, and loud. The women must be compliant, well turned out, and unopinionated. Image is everything. Money is power.

My father is now a very wealthy man, and, as a consequence, also very powerful. I'm not at all certain that I like power on my father. Being powerful seems to take up all of his time and makes him appear persistently exhausted.

How I long to return to a time when his business limped along and mother baked all day. It was of little consequence that I liked to indulge myself in words, whether reading them or writing them, or that I perhaps spoke up too often in matters of no business of mine. There was no one to impress, therefore lectures were a pointless task my father rarely wasted his time on. In fact, I think he enjoyed me biting around his ankles, squeezing him for all the information I could get. He let me sit on his knee while he worked. Answered my questions when I asked. Gave me more books to read, perhaps to keep me quiet. And Frank would always creep up on me whenever I was lost in those books and flick my ear. I'd punch his bicep. He would scowl playfully. Father would grin down at his quill. I would stick my tongue out. Then Frank would chase me around our father's desk while I screamed to high heaven and Papa laughed as he dealt with the poor state of his finances.

Now?

Now our address is Belmore Square, Mayfair, London. Father's newspaper is on course to become the biggest in England with the help of steam printing, and I long for the days when Papa laughed, even though we struggled to make ends meet. These days, all I have to look forward to is Latin and piano. Playing piano bores me to tears, and learning Latin seems like a pointless chore, since I am not permitted to travel to a place where I may have an opportunity to speak the language.

I scowl at the pane of glass, looking across the square to the corner of Bentley Street, where a house, individual in its architecture, stands alone, starkly separate from the rest of the homes on Belmore Square. It's fascinated me since I arrived here in London. It was once the Winters residence, until it burned to the ground a year ago and the family perished. I read the report that was written by Mr. Porter, a journalist who works for Father, about the tragic accident that wiped out the Winters family. Rumor has it that it was not, in fact, an accident, and it was the eldest son, Johnny Winters, who started the fire. That he acted in a fit of rage after a disagreement with his father over...what? No one knows. It's easy to fill mindless people with thoughts and conclusions when the accused is dead and unable to defend himself. Except Mr. Porter is a journalist, and, oddly, a respected one. I say *oddly respected*, because how anyone in their right mind could possibly trust a man who lives such a promiscuous life I do not know. He is loud, abrupt, egotistical, and dare I say it, a monster. And a power-hungry one at that. He mistreats his wife, ignores her in public, and beats her in private. He's also a raving Conservative.

In any case, the Winters house has been rebuilt and some-one is moving in.

But who?

Someone audacious, I am sure of it. Bold and unapologetic. There are thirteen houses here on Belmore Square. The old Winters residence is the only one that hasn't followed the uniform exterior so as to keep the rows of homes looking as pristine and neat as the gardens they circle. In fact, the new owner of number one Belmore Square seems to have gone out of their way to make the old Winters residence as different as possible from every other home. Better, actually. Bigger and grander in every way. It's a statement. A declaration of supremacy. Over the past few weeks since we have moved in, I have watched huge, exotic plants being off-loaded and taken into the property, along with the biggest, most sparkly chandeliers you ever did see, and beautiful, heavily carved pieces of furniture, which, after I had asked the men trusted to transport the pieces, I discovered were from India! So, whoever is moving into number one Belmore Square, I assume they are well traveled. How thrilling, to have traveled further than England.

So the finishing touches are being added, the wooden branches held together by hemp coming down from the exterior of the building, and now I, along with the rest of Belmore Square, wait with bated breath to see who will be moving into the sprawling, opulent mansion.

Hmmm, royalty, perhaps? Time will tell.

My attention is caught by the Duke of Cornwall, Lymington. His gray powdered hair is a beacon that could light the street better than the new gas lighting I have seen down in Westminster. He also happens to live at number two Belmore Square, with his son, Frederick, who I am yet to meet, which isn't such a hardship as I have heard he is an eternal bore. Lymington stops rather abruptly, and I follow his eyes to Lady Dare—she lives at number six Belmore Square and was widowed at the age of twenty after being married off to a decrepit lord at nineteen—breezing toward the gardens in a beautiful coat dress and an elaborately decorated bonnet. The woman does not walk, but floats. Her chin is constantly raised, her lips persistently on the verge of a suggestive, knowing smile, as if she is aware of the unspoken disapproval of the ladies of Belmore Square and the silent awe of the gentry who try and fail to ignore her beauty. Like Lymington right in this moment, who is still motionless, apparently caught in a trance, as he watches Lady Dare go. She is supposedly an exhibitionist, winning genuine disapproval from the ladies of the ton and false disapproval from the gentlemen. This rumor I know to be true, for I have seen the many men come and go from number six in the dead of night when I have been unable to sleep and have sat in my window wishing to be back in the countryside. Lady Dare is a ladybird, set free from the constraints of an arranged marriage by the fortunate death of her ancient husband, and now she will not bow to expectation, and yet she will also not flaunt nonconformity.

I purse my lips and peek down at my morning dress, an elaborate button-down piece trimmed with endless lace and sporting needlework that's really rather impressive. It's a status symbol, that is all. Along with this house, the staff, and the parties thrown most evenings by various members of the ton, this dress is merely here to demonstrate our wealth and standing. It's ironic, since no one will see it while I'm hanging around the house.

I lift the endless material so I can walk without tumbling, hearing the clanging and clattering of pots coming from the kitchen. Lunchtime. It has been only a few hours since breakfast, and it will be only a few more hours until dinner, and then tea, and finally supper. Eating five times a day is, apparently, a necessity when one is stinking rich. Because what else is there to do but hang around our mansion in a fancy dress constantly stuffing my face?

I pass the dining room, where one of our staff is laying the shiny mahogany table, and divert down the stairs to the kitchen. The smell of freshly baked bread is strong, the constantly raging stove and ovens making the underground rooms bordering unbearably hot. But it reminds me of home. I find Cook hunched over the flour-dusted table kneading more dough, probably in preparation for any one of the other three meals we will eat today. I release the bottom of my dress, not at all bothered by the mucky floor that will most likely dirty the crisp white muslin material. My hands are itching to sink into the mixture and get dirty.

"Miss Melrose," Cook cries, her doughy hands held up. "You mustn't be down here."

I pluck a plum out of the basket and sink my teeth in, something catching my eye. I slowly move around Cook's table. "*The*

Art of Cooking," I say quietly, looking down at the open page. "Mama had this when we lived in the country."

Cook wipes her hands on her apron, rounding the table, shooing me away as I sink my teeth into the ripe fruit. "I believe it is Mrs. Melrose's, Miss Melrose."

My chews slow, a sadness that feels perpetual since I left the countryside overcoming me. Mother doesn't have time to bake for us anymore. She's too busy being a lady in her shiny new manor. "Off you go now," Cook says. "We must serve lunch."

Silently, I leave Cook behind to finish her bread and climb the stairs, one hand holding up my dress, only to stop myself tripping and tumbling flat on my face, the other holding my fruit. By the time I have made it to the dining room, I have a band of grime around the bottom of my white day dress and a juice stain on the bust. "Oh dear," I murmur, brushing at the mark on the perfect dress.

"Eliza, you look like you belong in a slum terrace," Frank muses, looking up from the newspaper he is reading, seated at the far end of the table. "Perhaps even a gutter."

"I am not worthy, brother," I say, nibbling around my plum, eager to get every last piece of the juicy, sweet flesh as I present myself to the wall-hung mirror. I wipe my mouth and lean in, staring into my eyes that have always been described by my father as amethysts, and feeling at my hair that he says is rich like cocoa beans. I get both from my mother. And today, both seem significantly less…alive.

"I trust your mind is being suitably entertained by high-energy, top-quality, highly substantiated, educational reports about London and its residents," I say, looking away from my reflection and back to Frank, who, ironically, has blond hair and blue eyes, like our little sister, Clara, which they take from our father.

Folding his newspaper, he sets it aside. "Of course, since it really is I who writes the high-energy, top-quality, highly substantiated, educational reports which grace the pages of Father's newspaper these days." He cocks a brow, as if challenging me to challenge him. I would not, and he knows it. Frank wants to be a journalist about as much as I should like to be here in London. Not at all.

"And how are sales?" I ask.

His eyes narrow. "Sales are not something you should concern yourself with."

"Could be better, then?" I ask, feeling the corner of my mouth lift as I sink my teeth back into my plum. "I know a great writer who may help increase readership. Not everyone wants to read censored political and religious nonsense."

"Will you please sit down while eating?"

"Now if I did that, brother, I would be on my backside permanently." I lower to a chair, my back as straight as it is expected to be, my neck long. This is not through practice, but more my natural posture through years of horse riding. "What treasures will I find in today's edition of *The London Times*?" I ask, reaching for the newspaper. "Are the Catholics threatening to take over England?" I gasp, and it is wholly sarcastic. "Are they plotting to assassinate King George III?"

Frank scowls, unamused, pulling the newspaper out of my reach and standing, wandering over to the glass cabinet under the window. "You are caustic, Eliza," he breathes, unlocking the door and resting the latest edition atop the pile of newspapers, one copy of every edition since Father invested his last seven hundred pounds on a steam printing machine. The average and underwhelming two hundred copies per print are a distant memory, although, I hasten to add, Papa always sold more when I had written for his newspaper. Accepting my brother was named as the author was a small price to pay. I wanted not the accolades, only the satisfaction, fulfillment, and purpose. Now *The London Times* is slowly building, although I cannot help wondering if it is growing fast enough for Father and Lymington's liking.

About the Author

Jodi Ellen Malpas was born and raised in the Midlands town of Northampton, England, where she lives with her husband, boys, and Theo the Doberman. Her novels have hit bestseller lists for the *New York Times*, *USA Today*, *Sunday Times*, and various other international publications, and can be read in more than twenty-four languages around the world.

Find out more at:
  JodiEllenMalpas.co.uk
  Facebook.com/JodiEllenMalpas
  X @JodiEllenMalpas
  TikTok @JodiEllenMalpas